also by
SCARLETT ST. CLAIR

When Stars Come Out

HADES X PERSEPHONE
A Touch of Darkness
A Game of Fate
A Touch of Ruin
A Game of Retribution
A Touch of Malice
A Game of Gods
A Touch of Chaos

ADRIAN X ISOLDE
King of Battle and Blood
Queen of Myth and Monsters

FAIRY TALE RETELLINGS
Mountains Made of Glass

a GAME of RETRIBUTION

SCARLETT ST. CLAIR

Bloom *books*

Copyright © 2022 by Scarlett St. Clair
Cover and internal design © 2022 by Sourcebooks
Cover design by Regina Wamba

Sourcebooks and the colophon are registered trademarks of
Sourcebooks. Bloom Books is a trademark of Sourcebooks.

All rights reserved. No part of this book may be reproduced in any form or by any electronic or mechanical means including information storage and retrieval systems—except in the case of brief quotations embodied in critical articles or reviews—without permission in writing from its publisher, Sourcebooks.

The characters and events portrayed in this book are fictitious or are used fictitiously. Any similarity to real persons, living or dead, is purely coincidental and not intended by the author.

All brand names and product names used in this book are trademarks, registered trademarks, or trade names of their respective holders. Sourcebooks is not associated with any product or vendor in this book.

Published by Bloom Books, an imprint of Sourcebooks
P.O. Box 4410, Naperville, Illinois 60567-4410
(630) 961-3900
sourcebooks.com

Cataloging-in-Publication data is on file with the Library of Congress.

Printed and bound in the United States of America.
WOZ 10

*This book was brought to you by Hozier
and a really good editor.
Thanks, Christa.*

CONTENT WARNING

This book contains scenes that reference suicide
and scenes that contain sexual violence.

If you or someone you know
is contemplating suicide, please call the
National Suicide Prevention Lifeline at
1-800-273-TALK (8255) or go online to
https://suicidepreventionlifeline.org.

Are you a survivor? Need assistance or support?
National Sexual Assault Hotline
1-800-656-HOPE (4673)
https://hotline.rainn.org/

Please do not struggle in silence. People care.
Your friends and family care. I care.

Alcyonia
Ocean
Entrance
Elysium
The Cavern
Lake T
Den of
Monsters
Tartarus
Phlegethen
Forest of Despair
Fields of
Judgment
Asphodel M
Cell of the Titans
Phlegethen
Cocytu
Fields of Mou
Marshes
Styx
Cape Tenaron
Entrance

PART I

"His descent was like nightfall."
—HOMER, *THE ILIAD*

CHAPTER I
A Game of Retribution

Hades manifested in the shadow of the grandstand of the Hellene Racetrack. Soon, the divinely bred steeds of the gods would compete in the first of three races, which would ultimately place the fastest competitor on a path to becoming one of Poseidon's prized hippocamps—the fishtail horses that pulled his ocean chariot. But it was not this so-called honor that drew Hades's presence or even the usual thrill he got from the promise of a risky bet. He had come to test the validity of a supposed oracle who went by the name Acacius.

He was familiar with the name and his businesses—a well-known relic dealer whose front was a mechanic shop. Hades and his team had kept an eye on his affairs for several months. They were familiar with his routine, instruction, and correspondences, which was why, when he began to offer mortals a look into the future, Hades became suspicious.

It was not just the future Acacius offered. He'd

obtained a kind of omniscience that came only with divine blessing or the possession of relics, and since Hades knew it was not the former, it had to be the latter.

He had sent Ilias ahead to bet in his place, and now the satyr stood near the track, his disorderly hair slicked back and tied at the nape of his neck, making his horns look larger and more pronounced. Hades crossed the green, where twenty steeds would soon compete, heading toward him. At his approach, mortals gave him a wide berth. Despite their fear of his presence, they stared, curious too—more so now that he had openly shown affection to a person they believed to also be mortal.

Affection for Persephone, who was not mortal but insisted on acting as if she were, something that worried him far more than he was willing to admit.

He had few vices, among them racing, whiskey, and Persephone, his Goddess of Spring. Two of the three had never interfered with his routine, had never provided enough of an escape to be called a distraction.

But Persephone was more than that—she was an addiction. A craving he could not sate. Even now, he fought the visceral urge to return to her despite having spent most of the weekend with her, exploring her, buried inside her. She was why he was late. He had not wanted to leave her side, in part because he worried over whether she would remain despite her promise that she would await his return to the Underworld.

A hot wave of frustration twisted through him at his doubt.

He had never doubted himself, but he doubted everything when it came to Persephone...even their fate.

"You're late," Ilias said, not looking at him but at the

starting gate where the horses and their jockeys marched into place.

"And you're a satyr," Hades replied, following his gaze.

Ilias glanced at him, brow raised in question at the comment.

"I thought we were stating the obvious," Hades said.

He did not like to be reminded of his mistakes, though those closest to him—in particular Hecate, Goddess of Witchcraft and Magic—reveled in reminding him that he was very much fallible.

Or, as she liked to say, an idiot.

"How are they looking?" Hades inquired, eyeing each powerful animal as they filed into their respective numbered stalls.

"I put money on Titan," Ilias said. "Just as you advised."

Hades nodded, his attention shifting to a large board where the odds glared back. Titan was favored for second place.

"I'm surprised you did not choose Kosmos," Ilias said.

Hades heard what the satyr did not say—*If you wanted to win, why go with Titan?* He was familiar with Kosmos and his trainer. He knew that he was a favorite of Poseidon's. Given that, it was likely no other horse in the running had a chance.

Then again, this was a race of divinity, and that meant anything was possible.

"The bet is a test," Hades replied.

Ilias looked at Hades questioningly, but he offered no other explanation.

The horses and their riders were in place behind the gate, and the race would begin in minutes. There was a tightening in the bottom of his stomach, an anticipation for the race that was reflected in the enraptured and colorful crowd. Horse racing, like so many things in New Greece, wasn't even about the race for most; it was about the fashion and status, and while the outfits were not as extreme as those at the Olympian Gala, the hats and headdresses were.

"Lord Hades." A voice drew his attention, and he turned to find Kal Stavros standing a few paces behind him. Kal was the CEO of Epik Communications, the media conglomerate. He owned television, radio, news outlets, even theme parks. Among them, *New Athens News*.

Hades hated the media for many reasons, but Kal Stavros ranked near the top, not only for how he encouraged the spread of misinformation but because he was a Magi, a mortal who practiced dark magic and already had two strikes against him for misuse.

A third and he would be banned, possibly punished.

Like many, the mortal kept his distance, though his pose was casual—his hands were stuffed into the pockets of his pressed navy slacks. His bright-blue eyes seemed to glitter, and Hades knew it wasn't from admiration. When Kal looked at the God of the Dead, he saw power, potential.

Neither of which he possessed.

Kal took his hands out of his pockets to bow, and Hades glared—not only at Kal but those who stood near, warning off any approach they may have been considering after watching this exchange.

"A pleasure," Kal said, grinning as he straightened.

"Kal," Hades said. "To what do I owe the interruption?"

The words fell from his tongue, heavy with disgust. If the mortal caught on, he ignored it.

"Forgive me," Kal said, though he did not sound all that sorry. "I would have approached you elsewhere, but I have been requesting a meeting for weeks and have heard nothing."

Hades's irritation increased, a subtle heat that burned the back of his throat.

"Silence is usually taken to mean no, Kal," he replied, focusing on the gate again. If it had been anyone else, they would have understood this to be a dismissal, but Kal had always made the mistake of flying too close to the sun, and it seemed that everyone understood the implications but him.

Kal dared to step closer. Hades's spine went rigid, and he clenched his fist, noting Ilias's warning glance.

"I hoped to discuss a possible partnership," Kal said. "One of...mutual benefit."

"The fact that you believe you could possibly benefit me, Kal, illustrates a significant amount of arrogance and ignorance."

"Considering your recent experience with a certain journalist, I think not."

There was a note of irritation in Kal's voice, but it was his words that drew Hades's attention—and made that small scratch of irritation a full-on inferno.

"Careful with what you say, Kal," Hades warned, uncertain of where this conversation was heading but disliking the possibility that Persephone's name would soon pass this mortal's lips.

Kal smirked, oblivious to the danger, or perhaps he wished to antagonize him, force him to act out in public merely for the benefit of his reporters.

"I could ensure your name never appears in the media again."

Those words hit like hot oil, though Hades did not outwardly react. Despite the fact that he was not the least bit intrigued by Kal's offer, he asked, "What exactly are you suggesting?"

"Your public relationship with one of my journalists—"

"She is not *your* journalist, Kal," Hades snarled.

The mortal stared for a moment but continued. "Regardless, you allowed her to write about you, which will encourage others to do the same with an emphasis on your relationship. Is that what you want?"

It wasn't what he wanted at all, mostly because it placed Persephone in more danger.

"Your words ring eerily threatening, Kal," Hades said.

"Not at all," the man said. "I'm merely pointing out the consequences of your actions."

Hades was not certain what the mortal meant by actions. Was it that he had let Persephone write the articles? Or was he referring to their public reunion outside the Coffee House, when she had run and jumped into his arms, both heedless to onlookers who had photographed and filmed the entire thing?

"I can help ensure your privacy."

"For a price, you mean?"

"A small one," Kal said. "Only a share in the ownership of Iniquity."

Kal's voice was drowned out by a loud bell, followed by the clang of the gates opening and the thundering of hooves as all twenty steeds sped down the track. The announcer's voice rose over the roaring crowd, narrating with a lyrical inflection.

"Kosmos has an early lead as expected, then it's Titan…"

He rattled off more names—Layland has the rail, Maximus on the outside. Throughout, Kosmos maintained the lead, with Titan only a length behind. The continued reporting from the announcer made Hades's chest tighten and his teeth grind together, exacerbated by the crowd's cheering, but then there was a shift in the race. Titan seemed to gain a better foothold and practically sailed past Kosmos across the finish line.

The announcer's voice rose with excitement as he announced the winner.

"Titan, the dark horse and Divine superstar, wins the Hellene Cup! Kosmos is second!"

In a matter of minutes, the race was over, and Hades turned from the rail to make his escape when a hand landed on his arm.

"Our bargain, Hades," Kal said.

The god turned quickly, catching Kal's wrist within his grip and shoving him away.

"Fuck off, Kal."

He offered nothing else before he vanished.

―――

Hades manifested at the Nevernight bar.

The club was pristine, the floor empty, though he knew his employees lurked, navigating within the shadows of the club to prepare for opening tonight—an event that never saw peace. Inevitably, someone always assumed their status would grant them access and, depending on their sense of entitlement, always led to a very public tantrum that Mekonnen—or, in very serious cases, Ilias—would have to handle.

Mortals and immortals alike never ceased to illustrate the faults of humanity. There were moments when Hades wondered if he had done right to create such a paradise in the Underworld. Perhaps it was best when they feared the afterlife—feared him, even. Then people like Kal would never dare approach with such imperious requests.

Another wave of frustration ricocheted through him at the man's audacity.

Worse, Kal's offer brought up another concern—Persephone's safety. Hades had an unlimited number of enemies. He hated to regret anything about their reunion, but he should have been more careful. He could have draped them in glamour, teleported, anything to prevent the public from having access to their lives and leave her exposed.

But the damage had already been done, and the world was watching.

Was Persephone prepared? It was one thing to be favored, another to be the chosen lover of a god. She did not wish to be known for her divinity. Would she tire of being known as his lover?

He took a bottle of whiskey from the backlit wall and drank it straight. As he did, he sensed he was not alone and turned to find Hera, Goddess of Marriage and his begrudging sister-in-law. She stood at the center of the floor, impeccably dressed in white, her face angled, proud.

Only slightly less severe than Demeter's, he thought.

"A little early for a drink," she said, her voice tinged with disgust, though he knew she had come to make requests. She never bothered to approach him otherwise.

"A little early for your judgment," Hades replied, returning his attention to the bottle, effectively dismissing Hera, who stood quiet for a moment before taking a breath and moving a step closer to the bar.

Hades braced himself for whatever came next.

He knew he would not like it.

"Before I begin, I hope my visit to you remains anonymous."

Hades raised a brow. "That depends on what you have come to say."

He took another drink, just to drive the point home.

Hera's features turned stony.

Hades did not dislike the goddess, but he also did not like her. For him, she was neutral territory. Her vengeful nature was often spurred by Zeus, his infidelity the crux of many of her outbursts. In most instances, Hades had a hard time blaming her for her outrage. After all, Zeus and Hera's marriage was built on deceit, but her cruelness was misplaced, always directed toward those who were often victims of Zeus themselves.

Hera lifted her chin, glaring.

"You are well aware of Zeus's exploits," she said. "The havoc he wreaks upon the human race."

She was not wrong, and though no god was particularly innocent, Zeus was probably the hardest on humanity.

"I'm well aware of yours as well," Hades replied.

Hera's mouth hardened and her voice shook as she spoke. "I have reason. You know I do."

"Call it what it is, Hera—revenge."

Her fist clenched at her side. "As if you haven't sought revenge."

"I was not passing judgment," he said and, after a moment, prompted, "Why have you come?"

She stared at him, and Hades remembered that he did not like Hera's eyes. It was easy to forget as she was often with Zeus, and when he was by her side, she presented herself as being uninterested and almost aloof, but being the center of her attention meant feeling the stab of her gaze.

"I have come to obtain your allegiance," she said. "I wish to overthrow Zeus."

He was not so surprised by her statement. This was not the first time Hera had attempted to dethrone Zeus. In fact, she had tried it twice and had managed to enlist the help of other gods—Apollo, Poseidon, and even Athena, and of the three, only one had managed to escape Zeus's wrath once he was free.

"No."

His answer was automatic, but he did not have to think long about this decision. Hades disliked Zeus's tyranny just as much as the next god, but he knew Hera's intentions, and he'd rather his erratic brother have the throne than her.

"You would decline, knowing his crimes?"

"Hera—"

"Don't defend him," she snapped.

He had not intended to defend Zeus, but the reality

was, Zeus was only king because they had drawn lots. He had no greater power than either Hades or Poseidon.

"You've tried this before and failed. What makes you think this time will be any different?" Hades asked because he was truly curious. Had Hera come into possession of some kind of weapon or alliance she believed would change the course of fate?

Instead of answering, she said, "So you are afraid."

Hades gritted his teeth. Zeus was the last person in the cosmos Hades feared. He was merely cautious. There was a difference.

"You want my help?" Hades asked. "Then answer the question."

A bitter smile spread across her face. "You seem to think you have a choice, yet I hold your future in my hands."

Hades narrowed his eyes. He did not need to ask what she meant. Hera also had the ability to bless and curse marriages. If she wanted to, she could ensure that he never married Persephone.

"Perhaps I will find reason to side with Demeter. I *am* the Goddess of Women, you know."

While many had known that Demeter had a daughter, she had kept her identity a secret, which meant that few gods knew of Persephone's divinity. The most recent exception was Zeus—and, by default, Hera—when Demeter had gone to him to demand the return of her daughter. Zeus, however, was not interested in opposing the Fates and had refused.

"If you wish to embody that role, then you'd do well to listen to Persephone herself and not her conniving mother. Do not fuck with me, Hera. It will not end well."

She offered a bark of laughter, her chin dipping so that she glared back at him. "Is that your answer?"

"I will not help you overthrow Zeus," Hades repeated.

He would not do anything on anyone else's terms. Overthrowing Zeus was far more complicated than gaining alliances. The God of Thunder was always looking for hints of rebellion, consulting prophecies and moving pieces to prevent the conception of someone far more powerful than himself. It was perhaps the plight of being a conqueror—a fear of the cycle repeating as it had with the Titans and the Primordials. Zeus feared ending up like their father, Cronos, and their grandfather, Uranus.

Hades had no doubt that eventually the tides would turn and the Fates would weave new rulers—a fact that would make the Olympians a target. He'd already suspected Theseus, his demigod nephew, of making such plans, though he did not know the extent. Theseus led Triad, an organization that rejected the influence and interference of the gods. Ironic, considering Hades was certain Theseus hoped to obtain full divinity, or at least equivalent power.

"Then this will not end well for either of us," Hera replied.

They stared at each other, a quiet tension building.

"If you will not help me overthrow Zeus, then you shall have to earn your right to marry Persephone."

Hades's fingers curled into his palms.

"This is not about Persephone," he said, the words slipping between his teeth.

"This is the game, Hades, and all gods play it. I asked for your aid and you declined, so I shall seek retribution all the same."

She spoke as if this were mere business, but Hades knew Hera, and her threats were not idle. The goddess would do just about anything to ensure she got her way, which meant she was not above hurting Persephone.

"If you touch her—"

"I will not approach her if you do as I say," she said, then tapped her chin, eyeing Hades from head to toe. "Now, how best to earn the right to marry your beloved Persephone."

Her musing made Hades cringe. Clearly her intention was to wound. She knew Hades wished to marry Persephone just as much as she knew he felt unworthy of such a gift. This was as much a punishment as it was entertainment for the goddess.

"Ah! I have it," she said at last. "I shall assign you to twelve labors. Your...completion of each one will show me just how devoted you are to Persephone."

"Pity Zeus never had to do this for you," Hades replied tightly.

It was the wrong thing to say—and hateful, he had to admit. Hades despised how Hera had come to be wed to his brother. It had been through deception and shame, and Hades's words had only brought those memories to the surface, causing Hera to go pale with rage.

"Kill Briareus," she sneered. "That is your first task."

Hades could barely breathe hearing her words.

Briareus was one of three Hecatoncheires, unique in his appearance, as he had one hundred arms and fifty heads. The last time Hera had tried to overthrow Zeus, it was Briareus who freed him, earning Hera's wrath, so while it was no surprise that she would seek her revenge, to execute him through Hades's hands was another thing entirely.

Hades liked Briareus and his brothers. They had been allies during the Titanomachy and ultimately were the reason the Olympian gods had been able to overthrow the Titans. They deserved the gods' reverence, not their blades.

"I cannot take a life the Fates have not cut," Hades countered.

"Then bargain," she replied, as if it were that simple.

"You do not know what you ask," Hades said.

A soul for a soul was the exchange the Fates would make—a give or take, depending on the havoc they wished to create.

The Fates did not like the gods meddling in their threads. This would have dire consequences. Hades could feel it moving beneath his skin as the phantom threads of the lives he'd bargained away tightened.

"You have one week," Hera replied, heedless of his words.

Hades shook his head, and while he knew she did not care, he said it anyway. "You will come to regret this."

"If I do, then you will too."

He had no doubt.

When she vanished, Hades stood in the quiet of Nevernight, recalling their exchange. The Goddess of Marriage had been right. This was a game that all gods played, but she'd used the wrong pawns.

Hades would get his way eventually, and the goddess would come to rue the day she decided to test him.

He took another swig of whiskey before hurling the bottle across the room, where it shattered in an explosion of glass.

"Fucking Fates."

CHAPTER II
An Element of Dread

Kill Briareus.

The two words felt thick and heavy in his chest, a binding that made it hard to breathe or think as he made his way to the Underworld.

He had imagined his return very differently. He had intended to occupy himself with erotic thoughts of how he would conclude his weekend with Persephone and see them through to the early morning when they would both face the harsh reality of their choice to go public with their relationship, a decision Hades was not certain either of them was prepared for. Given Kal's earlier attempt at some kind of blackmail, the sharks were already circling.

Now he was distracted by Hera's singular order and devising plans to avoid her labors. Hera was not the only god with the power to bless marriages, though her power to curse marriages was far more dreaded. Ultimately, though, the decision was up to Zeus, and Hades did not think his brother would be so approving if Hades were responsible for Briareus's death.

Gods, he hated his family.

Hades appeared in his office, intending to go in search of Persephone, but found he was not alone. Thanatos was already waiting. The God of Death often kept Hades informed on the daily activities of the souls—especially when things went awry, and it was that thought that gave Hades pause.

"Is something wrong, Thanatos?" Hades asked as the god swept into a deep bow, his long white-blond hair veiling his face.

"No, my lord," Thanatos replied as he straightened, his dark wings rustling. He looked like a slender shadow, his head crowned with a pair of black gayal horns. "I merely wished to make you aware of an…occurrence."

"An…occurrence?"

"At the Styx," he said. "Lady Persephone greeted the souls."

There was nothing inherently wrong with Persephone greeting the souls, though the way Thanatos was presenting the information made Hades's heart race.

"Get to the point, Thanatos," Hades snapped. "Is she okay?"

The God of Death blinked.

"Why yes, of course," he said quickly. "I did not mean to imply otherwise. I thought you would want to know and perhaps…caution her. You know new souls can be very unpredictable."

Hades's relief was instantaneous, though his irritation with Thanatos spiked.

"Are you…*tattling*, Thanatos?" he asked, raising a brow.

The god's eyes widened. "I— No, that was not my intention. I only thought you should know..."

The corner of Hades's mouth lifted. "I will speak with Persephone," he said. "Though the next time you intend to inform me of her exploits, I suggest you begin with how it ended."

Thanatos's pale face turned red. "Yes, my lord."

Without another word, Hades left his office to find Persephone.

It was not difficult to locate her. He could sense her within his realm, her presence a steady pulse that beat in tandem with his heart. He followed it, drawn to it, and found her in the library, seated in one of the overstuffed chairs near the fireplace. Even if he had not been able to sense her, he would have guessed she took solace here. His library was one of her favorite places in the palace, and he found it comforting that even after their time apart—though he hated to be reminded—she found it so easy to return to her previous routine.

From his place at the door, he could see the very top of her golden head, and as he approached, he found her reading. A chaotic mix of emotions erupted inside—a warm relief and a cold dread.

She was here now.

She was present now.

But the past month had taught him that it could end in an instant, and Hera's labors did not ease his turmoil, though he managed to suppress the feelings as he drew close.

"I thought I would find you here," he said and reached for her, seeking her mouth. He curled his fingers beneath her chin, tilted her head, and pressed his lips to hers. She arched to reach him, her hand clamping behind his neck as they fused together.

Hades liked this. It grounded him, reminded him that she was real—that they were real.

He pulled away and brushed her jaw with this thumb, studying her face, lingering longest on her lips, which he wanted to taste once more. Her eyes were brighter today—like the vibrant green of her meadow—and he liked to think it had something to do with him.

"How was your day, darling?" he murmured.

"Good," she answered, and her breathlessness made him smile.

"I hope I'm not disturbing you. You appeared quite entranced by your book." He glanced at it before straightening.

"N-no. I mean...it's just something Hecate assigned."

"May I?" he asked.

She handed it over and he noted the title, *Witchcraft and Mayhem*. He refrained from rolling his eyes at Hecate's choice of assigned reading. Though it was no surprise the Goddess of Magic would choose to teach his lover the art of chaos. It was a type of magic that could be both harmless and destructive, and Hades had no doubt that Hecate had intended to teach Persephone the whole spectrum.

He would have to speak with her later.

"When do you begin training with Hecate?" he asked.

"This week," she said. "She gave me homework."

"Hmm," he acknowledged and leafed through a few more pages before closing the book. "I heard you greeted new souls today."

He spoke casually, yet as he lifted his gaze to meet hers, she straightened, ready to defend her choice.

"I was walking with Yuri when I saw them waiting on the bank of the Styx."

"You took a soul outside Asphodel?" That was far more concerning to him than the fact that she had greeted souls.

"It's Yuri, Hades. Besides, I do not know why you keep them isolated."

"So they do not cause trouble."

He admired Persephone for her trust, and of all the souls, Yuri was probably the least likely to break protocol, but offering them free rein of the Underworld would only prove difficult. Even Persephone could not manage to stay out of trouble. The last time she'd wandered into the wild of his realm, she'd found herself face-to-face with Tantalus.

She must have forgotten that encounter because she laughed, her eyes bright with amusement—an amusement that died with his stare. His eyes fell to her lips, which were now parted as she studied him, and his thoughts took a drastic turn.

He drew in a breath and tried to swallow, but his throat was dry. Suddenly, all he wanted to do was close the distance between them. Perhaps he could still have the evening he'd imagined with Persephone before Hera had ruined it all, but then Persephone dropped her gaze.

"The souls in Asphodel never cause trouble," she said.

"You think I am wrong."

He wasn't at all surprised.

"I think you do not give yourself enough credit for having changed and therefore do not give the souls enough credit for recognizing it."

Her words surprised him and stirred something warm within him.

"Why did you greet the souls?" he asked, curious about what had motivated her to approach.

"Because they were afraid, and I didn't like it."

He wanted to laugh, but he managed to suppress it. "Some of them should be afraid, Persephone."

"Those who should will be, no matter the greeting they have from me. The Underworld is beautiful, and you care about your peoples' existence, Hades. Why should the good fear such a place? Why should they fear you?"

Once more, he would have laughed at her assessment if she weren't so serious. If anyone had been listening, they would never suspect she was talking about him, the God of the Underworld, and though there was perhaps a grain of truth to what she said, it was only that, and he feared the day she discovered otherwise.

"As it were, they still fear me. *You* were the one who greeted them."

"You could greet them with me."

She spoke as if she feared he might reject her suggestion as quickly as she had made it.

"As much as you find disfavor with the title of queen, you are quick to act as one," he observed.

The smile her words initially brought to his face vanished as he noted how she hesitated, asking, "Does… that displease you?"

"Why would it displease me?"

"Because I am not queen."

Hades did not like those words. It was as if she were distancing herself from the idea, and as she stood and took the book from his hands, he spoke. "You will be my queen. The Fates have declared it."

He noted how she straightened, her chin jutting in defiance. She had not liked what he said, and instead of confronting him, she turned and headed into the stacks, book in hand.

Hades followed, appearing before her as she made her way down one of the aisles.

"Does that displease you?" he asked.

"No," she said, brushing past him, and while he followed, she continued to speak. "Although, I would rather you want me as queen because you love me, not because the Fates have decreed it," she said as she returned the book to its place.

He frowned, waiting for her to face him before he said, "You doubt my love?"

Her eyes widened, and her lips parted. "No! But...I suppose we cannot avoid what others may perceive about our relationship."

Hades raised a brow and drew a step closer. "And what will others say, exactly?"

Again, she averted her eyes and shrugged as she answered, "That we are only together because of the Fates. That you have only chosen me because I am a goddess."

His brows slammed down over his eyes. Those sounded oddly like things her mother would say.

"Have I given you reason to think such things?"

He hadn't.

He already knew the answer.

"Who has given you doubts?"

"I have only just started to consider—"

"My motives?"

"No—"

He narrowed his eyes. "It seems that way."

She took a step away, though she had little room to put distance between them as her back hit the bookcase, which did nothing to dispel the tension between them.

"I am sorry I said anything," she snapped, her arms crossing over her chest, as if to put a barrier between them.

"It is too late for that."

"Will you punish me for speaking my mind?" Her eyes flashed, full of defiance, but those words interested him.

"Punish?" he asked, closing the space between them. He guided her hands away from her chest, his cock growing thick and heavy as he rested against her hips. "I am interested to hear how you think I might punish you."

She inhaled, her chest rising, and Hades could see the want in her eyes, yet she fought it, unwilling to give in to temptation. "I am interested in having my questions answered."

He'd forgotten everything that had come before her suggestion of punishment. "Remind me again of your question."

She looked at him shyly and took a moment to speak. All the while, he grew harder, still pressed between her thighs.

"If there were no Fates, would you still want me?"

An unsettling shock rippled through him as he considered her words.

If there were no Fates, would you still want me? He took a moment to comprehend them, to let them cycle through his mind, but there was a part of him that could not quite grasp why she felt inclined to ask such a question. In the end, did it matter?

The Fates were.

And so they were.

That was all.

Those were not the words she wanted to hear, though, and in truth, they were not enough, because Hades knew that what was between them had gone beyond fate.

And even if their future were to unravel, he would fight for it.

Desperately.

She began to lower her eyes and shift from between him and the shelf, seeking an exit, but he clasped her jaw, forcing her to look at him once more.

When he had captured her attention, his fingers brushed along her cheek as he spoke, low and rough. "Do you know how I knew the Fates made you for me?"

She shook her head.

He leaned in, allowing his parted mouth to touch her skin. "I could taste it on your skin," he said, and his lips followed the trail of his fingers—along her jaw, over her cheek. "And the only thing I regret is that I have lived so long without you." His teeth grazed along the shell of her ear and down her neck, a light caress that had her breath seizing. Then he pulled away.

She wavered a moment, and a look of confusion crossed her face before her brows lowered. "What was that?" she demanded.

He smirked, chuckling at her anger, and answered, "Foreplay."

And then he swept her over his shoulder and left the library.

"What are you doing?" she demanded, her hands pressed into his back as she tried to hold herself up.

"Proving that I want you," he said.

Since his obviously erect cock wasn't enough.

"Put me down, Hades!"

He grinned at her breathlessness, and his hand slipped up the back of her thigh and under her skirt, fingers finding her heated intimate flesh. Her moan ignited him, and he suddenly did not care to find a private place for what he intended to do to her. He shifted, bracing her against the wall just as her hands tangled into his hair and their mouths collided. He clasped her jaw, plying her mouth with his tongue while his other hand gripped her ass, grinding his hard and throbbing length into the soft cradle of her hips.

This was a need, he thought. A tonic that cured his frenzied mind.

"I will punish you until you scream," he promised, feeling the truth of the words swell within his chest. "Until you come so hard around my cock, you are left in no doubt of my affection."

He didn't think it was possible to grow any harder, but then her magic surfaced, smelling warm and sweet. He could feel it on the tips of her fingers like lightning, calling to his—to the shadows and threads that moved beneath his skin—and it only added to his excitement, to the heady anticipation of feeling her around him, hot and pulsing and coming.

He drew back to meet her gaze, to gauge her readiness, and then she spoke. "Make good on your promises, Lord Hades."

His lower stomach tightened, the head of his cock

throbbed, and he was suddenly so fucking desperate for her flesh, he could wait no longer. He worked his hand between them, intent on freeing himself and taking her against the wall—until it collapsed, and he stumbled forward with Persephone in his arms, catching himself before they tumbled to the floor.

As he straightened, he lowered her to the ground but kept her pressed to him because they had an audience—a large one, in fact, made up of mostly his palace staff, in addition to Thanatos, Hecate, and Charon.

Thanatos looked in their direction and away, a slight tint to his pale cheeks. Charon's dark eyes widened before he too averted his gaze, breaking into a wide smile. Hecate was the only one who stared openly, a brow raised, a tilt to her lips.

There was a part of him that acknowledged he should have been more mindful of where he chose to take Persephone, yet at the end of the day, the palace was his in its entirety.

He could fuck where he wanted.

Hades cleared his throat, and Persephone cast a glance behind her before pressing her forehead into his chest, and for a moment, he imagined he could feel the heat of her embarrassment through his shirt.

"Good evening," he said. "The Lady Persephone and I are famished, and we wish to be alone."

Her hands rested on his sides beneath his jacket until he spoke and she jabbed him in the ribs. He grunted, tightening his hold as his staff scrambled to clean up. They filed out of the hall, carrying platters of food, addressing them as they went, and with each "Good evening, my lord, my lady," Persephone burrowed farther into his chest.

Hecate was the last to leave, and as she passed, she popped a grape into her mouth before closing the door behind her.

"Now," he said, guiding her back until she came into contact with the table. "Where were we?"

"You cannot be serious."

"As the dead," he answered.

"The…dining room?"

He did not understand her hesitancy, not when they had done this before, but perhaps she had envisioned something far different when he had promised punishment.

"I'm quite hungry, aren't you?"

He lifted her onto the table and took her mouth, tongue sliding out to caress her lips and then dipping to collide with her own. His hands slipped up her waist to her breasts. He wanted to touch her smooth skin but settled for teasing her nipples before taking each into his mouth through her dress. Her legs tightened around him, heels digging into his ass, urging his hips forward. He indulged for a moment, surging forward to kiss her as he guided her to her back. Once she was settled, he straightened and took her in—a literal goddess, a queen in her own right, spread before him, golden hair spilling off the edges of the table. Her chest rose and fell, her eyes gleaming with a hunger he could feel in the pit of his stomach.

She was a dream—one he never wished to wake from.

He drew each of her legs up, so her heels rested on the table, and kissed the inside of each of her knees. The skirt of her dress was pooled at her hips, and he pressed her legs apart, exposing her hot flesh as his mouth closed over her clit.

She arched, her legs coming up to cradle his body, and while he liked the feel of her thighs against his face, the position did little for her pleasure and his access, so he pushed them down once more and continued to caress her with his tongue. She tasted warm and wet, and he was consumed by her as she writhed and moaned and whispered encouragement.

Then she stretched her leg, her foot rubbing his engorged flesh, and as much as he would have liked to free his sex and slide inside her, what he wanted most was to make her come.

And she was close.

Her body was a bowstring pulled taut, and Hades was desperate to feast, but his chase was hindered by a knock at the door.

Persephone tensed, and a wave of frustration roared through him.

"Ignore it," he snapped, glancing up at her from where he still knelt, unceasing as he continued his work. His face grew hot, ears ringing as he pushed Persephone toward the edge, preparing to wring every bit of pleasure from her body, and in the aftermath, he would pour his own into her.

It was just as much a cycle of life and death—a give and take—one he would never bargain away.

The knocking sounded again.

"Lord Hades?"

"Go. Away."

Another word from the other side of the door, and he would send whoever it was to Tartarus.

"It's important, Hades."

Fuck. He recognized the voice now—Ilias.

He straightened completely, and Persephone followed.

"A moment, my darling."

He tried to keep his frustration at bay, but it was difficult given the nature of this interruption, made worse by Persephone's roving eyes, which lifted from his hard cock to meet his gaze.

"You won't hurt him, will you?" Her voice was low and silky, urging him to return.

"Not too terribly," he said, though he was already weighing options.

He stepped away, gaze lingering on her flushed skin, the evidence of how hard he'd chased her orgasm, and slipped outside to find Ilias waiting.

"This better be important," Hades hissed, "or I will send you to Tartarus—a year for every word you speak. Choose carefully."

Ilias did not seem fazed by Hades's threat as he replied, "It's urgent."

Hades stared at the satyr for a moment, recognizing that he never summoned Hades unless absolutely necessary, which meant whatever had occurred was not good. He wondered if it had anything to do with Kal or Hera, and he stiffened at the thought.

"I will be along soon," he said.

Ilias nodded. "I'll be in security."

That made Hades curious and slightly concerned, but he pushed those thoughts to the back of his mind as he returned to the dining room before he could watch the satyr leave. Persephone had moved from her perch on the dining table and now stood, staring up at the ceiling. Hades wondered what she found so appealing, but he did not ask, remaining silent as she turned to face him.

"Is everything okay?" she asked, keeping her arms crossed tight over her breasts, as if she wished to put up some kind of wall between them. A wall he refused to allow.

He drew closer, and her hands went to his waist. "Yes," he said. "And no. Ilias has made me aware of a problem better dealt with sooner than later."

"When will you be back?"

"An hour. Maybe two," he guessed, depending on what Ilias wanted, but he did not wish to worry Persephone.

Disappointment darkened her eyes.

He placed a finger beneath her chin to hold her gaze. "Trust, my darling, that leaving you is the hardest decision I make each day."

"Then don't," she said, and her arms wound around his waist, sealing their bodies together. "I'll go with you."

Her suggestion made him stiffen. Though he did not know what Ilias had to show him, he could not imagine anything good coming from Persephone's presence in his work, at least aboveground.

"That is not wise."

"Why not?"

"Persephone—"

"It's a simple question."

"It isn't," he snapped and regretted the loss of his temper as her eyes widened and her mouth hardened. He sighed. All he wanted to do was get this over with so he could return to her. Could she not see that?

"Fine," she said and took a step away. Her distance felt like more than the loss of physical touch. "I'll be here when you return."

Was she only saying that to appease him?

"I will make it up to you," he promised.

She arched a brow and, like a queen, commanded, "Swear it."

He offered the slightest smile, his still-heavy cock spurring his mischief. "Oh, darling. You don't need to extract an oath. Nothing will keep me from fucking you."

Though it felt like sacrilege to leave her without having made her come.

CHAPTER III
Return of the Nymph

Hades met Ilias on the top floor of Nevernight, which was dedicated to security. It was a large room, but the walls and ceiling sloped inward to a shadowed point just like the exterior of the building. The room was awash in the pallid light of computer screens, illuminating the stern faces of Hades's security team, though this was only a fraction. The others roamed the floors below and the dark alleys of the exterior, eyes peeled for anything untoward.

Ilias was positioned before a set of screens on the far wall, one for every holding room. Of the six, four were occupied. They were reserved for anyone who broke Nevernight rules, which occurred nightly and ranged from taking photos to card counting and, on rare occasions, spying.

It was the latter Hades expected to hear about from Ilias, considering his most recent visitors, but as he scanned the screens above the satyr's head, he caught sight of a familiar face, one that shocked his system.

"Is that Leuce?"

Though he asked the question, he knew the answer. There was no denying the ocean nymph's white hair and pale skin. It had been a long time since he had loved her, since she had betrayed him, since he had turned her into a poplar tree and forgotten her.

Yet here she was, returned from her prison.

How?

He certainly had not freed her.

"It is," Ilias said. "She made a scene when she arrived."

Hades wondered how many people glimpsed her outburst before it was contained. As if Ilias knew what he was thinking, he added, "We have begun damage control."

"Has she been questioned at all?"

Ilias shook his head. "I figured you would want the opportunity."

He would, though she had already had plenty of time to herself. Time to think up lies and believe them enough to avoid detection. It was a tactic she knew well and would not have forgotten, given she had spent her years as a tree unconscious. She would have woken up today believing he had only just confronted her about her infidelity—what a shock to learn that more than two millennia had passed. He wondered now if he had done her a cruelty or a kindness.

He watched her on the screen once more. She had pushed her chair against the wall, away from the table. Her knees were drawn to her chest and her thin arms were wrapped around them. She looked small, innocent, though that was not how Hades remembered her.

"What will you do with her?" Ilias asked. Hades

knew the satyr wasn't asking out of concern; he was asking because he wanted to know what he would be tasked with next, which was likely handling the nymph.

Hades looked at Ilias. He had not thought beyond this moment, save that he did not see any reason for Persephone to ever find out about Leuce. He could just imagine how she might react to not only discovering that his lover from the ancient world had returned but how he had handled her treachery—and it wasn't good.

Leuce was a complication.

"I do not know," Hades said. "Just...be on standby."

Ilias nodded and Hades left.

He could teleport into the room, and he often did when he confronted those who had committed wrongs against him, but he wanted time to think, to prepare to face the lover he had forgotten, so he moved from floor to floor, invisible to the crowd, growing more and more frustrated.

Of course Leuce would return only a day after he had managed to reunite with Persephone, he thought bitterly and then halted. That thought gave him pause. Perhaps it wasn't just a coincidence. Perhaps it had been more purposeful.

Perhaps it had been Demeter.

Suddenly, he was more than eager to confront her, and he did not hesitate. A cloud of thick, heated air hit him as he opened the door. Leuce pinned him with a chill gaze, her blue eyes narrowed in contempt.

"You."

It was all she said, but she spoke with venom in her voice and then launched herself at him.

She was lithe and willowy, and she moved as if she

had wings, cresting the table between them like it wasn't there at all. While her anger was justified, he was not interested in allowing her near, so he flung out his hand, and his magic became shadows that restrained her midair.

"You have every right to be angry," he said. "But if you have come here to ask for my aid, as I suspect you have, then you will do well to keep your hands to yourself."

She spit in his face, and he released her quickly. She collapsed to the ground, a pile of bony, white limbs. She glared up at him.

"Haven't you hurt me enough?"

He hadn't heard her voice in so long; he had forgotten the sound. Despite her anger, she spoke softly, yet each word was deliberate, another stone stacked, a greater guilt to bear. He wanted to flinch at her words but kept his cold composure. He did not want Leuce to think she was welcome to return to his side. In fact, he'd prefer she kept her distance.

Then he noticed the tears.

"What is this place?" she whispered, once again resuming the position she had taken in the chair and drawing her knees to her chest.

Hades was confused and taken aback, both by her tears and her question, but he recognized suddenly that he had given little consideration to how much of a shock this had all been. He had merely assumed ill intent, and he still did, but that did not take away the trauma of returning to a world that looked nothing like the one you remembered.

He crouched low before her.

"What do you wish to know?" he asked.

She froze a little, probably caught off guard by the change in his demeanor. After a moment, she spoke. "How long has it been?"

Dread crept up the back of his throat. He did not want to answer. Somehow, he felt that if he said it aloud, it would make him crueler.

"Over two thousand years."

She blinked, and for a moment, there was nothing behind her eyes. "Two thousand," she repeated, as if saying it would help her comprehend just how much might have changed over all those years. Then her eyes focused on him, and he thought she was recalling what he had looked like the moment he had turned her into a tree.

Perhaps he'd been wrong to think he could question her. She was clearly in shock.

"Why?"

Hades was not prepared for the way her voice broke. Guilt twisted his stomach, and because he had no explanation, he remained quiet.

"Why?" she said again, more demanding. Her watery eyes, rimmed with red, made her anger all the more apparent.

He gritted his teeth. "At first, because of your infidelity."

She shook her head a little, as if she didn't understand. "It took you two thousand years to get over my treachery?"

Hades's jaw tightened. He wanted to deny her statement, did not want her to think he had pined after her all these years, but he also did not want to admit the truth—he had forgotten.

"And Apollo? What was his punishment?"

Once again, Hades did not reply because the truth was shameful. He had not punished Apollo as he had Leuce. Indeed, he had done nothing to the God of Music, and at the time, that had seemed more than fitting, given that Apollo had seduced Leuce in retaliation for Hades's refusal to allow him to reunite with his lover Hyacinth. So he'd left the god alone with his misery.

She scoffed and looked away, more tears sliding down her cheeks. "You're all the same," she whispered.

Hades frowned, brows knitting together. He wanted to say something about how he had changed like the new world she found herself in, but what good did that serve? She was a victim of his wrath, and no matter how he had moved forward, nothing changed that.

He rose to his feet. He had been wrong to think he could question her now, but that only meant he would have to keep a close eye on her longer.

"You have much to learn if you are going to return to this world," Hades said.

"That's all you have to say?"

He stared back at her, uncertain of what she wanted from him and feeling like there really were no words great enough for this moment.

When he said nothing more, she spoke, her words bitter. "I see you haven't changed."

"If that were true, I'd have told you I owe you nothing beyond the life I have granted you and turned you away." He recognized the irony of his words. As much as he had granted her life, he'd also taken the majority of it away.

"I don't need your charity."

"Don't you?" he asked. "Or is the one who returned you to your human form offering a hand?"

Her brow creased at his comment. "Was it not you?"

He was concerned by the genuine confusion in her expression and asked, "Exactly how did you come to be here tonight?"

"I woke up," she said. "I screamed your name until someone brought me here."

He stared at her for a long moment. He did not sense a lie, and though she may have omitted parts of the truth, he supposed it wasn't impossible that she had not seen the person who had restored her to her natural form.

Still, Hades did not trust her. Ilias would have to keep an eye on her activity once she was settled.

He turned to the door.

"I will have my people help you make the transition into this world," he said. "But beyond that, never contact me again."

With that, he left.

Someone was fucking with him, and he did not like it.

First Kal, then Hera, now Leuce.

He had wanted his confrontation with her to be short, concise, and final, but he knew he'd have to talk to her again. He needed more information on her sudden transformation. He had a hard time believing she didn't know who was responsible, and her connection to him was too great for someone not to use it against him.

Hades instructed Ilias to find Leuce a place to stay and assign surveillance before returning to the Underworld, and while he'd have liked to return to Persephone, he had one other unpleasant task ahead—visiting the Fates.

Dread pooled low in his stomach, a weight as heavy as the guilt he carried for Leuce. Hades never enjoyed visiting the Fates, but he liked it less when it was personal. They were deities who understood their power and used it to mock, tease, tantalize, and provoke, and he knew that he would not escape their ridicule tonight, which would make the horror of his labor worse.

He manifested outside the Fates' mirrored palace, the size of which was impossible to detect given that the structure was almost consumed by evergreens and ivy. When Hades had created their isolated realm, the sisters had insisted on many things. Among them, the palace was to be made of mirror and glass.

"*To reflect the truth,*" Clotho had said.

"*To show what is,*" Lachesis explained.

"*To illustrate reality,*" Atropos added.

Hades had no doubt the Fates used the mirrors for more than just truth. They represented possibility, and while possibility could be grand, it could also be devastating. The Fates were supposed to be neutral deities, but truthfully, they had a tendency to favor tragedy.

"The King of the Underworld is troubled." Lachesis's voice was the first to reach him, yet the Fate had not yet materialized.

"The Rich One is in despair," Atropos said.

"The Receiver of Many is bothered." Clotho materialized as she spoke.

All the Fates looked the same, even in age, though Clotho was the youngest. They had long, dark hair and wore white. They did not have horns but wore crowns that resembled a nest of gold twigs.

"What is it, King?" Atropos inquired, appearing next.

"Tell us why you have come, Your Majesty," said Lachesis, incarnating last. They stood in an arc before Hades, and he gritted his teeth. They knew why he had come. He needed to know if they had woven Briareus's fate and if he could fight it.

"I need the thread of Briareus," Hades said.

"Demanding, aren't we?" Atropos said.

"Gruff," Clotho replied.

"Brutish," Lachesis agreed.

"Ask nicely," they said in unison.

His jaw hurt as he glared back at the three so hard, his eyes burned.

"Please," he gritted out.

The three broke into wicked smiles.

"Well, since you asked so politely," Lachesis sniffed.

"Pleasantly," Clotho added.

"Kindly," Atropos said. "What do you wish to know?"

"I must know Briareus's fate," Hades said, hating the way the Fates' eyes gleamed.

"Briareus, you say," said Lachesis.

"One of the Hecatoncheires," observed Clotho.

"The storm giants," Atropos affirmed.

"Why?" they asked in unison.

"As if you do not already know," he gritted out.

They were all quiet, and Hades recognized his own behavior in them. They would not continue until he gave them the answer they wanted.

"What will it cost me when I kill Briareus?"

He hated asking the question before he'd even tried

seeking a loophole, but he knew how this worked. He had seen the cycle repeat over centuries. There would likely be no other way to appease Hera, and the one thing he was not willing to sacrifice was Persephone and their future together.

"You wish to end a life I have spun?" Clotho said.

"A life I have measured?" Lachesis continued.

"A life I haven't cut?" Atropos asked, affronted.

As they spoke, a gold thread shimmered in the dark, twisting and looping around each of the Fates. He watched it, a thin line of energy that made up the fabric of the world.

"I do not wish to," Hades said, but the alternative was a price he would not pay, so he had to know this one. "As you are aware, this is Hera's vendetta."

"And you she has chosen for the deed," said Clotho.

The thread morphed into a silhouette of Hera, Persephone, and himself. The Goddess of Marriage stood between them and used her spear to sever the thread that connected them. That was not the end of Hera's rage, however. The threads continued to depict her pursuit of Persephone until she descended into madness.

Hades closed his eyes at the scene, and when he focused on the Fates again, the threads were gone.

Atropos spoke. "And the consequences of refusing her are so great, you are willing to face our wrath."

It was not a question, and Hades did not speak.

"A life like Briareus will cost you dearly, King," said Lachesis.

"The consequences are the same—a soul for a soul," said Clotho.

He did not bother asking which soul would replace the one he was about to take, though he knew a life like Briareus would come at a great cost. He was an immortal being, a monster, and whatever took his place would have to be powerful.

"Where does this path leave Persephone?" Hades asked, focusing on what was important.

If one path led toward madness, he did not trust that the other would not lead to hardship.

"Oh, dear king," said Clotho.

"There is no path," said Atropos.

"That will leave her unbroken," said Lachesis.

There is no path that will leave her unbroken.

Those words crowded his thoughts, pressing hard against his skull as he watched Persephone sleep from his position near the fireplace. She lay on her side, draped in black silk. Her hands were curled under her head, her breathing even and undisturbed.

She was safe.

If he were true to his nature, he would never let her leave his realm. It was the life above that would damage her...or would it be him?

He frowned at the thought and then downed what remained of the whiskey in his glass before shedding his clothes and climbing into bed. He hovered at the end and pulled the sheets from her body. As the silk slid over her skin, exposing her nakedness, she opened her eyes and turned her sleepy gaze to him.

"You're back," she said groggily.

She rested on her elbows, and her breasts filled his

vision. They swelled as she breathed, her nipples peaked and rosy, contrasting beautifully with her creamy skin. Hades leaned forward and took each into a hand, lavishing her with kisses. As his tongue teased, she let out a moan, fingers tangling into his hair and tightening as she pulled, urging his lips to hers, and he obliged, crashing down on her mouth. He let his body mold to hers for only a moment before his knee parted her thighs to tease her, feeling the wetness of her arousal. Another wave of sheer pleasure rocketed through him, straight to his already-hard cock, and as much as he wanted to be inside her, he wanted to prolong this more.

He left her lips, trailing kisses down her body until he reached the apex of her thighs, and as he went down on her, he held her gaze. She had returned to her original position, leaning back on her elbows, watching with lust-clouded eyes. She inhaled deep, and Hades focused on the sound of her quickening breaths as he continued. He loved the taste of her, the feel of her heated flesh against his tongue. All the while, his cock throbbed and the anticipation of plunging into her warmth made his balls tight.

"Fuck," Persephone breathed, and Hades glanced up to see her head had fallen back, her fingers crushing the sheet beneath her. Then she began to move against his mouth, chasing the friction that would make her come. That was when Hades pulled back. Persephone watched him, and then her eyes fell to his length, heavy with arousal.

"Let me pleasure you," she said.

He did not argue as she moved to her knees before him and took him into her mouth.

He intended to release his breath in a slow stream, but it came out as a gruff exhale. In their time together, she had gained a rhythm, and she used it now—her hand cupping his balls, her mouth working the crown of his cock.

"Yes," he hissed as her mouth moved down his shaft while she continued to stroke him. The pressure made his ears ring, and all he could focus on was her touch, her smell, her presence. She filled all his senses, and as her mouth popped off his cock, he guided her onto her back. Her legs fell open, and he jerked her close, stroking himself before guiding his cock to her entrance. She slid on with a practiced ease and they moved together. Hades kept himself upright, one hand on Persephone's shoulder, as they slammed together. Her breaths turned to cries as he moved, alternating between long, slow strokes and rapid thrusts. He wanted to kiss her, but he also wanted to watch her expression continue to morph as he fucked her into oblivion.

"It feels so good," she whispered, her head hung back, her throat exposed.

Hades bent and kissed her there. "I thought about this all day," he said. "How I would make you come."

At his words, she met his gaze and he pulled back, bringing her with him, lifting her into his lap. Her legs framed his body, giving her the leverage she needed to move with him. He liked this position—he could feel her breasts and her swollen clit rubbing against him, and when she grew too tired to move, he rolled with her, moving to their sides. He pulled her thigh up and behind his knee, continuing to thrust. The pressure at the base of his cock was building, moving upward, and he wanted to go faster but also make all this last forever.

Persephone's cries became keen, and he could feel her muscles contract around him.

"Fuck," she breathed, her hand sliding down her stomach to her clit, rubbing vigorously.

"Come," he commanded, and as her orgasm tore through her, he followed, body stiffening as his release spilled inside her. Hades drew his arm around Persephone's waist and pulled her close, their breathing evening as their bodies relaxed.

"Was everything okay?" Persephone asked, her voice heavy with sleep.

"Fine," he replied, even though it was a lie.

CHAPTER IV
The False Oracle

"Are you sure you do not wish for me to take you to work?" Hades asked, standing outside Nevernight. He gripped Persephone's ass, his cock growing harder the longer he held her close, but he found that he did not want to let her go, even with Antoni waiting to take her to work.

"I am sure you have more important things to do than take me to work," she said.

"Nothing is as important as you," he said.

She arched her brow. "My life will never be the same now that all of New Greece knows about us," she said. "I'd like to keep parts of my routine, even if they seem... impractical."

He had anticipated this and did not argue, though he glanced at Antoni, who had instructions to see her safely to work and report on anything amiss.

"Will you come to me tonight?" he asked.

"I think I should stay at the apartment tonight," she said. "Lexa misses me."

Disappointment made his body heavy, though he tried to mask it by pressing a kiss to her forehead. He knew this was what she had wanted—a balance between the life she shared with him in the Underworld and the one she had here with her friends and roommate.

"Of course," he said.

"You aren't...mad, are you?" Though she peered up at him, she almost seemed to shrink, as if she were either embarrassed by her question or expected him to express his anger.

Instead, he frowned, brows lowering over his eyes. "Why would I be mad?"

"I just...didn't want to disappoint you."

Her words confused him, but he thought he could guess where this was coming from, and it had everything to do with her mother.

He lifted her chin. "Will I miss you?" he asked. "Yes, but I am not disappointed."

Persephone stared at him for a moment, then lifted onto her toes and kissed him on the mouth. She took a step away before he could hold her any tighter or deepen the kiss. It was time for her to go.

A new sense of dread filled him at the thought of what she would face today. Given their public reunion, it was likely she would endure not only questions from her curious coworkers but an onslaught of other media.

As Persephone slid into the back seat of his black Lexus, Hades's gaze shifted to Antoni. The cyclops nodded and then shut the door, rounding the car to enter the driver's side. Hades watched as the car slipped into traffic and disappeared down the street.

He took a deep breath. It was an attempt to loosen the knots in his stomach, the strange dread that still consumed him at letting Persephone out of his sight. It was ridiculous. He knew she needed freedom, and he had no desire to be like her mother, to keep her sequestered and sheltered from the world at large. Those actions would only make her wilt, but he did want her to recognize that the world was a different place when people knew her name, and he feared that she would come to understand that too late.

Hades returned to the Underworld, teleporting to his office. He approached the bar to pour a glass of whiskey when he found his cabinet was empty.

Strange, he thought, and surveyed the room, noticing that the door to the balcony was slightly ajar. He approached and stepped out, looking down to find an explosion of broken glass on the cobble-stoned courtyard below.

"What the fuck," he said under his breath and teleported to the ground. The glass crunched beneath his feet as he appeared, once again looking around in confusion. It appeared that every bottle of alcohol he owned had found its way over the edge of his balcony.

In all the time he had existed, this had never happened.

The air changed suddenly, filling with a smoky, earthy smell.

Hades turned to see Hecate appear, cloaked in black velvet. The Goddess of Magic often wandered the world at night, wrapped up in various missions of her own making. Hades never questioned her whereabouts, trusting that whatever she was up to was warranted.

Except that today, he suspected she had something to do with the mess at his feet.

"Where have you been?" Hades asked.

The goddess turned toward him, removing her hood, revealing her dark, braided hair. "Meddling," Hecate replied sheepishly.

Hades had no doubt and indicated the glass littering the ground. "What happened here?"

Hecate let her gaze fall, though Hades suspected she didn't need to look.

"Persephone and I had a little fun after you left last night," Hecate answered.

"A little *fun*?"

The goddess did not even blink, her dark eyes as passive as ever. "We needed to find another way to expend her energy since you couldn't."

"It wasn't that I *couldn't*," Hades grated out.

"So you wouldn't? Even worse."

"Hecate," Hades warned.

"Do not be upset with me when it is you who could not perform."

Hades snapped his fingers, and pieces of the glass assembled into the shape of a bottle in his hand, full of amber liquid. He took a drink.

"If you are going to continue to question my ability to give my partner pleasure, I would be more than happy to prove otherwise with a detailed account of how I spent my night."

"Hmm," Hecate hummed, almost warmly, and answered, "I think I'll pass."

"If you're finished critiquing my sex life, I'd like you to accompany me on a business trip."

Despite the labor Hera had assigned, the pressing matter of Leuce's return, and the unrelenting media Persephone would face today—which Hades mostly blamed Kal for—he still had to deal with Acacius, the false oracle who was carelessly offering prophecy without any consideration for the consequences.

"Is that what you're calling your interrogations?" she asked.

"Do not act as if you disapprove," he said.

"Oh, I fully support persecution when it's deserved," she said.

"This is deserved," Hades said. "I have reason to believe this mortal has obtained a kind of relic that allows him to see the threads of the present and future."

"So what has he done to incur your wrath? Tell people when they will die?"

"No," Hades said mildly. "He's offering outcomes—athletics, cards, racing."

Hades had to admit it was unusual. In the past when he had handled a mortal who'd come into possession of a relic with sight, they'd already traumatized themselves and others by offering insight into death dates, lovers, the potential for children.

Everyone wanted to know the future until they didn't.

"What a waste," Hecate said, and Hades wondered if she was more upset that there was no particular drama to this case. Then she yawned. "But you know I do not go out in the daylight."

"Are you saying you would forgo the chance to punish a false oracle who sacrifices cats for divine favor?"

Hecate cringed noticeably. "How criminal. I'll be ready in ten minutes."

Hades did not often shape-shift and rarely had reason to, even when he was confronting those who broke the rules of his Underworld, but this was a special case. He had used this tired, mortal skin upon his initial visit to Acacius a few days prior to the race, begrudgingly approaching the greasy, dark-haired mechanic to evaluate his so-called skills. When he had entered the musty shop, Acacius stood behind a counter, pen in hand, filling out forms. He had not even looked up as he'd asked in a bored monotone, "What can I do for you?"

The man would likely not have been so dismissive if Hades had been in his usual form, but he reminded himself that he was there to bargain. He took a breath to release his frustration before resting a coin on the countertop. Hades pushed it closer, then let his hand fall to his side.

Acacius looked at the coin for a few seconds—long enough for Hades to know he was interested. Obols were not used as currency in New Greece, and while Charon no longer demanded them for entrance to the Underworld, they were a prized form of payment in the black market, one that granted access to Hades's club, Iniquity.

"What do you want?" Acacius asked.

"The winner of the Hellene Cup," Hades replied.

Acacius took a moment to respond, and in that brief silence, Hades searched for any signs that he was using a relic. Often, a user had to touch the item to channel its power, but Acacius did not stop writing notes, nor did Hades sense a burst of energy that would signal the use of magic.

"A second obol," Acacius said.

Hades's hand curled into a fist, but he said nothing and instead summoned another coin, placing it on the counter.

He would take them back later.

"Titan," Acacius said.

"Titan is not favored," Hades replied.

"You asked for the winner of the Hellene Cup. I gave it." Acacius dragged the coins toward himself, letting them scrape loudly against the counter. Hades ground his teeth. "Now leave."

The dismissal had ignited Hades's magic then, just as it did now, making it vibrate against his skin. He could have dropped his glamour and reveled himself to the mortal, but he felt he'd have more leverage later.

Threatening death and eternal torture did not always work on the underbelly of society. They tended not to fear him as much as those on the straight and narrow, which was why Hecate's presence was necessary. Every mortal feared her, even if they didn't know it quite yet.

New Athens was made up of districts. Some were known to the world at large and their purpose evident—the fashion district and the pleasure district were two examples. Then there were those that were unknown, pockets of New Athens that might look pleasing enough in the daylight, but when night fell, they transformed into terrifying and violent landscapes.

The worst of these was called Hybris, named after the daimon of the same name who presided over violence, recklessness, and hubris. Its proximity to a major motorway, a railway, and a port meant that it was the perfect area to move a combination of illegal materials across

New Greece. Despite this, the district proved useful to Hades, and he had even made use of its inhabitants' abilities to gain various weapons, relics...even people.

It was one reason he allowed it to continue, but not without oversight.

Hades and Hecate appeared before a large, metal building. A matching metal fence kept most of the building obscured from view, so it was impossible for outsiders to tell how large it was, but Hades knew it was extensive. Behind its facade as a mechanic shop was a business that received stolen goods, sold them, and moved them across New Athens, and it was all owned by Acacius.

"Charming," Hecate said, but it was clear she was not impressed. She stood beside Hades, concealed in her black robes.

He glanced at her. "You look like Thanatos."

"Better Thanatos than a greasy mortal," she replied. "Why are you hiding anyway? You're not one for dramatics outside your relationship."

Hades glowered. "I'd rather Acacius not realize he's dealing with me until the last possible moment."

The two entered the open gate. There were six garage doors, each open and occupied by a variety of cars. A few of the men who milled about in the lot stared openly, probably because Hecate looked like Thanatos.

Hades groaned inwardly.

"Can I help you?" A man approached, wiping his hands on an oil-stained towel. He was dressed in a blue button-up with the name Giorgos embroidered on the left pocket.

"Is Acacius here?" Hades asked.

"Who's asking?"

Annoyance made his spine stiffen, and for a moment, he forgot he wore the skin of a mundane mortal. At the same time, Hades felt the energy shift between them. Hecate was casting a spell. The smell of her magic permeated the air, likely undetectable by the man opposite them. Hades could tell when the spell hit because the man's expression shifted to friendly confusion.

"Sorry. Let me take you to him."

Hades glanced at the goddess whose face he could not see beneath the hood she had pulled far over her head.

"What would you do without me?" she asked.

"Be far more inconspicuous," Hades replied.

The garage felt humid and smelled like oil and gasoline, and while it was lit by rows of fluorescent lights, there were dark pockets throughout the warehouse-like shop. Hades imagined they concealed various illegal goods. Now and then, the sounds of an engine revving or a car squealing interrupted the chatter of the workers.

Acacius was working under the hood of a red car. Hades recognized him even before Giorgos called out his name.

"You have visitors."

Acacius kept his back to them, continuing to work beneath the hood of the car. He was taking his time to greet them. It was the behavior of a man who believed he had both time and power, and Hades supposed that, as of right now, that was still the case. Beside him, Hecate grew impatient, and when he felt her cast another spell, he gave her a warning look. He needed this to unfold as naturally as possible.

When Acacius finally straightened and turned to face them, he had a cigarette in his mouth, which he removed only to blow smoke in their direction. He was a round man with a swath of dark, curly hair. His lips were thin, and when he spoke, he revealed a set of uneven, oddly spaced teeth.

"I don't return payment," he said, then his eyes shifted to Hecate. "So you and your friend can go back the way you came."

His soul was almost as unpleasant as his exterior, the only bright spot being the dedication he had to his family.

"I haven't come to seek repayment," Hades replied. "Your prediction was right."

"So what? You want to strike another deal?"

"Of sorts," Hades replied.

Acacius stared and was either smiling or scowling. Hades could not tell which. Acacius placed his cigarette in his mouth and spoke as he turned to close the hood of the car.

"Let me guess. Another horse race?"

"Not quite."

The man turned, narrowing his oily eyes at Hades. He stepped closer and took the cigarette from his mouth. This time, he blew the smoke directly in Hades's face.

"Your gambling habit is low on my priority list, got it? So unless you have something far more valuable to trade, I suggest you leave."

Hades had already sensed that they were surrounded—the mechanics in the shop had formed a circle around him and Hecate.

"How adorable," she said, her covered head moving from left to right. "They're trying to threaten us."

"Shut your friend up," Acacius said, poking his fingers in Hades's face.

The best thing about this disguise and why Hades

had wanted to wear it was that Acacius and his gang would underestimate him, which made the next few seconds more satisfying than ever.

The god snatched Acacius's fingers and bent them back. A crisp, clear snapping sound preceded Acacius's pained screams.

Simultaneously, his men jumped into action. Hecate whirled, throwing off her hood, sending a wave of magic through the air that halted everyone in their stride.

Hades stepped toward Acacius, who knelt on the ground, cradling his hand. As he approached, he smothered the mortal's smoldering cigarette with his boot and knelt face-to-face with him. With his stern expression gone, Acacius looked younger—a boy playing a man's game. Hades was about to show him just how unprepared he was to deal.

"Now, about that bargain."

"Wh-who are you?"

At that question, Hades let his glamour fall away.

Acacius's eyes widened, but he did not tremble, and Hades wasn't sure if that was something to be respected or concerned about.

"Hades," Acacius breathed his name, and the god rose to his feet. The mortal remained on the ground, lifted on his elbow so his bruised and broken fingers were visible. "What do you want?"

"Nothing too taxing," Hades said. "Just your cooperation."

Acacius made his way to his feet before he asked, "In exchange for what?"

He was a foot shorter than Hades, yet still managed to appear hardened and unafraid in the face of death.

"Let's not pretend you have anything to bargain with," Hades replied. "We both know I could dismantle your empire with a snap of my fingers, so what will it be?"

"Depends on what you want from my cooperation."

Hades stared, unamused. "The audacity," he said, though he had expected this behavior. "I know you possess some kind of relic. Something that allows you to see the future. I want it."

"That is a hefty price."

"Give it to me, or I take it by force. Can you survive a bruised ego in this part of town?"

The answer was no, and Acacius knew it. His lips slammed into a hard line. "Follow me," he said and turned to leave the garage.

Hades started to follow but paused when Hecate did not. "Are you coming?"

"No," she said, a smile curling her lips. "I think I'll stay."

Acacius led him to an office inside the garage. It was lit with low, amber light, and as Hades entered, he noted several expensive furnishings, among them an ornately carved executive desk and accompanying leather chair, the back of which faced the door and a wall of windows, something Hades found odd. Usually, people of Acacius's caliber did not sit with their backs to doors or windows for fear of assassination, but perhaps he felt comfortable in his own space.

Hubris, Hades thought.

Acacius moved behind the desk, removed a set of keys from his pocket with his uninjured hand, and opened one of the drawers. Hades watched him closely, not trusting that he wouldn't try something stupid, like drawing a gun on him. While those weapons were known to be useless against gods, people still made the attempt. The last one to try was Sisyphus, and that had ended with the gun melted to his hand.

Instead, though, the mortal set a small box on the desk. It appeared to be a ring box, but what was inside surprised even Hades.

It was an eye.

"Is that what I think it is?" Hades asked.

"That depends on what you think it is," said Acacius.

"You are wearing your chances thin."

"It is the eye of the Graeae."

It was exactly as Hades thought. The Graeae were three sisters who wore the skin of hags, though their true form was rather monstrous. The three had the bodies of swans, though their heads and arms were human, and between them, they shared a tooth and an eye.

"How did you come to possess it?" Hades asked.

"I took it from them," Acacius said. "The Graeae."

"You took it from them?" Hades repeated. "When?"

The Graeae had not been seen in centuries, choosing to self-isolate, fearing the evolution of man—and rightly so, as Acacius had demonstrated.

"They were obtained by hunters and brought to me," he said. "Monsters are worth a fortune in the market."

"So you sold them."

There was a moment of silence, then Hades pounced. He grabbed a handful of Acacius's shirt and slammed him down on his desk.

"Who did you sell them to?" he demanded.

The mortal's hands dug into Hades's arms as he held him down—even the broken ones.

"Di-Dionysus!"

Hades released the man.

"How long ago?"

"They were shipped off just yesterday."

The God of Wine was as much a collector of monsters as Hades, and while Dionysus probably thought the Graeae would make a nice addition to his collection, it was likely what he really wanted was the eye, and Hades wanted to know why. What information did he hope to obtain?

Hades reached for the box and placed it inside the pocket of his jacket before heading toward the door.

"You cannot just *take* what's mine," Acacius said. "That eye was bought and paid for."

"Perhaps my generosity has led you to believe you are entitled to make demands," Hades replied. "It doesn't." At the door, Hades paused. "Dionysus will come for you. He always does. I would remain alert, not that it will do you much good."

"You cannot leave me to him," Acacius argued.

"Tell me one more time what I can and cannot do," Hades said, and as he stepped outside, he found that Hecate had transformed many of Acacius's men into topiaries.

"I think they look better this way," she said. "I trimmed them after."

Hades raised a brow. "I'm assuming they did something to deserve this?"

She shrugged. "They didn't like cats."

CHAPTER V
Power Play

While Hecate returned to the Underworld, Hades went to Nevernight and informed Ilias of the situation with Acacius, advising him to maintain surveillance on the mortal's shop. It was not so much with the intention of providing protection as much as it was to see who visited.

"I'm not so certain that man will live long," said Ilias.

"Agreed," Hades replied. "He fucked with a god."

Ilias shook his head. "Acacius established himself as someone who has answers. Now he doesn't. He'll find himself at the end of someone's gun soon enough."

Hades did not doubt it. It was just another consequence of using relics.

"Wonder what Dionysus wants with the Graeae," Ilias mused.

Hades did not know, but he would find out.

In the meantime, he also had to deal with Hera's fucking labors, the thought of which filled him with both anger and dread. It tightened his muscles and filled his stomach with an almost arresting feeling that he couldn't shake when he thought of the daunting task of executing someone he cared for. And what happened after? What if she asked him to murder again? He could only hope that by then, he found a way out of these labors that left his future with Persephone intact—not only their future, Persephone's future.

Hera was not above torturing gods, and Hades knew if she did not get her way, she'd set her sights on Persephone.

It would be a move the goddess regretted for the rest of her life.

Hades crested the stairs that led to his office and paused outside the gilded doors. Something was wrong. The feeling raised the hair on the back of his neck and trickled down his spine. He noted it and continued inside to find his office empty. He started across the room, intent on heading for the bar, when something snuck up behind him.

"Boo!"

Hades whirled and punched Hermes in the face.

The God of Mischief stumbled back and clamped his hands over his nose. "Motherfucker! Why did you do that?" he demanded.

"You scared me," Hades said simply, lips curling at the sight of the god's pain.

"I did not," Hermes said, dropping his hands. Any evidence of the strike to the face was already healed. "You *wanted* to punch me."

"Don't give me an excuse," Hades said, making his way to the bar, where he poured himself a drink. "To what do I owe your visit, and what can I do to prevent it in the future?"

"Rude," Hermes said, sauntering to the bar. "You're talking to a hero."

Hades raised a brow.

"You should be thanking me," he continued. "I distracted a whole crowd of screaming fans so Sephy could go to work."

Hades frowned. "Was she not escorted to the door by Antoni?"

Hermes's face fell, as if he realized he'd brought something to Hades's attention that he shouldn't have.

"Well, I could be wrong, but she kept repeating that she wanted a normal, mortal life, which is hard to do when you arrive at your day job in the God of the Underworld's personal car and allow his personal driver to escort you to the door."

"She's a *goddess*," Hades countered.

"A new one by her standard and ours," Hermes argued. "You have to give her time to transition into her role. She's played mortal for the past four years, and she's liked it. She will resent you if you take her normalcy away too quickly."

"You sound like Hecate," Hades accused.

"I *resent* that," Hermes sniffed. "I can be wise."

Hades sighed, frustrated. The problem was, she was no longer normal. People saw her differently just by her association with him.

"We've been famous all our lives," Hermes said. "Persephone hasn't, and she will not learn how to live this life without mistakes, so you might as well let her make them."

"There is no room for mistakes, not when it comes to her safety."

"Not everyone is a threat to her well-being."

Except that anyone who was a threat to him was a threat to her—and that very nearly included everyone.

Hades was doubtful, and then Hermes leaned across the bar so far, his chest almost touched the counter, and he whispered, "Has anyone ever told you...you need therapy?"

Hermes had, in fact, told him often.

"Pot, meet kettle," Hades replied.

Hermes straightened and narrowed his eyes. "Since when did you start using mortal expressions?"

"I thought you might appreciate it."

"Well, I don't," he said, crossing his arms over his chest, but after a moment, he dropped them. "What does it mean?"

"It means," said Hades, "that you are a hypocrite."

"Rude! That's twice in one conversation, Hades."

"Perhaps you should stick to what you do best, then."

"And what is that?"

"Fuckery," Hades replied and downed his drink.

"Are you saying that's all I'm good for?" Hermes asked.

It was a trick question, and Hades did not bite. Instead, he was quiet for a moment before he asked, "How long has it been since you visited Bakkheia?"

Bakkheia was one of Dionysus's nightclubs. Of those he owned, it was considered rather tame, but it was just as difficult to gain entry into as Nevernight.

"Dionysus's club?" Hermes asked. "Why would I go there?"

Hades raised a brow. "Orgies."

Hermes's mouth opened and then closed before crossing his arms over his chest. "I was there last week. Why?"

"I'd like you to go again," Hades said.

"You're...asking me to have an orgy?"

"No," Hades said. "I'm asking you to take Dionysus a message."

Hermes sucked air through his teeth. "Can't you send an email?"

"These words are better delivered in person."

"Hades!" Hermes whined. "You're going to get me kicked out."

"I am certain you will have no lack of orgies in the future," Hades replied. "Tell Dionysus I'd be happy to chat about his recent acquisition at a time that is most convenient for him."

"No one talks like that anymore, Hades."

"I just did," he replied.

"And look how long it took you to get a girlfriend."

Hades glared.

"You know what I think you should do?" Hades did not reply, but Hermes continued anyway. "Just castrate him."

"Castrate him?"

"Think about it, Hades. Who'd mess with you if you started chopping off balls?"

"Nothing good comes from castrating gods," Hades replied.

Divinity could still be born from the flesh of the gods, as his grandfather, Uranus, had demonstrated with the birth of the Furies, giants, nymphs, and Aphrodite after his testicles were dropped into the ocean.

"It's just a suggestion," Hermes said and made his way to the door. "One you'll want to keep in mind once I deliver this message to Dionysus."

Hades was aware of Dionysus's difficult personality, and despite the fact that the God of the Vine was in possession of the Graeae, Hades still had the advantage.

Hermes paused a moment, as if he'd just remembered something, and faced Hades. "Be patient with Sephy. She tries so hard to be independent, she thinks relying on anyone is a weakness."

Then he left.

Hades gritted his teeth against Hermes's words. He didn't like how the god acted as if he knew Persephone better. Hades understood her need to be independent, knew that it stemmed from Demeter's overprotectiveness, but this was different. People were unpredictable, obsessive, and cruel. He did not trust them, and perhaps it was because he saw the impact of one bad seed. It took one man or woman to turn against a culture, and after a few well-delivered words, a nation was suddenly at war.

Persephone was just now learning the world she would battle, and it was nothing like the one she was used to, because it was his and there was nothing in his life that did not become darkness.

Hades sighed and polished off what remained of his drink before taking the small box out of his pocket. He sat it on the bar and stared at it, unopened. It was tempting to use its magic. Just holding the eye would reveal his future, though Hades knew it was ever-changing, hinging always on the threads the Fates wove into the world.

And if they discovered his use of the eye, he knew

they would retaliate, but there was only one thing they could take from him that would damage him beyond repair: Persephone. And while the Fates were vengeful, they were not rash. Even if they considered taking Persephone away, they'd weigh all possible futures, and once they perceived how each ended—in death and fire and darkness—they'd leave their threads entangled.

He opened the box.

The eye that stared back had a large, black pupil, and it was misshapen and gelatinous. He stretched his fingers on the table and curled them into a fist—even gods were not immune to curiosity. Zeus was obsessed with the future, with prophecy, constantly using his oracle to determine who was a threat to his throne.

All Hades wanted to know was that Persephone had a place in his future.

But knowledge always came with a price, and Hades wasn't willing to pay, even for the certainty. He couldn't.

There was too much at stake right now.

He closed the box, shoved it in his pocket, and left Nevernight to go in search of Persephone.

He wanted to hear about her day.

Hades found Persephone in her room, standing with her eyes closed. Her head was tilted slightly upward as if she were inviting him to kiss her full lips. As he observed her, she took a breath, shivering, and her shoulders rose with it. She looked…adorable, and he found himself smiling at how much he loved her.

Despite everything that had transpired today, this moment made it all worth it.

He touched her chin and pressed his mouth to hers, and his mind went blank, consumed by her smell and her taste and her touch. Her hands splayed softly across his chest, kindling heat in the core of his stomach. He stepped closer, tangled his hand in her hair, and kissed her harder. He wanted nothing more than to take her home to the Underworld and continue this worship, especially if it meant avoiding the world that existed beyond them.

Yet there was a part of him that did not wish to use Persephone in that way, so he pulled away. Hades pressed his palm to her cheek, searching her gaze. She seemed a little anxious, and while he could feel it tangled between them, he did not know what it stemmed from.

"Troubled, darling?"

Suspicion bled into her gaze. "You followed me today, didn't you?"

"Why would you think that?" he asked, especially since he hadn't, but he was curious about her reasoning.

"You insisted Antoni take me to work this morning, most likely because you already knew what the media was reporting."

"I didn't want to worry you." And while he had assumed she would be under the scrutiny of both the media and the public at large, he had to admit that he hadn't expected the crowd that had gathered today, but it appeared the public did not yet connect their fear of him to Persephone.

"So you let me walk into a mob?"

"*Did* you walk into that mob?" he asked, knowing better.

"You *were* there! I thought we agreed. No invisibility."

"I wasn't," he said. "Hermes was."

Her eyes flashed with a note of frustration and then dread as Hades spoke.

"You could always teleport, or I can provide an aeg—"

"I don't want an aegis. I'd rather not use magic, not…in the Upperworld."

"Unless you're exacting revenge?" He raised a brow, knowing full well she had no trouble turning Adonis's limbs into vines and Minthe into a mint plant.

"That's not fair. You know my magic has become more and more unpredictable. And I'm not eager to be exposed as a goddess."

"Goddess or not, you are my lover."

He had said it to emphasize his point, that things had changed. Even the attention she had received from writing about him was different from this, but he noted how rigid she became and glowered. "It is only a matter of time before someone with a vendetta against me tries to harm you. I will keep you safe."

At his words, Persephone hugged herself, and at least he knew some of them had gotten through.

"You really think someone would try to harm me?"

"Darling, I have judged human nature for millennia. Yes."

"Can't you, I don't know, erase people's memories? Make them forget about all this."

He frowned at her question. *All this*, he thought. What she really meant was *them*.

"It is too late for that. What is so terrible about being known as my lover?"

"Nothing," she said instantly. "It's just that *word*."

"What's wrong with 'lover'?"

"It sounds so fleeting. Like I am nothing but your sex slave."

One corner of his lips curled. "What am I to call you, then? You have forbidden the use of 'my queen' and 'my lady.'"

"Titles make me uncomfortable," she said and hesitated. "It's not that I don't want to be known as your lover...but there has to be a better word."

"'Girlfriend'?" Hades supplied. He had to admit, it was an odd choice given the circumstances of their fate, but it was modern enough.

She laughed and Hades glowered.

"What's wrong with 'girlfriend'?"

"Nothing. It just seems so...insignificant," she explained, growing flustered, and Hades felt less defensive as her cheeks reddened.

He touched her chin once more, holding her gaze as he stepped even closer. Their faces were inches apart, his lips hovering near hers, ready to take her mouth against his once more as he whispered, "Nothing is ever insignificant when it comes to you."

They stared at each other, and a sweet tension built between them at the faint brush of his lips against hers.

A knock sounded at the door, and Lexa shouted from the other side. "Persephone! I'm ordering pizza. Any requests?"

The sudden interruption had caused Persephone's heart to race. He could hear the steady thrum vibrating against his own skin, and there was a part of him that wanted to maintain that beat as they descended into a frenzied passion.

Neither one of them moved, and Hades was

unwilling to lose this moment, kissing down the column of her neck as she cleared her throat and spoke, flustered. "N-no. Whatever you order is fine."

"So pineapple and anchovies. Got it."

Persephone's reply was lost as Hades's hand came up behind her head and he sucked her skin into his mouth, his teeth gently grazing, sending shivers through her body.

"Are you okay?" Lexa asked, clearly not satisfied with Persephone's lack of response.

Hades chuckled and released her skin and continued his exploration. All the while, Persephone clung to him, her fingers digging into his upper arms. He liked it, liked knowing that the more pressure he felt there, the more tension he was building inside her.

"Yes," she hissed.

Lexa paused and then asked, "Did you even hear what I'm going to order?"

"Just get cheese, Lexa!" Persephone snapped.

"Okay, okay, I'm on it."

Lexa left after that, clearly amused, though her interruption seemed to have succeeded in distracting Persephone enough because she pushed against his chest to create distance between them.

"You shouldn't laugh."

He was confused by her comment—did she feel insecure about her reaction to him? If it was any consolation, he rarely had the ability to think beyond her when they were together.

"Why not? I can hear your heart beating. Are you afraid to be caught with your boyfriend?"

Persephone rolled her eyes. "I think I preferred lover."

He laughed, and he liked the way she looked at him when he did…like she wanted to make him laugh forever. "You are not easy to please."

"I would give you the chance, but I'm afraid I don't have time."

"I don't need long," he said, gripping the fabric of her dress. "I could make you come in seconds. You won't even have to get undressed."

The way she looked at him made his cock harder. It was sensual, almost a dare, yet she denied him.

"I'm afraid seconds will not do. I'm owed pleasure—hours of it."

He could not argue with that, but he could bargain. "Allow me to give you a preview, then."

He pulled her tight against him, and the bulge of his cock settled against her stomach, but she pushed against him.

"Perhaps later," she said, and he wasn't that surprised. She had been adamant about spending time with Lexa, and he knew that was important to her.

He could be patient.

"I'll take that as a promise," he said and vanished before he decided against waiting.

CHAPTER VI
The Past is a Shadow

When Hades returned to his room in the Underworld, he was exhausted but wired, his whole body alive with a need to come. He poured himself a glass of whiskey only to down it immediately. It slid down his throat like fire, and he gritted his teeth against the sensation. It did nothing to relieve the ache.

He raked his fingers through his hair, pulling it free from its tie before pouring a second glass. When that did not work, he discarded his clothing, lay down in his bed, and took his cock into his hand.

"*Fuck.*" The word left his lips in a low growl. He was engorged and hot, and the first pumps of his own fist made his head feel light. There was nothing compared to being inside Persephone, but at least he would sleep after this.

He stroked himself, rubbing his thumb over the head of his cock. He smoothed the come that had already beaded there down his shaft, but it wasn't enough, so he spit into his hand and gripped himself again, stroking roughly, closing his eyes so he could better imagine what it was like instead to have Persephone's body beneath his, fully sheathed in her warmth. He groaned at the thought and thrust harder into his hand, hips driving forward as if he really were inside her. Pressure built in his balls, and it rose higher and higher, and just as he thought he might come, he stopped.

His breath came harshly and he was so erect, his cock practically pointed at the ceiling, but he liked this high—the rush to an end that never came because it meant he could build it again and again. It is what he would have done if Persephone were here—draw out pleasure until he could not stand the tightness in his arousal and the heaviness in his balls.

When his breathing had returned to normal, he took himself again and closed his eyes, imagining that Persephone was straddling him. He sought the friction that this position usually offered. He thrust upward into his hand and stroked himself almost violently while his other hand tugged at his balls, heavy with a release threatening to come.

Once more, he felt the familiar stirring of an orgasm rippling from the pit of his stomach, tightening in his thighs and ass. This time, he came as a guttural sound tore from his throat, and in the aftermath, he continued to pump his fist along his cock, expending every last drop of come.

He lay there for a moment, feeling weightless, before rising to clean up and pour another glass of whiskey. This one he sipped, and when he was finished, he lay down to sleep.

Hades had only slept deeply a handful of times in his entire life, and most of those had occurred over the past few months with Persephone by his side. Usually he wavered somewhere between wakefulness and sleep, too on edge to let himself fully rest, which was why, when he felt something touch his face, he reacted quickly, his hand clamping down on the intruder's only to open his eyes and realize it was Persephone.

"Fuck!" He jackknifed into a sitting position and drew her to him, pressing kisses to the wrist he had snatched. "Did I hurt you?"

When she did not answer, he met her gaze and found she was staring at him, her eyes wide and her lips slightly parted. She looked flushed and sleepy, her wild curls falling haphazardly around her face.

"Persephone?" he said again, hoping to catch her attention.

She seemed to come to then, and she smiled, brushing a piece of hair from his face. "I'm fine, Hades. You only scared me."

He felt a wave of relief at her words and kissed her palm, only to draw her against him and lie down. Her weight was a calming presence, and he reveled in the feel of her draped atop him.

"I did not think you would come to me tonight."

"I can't sleep without you." She whispered the words against his skin, and his chest tightened at her admission.

He should say the same, but instead, he ran his hands down her back to her ass, grinding her middle into his growing erection and responded, "That is because I keep you up so late."

Persephone lifted her head and rolled her eyes, sliding

into a seated position, her thighs hugging his waist, her fingers threaded through his.

"Not everything is about sex, Hades."

"No one said anything about sex, Persephone."

She planted her hands against his chest and moved against his cock, and he could feel the heat of her through the thin sheet that separated them.

"I don't need words to know you're thinking about sex."

Well, that was true, and since it was no secret, he let his hands trail up her sides and to her breasts. He loved them—their fullness, their weight, the color of her hardened nipples. He wanted them in his mouth, and though Persephone inhaled against his touch, her hands stilled his.

"I want to talk, Hades."

"Talk," he said. "I can multitask...or have you forgotten?"

He sat up, and Persephone's arms wrapped around his neck while he lowered his head to tease her nipple through the fabric of her nightshirt. Meanwhile, his hands moved up her naked thighs.

"I don't think you can multitask this time," she breathed, her fingers twisting into his hair. "I know that look."

"What look?" he asked, pulling away with the intention of lavishing her other breast with just as much attention, but Persephone clasped his head between her hands.

She might be able to stop his mouth, but his hands continued his exploration, moving beneath the hem of her dress, skimming up her sides.

"You get this look. The one you have now. Your eyes are dark, but there's something...alive behind them. Sometimes I think it's passion. Sometimes I think it's violence. Sometimes I think it's all your lifetimes."

He said nothing, but he felt every word she spoke and knew they were all true. His hands tightened around her waist, and as he moved to kiss her, she spoke his name, but whatever she intended to say was lost as his mouth closed over hers. He rolled so that she was beneath him, parting her lips with his tongue, kissing her deeply before shifting, trailing kisses down her neck and over her breasts, but he was halted by Persephone, whose thighs clamped down on his waist.

"Hades. I said I wanted to talk."

"Talk." It wasn't as if they hadn't managed a full conversation during sex.

Then she spoke, and what she said drained the heat from his body. "About *Apollo*."

Fuck Apollo, he thought as he sat back on his heels. Why was he suddenly haunting his days? First Leuce and now Persephone?

"Tell me why the name of my nephew is on your lips."

"He's my next project," she said, as if that explained everything, but Hades felt agitated to the point that his jaw hurt from clenching his teeth. Apollo was not the kind of god one turned into a *project*, and if *project* meant what he suspected—that Persephone hoped to write one of her articles about the God of Music—the answer was no.

She seemed to see his frustration and continued in an attempt to convince him. "He fired Sybil, Hades. For refusing to be his lover."

He was not surprised. Apollo's response to rejection was revenge.

Spurn Apollo once, and never again.

Which was why Persephone could not write about him, but even as he looked at her, he knew this was going to be an argument. He could see the flash of determination in her eyes. She wanted to change Apollo, but Apollo was power, and power did not necessitate change.

Hades left the bed. Once again, he needed a drink.

"Where are you going?" she asked.

"I can't stay in our bed while you talk about Apollo."

He was honestly surprised by how triggering it had been to hear her speak his name, but perhaps it had something to do with Leuce's return. She was a reminder of Apollo's fury, and Hades could only think that if given the chance, Apollo might continue to execute his revenge.

Persephone pushed off the bed and approached as he poured himself a drink.

"I'm only talking about him because I want to help Sybil! What he's doing is wrong, Hades. Apollo can't punish Sybil because she rejected him."

"Apparently he can," Hades said, glancing at her as he took a slow sip from his glass.

Her features hardened and her eyes turned a vibrant green. Her glamour was burning away, which was how he knew she was truly mad.

"He has taken away her livelihood! She has nothing and will have nothing unless Apollo is exposed!"

But his frustration was growing too, and he drained his glass only to pour a second. He started to drink this one too but paused, staring at the amber liquid, one hand braced against the bar top, knowing that what he said next would just exacerbate the situation.

"You cannot write about Apollo, Persephone."

"I've told you before, you can't tell me who to write about, Hades."

He set the glass down and turned to face her. He felt like a fucking giant, towering over her, yet she just seemed to grow braver.

"Then you should not have told me your plans."

He regretted those words as soon as he spoke them. He was glad she had shared her intentions, but would she again given how this was turning out? He wasn't so sure.

"He won't get away with this, Hades!"

Her fists clenched, and he could sense her magic awakening beneath her skin. There was a part of him that wanted to reach out and touch her, urged on by his own magic, which always seemed desperate to tangle with hers.

"I'm not disagreeing with you," he said, realizing that he had to change his approach or she would never see reason. "But you aren't going to be the one to serve justice, Persephone."

"Who, if not me? No one else is willing to challenge him. The public adores him."

And they always had.

Apollo was the golden god, the light bringer, the epitome of youth and male beauty in ancient Greece. He had numerous temples built in his honor and even more today. His most basic role was driving away the darkness—something all mortals feared. He was their hero, the representation of everything good in their society. If they let themselves see the bad, they'd be forced to acknowledge the cracks in their own world.

And no one wanted that.

"All the more reason for you to be strategic," he said. "There are other ways to have your justice."

She glared at him. "What are you so afraid of? I wrote about you, and look at the good that came out of it."

If she was referring to their relationship, that would have been achieved by their bargain without her scathing articles, though he could admit that her words made him want to prove her wrong, to be better, and some good had come from them. The Halcyon Project, for example. But everything else was a thorn in his side, especially the public's obsession with both of them.

"I am a reasonable god," he said, though Persephone raised a brow at his response. "Not to mention you intrigued me. I do not want Apollo intrigued by you."

Her features softened for the first time since they began this argument.

"You know I'll be careful," she said, taking a single step closer. "Besides, would Apollo really mess with what's yours?"

She really had no idea.

He frowned and held out his hand.

"Come," he said, sitting in a chair before the fire. He pulled her to him, her knees framing his thighs. She leaned against him enough so that he could feel the softness of her breasts against his chest and still hold his gaze.

"You do not understand the Divine. I cannot protect you from another god. It is a fight you would have to win on your own."

Hades could not prevent retribution between a god and their target, even if it was Persephone. The only possible way was to bargain, and no god wanted to owe another.

Especially Hades.

But for her—for this goddess whom he loved more than anything—he would bargain, and that made what she asked next somehow more painful.

"Are you saying you wouldn't fight for me?"

He wouldn't just fight.

He would dismantle the world, and he would only feel remorse for Persephone, who would grieve for humanity. As he stared at her, innocent and beautiful, he thought he could see a hint of fear at whatever she saw in his eyes. He hated it but could not deny this darkness. It was as much a part of him as his magic—as her fate was woven with his.

He brushed a piece of hair from her face before trailing his fingers over her cheek.

"Darling," he said, his voice low and fierce. "I would burn this world for you."

Then he kissed her and cupped her face with his hands, moving them into her hair. Her lips parted for him, and his tongue slipped into her mouth. When her arms closed around his neck and her body melded fully to his, he felt as though he were no longer grounded. The world had fallen away, and it was only them and sensation. It was how he knew he could end worlds for her.

He pulled away only to rest his forehead against hers, their breath coming harshly against their lips.

"I am begging you," he said, drawing back only a

fraction to meet her gaze, his voice barely a whisper. "Do not write about the God of Music."

She nodded. "But what about Sybil? If I do not expose him, who will help her?"

He understood her worry for Sybil. Being the chosen oracle of Apollo was no easy task. They were part of the reason he got away with so many of his antics and how he maintained his status among the public. Sybil knew Apollo's behaviors, and she had stuck to her values when she had denied the god. It was that fact that led Hades to believe she would be okay.

But Persephone could not see that, and it was likely Sybil couldn't either. They, like everyone else, were caught up in the very human tendency to care what others thought.

"You cannot save everyone, my darling."

"I'm not trying to save everyone, just the ones who are wronged by the gods."

He brushed another strand of her wild hair away, studying every feature of her face—her bright eyes and freckled nose, her pink lips, raw from their kiss. "This world does not deserve you."

"Yes, they do. Everyone deserves compassion, Hades. Even in death."

"But you are not talking about compassion. You are hoping to rescue mortals from the punishment of gods. It is as vain as promising to bring the dead back to life."

"Because *you* have deemed it so."

His frustration was so immediate, he had to remove his hands from her body and grip the arms of his chair. He looked away, toward the fire. He wanted to argue with her, to point out that he had lived thousands of years with these gods and they had never changed. What made her think they would listen to a new goddess whose life was shaped by a mother who was too afraid to teach her about the harsh world save for a few false tales about the gods she hated most?

She placed her hands on his face and drew his gaze back to hers.

"I won't write about Apollo." She spoke quietly, sounding almost defeated, and though guilt twisted through Hades's stomach, he was relieved by her promise.

"I know you wish for justice, but trust me on this, Persephone."

She thought she knew the gods, but their histories were long and dark. It made them unpredictable.

It made them all dangerous.

"I trust you."

You don't, he thought, though he desperately wanted her to. He couldn't blame her, especially given what he'd just been thinking.

In the next moment, he stood, gripping her ass as he carried her to bed.

He was done talking.

He set her down and drew her nightdress up and over her head, and as he knelt before her, she held his gaze with a sensual stare that had his cock throbbing. He kissed the insides of her knees and then lifted himself enough to kiss her.

"Lie back," he whispered, and she did.

He pulled her legs apart, kissing her thighs and her center, growing warmer with each soft breath she took. His teasing made her restless. Her legs sought purchase on the edge of the bed, her fingers twisted into the sheets beneath her, and her body arched off the bed. Hades splayed a hand across her belly to keep her in place, and when she was still once more, he licked each side of her slowly, then used his fingers to spread her so he could access the soft silk of her center.

She was wet, heated, and his touch made her moan his name, which only succeeded in encouraging him to continue at his pace—a slow and steady mix of kissing, sucking, and blowing on every sensitive part of her. The teasing ceased when he curled his fingers inside her, pressing into a part of her that made her legs clench and her body tight. She seemed lost, her head thrown back, her eyes closed, her hands kneading her own breasts.

This. This is what I can do to her—for her. I can please her, he thought.

"Come, my darling," he said. "I want to taste you on my tongue."

He took her higher until her muscles contracted and a sweet warmth coated his fingers, and when he withdrew, he took them into his mouth.

"You are my favorite flavor. I could drink from you all day."

Persephone had rolled onto her side, breathing hard and spent, but Hades was just getting started. He gripped her hips and pulled her to him. The angle was odd because he was so tall, but as he slid inside her, Persephone offered a guttural cry. She didn't seem to know what to do with her hands. They tangled into her hair and then fell to her breasts and then to the bed, where she lifted herself enough to stare at where they were joined, where Hades thrust into her.

"Gods," she breathed, choking on a moan.

"Say my name," Hades commanded, but only keen cries escaped her mouth. "Say it!" he said again.

"Hades!"

"Again," he said as he thrust into her, moving so that his palms were on the bed beside her head. They were closer now, their heat building between them to an impossible level.

"*Hades.*"

"Pray to me," he continued. "Beg me to make you come."

"Hades. Please." She could barely form words, but he could scarcely think. He felt her everywhere.

"Please what?" he breathed.

"Make me come," she said, desperate, frustrated. "Do it!"

He drove into her until the pressure was too much and he erupted, releasing a guttural sound from his throat. He remained inside her, coming in waves, suspended on shaky arms, only to collapse atop her when he was finished. He kissed her, taking her into his arms and teleporting to the baths. While they showered, he took her against the wall. It was desperate and rough, and it wasn't until they lay in bed later that he realized why.

The conversation about Apollo did not feel finished, and as he lay by Persephone, her body pressed against his, he realized he was not okay. What if history repeated itself? Unlike Leuce, Hades did not believe Persephone would willingly sleep with Apollo, but the god was not above deception.

"Persephone?"

"Hmm?" She was almost asleep, and with only an hour left before she had to be up for work, he didn't feel he should bring up Apollo again, so instead, he let himself be jealous and vulnerable and offered a threat.

"Speak another's name in this bed again and know you have assigned their soul to Tartarus."

For some reason, it made him feel better.

CHAPTER VII
An Unwelcome Introduction

Persephone's alarm came too soon.

He opened his eyes and watched her rise and stretch. The silhouette of her body was haloed by the warm light from the fireplace, and his chest tightened at the sight. She did not seem to notice he was awake, and she disappeared into the bathroom. When the shower came on, he rose and dressed. As he poured himself a drink, he summoned coffee for Persephone.

When she returned to the room, she had a towel wrapped around her, and he sat, growing hard as she dressed. She looked at him as she finished buttoning her shirt, eyes falling to his very prominent arousal.

She smirked, smoothed her skirt, and approached, reaching for her drink.

"Thank you for the coffee."

"It's the least I could do," he replied, weighed down by guilt at seeing how exhausted she was.

She took a sip and then set it aside, going to her knees.

And despite his excitement at seeing her kneel, he touched her chin and asked, "Are you well?"

"Yes," she replied. Her voice was a low whisper. She pressed her hands flat against his thighs, inching her way toward his cock. Then she touched him, and his throat felt thick.

"Would you like release?"

He swallowed. "You will be late."

She shrugged. "Perhaps the waiting crowd will disperse some, then."

He said nothing, just stared at her as his skin grew warmer. She unzipped his trousers and pulled his sex free, rubbing him up and down before licking him from root to tip. He took a breath, letting it out slowly, watching as she swirled her tongue over the crown of his cock. His mind went blank, focused only on her warm and wet mouth, and his body responded, his chest expanding, his head light, his body hot and tingling. He had a moment when he wondered if he should come in her mouth, but she seemed intent, increasing the pressure and pace, and suddenly his want to come became a need, and he could no longer hold on to the tension in his body. His release came hard and fast, in a surge of electricity that left him feeling completely euphoric.

Persephone released him, standing to return her attention to her waiting coffee. Hades restored himself and stood, touching her jaw with a gentle brush of his fingers.

"You are far too generous, my darling."

She smiled, her face flushed. "I have no doubt you will return the favor."

"Eagerly," he said.

Despite how intimate they'd just been, Hades wasn't able to convince Persephone to let him take her to work, so he saw her off with explicit instructions for Antoni to escort her to the door and started his day with a visit to Iniquity. While Hades had many clubs, this one was... unique. There were two parts. One side entertained the public with burlesque dances, loud music, and alcohol. It was also the entrance used for those who sought help from Magi. Of all the criminals Hades worked with, he disliked the Magi most, and while he'd rather not entertain their so-called gifts at all, he liked having his thumb on their pulse so he could send Hecate to clean up their messes.

The other side of the club was a lounge for the most powerful criminals in New Greece. Criminals who had gained traction via Hades's influence—from brothel owners to the Mafia, relic dealers to assassins. His empire ran deep, and he pulled the strings. One mishap and they tumbled.

Today he came to speak to Ptolemeos Drakos, who led one of the greatest smuggling rings in the whole of New Greece. He was a hardened man with deep lines on his face and a shaved head. His eyes were dark and slightly narrow, his thin lips turned down at the corners, but he always dressed sharply in a tailored suit and colorful tie. When he entered Hades's office, he did not move to sit, which the god appreciated—this assignment would not take long.

"My lord," he said, his voice so deep, it was almost hard to hear him.

"Mr. Drakos," Hades said. "I'd like you to keep an eye out for any monsters that happen to make their way into the market. Make note of where they go and inform me immediately."

Hades wanted to know if Dionysus was making a habit of collecting monsters. It wasn't unusual considering many gods gave birth to said monsters, but Hades liked to know what all gods had, considering they could be used as weapons.

"Is that all, my lord?"

"For now."

"Very well," Ptolemeos replied, bowed, and left.

Hades was only alone a moment when the door opened once more. He looked up and found a woman standing in his office. She had long, dark hair and dark eyes. She was thin, dressed in a button-up shirt and slacks. He noted the badge on her hip.

"Who are you?" Hades asked, already irritated by her presence.

"My name is Ariadne Alexiou," she said. "Detective Alexiou."

"I'm not held to mortal law," Hades said. The police never interfered with the gods—not in their exploits or their quests for divine retribution. "So I cannot imagine why you're here."

He expected the woman to react in some kind of way—with frustration, or perhaps defensiveness. While they'd never supported them publicly, Hades knew the Hellenic Police Department supported Triad's idea of fairness, free will, and freedom. They did not like the idea that the gods intervened in justice and that there was nothing they could do about it. Divine justice ruled all.

Instead, the woman said, "I need your help."

Hades raised a brow. "You don't want my help."

"Do you make a habit of telling women how they think?"

"Well, aren't you bold," Hades replied, staring at the woman for a moment. It was only then he saw a bit of her confidence waver, and that was the root of her soul—a once self-assured woman who was crumbling on the inside. But why?

"I would not have come here if I wasn't serious," Ariadne said, and she crossed the room. "There are women going missing all over New Greece, three in the past week." She opened the folder she had held under her arm and laid three photos on his desk, each facing him. "Niovi Kostopoulos, Amara Georgiou, Lydia Lykaios. I must know...are they dead?"

"If I answer you, this can go no further. You don't get to question the dead." She nodded and he answered, "They are not."

"Then I believe their disappearances are connected, but I can't find anything concrete to link them. There are no commonalities in their background or appearance, nothing. It's like they vanished into thin air except for this one..."

She pulled out another folder and placed it atop the others. The woman in the photo had thick auburn hair, and she was smiling.

"Megara Alkaios. Her friends tell me she was last seen at Bakkheia. They swear she went inside and never came out."

The irony that this woman was here speaking of Dionysus when Hades had just discovered his acquisition of the Graeae yesterday was not lost on him.

"You still have not said why you require my help," Hades replied.

"I'm asking you to help me get into Bakkheia."

"Why?"

"Have you heard nothing I just said?"

"I heard every word, Detective," Hades said. "You have one instance of a woman going missing after entering Bakkheia, and suddenly you are accusing Dionysus of what? Trafficking?"

She raised a brow. "You said it, not me."

"Those are big accusations."

"You cannot tell me you aren't curious yourself," Ariadne said.

After the incident with the Graeae, he was.

"I am," he admitted. "But why do I need you?"

"It's my investigation!"

"One, if I had to guess, your supervisor would not approve of. So I will ask you again, why do I need you?"

"I'm putting everything on the line for this case. It will make or break my career. Do you understand?"

She might be putting her career on the line by coming to him for help, but that did not answer why she was invested in the case.

Hades was about to reply when his phone rang. He might have ignored it, but he noted that it was Ivy, the office manager at Alexandria Tower, the headquarters of his charitable organization, the Cypress Foundation—and she never called.

"Yes?" he answered.

"Lord Hades," Ivy said, breathless. "You did not tell me Lady Persephone would be by for a visit. I was grossly underprepared to serve her."

Hades's brows rose in surprise, though he supposed it was just a matter of time. He had hired Lexa, after all, though he berated himself for not being the one to introduce her to the ins and outs of Alexandria Tower. He could only imagine how overwhelmed she might be.

"I was not aware," Hades replied, glancing at Ariadne, who glared back, a sour look on her face. She apparently did not like being ignored, but all the same, Hades did not like being interrupted by unwanted guests. "Accept my apologies. I shall arrive soon."

He hung up the phone and picked up the folder Ariadne had placed on his desk. He would hand it over to Ilias.

"What are you doing with my file?" she demanded.

"You'll forgive me for wanting to conduct my own investigation into this matter," he said. *And you*, he added silently.

"I have done a *thorough* investigation."

"By mortal standards, I am sure," he said as he headed for the door. "As a rule, Detective Alexiou, it would be wise to never place all your money on one bet. My men will be in touch. Please, see yourself out."

With that, he left.

———

Ariadne's file felt heavy in Hades's hands, and while he was curious to figure out what exactly Dionysus was up to, he also wanted to proceed cautiously. The God of the Vine was neither an enemy nor an ally, though he represented a part of Hades's past he did not really like to recall. Still, this was the second time Dionysus had come up within a week.

He was up to something.

Hades took the folder to his office at Nevernight for safekeeping until he could meet with Ilias, then he teleported to Alexandria Tower. He used his glamour to remain unseen among his staff. He wanted to locate Persephone uninhibited, which was easy given that she was in his territory. He could feel her presence just the same as when she was in the Underworld. It was comforting to have her near, and the tension that had crept into his muscles while speaking with Ariadne lessened.

"Here it is!" he heard Lexa say as she walked ahead of Persephone into his office. Persephone stood in the doorway, her head tilting up and around as she took in the space. He wondered what she was thinking—probably something sarcastic about how he never used this office, though he'd like to make use of it now that she was here.

"Lexa," a woman called from her cubicle. "Have you finished the posters for the gala?"

Hades appreciated the interruption, as it left Persephone alone and Lexa occupied.

He made his way into his office, still undetected. She had moved beyond his desk, which he kept free of clutter, save a vase of white narcissus Ivy insisted on refreshing daily...and a picture of her. He had taken it when she was unaware as she wandered in the gardens outside his palace. He could recall exactly why he'd been drawn to capture the moment too...because she'd looked so perfect among his flowers, and he remembered not understanding how he'd gone so long without her presence among them.

The picture was a reminder of his awe that she was his.

Persephone reached for it, and Hades appeared behind her.

"Curious?"

Persephone startled, and the frame fell from her hand. Hades reached around her and caught it, returning it to its place on his desk before she turned toward him.

There was so little space between them, Hades could feel the brush of her breasts as she breathed.

"How long have you been here?"

Hades raised his brows. "Always suspicious."

She was wary of his power of invisibility, and while he did not blame her, he had promised not to use it to spy on her, and he had held to that, except for today, though spying had not been his intention.

"Hades—"

"Not long," he assured her, wondering if she was merely embarrassed by the fact that she'd been caught looking at his things. "I received a frantic call from Ivy, who chastised me for not letting her know you were stopping by."

She started to smile, then her brows furrowed. "You have a phone?"

"For work, yes."

"Why didn't I know that?" There was an edge to her voice, more frustrated than suspicious.

"If I want you, I will find you." He did not need modern technology to locate her, just magic.

"And what if I want you?" That question was innocent enough and shouldn't have made him feel anything at all, but the idea that she might ask him for help—and accept it—sent a strange sort of thrill through him.

"Then you have only to say my name."

The hope that had swelled in his chest quickly dissipated with her frown, an expression he matched.

"You are displeased."

"You embarrassed me," she murmured, staring at his chest.

Hades lifted her chin so he could study her face. He did not understand. "Explain."

She took a breath, like she was warring with herself, but her frustration won out. "I should not have to learn about all your charities through someone else. I feel like everyone around me knows more about you than I do."

No one knew more than she did, except, perhaps, Hecate, who sometimes obtained information via her spells, something Hades considered a nuisance.

"You never asked."

And had there been a time to even bring up the matter of his business ventures? Though he supposed he should have anticipated that others would be eager to disclose elements of his life to her. Aphrodite had done the same when she had told Persephone of their bargain.

"Some things can be brought up casually, Hades. At dinner, for instance: Hi, honey. How was your day? Mine was good. The billion-dollar charities I own help kids and dogs and humanity!"

Honey? That was not a name he had tried out before.

Her words amused him, and as the corners of his mouth lifted, Persephone placed a finger to his lips. He had the very primal urge to take it into his mouth.

"Don't you dare. I am serious about this. If you wish for me to be seen as more than a lover, then I need more from you. A...*history*...an inventory of your life. *Something*."

She was asking to know him, to understand him better. He could not deny that thought gave him anxiety. What if she did not like all parts of him? As he knew she wouldn't.

He took her hand and kissed her fingers.

"I'm sorry. It did not occur to me to tell you. I have existed so long alone, made every decision alone. I am not used to sharing anything with anyone."

It was the truth, especially his past. He had never placed much value in reliving it.

"Hades." She said his name quietly and placed her hand on his cheek. "You were never alone, and you certainly aren't alone now."

He liked her words, even if they were only half true. When she dropped her hand, she took her warmth, and he was eager to have it back, though she had moved, putting distance between them by stepping out from between him and the desk.

"Now." She turned to look at him, planting her hands on the desk. "What else do you own?"

"Lots of morgues," he said.

Persephone stared for a moment. Her mouth opened as if she were going to speak, then she closed it again. Finally she asked, "You're serious?"

"I am the God of the Dead."

Her eyes brightened, and a beautiful smile broke across her face.

"Tell me," he said, rounding the desk to be closer to her. "What else can I share with you now?"

She had turned toward him as he approached, and a pleasing tension grew between them. Persephone hesitated for a moment, then touched the picture on his desk.

"Where did you get this?"

He wasn't sure why he stayed quiet so long. Perhaps it was because he could not read exactly how she felt about the photo, but it also meant revealing a part of himself he had never shared with anyone at all.

"I took it."

"When?" A note of surprise colored her voice.

He smirked, humored. "Obviously when you weren't looking."

She rolled her eyes, and he drew closer. He wanted to take her mouth into a punishing kiss and worship her on this desk, though he knew her thoughts were much more wholesome.

"Why do you have pictures of me and I do not have pictures of you?"

"I did not know you wanted pictures of me."

"Of course I want pictures of you."

"I may be able to oblige. What kind of pictures do you want?"

"You are insatiable," she said, hitting his shoulder playfully.

Hades's hands locked on her waist, and he pulled her toward him, their bodies colliding hip to hip. "And you are to blame, my queen," he said, mouth falling to her neck, his tongue touching her skin as he kissed down to her shoulder. "I'm glad you are here."

"I couldn't tell," she said mildly. A tremor made her body vibrate beneath his hands.

He pulled back, but only enough to meet her gaze. His mouth lingered near hers as he spoke, hushed. "I've wanted to pleasure you in this room, on this desk, since I met you. It will be the most productive thing that happens here."

"You have glass walls, Hades." Her tone matched his, wavering.

"Are you trying to deter me?"

She tilted her head, her hands pressing into his chest, not to push him away but because he was holding her tighter.

"Exhibitionist?"

"Hardly." He was not interested in sharing in any form, and he had said so before. He bent closer, his lips brushing hers as he spoke. "Do you really think I would let them see you? I am too selfish. Smoke and mirrors, Persephone."

He liked the way she stared at him now. A light burned behind her eyes, and he knew she was aroused. He could sense it in how her body arched to his, the way her magic started to scent. She stared at him, then focused on his mouth and whispered, "Then take me."

He was not one to deny her command, and as his arm tightened around her waist, intent on lifting her to the desk and calling up his glamour, someone cleared their throat.

Their heads whipped toward the door to find Lexa standing there, smiling.

"Hey, Hades," she said brightly. "Hope you don't mind. I brought Persephone for a tour."

Persephone pushed against him to create distance, and he worked to stifle his disappointment.

"I have to get back to work," she said, making her way to the door, but before she left, she turned to look back at him.

He realized he saw her nearly every day, had memorized every curve and detail of her body, yet she somehow still managed to arrest him.

"I'll see you tonight?"

He would never say no, despite all the fires raging around him at the moment, and when he nodded, he knew he had made the right decision because she smiled so bright, it made his heart race.

After she left, Hades remained standing for a few minutes before sinking into the chair behind his desk. His gaze fell to the picture of Persephone, which he straightened, then he leaned back and closed his eyes, waiting for his lust to subside.

"There you are!"

"Go away," Hades groaned.

"Excuse the interruption, my lord, but you are rarely here," said Katerina.

Hades opened his eyes and stared at the director. Her eyes were lively, and she seemed far more energetic than usual, which was saying something, because she was always rather enthusiastic. It made her a better leader, as she was able to motivate people to do just about anything.

Even Hades.

"Which is why I have *you*," he replied. "Actually, though, I may have something for you."

He summoned Ariadne's file, and Katerina approached.

"I need to know if any of these women sought sanctuary at Hemlock Grove," Hades said, which was a safe house operated by Hecate. Katerina, like many of his staff, volunteered there.

Katerina frowned as she leafed through page after page of missing women. "There are so many," she said.

"A true tragedy," Hades said, and he meant it.

Katerina hugged the folder to her chest. "I'll work

on this today," she said. "While you are here, I need your approval on a few things."

"Fine," Hades replied. "As long as it doesn't take long."

CHAPTER VIII
Secrets Unravel

It was two hours before Hades was finished signing off on designs and approving new fundraising opportunities for the Halcyon Project. As he went to leave, he dropped everything by Katerina's office. She was hard at work, Ariadne's folder open on her desk.

"That was not a few things," he said.

"Relative," she said. "Besides, you're the one who was explicit about being involved in the project. I am only following your instructions."

He did not always need to have control, especially if he found people he trusted to see his visions through, and while he did trust Katerina, the Halcyon Project was personal. He wanted it to capture the essence of Persephone, and he felt like the only one qualified to do so.

He nodded to the folder. "Let Ilias know as soon as you find something. He's on the case too."

Katerina nodded grimly, and there was a part of him that hated to have given her something so heavy.

Katerina was a fierce advocate for women, having her own history with domestic violence.

"Will you be okay?"

"I will," she promised. "I'd just like to find them."

Hades agreed and, with that, left to return to the Underworld. Persephone would be off work soon, and he did not wish to break his promise of seeing her tonight. There was an ever-present thought in the back of his mind that at any point, he could be drawn away to deal with some threat. If not ones that already existed—Hera, Leuce, Dionysus—it would be something new.

Because of that, he used this time to unwind, wandering into the fields and summoning Cerberus, Typhon, and Orthrus, only as the dogs approached, he found they had morphed into their singular form—a single body that shared three similar heads. Despite this, the three always maintained distinct personalities, which were very evident even now. Cerberus, the middle, had a stoic expression. Typhon, on the right, was calm, though his ears were up and alert. Orthrus, on the left, had his tongue lolling out of his mouth, and the right foot of their large body bounced.

Hades raised a brow. "Were you part of Hecate's punishments today?"

The three Dobermans took whatever form they pleased, but Hecate often used this one—their monstrous form—to chase deserving souls across Tartarus. In some cases, she allowed the three to devour their prey.

In answer, the three barked.

"I see," Hades replied. "Does that mean you are too tired for a bit of fetch?"

All three perked up, and Hades smiled, manifesting their favorite red ball.

"I thought not," he said, throwing the ball up and down. Their eyes followed. "Question is, will you three work together or not?"

Hades reared back.

"Not yet," he ordered and tossed the ball clear across the Underworld. Three pairs of eyes watched him, body wiggling in anticipation of chasing their new target.

He smirked. "Go."

The three let out a growl as they twisted, kicking up dirt as they took off in the direction he'd thrown the ball, and as he watched them bound across the green fields, dipping into rolling hills and parting tall grass, they broke apart, departing into their three bodies once more.

It looked like it was going to be a competition.

While Hades's strength meant he could throw far, his dogs were monsters, and they had their own power, strength, and speed, which meant that while it would take a normal animal hours to retrieve the ball he'd thrown, it took seconds for them to return. As he stared across the horizon, he saw Orthrus in the lead, red ball clasped in his jowls, yet neither Typhon nor Cerberus were ready to lose. They kept on Orthrus's heels, nipping at his feet to trip him up.

Still, Orthrus managed to make it to Hades without sabotage. He sat dutifully and dropped the ball at his feet. Typhon and Cerberus took their places beside him, waiting once more for another round.

Hades continued the game until his body glistened with sweat and the light in the Underworld was fading. He returned to the palace through the garden and found himself choosing flowers that made him think of Persephone either in color or beauty—irises and lilies, aster and bellflower—until he had a substantial bouquet.

He had to admit, until Persephone, he had not paid much attention to flowers, especially these—the ones he'd created via illusion. They were for the pleasure of the souls and staff and only managed to remind him of how he'd been born into this world, the war that followed, and the many dark days after. He built feeble walls around the darkness and decay, and while it looked nice enough, what lay beneath was never far from his mind, and he found himself wondering how he could manage to disclose such things to Persephone. How did one communicate lifetimes of turmoil and strife, mistakes and regrets?

"What are you doing?" Hecate asked.

He had been so lost in thought, he had not sensed her approach. He refocused and continued choosing flowers. "What does it look like?"

"Like you are about to add datura to your bouquet," she said, and Hades's hand hesitated over the white, trumpet-like flower. "It's a nasty nightshade. Best leave it be."

He straightened and turned to face the witch goddess.

"I'm ridiculous," he said.

"You are ridiculous often," Hecate said. "But you are not ridiculous for picking flowers for your lady love, if that is what you are insinuating."

Hades wasn't certain. He wasn't even sure why he'd begun this. Why would the Goddess of Spring want a bunch of soon-to-be-dead flowers?

"I am going to fuck this up," he said.

He often shared his doubts with Hecate, and while he knew they were safe with the goddess, her responses were not always comforting.

"Probably," she said. "But Persephone is forgiving. You'll remember that when you need to forgive her, won't you?"

Hades's brows rose. "Do you know something I don't?"

"I always know something you don't," she replied. "And yet you still do not listen to me. You'll always need to be forgiving, but especially with Persephone, who has yet to learn the cruelty of the world."

Hades frowned. "I'd protect her from it if she'd let me."

"You can't," Hecate said. "Nor should you. How else do you expect her to become a goddess otherwise?"

Is that what it takes to embrace divinity? Hades thought. *Strife?* He supposed it was true of every god he knew. Despite the differences among the Olympians, one thing always united them, and that was the shared trauma of war.

Hecate moved to his side and instructed, "Choose more greenery and those lilies that have yet to bloom."

Hades paused for only a brief moment before doing as she instructed, noting that Hecate picked the datura.

"I thought you said that was poisonous," Hades said, eyeing it in her hands.

"It is," she replied and continued to pick the deceptive flower, root intact.

They spent a few more minutes in the garden before heading inside, where Persephone's voice echoed in the hallway.

"Good boys!" she said, and they found her kneeling on the ground, rotating between rubbing Orthrus's belly, Typhon's neck, and Cerberus's ear.

"Spoiled beasts," Hecate chided.

"They are not spoiled. You're not spoiled, are you?" Persephone asked. They preened beneath her hands, and Hades did not blame them. He liked being fawned over by her too. "You are all very good boys."

She finally looked up and seemed to realize that he was also present. Her smile faltered, but only for a moment. She rose to her feet and spoke shyly.

"Hi."

Hades was amused but no less flustered by her. He liked seeing her so at home in his realm. It made him feel like this could last an eternity.

Her eyes darted to the flowers in his hand. For a moment, he forgot he was holding them.

He cleared his throat and held them out. "I...picked these for you."

Persephone smiled sheepishly and took them. "They are beautiful, Hades."

There was a brief moment of strained silence, and Hecate cleared her throat. "Let's go, beasts. The lovers would like time alone. Not in the dining room, please."

The Goddess of Witchcraft turned and wandered down the palace hallway with the dogs in tow.

Persephone held Hades's gaze. "What are these for?"

Hades rubbed the back of his neck. "I just thought you might like them."

"I love them," she said. "Thank you."

There was a beat of silence, and Hades wondered why things felt so awkward between them. Had it been the flowers? Or did it have something to do with their earlier conversation? Was Persephone expecting him to dive into an explanation of his past and present?

"How was work?" he asked, disliking the doubt that twisted through him when she hesitated.

"Fine," she answered quickly.

"Sounds frustrating," he observed.

"I don't want to talk about work," she said, fixating on one of the lilies, drawing her finger along one of the petals.

Hades frowned. This had already gotten off to a bad start. "Then we won't," he said, and she looked at him over the bouquet.

"You said you took my picture," she hedged. "Do you have a camera?"

"I do," he said, and he couldn't quite place how he felt about sharing it and its contents. Perhaps the closest feeling to describing it was embarrassment, though he also felt a little shameful. He should want to share this with Persephone. He supposed his only fear was what she would think, as always.

"Do you take pictures often?"

"Occasionally. When I find something worth immortalizing."

Her lips curled. "But you are immortal."

"I am, but moments are not. They are fleeting."

"Can I see?" she asked.

"Of course," he found himself saying, despite his concerns, and led her to his office.

"When did you begin this hobby?" Persephone asked as he made his way behind the desk.

"Years ago," he said. "The technology of mortals never ceases to amaze me."

And terrify him, if he were being honest.

He pulled the camera from a drawer behind his desk, turned it on, and handed it to her. While it was old, he liked the results he got from the pictures he took.

As she looked through the photos, he walked across the room to pour a drink, hoping it would settle the unfamiliar, nervous energy moving through him.

She was quiet for a moment and then said softly, "These are beautiful."

A faint smile touched his lips, and he heard a click. When he looked, she was lowering the camera.

"There is a moment I want to keep." Her voice was quiet.

He stared for a minute and then approached, setting his glass on the desk. He touched her chin with his thumb and forefinger and kissed her, pulling back when he heard the click of the camera.

"This moment too," she whispered.

Hades wasn't sure what to think, but he did not dislike this. "Will you let me take pictures of you?"

"You already have," she said.

He swallowed something thick in his throat as he clarified. "Bare."

She paused for a moment and then answered, "If you let me do the same."

Hades held her heated gaze and took the camera from her before instructing, "Take off your skirt."

He stepped back, camera in hand, and snapped a few pictures as she shimmied out of it. When it puddled on the floor, he approached and lifted her onto the desk, drawing her shirt over her head. He took a moment to kiss her mouth and the part of her breasts that pillowed over the top of her bra before handing the camera to her.

"Take pictures of yourself," he said.

She stared at him for a moment, as if uncertain, so he prompted, "What would you send me when we are apart?"

Her eyes darkened. "And what will you do?"

"Watch," he said. He took his glass, moved a few steps back, and sank into one of the chairs in front of the desk.

It took her a few minutes to get comfortable, but soon she was taking teasing pictures and explicit ones, and the longer Hades watched, the harder he grew. When she was finished, she sat on the edge of the desk with her legs crossed and took a final photo of him. He could not imagine how he looked—half crazed with lust, overcome by a primal need to claim her.

He thought he would go to her, but she came to him, straddling his thighs. She set the camera aside and unbuttoned his shirt. Her hands were hot against his skin as they made their way down his stomach to his erection, painfully restricted by his slacks. She freed it, only to reach for the camera.

Before she captured this moment, she looked at him. "What will you do with these?"

"Can you not guess?"

"Show me," she said, her voice a breathy whisper.

It was so fucking hot in this room.

He reached between them and stroked himself, timing each movement with the click of the camera.

What the fuck was happening? He had never let anyone take pictures of him before, much less this, something so personal and so fucking intimate, yet he let it happen, and there came a point when the camera was set aside and their mouths collided. Persephone rose up onto her knees to guide Hades's cock inside her and they rocked together. As their bodies grew slick and their breaths became ragged, Hades had never quite felt so desperate before, like everything that had come before this moment had made the chase for release so much sweeter. When they tumbled over the edge and lay in a breathless entanglement, Persephone shifted, reached for the camera, and took a picture of their faces.

"I want to remember this," she said and kissed his raw lips.

He didn't think he'd ever forget.

Hades had never consistently offered his time to mortals seeking bargains, and he had found since Persephone's arrival, he had made himself available less and less, but the weekend was upon them, and there was a general discontent to the crowd gathered on the floor of Nevernight, a desperation that he thought he may as well attempt to cull.

So he bargained.

He had been right about the hopelessness he'd sensed. Every mortal who came to him was offering far more than they were at liberty to give.

"Please," a woman had begged after her loss to Hades. "I will do anything... T-take my firstborn!"

Unease slithered through him at her offer.

"Money in exchange for a soul is a bitter bargain." Hades frowned. "I pity the child who is born to you."

She seemed to brighten. "Is that a yes?"

Hades scowled. "Out!"

Hades's tone must have frightened her because she fled for the door. The next mortal was a man, desperate for money, who offered Hades the pick of the hetairai employed within his brothel.

Hades raised a brow. "I have no interest."

The man's face fell. "But, my lord, no singular woman can meet a man's needs."

Hades considered listing the faults of this man's soul, hoping each one might hit like a bullet to the chest—insecure, lonely, dishonest, cruel—but there would be no benefit and would only mean that the man would linger longer in his presence, so he offered a threat instead.

"If you want to exit this club no worse than when you arrived, I suggest you leave. *Now.*"

The man scrambled from the room, and Hades was left far more frustrated than when he'd begun. He was reminded everyday how the public looked at him... which, sometimes, was no different from how they viewed Poseidon or Zeus. Neither of his brothers were particularly loyal gods, and it was likely they would have jumped at the menagerie of offerings tonight, but Hades was not like his brothers and he never would be.

The proposed deals were no better after that—just a string of beggars hoping for money, truly believing that a bargain with the God of the Dead would make their lives better.

The last client of the night was a young man around twenty or so, and while he presented clean shaven and well dressed, a darkness lingered beneath his skin, a corruption that had made his life spiral out of control. He was addicted to drugs, and if Hades had to guess, he'd say it was Evangeline, possibly one of the most destructive and common street drugs on the market. Its creation had originated with Eris, the Goddess of Destruction.

"What is it you wish to bargain for?" Hades asked.

"I...uh...I need money."

"For drugs?" Hades asked.

The man's eyes widened. "No... I need to replace the money I spent on..."

He did not finish his sentence, and Hades guessed it was due to shame.

The man took a breath and explained, "I'm supposed to be in college, but I haven't gone all semester. I've been lying to my parents...but if I can get the money back, I can return. They won't have to know."

Hades raised a brow. "You think you can return to college with an addiction so severe?"

Just as the man was about to open his mouth, Hades felt the familiar tendrils of Persephone's magic call to his own, which meant two things—she was here and she was angry. A particularly fierce dread took hold of his heart.

What had she discovered?

The door swung open, and Persephone was framed in the dim light from the hallway. Her glamour peeked through to reveal the goddess beneath—gleaming eyes and glowing skin. She was also livid. A deep flush kissed the high parts of her cheeks, and her lips and jaw were set hard.

The mortal turned to look at her, so desperate for his own bargain that he did not even notice her faltering glamour.

"If it's him you want, you'll have to wait your turn. Took me three years to get this appointment."

She did not even glance at him. All her anger was directed at Hades. He straightened beneath her gaze.

"Leave, mortal."

It was unnerving to hear her say such a thing, when so often, she tended to relate more to human than god. The man must have picked up on the threat in her voice, because he clumsily got to his feet and darted out the door, which Persephone slammed shut.

"I'll have to erase his memory. Your eyes are glowing," Hades said, and despite himself, he found himself smiling. He liked when she seemed unafraid of her power. "Who angered you?"

"Can you not guess?" she asked. Her voice trembled, but only slightly.

Hades's brows rose and he waited.

"I just had the pleasure of meeting your lover."

Hades didn't have to think long about who she was referring to—Leuce.

Fuck.

"I see."

Her head tilted slightly. "You have seconds to explain before I turn her into a weed."

At the rate she was going, he wouldn't be surprised if he ended the night as a plant, so he began to explain.

"Her name is Leuce. She was my lover a long time ago."

"What is a long time?"

"More than a millennia, Persephone."

"Then why did she introduce herself to me as your lover today?"

Because she's an idiot, he thought. "Because to her, I was her lover up until Sunday."

Her power surged as she clenched her fists, and leafy vines erupted from the floor of the suite, covering the blue walls completely.

"And why is that?"

"Because she's been a poplar tree for more than two thousand years."

"Why was she a poplar tree?"

Hades took a breath. He'd been reminded of this too much over the last week when all he wanted to do was keep it in the past.

"She betrayed me."

"*You* turned her into a tree?" she asked, clearly stunned, and Hades wondered what had shocked her more, the fact that he had exacted revenge or the way in which he'd done it. "Why?"

"I caught her fucking someone else. I was blind with anger. I turned her into a poplar tree."

Persephone's features were still stiff with anger. "She must not remember that, or she wouldn't introduce herself as your lover."

She remembered, though he had a suspicion she blamed Apollo more than herself for the treachery, but he'd rather not get into specifics about why Leuce was still claiming to be his lover. It was likely only something she had used in hopes that she would get what she wanted, and it had backfired, so all he said was, "It is possible she has repressed the memory."

Persephone took a breath and looked toward the ceiling before she started to pace, and he thought that it had something to do with the magic building inside her.

"How many lovers have you taken?"

"Persephone." His tone was quiet. She could not

know that this question caused him so much discomfort. It was an impossible question, an unfair question, and to be honest, he didn't want to answer it.

"I just want to be prepared in case they start coming out of the woodwork," Persephone snapped.

Hades stared up at her from his place at the table. "I won't apologize for living before you existed."

"I'm not asking you to, but I'd like to know when I'm about to meet a woman who fucked you."

He could understand her anger to a point. He would not have liked for these roles to be reversed.

"I was hoping you'd never meet Leuce," Hades said, though he was realizing now how much of a mistake that was. "She wasn't supposed to be around this long. I agreed to help her get on her feet in the modern world. Normally, I'd pass the responsibility on to Minthe, but seeing as how she's indisposed—" He glanced at the ivy on the walls. "It's taken me longer to find someone suitable to mentor her."

Persephone halted and stared at him. She seemed even more shocked now than before. "You weren't planning to tell me about her?"

"I saw no need until now."

"*No need?*"

Persephone's magic surged, and Hades could hear the rustle of vines and leaves growing thicker and thicker, blooming with fragrant white flowers, the smell of which choked him.

"You gave this woman a place to stay, you gave her a job, and you used to fuck her—"

"Stop saying that!" Hades bit out. He obviously did not think about that as much as she did.

"I *deserved* to know about her, Hades!"

"Do you doubt my loyalty?"

"You're supposed to say you're *sorry*."

"*You're* supposed to trust me."

"And you're supposed to communicate with me."

Hades did not know what to say, though now he wondered if he could have prevented this if he'd just been honest about the nymph's return. Instead, he'd gotten exactly what he feared—Persephone's disdain.

Guilt and dread twisted uneasily in his stomach.

She took a breath, then she asked in a quiet, sad voice, "Do you still love her?"

"No, Persephone."

He hated that the question had even been asked. Even if she were questioning whether she knew him, how could she think he still loved Leuce? After he'd told her—shown her—how much he loved her?

He rose from his chair and came around the table, taking her face between his hands and threading one of his hands into her hair. At least she let him touch her. "I hoped to keep all this from you," he murmured. "Not to protect Leuce but to protect you from my past."

"I don't want to be protected from you," she said. "I want to know you—all of you, from the inside out."

He smirked, brushing her lips with his thumb. "Let's start with the inside," he said and kissed her.

He hoped kissing her would ease her worry and anger, and maybe she would let go of her magic before she suffocated him with the smell of sickly-sweet flora. For a moment, it worked. Her hands twisted into his shirt, and she pulled him closer as he gripped her harder, but then her palms flattened against his chest and she pushed away, ending the kiss.

"Hades, I'm serious. I want to know your greatest weakness, your deepest fear, your most treasured possession."

How could she not know the answer?

"You." His voice was low and rough.

"Me?" she said and shook her head. "I cannot be all those things."

"You are my weakness, losing you is my greatest fear, and your love is my most treasured possession."

"Hades," she said, averting her eyes, as if searching for words. "I am a second in your vast life. How can I be all those things?"

"You doubt me?"

She touched his face; the warmth of her fingers was a comfort despite all the anxiety this conversation had caused. "No, but I believe you have other weaknesses, fears, and treasures. Your people, for one. Your realm, for another."

"See," he said, a smile threatening his lips. "You know me already—inside and out."

He leaned in to kiss her once more, but she stopped him. Hades held her so tightly, he could feel her back arch as she drew back.

"I just have one more question," she said, and his heart fell. "When you left Sunday night, where did you go?"

"Persephone—"

This time, when she stepped back, he released her.

"That's when she returned, wasn't it?"

As angry as she appeared, she could not hide the hurt that flashed in her bright eyes. It made Hades sick, made him want to heal her somehow, but how did one heal this kind of pain? Especially when it was of his own making.

"You chose her over me."

He stepped toward her. "It isn't like that at all, Persephone—"

"*Don't* touch me!"

He hated those words—hated that he was the reason they were being said at all, hated that they hurt too.

"You had your chance," she said. "You fucked it up. Actions speak louder than words, Hades."

She vanished before she could see him flinch.

Those were his words. He'd used them with her not so long ago.

Action, Lady Persephone. Action holds weight for me.

She was right.

He had fucked up.

CHAPTER IX
Overprotective

With Persephone gone, Ilias entered the room.

"Tell me Leuce has been detained," Hades gritted out, and when the satyr nodded, he teleported to her holding room. This time, he did not need to think about how he would approach her. His anger would decide.

When he appeared, she whirled to face him. Whatever warmth was left in her face drained away, and she staggered back until she hit the wall.

He imagined he looked a lot like a monster, because he felt like one.

"Did I not instruct that you were *never* to contact me again?" Hades seethed.

Despite her fear, Leuce rocked onto the tips of her toes and glared angrily. "I wouldn't have had to contact you if the people you pawned me off on had listened to my requests!"

"Your requests? What requests could you possibly imagine you are entitled to?"

"An agreeable apartment for one."

"Are you saying I was not charitable?" Hades asked, his words heavy with barely contained anger.

"*Charitable?*" Leuce asked. "I spent *years* as a tree, and the best you can do is a shitty apartment and a serving job?"

He had no idea what sort of lodging Ilias had secured for the nymph, but he doubted it was shitty. Likely it was just nothing compared to the finery of his palace.

"If your accommodations and work are not to your liking, then perhaps you do not need them at all."

"You would leave me without a home?"

"I have done much worse, would you not agree?"

He knew his words were hateful, but his anger and fear had manifested as an ache in his throat that made him feel like he couldn't breathe.

Leuce moved to slap him, but Hades caught her hand.

"Looks like I am not the only one who hasn't changed," he shot back, and she jerked free.

"This is about *her*, isn't it? That woman you're seeing?"

Seeing? It was such a minor word to describe the love of his life—a love that she had disrupted with her careless words. Now Hades had to hope he could rebuild trust between him and Persephone.

"Is that why you claimed to be my lover?" Hades asked. "Jealousy?"

"Hardly," she scoffed. "I was over you long before I slept with Apollo."

If she thought that would injure him, she was wrong. It did, however, make him feel particularly vengeful.

"What a timely admission," he replied. "It makes this next part much easier."

Leuce's eyes widened, and Hades gathered his magic. "I couldn't care less about your life and what you make it, but if it wasn't for *that woman*, you'd be a tree once more. She is your salvation."

And with that, Hades deposited her in a park, far from Nevernight, and cursed her to never set foot in his territory again.

Days passed, and Persephone had not returned to Nevernight.

It was strange to feel so uncomfortable in his own realm, but all he could think about was her absence. It was like his magic searched for her, and when it could not find her, it pulsed beneath his skin, a constant reminder that she had put distance between them.

Not just her.

Him. He was responsible too, as Hecate had so eloquently reminded him last night when she'd found him wandering the palace halls.

"What did you do?" she'd asked, already looking dour.

"That's very presumptuous of you," he replied mildly.

She arched her brow and pointed out, "You only get this angry with yourself."

He scrubbed his face, frustrated. "I fucked up. Persephone found out about Leuce. Of course the nymph would introduce herself as my lover. *Current*, not former."

"You say that as if one is better than the other."

"To Persephone, it might have been."

"Neither is better when they're both secret, Hades," Hecate replied.

He scowled at her. "I realize that now."

"I think you need to consider why you did not wish to tell her, and if the answer is because you were afraid… maybe you do not trust her as much as you think."

Now, her words tumbled through his head.

Did he trust Persephone?

He supposed he did not trust that her love for him meant she could overlook his past, and admitting that was both painful and embarrassing. In the end, he hadn't given her a chance.

He should never have kept Leuce a secret—which was what he wanted to tell Persephone. He had debated going to her, but he wasn't certain she was ready to hear his explanation, and when he'd finally decided to go to her, he was diverted by Ilias, who informed him that Acacius's shop had blown up with the relic dealer and his men inside.

Before he could even speculate about that information, Hermes arrived at Nevernight with a message from Dionysus.

"Well?" Hades prompted impatiently.

"I just really need you to understand, I'm only the messenger."

Hades waited, and after a moment, Hermes closed his eyes and lifted his middle finger.

"That's it?" Hades asked. "That's all he had to say?"

"He didn't even say anything. He just flipped me off."

Hades took a deep breath, and upon his exhale, he snatched a vase full of red flowers and threw it across the room. He was not surprised by Dionysus's reaction. The god did not like being told what to do, and he probably liked it even less that Hades was aware of his exploits.

"What will you do now?" Hermes asked.

"I'm not going to do anything...yet," Hades said. If Dionysus wanted to play childish games, Hades would too. "But you will."

"What? Nuh-uh," Hermes said. "Not this time. I always help you, and what does it get me in return? Nothing. I haven't even gotten a thank-you for today."

"Fine," Hades said. "I suppose I'll have to find someone else to plague Dionysus with dreams of bloody castration."

Hermes pursed his lips as if considering.

"I suppose I can ask Morpheus or Epiales," Hades said. "He *is* the personification of nightmares after all, and he would do a fine job."

"Fine?" Hermes scoffed. "Let me do it. I'll show you bloody castration."

"But you have already declined," Hades said.

"I take it back," Hermes said. "And you know what? Thank you, Hades."

"For what?"

"For being you," Hermes said. "Now, can I set Dionysus's dick on fire?"

"I wouldn't give the task to anyone else," Hades replied.

"Yes!" Hermes hissed, pumping his fist in the air. "I'm off to make plans."

"How much planning can possibly go into castration?"

"It's an art," Hermes replied before vanishing, and while there was an initial satisfaction to the errand Hades had sent Hermes on, he soon felt the exhaustion of it all and found himself on the empty floor of Nevernight in the early morning, nursing a glass of whiskey until Ilias arrived.

"Did you sleep?" the satyr asked as he approached, rounding the bar so he stood opposite Hades.

"No," he replied, taking a sip of his whiskey.

"You sure you don't want something else? Coffee, perhaps?"

"No."

"Well, I would ask you if you were all right, but I think I know the answer."

Hades met Ilias's gaze. "Are you here to judge, or do you have something to tell me?"

"I'm not one to judge," Ilias replied. "But I do have something to tell you. I spoke with Katerina this morning about these missing women."

The satyr placed Ariadne's folder on the table.

"They are all running from something—a partner, parents, all kinds of trauma. Our detective probably missed it because their families all claimed they were happy and they had all made plans for their future. She's not wrong about how they went missing, though. None of them could be traced to a specific location aside from Megara, who, as you know, seems to have never left Dionysus's club, which cannot actually be confirmed."

"And none of them went to Hemlock Grove?" Hades asked.

Ilias shook his head. "No one named in this folder."

It seemed Hades was going to have to begin with the only lead he had—Dionysus.

"Now for the bad news," Ilias said, and Hades's brows rose. Was this not bad enough? "This was left at the doors this morning."

Hades could very much say he was not prepared for

what the satyr had to share. He placed a folded newspaper on the counter in front of him so that the title glared at him in bold black.

APOLLO CASTS A GRIM SHADOW ON PAST AND PRESENT LOVERS

His heart beat unevenly in his chest as he picked up the paper and read:

Apollo, known for his charm and beauty, has a secret—he cannot stand rejection.

The evidence is overwhelming. I would have his many ex-lovers vouch for me, but they either begged to be saved from his wily pursuits and were turned into trees or died horrible deaths as a result of his punishment.

You are familiar with a few of these lovers. Daphne, the river nymph who Apollo pursued relentlessly until she begged her father to turn her into a tree. Cassandra, Princess of Troy, who cried that Greeks were hidden in the Trojan Horse but was ignored. Which begs the question, how noble can Apollo truly be when he fought on the side of Troy yet compromised their victory, all because he was given the cold shoulder?

Perhaps the greater issue at hand is that the public is very much aware of these transgressions yet continues to elevate a god who should instead be held accountable for his actions. Apollo is an abuser—he has a need to control and dominate. It's not about communication or listening; it's about winning. Is this who we really want representing New Greece?

Hades read the article once more, his fingers curling into the paper. All he could think was that she'd promised not to write about Apollo. Except that he knew she'd never actually promised.

"*Trust me on this, Persephone.*"

"*I trust you,*" she'd said.

But she didn't, or at least if she did, she'd disregarded his warning. Was this her way of seeking revenge because of Leuce? The irony was, she had no idea why he'd turned the nymph into a tree or that it had been because of Apollo.

"If that makes you angry, you won't want to see what else is in the news today."

The satyr was likely right, but Hades wanted to know anyway. He had a feeling it had everything to do with Persephone.

Ilias pulled out his phone to show Hades a video. It was a news report from earlier, and a red banner at the bottom of the screen drew his eye.

HADES'S LOVER ATTACKS BELOVED GOD

He grimaced, his anger growing the longer the reporter talked about Persephone as if they did not fear his retaliation.

"Guess she didn't gain enough fame by sleeping with Hades. She had to go after Apollo too?" the reporter said.

Those words went right through him, and he pushed

the phone back toward Ilias. After a moment of silence, he asked, "Is she safe?"

"She made it to work," he replied.

He didn't like that he'd had to ask that question, did not like that Ilias had to qualify his answer, knowing that she'd now have to make it home.

"If she'd known this would be the response, I doubt she'd have done this," Ilias said.

"She knew," Hades said curtly. "I *warned* her."

Ilias did not respond, though Hades could tell the satyr was holding back.

"What is it?" he snapped.

Ilias shrugged. "I don't know. I just think she probably thought you were being overprotective."

Hades bristled at those words.

Overprotective.

It almost made him sound controlling, and he hated that.

"*You can't tell me who to write about, Hades,*" she'd said, and while he'd have liked for her to have been able to write about anyone and anything she wished, the reality was, it wasn't possible without fallout. She was about to learn the hard way.

"When it comes to Apollo, there is no such thing," Hades replied.

Ilias did not disagree. "He will hunt her."

Hades did not need to be told. He knew what the god was capable of. He'd pursue Persephone until she paid for her alleged slander, but Hades wasn't willing to lose another love to the God of Music.

"That's not all I have for you," Ilias said. "This came pinned to the newspaper."

Ilias handed him a piece of white parchment. The top of the page was embossed with a gold peacock. Beneath the icon was printed *From the desk of Hera, Goddess of Marriage* and below that was a handwritten message.

I see your lover has caused quite a stir. With your allies growing fewer and fewer among the Olympians, it will be no easy task to convince Zeus to agree to your hopeful matrimony.

It was as much a threat as it was a reminder of the labors Hera had sentenced Hades to. He knew he was running out of time. He would have to kill Briareus soon.

Hades crushed the note in his palm and set it ablaze with black flame. It curled into solid ashes that dissipated into a fine dust, leaving behind a sharp, clean smell and pale-white smoke.

"Anything else?" Hades asked.

"I think that's enough for today, don't you?"

Hades rose from his chair, drained his glass, and left the club.

———

Hades waited for Persephone in the darkness of her room. He wondered if she had dreaded this encounter. Had the thought of facing him invaded every part of her day? While he would have preferred to occupy her thoughts for a different reason, she had to know he was coming for her, yet she did not hesitate as she entered her room, did not pause to scan the area for signs of his presence. She walked straight to her bedside table, turned on the light, and stepped into the bathroom. She turned on the faucet and returned to her room, arms tangled behind her back as she managed to unzip her dress.

They had not been apart long, but the anger and betrayal between them made it feel like months. His fingers itched to touch her, to help her out of her dress, to ignore the past few days of fury and frustration in favor of something far more pleasurable, but even he knew that was foolish, because all those feelings would be waiting on the other side of that intimate high.

Her dress puddled around her feet, and her skin glowed softly, bathed in the warmth of her lamplight. She straightened, dressed only in black lace, but before she could remove that too, she must have caught sight of him, because she glanced his way and startled.

"Please continue," he implored, leaning against the wall opposite her. Despite his frustration with her, he'd happily watch her strip, especially knowing he was soon to be the recipient of her anger, given what he'd come here to do.

She stared, speechless, and he wondered what she was thinking as her eyes roved over his body, but there came a time, all too quickly, when she met his gaze, narrowed her eyes, pressed her lips tight, and bent to pull her dress up, holding it to her chest as if they were not lovers at all but strangers.

That simple act made him feel many things but mostly hopeless.

He offered a humorless laugh. "Come now, darling. We are beyond that, are we not? I have seen every inch of you—*touched* every part of you."

A tremor shook her, but at least she did not cringe.

"That doesn't mean you will tonight," she snapped. "What are you doing here?"

Hades's impatience made his body vibrate. Why did she feel entitled to anger? She had defied *him*.

"You are avoiding me."

He wondered how long it would have taken her to return to the Underworld if he had not sought her out tonight.

"I'm avoiding *you*? It's a two-way street, Hades. You've been just as absent."

"I gave you space," he argued, because he'd assumed that was what was best, yet Persephone rolled her eyes. "Clearly that was a bad idea."

"You know what you should have given me? An apology."

She tossed her dress aside and whirled around, heading into the bathroom, where she removed the rest of her clothes. Hades followed as she stepped into the bath and sank into the steaming water. She didn't seem to mind the heat, though it had already turned her pale skin a bright red. She kept her knees pressed to her chest, and as he spoke, her arms tightened around her knees.

"I told you I loved you."

It wasn't as if he had hoped to keep Leuce a secret for malicious reasons. As selfish as it may have been, he hadn't wanted to admit to turning her into a tree. It was abhorrent behavior and something she had criticized Apollo for.

"That's not an apology."

"Are you telling me those words mean nothing to you?"

She tilted her chin, anger flashing in her eyes. "*Actions*, Hades. You weren't going to tell me about Leuce."

"If we are going to speak of actions, then let us speak of yours. Did you not promise me you wouldn't write about Apollo?"

He knew he was being a little unfair, but of the two things they were discussing, Apollo took precedence. He was a god with power and a taste for blood.

"I had to do it—"

"*Had to?* Were you offered an ultimatum?"

He couldn't keep the bite from his voice, and his tone drowned out the part of him that was actually concerned she might have faced some kind of demand from her job. *New Athens News* was owned by Kal Stavros. At his question, Persephone looked away, setting her jaw.

"Were you threatened?" he continued.

She did not respond. She was digging her heels in against his anger.

"Did any of it have *anything* to do with you?"

She stood from the bath without warning, water rippling off her body, and clutched a towel to her chest.

"Sybil is my friend, and her life was ruined by Apollo," she said, standing so close he could feel the heat coming off her body. "His behavior had to be exposed."

Hades inched closer, tilting his head as he did.

"Do you know what I think?" he whispered furiously, letting his arms fall to his sides, fingers curling into fists to keep from touching her. "I think this is all a game to you. I pissed you off, so you wanted to piss me off, is that it? One for one—now we're even."

She scowled. "Not everything's about you, Hades."

He gripped her hips and drew her close, voice rough.

"You promised me you wouldn't write about Apollo. Is your word worth nothing?"

She flinched, and he felt it in her whole body, a desire to create distance between them.

"Fuck you," she spat with tears in her eyes, and as much as he hated to see it, he smiled.

"I'd rather fuck you, darling, but if I did right now, you wouldn't walk for a week."

He snapped his fingers and teleported to the queen's suite. It was where she usually got ready for events in the Underworld, and it would be her home for however long it took to end Apollo's hunt.

As soon as they had appeared, Persephone pushed away from him.

"Did you just abduct me?"

"Yes. Apollo will come after you, and the only way he will have an audience with you is if I am present."

"I can take care of this, Hades."

"You can't and you won't." He hated to say it, but in this instance, it was true. She couldn't go up against a god—not one as seasoned as Apollo.

Her eyes glinted, lifting her chin in defiance as she tried to teleport. When it didn't work, she stomped her foot, and from there, a mass of vines erupted from the floor and crawled toward him.

"You can't keep me here."

Hades's responding chuckle only seemed to infuriate her more. "Darling, you are in my realm. You're here until I say otherwise."

He turned and headed for the door.

"I have to work, Hades. I have a life up there. Hades!"

He kept walking, though with each step, her magic

surged, and in seconds, the harmless vines she'd sent his way earlier became thick thorns, rising from the broken floor to attack.

Hades turned quickly, dismissing her magic with a wave of his hand.

She stared, mouth ajar. After a moment, she swallowed, and there was a flash of something in her eyes that hurt his chest, a pain he did not understand but had seen in many mortals. It was the shock of suddenly understanding just how powerless she really was.

He let his hand fall, and despite everything inside him that wanted to go to her, to comfort her, he turned to leave once more.

As he did, she yelled after him, her voice breaking with a distinct crack he could feel in his heart. "You will regret this!"

At the door, he turned his head a fraction and answered, "I already do."

When he stepped out of her room, he found Hecate waiting. The goddess's eyes were glassy with anger. Hades wasn't certain what had summoned her, but he had a feeling it had something do with the surge in Persephone's magic.

"Don't," he warned, and while his voice did not waver, his insides shook.

He didn't want to hear what Hecate would say, because he already knew he had fucked up. He knew it with every beat of his heart, but if he hadn't gotten her out of the Upperworld and into his realm, there was no end to the list of the things Apollo might do.

At least here, she was safe—and he'd take that in the

end, because the one thing he wouldn't live without in this world was her, even if she hated him.

To her credit, Hecate said nothing, and Hades made a wide arc around her, leaving the palace altogether.

CHAPTER X
Bakkheia

Hades was distracted, his mind on the final moments before he'd left Persephone in the queen's suite of his palace the night before. The broken note in her voice tortured his thoughts and clawed at his chest. That night, he'd watched her from his balcony, wandering through the garden. She fit so perfectly among those flowers, like his soul had known to make it for her before she existed.

Even then, with all the knowledge that their fates were entwined, he could not manage to talk to her, to make this rift between them right. In some twisted way, he feared comfort would only seem like he approved of her actions, and he wanted her to know the consequences of dealing with gods.

"My lord?" Antoni queried, and Hades looked up, meeting the cyclops's gaze in the car's rearview mirror. "Apologies. We have arrived. Would you like for me to wait for you?"

Hades had asked Antoni to take him to Bakkheia. He'd decided to put this anger to good use and confront Dionysus over his involvement with Acacius, and he preferred to arrive in a mortal fashion, as it would announce his presence. Not only that, but teleporting into a god's territory was usually frowned upon, though Hades would have been able to do so, given that he shared control of the Upperworld with his brothers.

"That won't be necessary," Hades replied. He would choose a far quicker exit when he was ready to leave the God of Wine's territory.

Antoni looked at him in the rearview mirror.

"Pardon the observation, my lord, but you seem... off tonight."

That was an effective way to describe how he felt.

He was *off*. He had been since the night Persephone had confronted him about Leuce, and things had spiraled from there. Now he agonized, replaying every decision he'd made prior and since, and he felt ridiculous.

A horn blared as an impatient driver pulled in behind them, and Hades curled his fists at the sound.

"Apologies, Antoni," Hades said and stepped out of his limo. As he did, he straightened his tie and turned his head toward the waiting car. The driver's eyes widened, and he backed up into the vehicle behind him in an attempt to flee.

That was a satisfying enough punishment for Hades, and he strolled to the black doors of Bakkheia, illuminated on either side by strands of red light. The bouncers, two large satyrs, allowed Hades past with only a nod, though he knew they'd already alerted Dionysus of his presence the moment he stepped out of the car. And while he hoped that meant he wouldn't have to go in search of the god, he had a feeling Dionysus was going to make this very difficult.

Once Hades stepped through the doorway, he was greeted by a loud and crowded club. The music was so loud, it vibrated his bones. Red laser light cut through the darkness and billows of white smoke clouded the air. It was supposed to be hypnotizing, but Hades found it suffocating. He edged along the dance floor to the stairs and headed to the second floor, where it was quieter and far more intimate. A few people leaned over small tables, talking in hushed voices, while some shared space, taking up large plush chairs to kiss and explore. Then there were some who openly fucked, the darkness unable to mask the sounds of pleasurable intercourse.

No one seemed to mind, not the exhibitionism or the voyeurism, but Hades had no intention of lingering. Being on this floor reminded him of how badly he'd wanted to comfort Persephone when he'd taken her to the Underworld. He'd wanted to touch her, kiss her, caress her. He'd wanted her to find pleasure in his arms, but he'd left instead, and now the distance between them felt like a hopelessly deep and jarring chasm.

He continued down the hall, which was wide and full of seating. A wall of windows overlooked downtown New Athens, providing a glittering backdrop for the sin that took place here.

Dionysus had a unique repertoire of powers, among them the ability to inspire madness and ecstasy, and he could apply them to myriad situations—from the murderous to the erotic. It was no surprise, given that the god was the first to create wine, a drink responsible for lowering the inhibitions of many mortals. At the root of it, Dionysus was the cause for much disruption, and he reveled in the chaos.

It was just one reason Hades preferred to keep his distance, yet here he was, seeking him out for the discord he'd caused.

He came to the third floor, reserved for private suites. The hall was dark, and doors bearing red numbers ran the length of it. There was an energy to the air that put Hades on edge, and while he knew part of it had to do with being in another god's territory, there was something darker beneath—a desperation that called to death. He may have ruled over that realm, but it was unnerving to feel how it lingered within these walls.

Hades paused before the seventh door and entered.

Inside, the suite was dim, but Hades did not need any more light to know what was occurring before him. Dionysus relaxed in a large chair, arms stretched out over the back, while a woman knelt between his legs, working her mouth and hands over his cock. There were other people in the room too, all engaged in various sexual acts, and Dionysus's magic hung heavy in the air, magic that had worked these mortals into a frenzy, unable to think of anything but their carnal need to fuck.

"Hades," Dionysus said in acknowledgment, and as he nodded, the gold coiled in his hair glinted in the light.

"Dionysus."

"Excuse the display," he said. "Just making sure everything is in working order, given I have been plagued with dreams of castration."

"How unfortunate," Hades commented.

He shrugged. "I quite like the pain."

Of course he would, Hades thought.

"I've been expecting you," Dionysus said with no hitch in his voice despite the woman's vigorous work between his legs.

Hades was not surprised. "You've been busy, from what I hear."

"What have you heard?"

Hades only waited a beat before responding. "A lot," he replied.

"From which you have made a lot of assumptions."

Hades raised a brow. "I do not assume," he said, though there was an element of guilt that accompanied those words as he recalled how much he assumed when it came to Persephone.

"Isn't that why you're here?"

"Look who's assuming," Hades replied. "And here I thought to give you the space to explain yourself."

That was the first comment to break Dionysus's cool facade. His eyes narrowed slightly, his fingers curled, then he sat up and his gaze fell to the girl, still valiantly engaged in her task.

"Leave," he commanded.

She looked up at him and obeyed, allowing his cock to slide from her mouth. She rose, using his knees for support, and left.

"I would apologize," Hades said, "but it does not appear she was able to hold much of your…attention."

Dionysus's lips flattened, and he stood to restore his appearance. He was just as tall and large as Hades. He wore a gray suit with purple accents, and his hair was long and braided.

"Usually I am not deterred by exhibitionism, but you tend to have an unnerving effect."

"I'll take that as a compliment."

"It isn't," Dionysus said flatly, navigating around entangled bodies as he made his way to the bar, where a glass of wine and a glass of whiskey already waited.

Dionysus handed over the whiskey.

"Since you've come for a visit, I hope you've brought along my eye."

"You illegally bought the Graeae. The eye is no more yours than they are."

"You missed the important part—bought *and* paid for."

"You missed the illegal part," Hades pointed out.

"What makes you think it was illegal?"

"Who does anything lawful on the black market?" Hades countered.

Dionysus took a sip of his wine and set it aside, watching Hades.

"I did not buy the Graeae. I bought their services. Imagine my...*surprise* when they arrived without their eye and no ability to do what I need."

Hades was skeptical. "And what did you need?"

Just then, the woman Dionysus had ordered to leave earlier burst into the suite.

"She's dying! There's a girl in the bathroom, and she's dying!"

Hades and Dionysus exchanged a look before leaving the room, scrambling for the restroom located at the end of the hall. Dionysus was the first to enter, throwing open the door with such force that it crashed against the wall. There, on the tiled floor, lay an unconscious woman whose life force was indeed fading, and the only reason she had yet to pass was due to the efforts of another woman who hovered over her, administering CPR. Hades recognized her immediately.

Ariadne.

"Get out of the way," Dionysus commanded, kneeling beside the woman.

"Fuck you!" Ariadne shot back.

"I said move!" the god roared, and Ariadne fell back, wedged between the wall and the countertop.

Dionysus produced a syringe from the inside pocket of his jacket and stuck the needle straight into the muscle of the girl's arm. When he was finished, he reached for Ariadne, dragging her back to the girl by the wrist.

"Do your compressions until she's breathing again."

She blinked, stunned, and while it took her a second to comply, she resumed without argument.

Shocking, Hades thought.

A few minutes passed, then Ariadne spoke. "She's breathing."

At that, the doors opened and two men entered, each lifting the woman up by an arm draped over their shoulders.

"Where are you taking her?" Ariadne demanded, rising to her feet. "She still needs medical assistance."

"My, you are presumptuous," Dionysus said.

"You expect me to believe you will see to her care?"

"I saved her life!"

"Excuse me? You are the reason she was in that state."

"I don't recall telling anyone to overdose."

"No? Then why do you carry Narcan?"

"Will you two shut the fuck up?" Hades snapped,

unable to take any more of their verbal sparring. He had work to do, and they were both fucking around.

Both Dionysus and Ariadne looked at him.

"What the hell are you doing here, Detective?" Hades asked.

Dionysus narrowed his eyes as she responded.

"What does it look like?" she countered. "And where were you? I didn't see you jumping to help us save that girl's life, *God of the Dead*."

"I highly doubt you wanted my intervention, Detective. It's in the name."

Silence followed his comment, and Ariadne crossed her arms over her chest.

"I take it you two are acquainted?" Dionysus asked tightly.

"We met briefly when Detective Alexiou accused you of trafficking women. Care to explain?" Hades thought they might as well cut to the chase. He saw no reason to keep Ariadne's secret, given that she had obviously decided to continue her own investigation. "By the way, it seems you had no trouble getting into Bakkheia on your own, Detective."

She glared.

"Trafficking women?" Dionysus asked, and Hades noted an edge to his voice that Ariadne did not seem to pick up on. Perhaps that was due to her line of work. He was certain she was used to being lied to, as well, much as Hades was.

"Megara Alkaios has been missing for two weeks," Ariadne said. "Her friends say she came here and never left."

"That is one woman," Dionysus pointed out.

"I have reason to believe you're also responsible for the disappearances of *many* more."

"Does reason equate to evidence, or is that just your opinion of me, Detective Alexiou?"

Hades knew very well she had no evidence and yet he found her response particularly amusing.

"If you were innocent, you would have said so, yet I don't hear you denying a thing."

"I'm not interested in gaining your favor," Dionysus replied.

"Well, you should be interested in gaining mine," Ariadne snapped.

That made Dionysus laugh, and he took a step closer to the mortal woman. Her head tilted back in defiance, and the tension between them grew as he asked, "Are you saying you have something to offer, Detective?"

"*I* have a lot to offer," said Hades, once more interrupting. "Including a stay in Tartarus if I have to hear this exchange any longer."

"No one said you had to stay," Ariadne shot back, glaring at Hades, then returned her gaze to Dionysus once she heard him chuckle. "Is something *funny*?"

"Oh yes," he said. "Something is definitely funny."

A woman entered the bathroom and hesitated at seeing it occupied by the three, but her expression quickly morphed to interest, and she sauntered inside.

"Want a fourth?" she asked.

Ariadne lifted the hem of her dress and drew a gun. "Get out."

The woman's eyes widened, and she fled just as Dionysus's hand clamped down on the weapon, wrenching it from Ariadne's hands.

"Tsk, tsk, Detective. Don't you know the rules? No weapons in the club."

"I see you pick and choose your morals."

"Like all gods," he said, and his eyes traveled down her frame. "Hiding anything else under that dress?"

"Wouldn't you like to know?"

"By the gods, I think I'm going to vomit," Hades said.

"Now you know how the rest of us feel about you and your lover," Dionysus said, finally looking at Hades.

He clenched his jaw at the comment, which only succeeded in reminding him once more of all the mistakes he'd made in the past couple of weeks.

There was a beat of silence as Dionysus placed Ariadne's gun inside his coat. "Follow me."

Dionysus left the bathroom first, and Hades gestured for Ariadne to follow.

"Ladies first," he said.

"What a gentleman," she replied dryly.

They followed Dionysus down the hall to an elevator tucked away in an alcove off the staircase. Once inside, he took out a key that gave him the ability to choose a level below the first floor that was unmarked. Hades wasn't surprised to discover that this club had a basement. If he had to guess, it had an underground tunnel too and likely connected to other properties owned by Dionysus.

As he suspected, when the door opened, it was to a large, concrete tunnel. A stripe of fluorescent lights ran down the center, casting the place in a painful, yellow light.

"Is this how you smuggle contraband into your club?" Ariadne asked.

"No," said Dionysus, stepping past her. "We bring that in the front door."

They followed him, and the tunnel led to a balcony that overlooked a large, warehouse-type room. It was accessible via a set of metal stairs. Several long tables ran the length of the space, and there were a few other cozier seating areas, some of which were occupied by women who were reading or cleaning weapons. There was a whole wall of shelving dedicated to leather-bound books, and another wall was taken over by a large screen that was currently displaying news streams from across New Greece. Several dark archways were located intermittently about the room, and Hades found himself curious as to where those led.

"This brothel looks terrible," Ariadne said.

"I didn't realize you were an expert," said Dionysus.

"It's not a brothel," Hades said.

"So now *you're* the expert?" Ariadne said.

"Megara," Dionysus called, ignoring her.

A woman looked up from one of the seating areas. It was evident she was the same girl from the photo Ariadne had presented to Hades earlier in the week—auburn hair, round eyes, slender frame. She had been reading a book, but when her name was called, she set it aside and stood, bowing.

"My lord," she said.

"This detective thinks you are in trouble," he said. "*Are* you in trouble?"

She shook her head and answered, "I am not in trouble."

Hades sensed no lie, but Ariadne moved ahead of the two gods.

"Do not lie for him," she said. "If he kidnapped you, you must let me know."

"He didn't," she replied. "I came here of my own free will."

Ariadne's brows furrowed, and Hades saw that her shoulders fell. "I...don't understand."

The woman looked confused, her eyes slipping to Dionysus, who said, "You do not have to tell her if you do not wish."

Ariadne's frustration must have boiled over, because she plowed ahead. "Look, I'm a detective with the Hellenic Police Department," she explained. It was the wrong thing to say, because every woman in the room looked up then, and Hades felt their collective apprehension, fear, and venom. Ariadne must have noticed it too because she hesitated. "Why are you all looking at me like that?"

"Because they don't want to be found," Hades said, and before Ariadne could speak, he stopped her. "Is it so hard to believe, given what you've seen? These women are in hiding."

"Did anyone happen to tell you where I was before I went missing?" Megara asked, and her voice trembled. "The hospital. It was my third visit. I decided it would be my last."

For the first time all night, Ariadne had nothing to say—but Hades did. He had a lot to say.

"You'll forgive me if I don't believe you've done this purely from the goodness of your heart," Hades said to Dionysus.

"What are you implying?"

Hades vanished and appeared behind one of the women, who had been cleaning a knife. In an instant, she was on her feet, and as soon as Hades appeared, the blade was at his throat.

He stared at the woman, no hint of fear in her eyes.

"Right," Hades said and took a step back. "So you've trained them."

Dionysus shrugged. "Why not give them the ability to defend themselves?"

"And assassinate your enemies. Two birds, one stone, right?"

The god did not respond.

"Are you saying you have an army of female assassins?" Ariadne asked.

"Well, this has been *most* satisfying," said Dionysus. "But you have worn out your welcome."

"Only just now?" Ariadne asked.

"That mouth really is something else," said Dionysus.

That made Ariadne smile, but in a way that communicated her disgust with the god.

"As much as I'd like to leave and never return," Hades said, "you've yet to answer my question."

Dionysus stiffened, and Hades felt everyone in the room tense around him. He got the distinct impression that Dionysus's assassins were poised for attack.

"I'd reconsider," Hades said. "Not even your assassins have a chance against death."

"Fine," Dionysus gritted out. "You want to know? I'll tell you."

"Fucking finally," Hades gritted out, relieved.

It had only taken discovering one of Dionysus's

weaknesses, which he was certain were few and far between. The God of the Vine was not overt about those he cared for, because it made them targets—it was a lesson he'd learned long ago, as he was a son of Zeus and had been the target of Hera's wrath for the majority of his life.

"I needed the location of a gorgon named Medusa," Dionysus said. "There is a rumor going around in the market that she has the power to turn men to stone. As you can imagine, that is quiet a useful skill in the hands of a mortal."

"One you want for yourself?" Ariadne asked.

"If I wanted to turn someone to stone, I could without a gorgon's gaze," Dionysus replied. "Shall I give you a demonstration?"

"Or you could finish your explanation," Hades interjected, his patience gone.

Dionysus and Ariadne were still glaring at each other when he continued.

"A few bounty hunters have put a price on her head, so I hired the Graeae to help me find her first."

"So she can join your team of assassins?"

"They're called maenads," Dionysus said, then shamelessly admitted, "And yes."

"As your weapon," Hades said.

Dionysus shrugged. "Her power makes her dangerous. She'll be on everyone's kill list. At least here, she would be safe."

"And what if that isn't what she wants?" Ariadne asked.

Dionysus looked at the detective and answered, "Not everyone has the privilege of choice."

Hades considered the information Dionysus had

given him. If it were true, if there were a bounty on Medusa's head, then it was just a matter of time before she was located. Still, he had questions. He was familiar with gorgons. He employed one—Euryale—to watch the doors to his lounge at Nevernight. Did she know Medusa?

"Why the Graeae?" Hades asked.

Dionysus stared.

"You have all these assassins," Hades continued. "A roomful of people who can search and spy, yet you purchased the Graeae. Why?"

"I purchased their *skills*," Dionysus clarified, as if he thought that were somehow better. "And because they are sisters to the gorgons. If anyone would know where Medusa resided, it would be the Graeae."

"And you think they will tell you?"

"If they want to keep her safe, then yes."

"It seems she's doing a fine job keeping herself safe," Ariadne pointed out, which was true. No one had been able to locate her, and if they had, it was likely that no one knew because she'd turned them to stone.

Still, Dionysus was right. Power like that was dangerous. Mortals would want to harness it—mortals like the Impious or even Triad—while immortals would want to destroy it. It was just a matter of time before someone figured out how to capture her.

Hades looked to Dionysus. "What will you do if she doesn't want to come with you?" It was an important question, one that Hades had to know the answer to before he decided how to proceed.

"I won't force her," Dionysus said. "But I have hope that her sisters will help convince her."

"Take us to them," Hades said, and before Dionysus could protest, he continued. "We'll learn the secret together."

Dionysus's lips flattened. "You hardly have the authority to command such a thing in my realm," he said.

"Last time I checked, the Graeae were not under your rule. Besides, I have the eye, and they cannot see without it."

Hades expected Dionysus to protest—to remind him that he had *bought and paid* for the services of the Graeae—and while his jaw ticked as he gritted his teeth, he gave a harsh nod.

"Fine."

Dionysus left the balcony, navigating to the floor where his maenads lingered, and led them through one of the darkened archways.

It turned out that they were dorms.

"I expected a dungeon," Ariadne said as they passed door after door.

"I have one," said Dionysus. "Though it's not exactly what you're imagining."

Ariadne scoffed, and Hades rolled his eyes.

Finally, Dionysus stopped at one of the doors and knocked.

"What are we waiting for?" Ariadne asked.

"For them to answer the door," Dionysus said. "They aren't prisoners."

But after a minute, no one had come, so Dionysus knocked again.

"Deino, Enyo, Pemphredo," he called, and still there was no answer. When he opened the door, they found the dorm was empty. "What the fuck."

Dionysus stepped inside the spacious room, which resembled more of a luxury hotel room with large beds, lush linens, and pleasing works of art. Hades and Ariadne followed. It was evident that the three sisters had occupied the room, as three of the four beds had rumpled covers and there were breakfast trays at the end of each, crowded with empty plates, glasses, and silverware, but the Graeae were nowhere to be found.

"You have a basement of assassins, and the Graeae still managed to escape," Ariadne said.

"They didn't escape," said Dionysus.

Ariadne raised a doubtful brow.

"They were taken," he said.

"Are you saying someone managed to steal from you?" she asked and glanced at Hades. "Twice."

Dionysus's body tensed.

"Seems your maenads aren't doing their job."

"It would be impossible for mortals, no matter how skilled, to go up against a god," said Hades.

"You think a god did this?" she asked.

There was no other explanation. Three monsters had disappeared from their room without a trace.

"If not a god, someone with divine blood," Hades said, knowing that demigods often took on powers from their mothers and fathers, which made the pool of culprits even greater. "The question is, who?"

Hades met Dionysus's gaze, but he shook his head.

"I have no fucking clue."

CHAPTER XI
A Battle of Wills

Hades expected to return to the Underworld only mildly frustrated after dealing with Dionysus tonight, but he had not anticipated adding to his long list of anxieties, among them the abducted Graeae.

The only thing that worked in either Dionysus's or Hades's favor was that he was still in possession of the eye. The way he saw it, there were two possibilities ahead of them—either he and Dionysus found the abductors, or the abductors would come to them. For now, at least the gorgon Medusa was safe.

Though for how long, Hades could not be certain, and that made him uneasy. In fact, everything about this made him uneasy. Something was at work here, and he felt like he could see it forming on the fringe of his vision, a slight shadow that hinted at darker days.

Whoever was in search of Medusa wanted a weapon.

A thick dread settled in his chest and tangled in his

lungs, making it hard to breathe and think of anything but...war.

He shook his head, frowning deeply at the turn his thoughts had taken, and it was made worse by the sudden, deep desire to see Persephone. When he felt like this—like chaos and turmoil—he turned to her to calm and soothe. She was everything he had never had upon entering this ravaged and bloody world—warm and loving and safe—and when this violence moved beneath his skin at the thought of his past, she always managed to ease it.

As he made his return to the Underworld, the need to see her blossomed. He was urged not only by these darker feelings but by far less rational thoughts, like what if Apollo had somehow found a way into the Underworld? He knew it wasn't possible, yet his mind would not ease until he laid eyes on her.

Still, he hesitated at her door. What if she did not wish to see him? He frowned, imagining what she might say.

Ensuring I remain in your prison?

He took a deep breath and knocked on the door.

There was no answer.

For a moment, he thought that perhaps she was ignoring him, but then he went in search of her presence and realized he could not feel her.

He opened the door.

It was dark, but he could see that the bed was untouched.

"Persephone?" he called and moved farther into the room, calling forth lights to burn away the darkness, leaving no part of the room in shadow. But she was not there, so he searched the baths, then the library, then the entire palace, and when he could not find her, he turned to the garden.

He walked the winding path that seemed neverending the longer he went without finding her beneath the branches of the willows or hiding among the flowers. Hysteria burned his throat when he came to the end of the garden where Cerberus, Typhon, and Orthrus waited, as if they sensed his discontent.

"Find Persephone," he ordered.

The dogs took off, their noses to the ground, but he could tell by the way they moved that they were not tracking her scent, which only made his fear more acute. As he followed their movement across the Asphodel Fields, he closed his eyes, searching his realm for her footprint, but he couldn't feel her.

On any given day, at any given time, he could feel her here, a soft caress, a burning ember. He could also feel her absence, a great disruption in the fabric of his world. That was how she felt now—gone. His growing unease turned to fear, churning hard in his stomach. Though this was his realm, it was still dangerous, and Persephone had found that danger readily enough in the past, wandering into Tartarus only to come face-to-face with Tantalus, a man who still wished to cause Hades pain, much like many who resided in his realm.

Except then, Hades had been able to track her to Tantalus.

He could not trace her now.

"Hecate, Hermes!"

Their names left his lips, a summoning command. There were no snide remarks or quips from either as they appeared before him. They knew he would not have called them if it weren't serious. If he did not need them.

"I cannot find her," he said, his voice shaking, his heart racing. "I cannot feel her."

They both paled hearing his words, and there was a shared sense of dread between the three.

"We'll find her," Hermes said confidently.

But would it be too late?

The two vanished, and Hades stormed across the field. The wind picked up speed, whipping around him, and the elegant stems of the asphodel wilted as he drained the lush ground around him of magic. Then the air rippled and grew warm with the energy of gods as Hades summoned the deities of the Underworld. They came to him disembodied, taking the form of shadow and lightning, whirling around him. He felt them acutely—grief and sorrow, sickness and panic, starvation and *want*. They whispered to him as they circled, monstrous things they used to infect mortal minds and drive them to madness.

And Hades felt mad.

Now and then, the deities flashed red eyes or gnashed long, sharp teeth. They were monsters more than they were human, and Hades needed them.

"Find. My. Queen!" he commanded.

The deities circled quicker, and their whispers became faster until they peeled away, dashing across the sky. Hades followed, still leeching magic from his realm as he went, his sole focus on finding Persephone.

His mind knew no bounds when it came to imagining what might have happened to her. His earlier thoughts of battle returned with a vengeance, and all he could think was that she must be hurt and that he would find her broken and bleeding. The images came to mind easily because he had seen many bodies in the same state. He had never allowed himself to think long on loss, not when it came to Persephone, though he'd always promised to end the world if anything did occur.

Now he was certain of it, but he'd not just set it aflame.

He would tear it to pieces.

It was Cerberus who came to him first, then Typhon, and they led him to a grove of poplar trees where Orthrus sat rigid, guarding Persephone, who slept beneath the silver of his strange moon. Even standing before her, he still could not sense her. It was as if, in slumber, she had managed to shield herself.

It took him a moment to move, to settle the chaos her absence had caused, and when he did, the wind ceased to roar and the deities he had called to his aid screamed as they were forced to return to the untamed wild beyond the gates of his realm. Though he managed to quell the external part of his frenzy, inside, he still felt the aftershock shudder through him, but that soon ebbed as he knelt to gather her into his arms.

He cradled her close as he rose, enjoying her warmth and weight and the smell of her hair, which was earthy and sweet, and soon, Hecate and Hermes had found them. None of them spoke, but there was a general sense of relief between the three. Hades moved past them, heading for the palace. While he could have teleported, he wanted more time with her like this—when all was well and peaceful, when she forgot that she hated him.

Cerberus, Typhon, and Orthrus led the way, and with each step he took, his world fell into place, and the Underworld became lush once more.

Hades took Persephone to his room, tucking her into his bed. She shifted once when he laid her down, moving to her side and curling her hands beneath her cheek, but she did not wake. He bent and pressed a kiss to her forehead, calm in the knowledge that she was safe, and ventured into the night, finding that he was far more disturbed by his behavior than he had expected to be.

He hated feeling like he had no control, and when he'd returned to the Underworld to find Persephone missing, he had lost it in more than one way. He returned to where he'd found her. This time, she had been far from the dangers of Tartarus, nearer to Hecate's meadow and the palace.

"She must have gone for a walk," Hecate said, appearing in the meadow beside him. "Perhaps she got tired and sat down to rest."

"I find myself wishing to destroy everything that poses a threat to her," he admitted.

"If you only try to insulate her, she will grow to resent you."

He knew Persephone well enough to know that Hecate was right. She would grow to hate him if she felt caged, and wasn't that the opposite of what he'd wanted for her?

He looked away. "I am afraid for her."

In the short time they'd been together, she had become collateral for Hera's whims and the focus of

Apollo's soon-to-be wrath. Not to mention her mother, Demeter, was likely still plotting ways to keep them apart, and he suspected that Leuce may be part of that scheme.

Worst of all, he knew this was only the beginning.

Persephone was a relatively new god, her powers untested, and in the end, she possessed a code of ethics that would never allow her to overlook injustice.

"So teach her," Hecate said.

Hades met the goddess's gaze.

"You want a queen," she said. "So teach her to live within your realm. Teach her to use her magic. Teach her to be a goddess, and stop trying to fight all her battles."

Hecate was right, and he would let Persephone fight her own battles—just not against Apollo.

Hades did not sleep that night.

He stayed in his office and kept himself occupied with thoughts of the Graeae. He wondered if there was a connection between their abduction and the bombing of Acacius's shop. He would have to see what Ilias discovered during his investigation. Outside of that and his inevitable encounter with Apollo, his greatest worry was still Hera and the labor he had not even attempted.

The murder of Briareus.

The last communication he'd had from the goddess was the note she'd attached to Persephone's article about Apollo, reminding him that she had control over their future as husband and wife. Though something she had said intrigued him—that allies among the Olympians might influence Zeus's decision. Hades knew his brother well enough, knew there was potential for that to be true, so how did he sway them to his side?

There was a knock, and he looked up as Hermes burst through the door.

"He's coming," Hermes said. "He's angry."

The God of Mischief didn't need to specify. Hades knew he was referring to Apollo.

"I want you to watch Persephone," Hades instructed. "Keep her occupied while I talk to Apollo."

Hermes raised his skeptical brow. "Because you're so good at conversing?"

"That's a big word, Hermes," Hades replied. "Have you been reading a thesaurus?"

Hermes narrowed his eyes. "Deflect all you want, King of Corpses, but I know you, and you aren't a talker. What are you planning?"

"I'm talking to you, aren't I?" Hades pointed out.

"Hardly, and I'm your best friend."

It was Hades's turn to raise a brow.

"Don't deny it. Do you ask Hecate for fashion advice?"

Hades scowled. "Don't make me regret my decision, Hermes."

"Regret? Excuse me. Did you get laid in those gray sweatpants I suggested you wear?"

He rolled his eyes.

"Then you can't regret it!"

"How do you know that was a yes?"

"Hades," Hermes said, as if he were about to point out something very obvious. "Because I dressed you for sex."

"Get Apollo, Hermes, and once he's here, go to Persephone."

"On it, *best* friend," Hermes said as he headed for the door.

Hades left his office. As he started for the throne room, he changed directions and headed for his bedchamber, where Persephone still slept, swathed in silk. She hadn't moved, still lying on her side, knees bent, hands curled near her face. He brushed a stray curl from her face, fingers lingering on her flushed cheek before teleporting to the throne room where Apollo already waited. He was like his mother, Leto, in appearance, crowned with dark curls and dark eyes that sometimes looked violet when he was frustrated enough, but that was where the similarities ended. Unlike her, there was no softness to his personality, nor his sister's for that matter.

"I knew you wouldn't let your little lover fight the war she started," said Apollo.

"What's the matter, Nephew? A few words have you ready for battle?"

"Her words were slander!"

"Is it slander if they are true?"

Hades noted the tightening of his fists. There was a part of him that wished Apollo would act against him in his realm. The affront would mean the god would be forced to end his pursuit of Persephone. While Apollo was often brash, he did not often challenge other gods, and it was likely he wouldn't challenge Hades, knowing something far more lucrative waited for him if he maintained his composure.

"Truth has nothing to do with this slight," Apollo replied. "Her blasphemy will be punished, Hades. Even you cannot stop divine retribution."

Hades took a moment to speak, working to relax his

jaw, and when he did, his words felt thick in his mouth. "And what if I offer to bargain?"

Apollo's eyes flashed, and he lifted his chin, intrigued. Hades hated the slight twitch to his lips as Apollo implored, "Go on."

"Forgive this *slight*, and in exchange, I offer a favor."

"A *favor*," Apollo echoed. "That is very generous."

"The offer is not for your benefit, though you will likely reap the rewards."

"You must really care for this mortal."

Hades said nothing. He did not have to. The offer of a favor spoke volumes.

"Fine," Apollo said. "But she will *never*—"

The doors to the throne room slammed open, and Hades's eyes lifted to Persephone, who stood barely dressed in her black robe. Though her exposed skin meant little to Apollo, Hades would have preferred he not see her at all. Every muscle in his body tightened as the God of Music turned to look at her.

"So," he purred, "the mortal has come to play."

Hades's body vibrated with frustration, his eyes sliding to Hermes, who had just come to a stop behind Persephone, looking a little too impish to be completely innocent. Hades glared.

"What?" Hermes asked, defensive. "She guessed!"

"The deal is done. You will not touch her," Hades said, both as a reminder and as a warning.

"What deal?" Persephone asked, taking a few more steps into the room.

He had not told her of his plans, and now that they were here in this room, he wished he had, even if there had been no time, and even though she wouldn't have approved, at least she wouldn't have had to find out this way. He knew it looked bad.

"Your lover has struck a deal," Apollo said, his disdain for Persephone evident in his tone. It was an insult, and Hades considered challenging the god, but it was a dangerous prospect now that he owed him a favor. "I have agreed not to punish you for your...*slanderous article*...and in turn, Hades has offered me a favor to be collected at a future time."

Persephone's eyes widened, which told him she understood perfectly the implications of his deal.

"Damn," Hermes whistled, and Hades's mood darkened. "He really does love you, Sephy."

"I will not agree to this," Persephone said.

Hades admired her words; they came out of a concern for him, no matter how futile.

"You don't have a choice, mortal," Apollo said.

"I'm the one who wrote the article. Your deal should be with me."

"Persephone," Hades warned. While he had accepted Hades's offer, there was nothing to prevent Apollo from also taking Persephone up on hers.

But Apollo laughed, such was his arrogance. "What could you possibly offer me?"

Persephone's eyes flashed, her fingers curled into her palms, and Hades allowed his magic to surface in response, hoping it would mask hers.

"You hurt my friend," she seethed.

"Whatever your friend did must have warranted punishment or she would not be in the situation she is in."

Apollo's response did nothing to quell Persephone's

anger, but at least it illustrated who he was, something that could only be witnessed—an asshole.

"You mean to tell me her refusal to be your lover warrants punishment?" Persephone asked.

Hades noted how rigid Apollo had gone, which told him he knew exactly who Persephone was talking about.

"You took away her livelihood because she declined to sleep with you. That is insane and pathetic."

As much as he enjoyed her insults, they were best kept between them. If Apollo wanted, he could take each word as a slight and ask for more in exchange.

"*Persephone*," Hades warned.

"You be quiet! You chose not to include me in this conversation. I *will* speak my mind." While he deserved her contempt, he'd have rather taken it without an audience. Hermes laughed, and to Hades's chagrin, she continued. "I only wrote about your past lovers. I didn't even touch on what you have done to Sybil. If you don't undo her punishment, I will dismantle you."

Hades assumed she meant she would do so with her words, and while he believed she was capable of writing something that hurt, she obviously had forgotten how poorly the public had taken her first article.

He expected Apollo to respond with aggression, but he chuckled, and that put Hades more on edge because it meant he was intrigued.

"You are a fiery little mortal. I could use someone like you."

"Speak further, Nephew, and you will have no reason to fear her threat, because I will tear you to pieces."

Apollo's gaze narrowed, daring him to try.

"Well?" Persephone asked, raising her voice to regain Apollo's attention.

The god studied her for a long moment, and Hades hated the smile that curled his lips.

"Fine," Apollo said at last, and Hades let his breath escape in a slow stream. "I will return your little friend's powers, and I'll take Hades's favor as well, but you will not write another word about me—*no matter what*. Understand?"

"Words are binding," Persephone replied. "And I do not trust you enough to agree."

Hades was quite proud of that.

Even Apollo grinned. "You have taught her well, Hades."

Then Apollo took a step toward her, and Hades fought every urge to fling him across the Underworld. He might have done it if he didn't think the God of Music was about to relent.

"Let me put it this way—you write another word about me, and I'll destroy everything you love. And before you consider the fact that you love another god, remember that I have his favor. If I want to keep you apart forever, I can."

You can try, Hades thought. *But it will be the last action you take.*

Apollo knew that, and Hades worried that perhaps that was what the god wanted.

Persephone's face was flushed, her jaw tight as she spoke. "Noted."

"I will warn you now, Apollo," Hades said. "If any harm comes to Persephone, favor or not, I will bury you and everything you love in ash."

As useless as the threat was, he still wished to make it, though he knew it had little impact on the god who felt he had already lost everything. Perhaps that was what made Apollo so dreadful to challenge.

"You'll only have me to bury, Hades. Nothing I love exists anymore."

With that, Apollo left, and in the silence that followed, Hermes spoke, still lingering near the doors. "Well, that could have gone better."

"Why are you still here?" Hades snapped.

"He was *babysitting* me," Persephone said, whirling to face him. "Or did you forget?"

Hades returned her angry stare.

"How can you say you wish for me to be your queen when, given the opportunity to treat me as your equal, you fuck it up completely? *Does your word mean nothing?*"

They were the words he had used against her, and they stung. But he deserved them. He wanted to speak, but Persephone turned, took Hermes's arm, and left the throne room.

CHAPTER XII
An Appeal for Trust

After his encounter with Apollo, Hades needed an outlet to channel his frustration, so he teleported to the Cavern, the oldest part of Tartarus, which was large and resonant. Stone formations made it almost mazelike and offered the opportunity for Hades to create designated spaces for various types of torture—and sport.

The room he had chosen was longer than it was wide. Opposite him was a wall of scarred wood, and at its center, a man was suspended. He was dead, an ax embedded in his chest.

Hades removed his jacket and shirt, hanging them on a hook just over a wooden table where he kept an array of tools and a whetstone for sharpening them. He also removed his shoes and socks, wishing to feel the sandy floor beneath his feet. Once he stood, wearing only his trousers, he approached the dead man, pulling the ax from his body and reviving him.

The man took a gasping breath, and it was a moment

before his eyes settled on Hades. Once they did, he began to weep.

"Not again," he begged. "Please."

Hades turned and walked away, speaking as he put distance between them.

"Are those the words your victims used while you raped them and before you murdered them?" he asked. He twisted the ax in his hand before laying it aside to prepare his station for sharpening it. This was a sacred process, and he believed it created a stronger bond between himself and the weapon. It meant that the tool would behave better, in battle or otherwise. So he took his time, soaking the stones and increasing the grit as his ax got sharper and sharper. When he was finished, he turned toward the man.

His name was Felix.

"Please, please, please," he whispered over and over, drool dripping from his mouth.

Yet there was one thing missing to his pleas. Actual tears.

Hades brought the ax over his right shoulder to throw, releasing when the handle was straight up and down. It landed with a crack in the wood, in the hollow between Felix's shoulder and neck, and the prisoner whimpered.

"Why do you do this?" he howled.

Hades turned back to the table and grabbed another ax.

He took aim again, and this time, it landed between the man's legs, only a hair from his balls.

"You motherfucker!" Felix roared. The veins in his neck popped, his eyes went wide, and the true nature of his soul surfaced, angry, terrifying. "Just kill me!"

"Killing you defeats the purpose," Hades replied.

The rapist's eternal torture was to be under a constant state of stress. Each time Hades took aim was another second spent wondering if this blow would be his last. It was the same horrible agony the man had put his victims through.

Hades ignored Felix and retrieved another ax.

"I will kill you!" the man seethed. "I will kill you and your lover!"

Hades paused and turned toward the man. "What did you say?"

This was not usual, not for Felix and not for any soul. They did not leave Tartarus. They were never aware of anything outside their eternal punishment.

"That's right," Felix said, a sickening gleam to his eyes. "I know about your lover. The blond. She takes up most of your time now…and your thoughts."

Hades did not want to ask how he knew, did not want to give him anything he might hold on to and repeat when he was revived again later.

"I'll find her. I'll have fun too. I'll taste her like you've tasted her and then I'll carve her from the inside out."

There was no way he could, of course. Even if he managed to escape his bonds, he would not make it out of this cavern.

The problem was, how did he know?

Hades let his arm fall, his fingers still tight around the ax handle.

The gleam in Felix's eyes dimmed, replaced by a subtle panic. He'd likely thought his words would lead to a quick death—and they would, but not in the way he'd imagined.

"You think you have power here, mortal?" Hades asked, gathering magic into his hand. It was energy that warmed his hand, and while invisible to the mortal's eyes, Hades knew he could feel it.

Everyone could feel death.

"How wrong you are."

Hades teleported and appeared before the man in a second, the magic in his hand manifesting in the form of a black spike he shoved into the bottom of his chin, straight through his head. Blood spattered on Hades's face, spilling from the soul's mouth and wide eyes. The kill was far less than he deserved. Hades had wanted to destroy his soul, but doing so would be the end of discovering how he knew about Persephone, which was of great concern to him. He would need to bring him back to life later to learn more. Knowledge of her should have ended at the borders of Tartarus. How then did this mediocre prisoner know of the existence of his lover?

"Thanatos!"

Hades jerked his hand free, allowing his magic to dissipate. As he turned, he came face-to-face with the God of Death. He was a pale wraith, cloaked in shadow. His deep-blue eyes, usually as bright as sapphires, hardened and darkened as his gaze slipped from Hades's to his bloodied prisoner.

"Are you well, my lord?" he asked.

"No," Hades said. "Tell me how a prisoner of Tartarus knew enough about Persephone to *threaten* her."

Thanatos's eyes widened. "I...I cannot say," he said, stumbling over his words, and then his mouth tightened. "But I will find out."

"See that you do," Hades replied.

He left Tartarus and bathed at the palace. Once he was dressed, he went in search of Persephone. Felix's words urged him to find her while Hecate's urged him to teach her and to be honest. All he wanted at this moment was to be near her. To know that she was safe.

This time when he went in search of her, he could feel the caress of her magic, though faint, and followed it to the silvery grove of trees he had gifted her. He found her kneeling in a patch of periwinkle and white phlox, her hands stretched out over a small, round section that had begun to wither. The energy around her was chaotic, and while there were moments when he felt her magic surge and focus on her task, it was soon overtaken by the turmoil of her thoughts.

After a few moments, she settled back, her body overwhelmed with her failure.

Hades stepped forward and settled behind her, letting his legs frame her body, drawing her back against his chest. He liked this, liked her scent, liked how her body settled against his in comfort despite the anger that had preceded this moment.

"You are practicing your magic?" he asked, voice quiet.

"More like failing," she said.

"You aren't failing," he said. He spoke near her ear and offered a small laugh at how desolate her voice sounded, only because she was wrong. "You have so much power."

"Then why can't I use it?"

"You are using it."

"Not...correctly."

"Is there a correct way to use your magic?"

He felt her frustration, obviously not understanding how he viewed her progress toward harnessing her magic. He wrapped his fingers around her wrists like cuffs, watching as chills pebbled up her arms.

"You use your magic all the time—when you are angry, when you are aroused…"

She had no trouble calling vines to ensnare him for the purpose of their pleasure, and at the thought, he let his lips trail across her shoulder, a light touch that made her shiver.

"That is not magic," she breathed.

"Then what is magic?" he asked.

"Magic is…" Her voice faded away as she considered what to say, finally answering. "Control."

Her response made him chuckle. Magic, in its most basic form, was wild.

"Magic is not controlled. It is passionate, expressive. It reacts to emotions, no matter your level of expertise."

Just like her, he thought as he moved his hands to hold hers.

"Close your eyes," he instructed, mouth near her ear once more. She obeyed without hesitation. He had to wonder if she did so to escape the sweet tension rising between them. "Tell me what you feel."

"I feel…warm."

He knew that, and his body was responding, tightening.

"Focus on it," he whispered, voice low and heavy, betraying his arousal. "Where does it start?"

It grew worse when she answered, "Low. In my stomach."

He wanted to press his hand there, to tease her until

she drew her legs up and granted him access to her heat. Instead, his hands tightened on hers.

"Feed it," he said.

He could feel her magic surge, an electricity that crackled between them. It called to him, the perfect light to his darkness. It sought balance just as he did.

"Now, where are you warm?"

"Everywhere."

"Imagine all that warmth in your hands. Imagine it glowing. Imagine it so bright you can barely look at it."

It was how he saw her—a moon, a star, a sun, a sky at the center of his universe.

"Now imagine the light has dimmed, and in the shadow, you see the life you have created." His lips touched the shell of her ear as he stared at the energy she'd summoned and used to paint a glimmering likeness of the periwinkle and phlox she'd wanted to grow.

"Open your eyes, Persephone."

Her lashes fluttered as she followed his instruction, inhaling a breath, and as Hades directed her hands to touch the ground, her magic solidified and the flowers became real—living and breathing. He released her hands then but did not put distance between them, watching as she touched one of the petals, smoothing it between her thumb and forefinger.

"Magic is balance," he said. "A little control, a little passion. It is the way of the world."

She turned her head only an inch so that her cheek was against his and her body began to tense. His hands were flat against the ground, but he kept his knees up, cradling her. He wondered what she would do. Would she tear away from him? Put distance between them once more?

Instead, she turned and came up to her knees to face him. Her hands went to his shoulders and she stared at him with glassy eyes, but before she could speak, he plowed ahead, needing to speak.

"I love you. I should have reminded you when I brought you here and each day since. Please forgive me."

"I forgive you, but only if you'll forgive me. I was angry about Leuce but angrier that you left me that evening to go to her, and I feel so...ridiculous. I know your reasons and I know you didn't want to leave me that evening, but I can't help how I feel about it. When I think about it, I feel...*hurt*."

Her admission made his chest hurt and his throat feel tight.

"It pains me to know I hurt you. What can I do?"

"I...don't know. I suppose what I have done must make up for it. I told you I wouldn't write about Apollo—I promised you—and then broke that promise."

All Hades could do was shake his head. "We do not make up for hurt with hurt, Persephone. That is a god's game. We are lovers."

"Then how do we make up for hurt?" she asked.

"With time," he said. "If we can be comfortable being angry with each other for a little while."

Tears slid down her face, and she whispered, "I don't want to be angry with you."

"Nor I with you." He brushed her tears away. "But it doesn't change feelings, and it doesn't mean we can't care for each other while we heal."

She swallowed and shook her head. "How is it that I was meant for you?"

Hades frowned. "We've discussed this."

"I just feel so…inexperienced. I am young and rash. How could you want me?" She could not know how those words hurt him.

"Persephone." He took her hands in his and spoke softly. "First, I will always want you. Always. I failed you here too. I was angry. I didn't take care of you. I didn't include you. Don't put me on a pedestal because you feel guilty for your decisions. Just…forgive yourself so you can forgive me. Please."

Her breath shuddered out of her, and his eyes lowered to her lips. He wanted to kiss her, to take her body into his and find the comfort they both needed.

She must have guessed his thoughts, because she moved forward on her knees until she straddled him, her arms twining around his neck.

"I'm sorry. I love you. You can trust me, my word. I—"

"Shh, my darling," he soothed, his hands moving from her waist to her thighs. "I will forever regret my anger. How could I ever question your love? Your trust? Your word? When you have my heart."

As his hands moved beneath the hem of her dress, she kissed him and he welcomed her, thrusting his tongue into her mouth. He had tasted her this way before, but it felt different, far more desperate, far more euphoric. His fingers pressed into her ass as he ground her against his erection, and while he was hungry for release, he was eager to please her more.

His mouth left hers, his tongue trailing along her jaw and neck. "Where are you burning?" he asked.

"Everywhere," she answered, her breath catching in her throat.

Her hands slipped eagerly beneath his jacket, guiding it off. Impatient, Hades helped, unbuttoning his shirt and shoving it off. With his chest bare, her hands smoothed over his skin. He moved to reach for her, hoping to bring her close once more, but she caught his wrists. Hades's eyes met hers, brow raised in question.

"Let me pleasure you." Her words were almost a plea, and he had no energy to deny her. He let her guide him to his back as she hovered over him and kissed him, her body shifting along his hard cock as she made her way there, freeing his sex just to wrap her soft hands around him.

He took a deep breath, and the air that escaped his mouth sounded like a growl.

"Keep looking at me that way, darling. I won't let you have control for long."

She smirked and bent to taste his flesh, and he lost all sense of his surroundings. He'd hoped to maintain some measure of control but found himself twisting his fingers into her hair, urging her to take him deeper. She didn't seem to mind, rising to the challenge of his need.

"Fuck," he groaned as he hit the back of her throat, and she released him, breathing hard only to continue using her hands and mouth to pleasure him. He did not last long after that, coming hard into her mouth. After a few moments, she climbed his body and kissed him, and he rolled so that she was beneath him.

"Such a gift," he whispered, stroking her face. "How shall I repay you?"

"Gifts don't require payment, Hades."

"Another gift, then," he said and returned his mouth

to hers. She drew her legs up and her hands moved between them, guiding him into her heat.

"This is what I want," she said, her legs tightening around his waist.

"Who am I to deny a queen?" he said and lost himself in the feel of her, in the way her body moved with his as they lay in her meadow surrounded by their magic.

CHAPTER XIII
At the Island of Euboea

Hades was almost asleep. His mind focused only on the continuous circles he drew on Persephone's skin, whose weight made his body heavy. They had stopped speaking when their responses had grown languid and short, and now they rested in a content silence.

"I'll mentor Leuce."

Hades opened his eyes and peered at her. She stared back, almost sheepishly, probably unsure of what he would say. Hades had to admit, he didn't really know what to think. How long had she been considering this, and what exactly had brought it on?

"I'm not sure how I feel about this," he admitted.

"Me either," she said but did not elaborate. Instead, she added, "And I need you to give her a place to stay and her job back. Please."

Of course he would agree. Still, he wanted to know why she'd offered to help his former lover.

"Why do you wish to mentor her?"

It took her a moment to respond, and she averted her eyes as she searched for her answer, her chin resting on her hands.

Finally, she said, "Because I think I know how she feels."

His mood darkened a little. "Explain."

She shrugged and the movement caused a lock of her hair to fall over her shoulder. "She's been a tree for thousands of years. Suddenly, she's normal again and the whole world has changed. It's...scary...and I know how that feels."

He could see how she might believe they had something in common. Persephone's mother had kept her hidden away from the world until she was eighteen, only letting her explore beyond the borders of her glass greenhouse on a short leash. She was just now learning what she wanted to believe and who she wanted to be as a woman and a goddess.

Still, while they might have this in common, Hades could not imagine two more different people than Persephone and Leuce.

"You want to mentor my former lover?"

She groaned. "Don't make me regret this, Hades."

"I don't want you to, but are you sure?"

Hades liked the way her lips pouted as she frowned. Still, she didn't look at him as she spoke. "It's weird, I admit, but...she's a victim. I want to help her."

He might have winced at her words, but he knew she was right, and even when Leuce had returned, he had failed to help her the way she deserved.

Yet Persephone was willing.

Hades drew her gaze back to his. "You amaze me."

She smiled and shook her head. "I am not amazing. I wanted to punish her at first."

"But you didn't," he said, letting his hand fall to her jaw. "There are no other gods like you."

"I haven't lived long enough to be jaded like the rest of you," she said and laughed. "Perhaps I'll end up like the others before long."

"Or perhaps you will change the rest of us," Hades replied.

They were still for a few seconds, then Persephone sat up, her hands planted on his chest, which made her breasts bounce. She rocked back so that her soft, wet center slid over his full, hard cock. Hades gritted his teeth, suppressing the urge to groan, to grip her hips and help her move.

"Eager for more, my lady?" he asked.

When she smiled, he smiled too.

"Actually, I'm afraid I must make a few demands," she said, lifting herself and guiding him into her body with a pleasurable sigh.

Hades could no longer stand not touching her. His hands dug into her thighs. He'd give her anything if she just kept moving.

"Yes?" he hissed.

"I don't want to be placed in a suite on the other side of the palace, ever."

Never, Hades thought as she slammed down on him.

"Not to get ready for balls. Not when you are angry with me. Not ever."

He closed his eyes for a few seconds, gathering thoughts that were so scattered, he could barely string a sentence together.

"I thought you would want privacy," he managed to grit out.

She paused, and Hades opened his eyes to find her bent over, lips hovering just over his. He took the opportunity to lift his knees, settling into her just a little more.

"Fuck privacy. I needed you, needed to know you still wanted me despite...everything."

He drew her to him, and as their lips met, he rolled, pinning her beneath him. He resettled himself inside her but did not move, laughing when Persephone wiggled in an attempt to make him.

She glared, but her expression softened as he spoke.

"I will always want you, and I would have welcomed you to my bed any night."

"I didn't know," she whispered.

He touched her lips, parting them beneath his touch. "Now you do."

Their mouths collided and Hades's hips surged forward. Persephone's moans encouraged him, drove him deep, and she clung to him like he clung to her until they drove each other to the edge and over.

Hades woke sometime in the evening. A day had passed since Apollo had come to collect retribution for his slight, a day since he and Persephone had made up on the floor of her silvery meadow, and the thought that pressed heavily on his mind as she slept soundlessly beside him was losing her.

He had never had much to lose, but she was everything, and since they had found each other, it felt like every god had tried—or would try—their hand at tearing them apart, and Hades would be damned if anyone succeeded.

He rose and dressed, taking a few straight shots of whiskey. While the drink didn't do much to intoxicate him, it did take the edge off his nerves.

Before he left the Underworld, he watched Persephone sleep, eyes following the outline of her body beneath the sheets, the way her chest rose and fell with her breaths. He placed his hand on her head and bent to kiss her forehead, then vanished, appearing on the island of Euboea.

It was an island off the coast of Attica. Once, long ago, it had been attached to the mainland, but earthquakes had separated the landmass and now it stood apart in the Mediterranean Sea. The island itself was not Hades's ultimate destination. It was one of three volcanic islands off its coast. They were each relatively small, made of layers of volcanic rock, visible from all sides of the island. Despite its rocky foundation, a sheet of green grass made the island look emerald next to the sapphire ocean, and in the fading twilight, it was beautiful.

The islands were connected by a wood rope bridge, both to the mainland and to each other. Hades started toward the one at the center, Lea, named after Briareus's wife, Cymopolea, Poseidon's daughter and Hades's niece.

The thought made each step heavier, yet he kept going, and when he made it to the island, he followed a path of round stones to a small cottage, nestled between two hills. The windows were full of warm and inviting light, and a plume of white smoke rose from a chimney atop its thatched roof.

Hades hesitated a step, his insides twisting mercilessly.

It had been a long time since he had reaped a soul, an innocent one at least. Doing so never got easier, and this one was somehow made worse by the fact that Briareus was merely a victim of a war between gods.

Still, he continued to the door and knocked.

He would give Briareus dignity, especially in his own home.

Hades was surprised when Briareus answered the door cloaked in glamour. He had taken on the guise of a middle-aged man with graying hair, face worn into happy lines, a mark of how content he had lived his life since ancient times. Still, Hades could see beneath his glamour, to the giant who towered above him, to his many heads and hands.

"My Lord Hades," Briareus said. His smile was so wide, deepening the lines around his mouth and making his cheekbones stick out sharply. The giant bowed.

"Briareus," Hades replied quietly with a nod. He could not raise his voice to match his enthusiasm, given his morose reasons for his visit.

There was a moment of silence, then Briareus's jovial expression faded. "It's time, isn't it?"

Those were cruel words given how Hades had come to be at this door. Still, he lied.

"It is."

The giant nodded and looked at his feet. Hades hated it, to see the peace leak from his eyes as he processed his impending death. "I could feel it, you know? In my bones."

Hades said nothing, but there was a part of him that wished Briareus would cease speaking, because each word was another knife to his heart.

After a moment, Briareus collected himself and took

a breath, an ounce of his previously joyful demeanor returning.

"I was just finishing up a meal," he said. "Care to join?"

Hades had no expectations when he had come to the giant's door. He had not known if Briareus would be distraught or angry, beg for his life or beg for it to end quickly.

But he had not at all expected to be invited to dinner.

"Sure, Briareus," Hades said at last. There was something morbid about accepting his hospitality, but Hades did not want to take away these last wished-for moments.

The giant smiled once more and stepped aside to hold the door open, allowing Hades entrance.

As soon as he entered the cottage, he was in the kitchen. It smelled of salt and fish and spices, though not unpleasant. There was a round, wooden table at the center of the room, and on it sat a small, clear vase with a handful of wildflowers.

Briareus returned to the stove and pulled on a white apron. As he tied it off, he offered, "Anything to drink, my lord?"

"Whatever you have, Briareus. It would be an honor to drink with you."

The giant chuckled. "You honor me, my lord."

"Hardly," Hades replied. "I am here to take your life."

"*You* are," Briareus agreed. "Not Lord Thanatos, nor another with ill intent. I am pleased."

Hades stared as the giant turned to his work, pouring Hades a glass of wine.

"It's sherry," he said. "I'll serve you something different with the lamb."

"Thank you, Briareus."

Hades accepted the glass and walked to the window. The view from his cottage was beautiful, mostly green hills, but the city of Euboea peeked through, still warmed by the golden light of the fading sun.

"You have lived here a long time," he said.

"Yes. I have not been beyond the bridge in some time. I imagine I would not even know the world now."

"It is very different," Hades said.

"I suppose in some ways it is fitting you are here," Briareus said. "I cannot imagine continuing to exist as the gods do, indefinitely."

There was a long pause, and when Hades looked at Briareus, he found the giant staring back.

"Are you not tired, my lord?"

"I am," Hades replied.

But he had been tired since the beginning. He just chose what to live for each day, and recently that happened to be Persephone.

The giant served a meal of lamb and roasted carrots. He held to his promise of serving fresh wine, choosing a red blend for dinner, and while Briareus had served Hades a healthy portion of food, it remained untouched.

"Are my brothers next?" Briareus asked.

"No."

"So I am the first."

Hades said nothing, guilt weighing heavily on him. He wished he had something to say, something to contribute to this conversation, but he rarely had anything to say and even less when he faced a person he liked and had to kill.

After a moment, Hades cleared his throat. "Your wife," he said, but before he could continue, Briareus spoke.

"Cymopolea spends most of her time in the ocean with her sisters. She visits now and then." He hesitated. "It's likely...she will find me."

"I won't let that happen," Hades promised.

"There is no one else," the giant replied.

Once more, Hades said nothing, but he did take a drink of the wine and tried not to grimace at the taste. They did not speak until Briareus finished eating. Hades wished he could be better company, but there was a thickness growing in his throat and a pressure building behind his eyes.

He did not want to do this.

Briareus sat back, his hands on his thighs, and spoke. "I'm not upset, you know? I understand."

You don't, Hades thought, and his jaw tightened. He wanted to explain that he had tried to think of ways out of this, that he had delayed it for as long as possible.

There were a few more beats of silence.

"How shall we proceed?" Briareus asked. "Do you want a knife?"

Hades should have winced, but he remained expressionless as he answered. "No."

He held out his hand, and Briareus took it. After a moment, shadows began to move beneath the creature's skin, breaking the surface like vines to wrap around Hades's own arm. It was the tendrils of the giant's soul coming out of his body.

He met Hades's gaze. "You're a good man, Hades," he said. "A great god."

The shadows disappeared into Hades's skin. If he were to drop his glamour, the giant would see a myriad of fine, black lines marring his body—a tale of the many bargains he'd made with the Fates, among them Briareus himself.

Briareus sat back in his chair and took a breath.

He was dead.

Hades remained for a few moments before he stood, turned, and punched straight through the wall. With his aggression spent, he drained what remained of the wine and left the cottage, only to come face-to-face with Hera.

The goddess looked triumphant, a smile curving her cold face.

"Well done, Hades," she said. "Your next trial will not have the luxury of time."

Hades's anger felt like a storm inside his body.

"Then stop wasting mine," he said.

Her smile widened. "Await my summons, Lord Hades, and don't forget what's at stake."

PART II

"Do the gods put this ardor in our hearts or does each man's desire become his god?"
—Virgil, *The Aeneid*

CHAPTER XIV
An Uncertain Future

In the immediate aftermath of Briareus's death, a dull ache formed at the front of Hades's head. It was only a matter of time before it turned into something far worse. He had known he would not be able to sleep, but all possibilities of rest were now out of the question.

So he headed to Iniquity.

He had only managed to take care of one task, though now that the first of Hera's labors was complete, a second would soon come. In the meantime, he had to figure out who had kidnapped the Graeae. There was the possibility that Dionysus was lying and he was still in possession of the gray sisters, but Hades doubted it. The God of the Vine had been too stunned, too affronted.

Hades wondered if the abductors of the gray sisters wanted the eye or just Medusa? What hope did they have in using her as a weapon? Who were their targets? There was a horrible dread that came with the unknown, and he hated it.

Once in his office, he found himself pulling the small black box from the inside of his jacket pocket and setting it on the desk in front of him. He stared at it for a long moment, wavering on whether he should use it. When he opened the box, he felt even less confident.

The eye stared back at him as if it knew his intentions.

He did not know exactly how the eye worked. Did it work like a crystal ball? Could he ask it to show him something? Was it sentient?

Hades turned the box on its side and let the eye roll out onto the desk. It was sticky, but it landed pupil up and seemed to glare back at him.

Definitely sentient, he thought. Fuck.

"I'm looking for your...owners," Hades said. "Can you show me where they are?"

He felt really stupid all of a sudden.

Idiot, he imagined Hecate saying.

He picked up the eye and was deposited onto a crowded street in the pleasure district. There was loud music and wicked laughter as people danced around him in a parade of colorful costumes. He recognized his surroundings, particularly the columns that decorated this square. They were gold, and even from here, he could make out the carnal scenes carved into their surface.

Dionysus was here.

Hades could not yet see him for the crowd, but he could feel his magic rising. It was slightly floral but acidic at the same time and possessed a heaviness unlike anything he had ever felt. To others, he imagined it must feel pleasant, but to Hades, it was cloying. Following the spike in power, those who had been dancing around him began to fuck.

The air was thick with carnality, and those present bent to the weight of it, tangled in passionate revelry, and as they fell, Hades saw Dionysus, sitting in his gold throne before those gold pillars. But it was not the sight of him that made his body go cold and fill with an unnerving heaviness. It was the sight of Persephone perched comfortably on his lap, dressed in matching white, the glamour she seemed so keen to hold on to around him gone.

Sitting there with her elegant white horns on display, her eyes as bright as the spring sky, she looked confident and queenly, and he raged at the heat in her gaze—a passion that should be reserved only for him.

What the actual fuck.

The vision flashed and faded away, and Hades was once again in his office at Iniquity, the eye of the Graeae clutched in his palm. He uncurled his clenched fingers, and the eye fell onto the table, bloodshot.

"What the fuck did you show me?" he demanded.

The eye sat silent, of course, but still seemed to be glaring.

"If there is an ounce of truth to that vision, I will crush you to a pulp," he threatened.

He had almost done so in the midst of the vision. He could still feel the stickiness of the eye on his palm.

He rolled the eye into its box.

"Useless," he muttered as he sat back in his chair. Obviously the eye would not help him locate the Graeae. And if it would not help him, it was likely it would not cooperate with Hecate either if the goddess attempted a location spell. With the eye's power, it was possible it would manipulate the spell anyway and send them on a useless hunt.

The fact was, the eye did not trust them.

Normally, he would make himself the target by feeding information into the market that he was in possession of the eye, to lure whoever had kidnapped the Graeae, but he had no doubt some bold idiot would attempt to hold Persephone for ransom as a result, and he wasn't willing to take the risk.

He had one other option, and the thought quite literally made him want to vomit. Not to mention he would probably be less helpful than the eye, and he required far too much coddling for a Titan.

Hades let out an aggravated growl and slumped farther into his chair.

"Fucking Helios."

Approaching the God of the Sun would take some planning, however, given that their last encounter had ended poorly. Hades had stolen every single one of his prized cows and refused to return them, though at least now he had a bargaining chip.

While Hades did not think it was likely that Helios would refuse the return of a cow, he couldn't be certain. The god was difficult, more of an asshole than Apollo. Hades would have to think of something else to hold over his head.

His thoughts were interrupted, though, by a call from Ilias.

"Yes?" Hades answered, dread already twisting through his body.

"I've got news for you, though you will not be happy."

"Am I ever happy to hear your news?"

"Do you want me to answer that question?"

"The answer is no," Hades replied. "If you want it to change, perhaps you should bring me better news."

"Then offer me a different job."

"And what would I offer? Flower picking for Hecate?"

"That is perhaps more dangerous than your workload," Ilias replied.

Hades managed a smirk.

"We've been tracking Dionysus's movements as you instructed. He has a few connections in the black market, but he is not trying to build a list of contacts like we thought. He *is* a contact."

"Any word on the kind of jobs he's running?"

Hades guessed he was sending his maenads on assassination missions, but assassins were also good spies.

"He seems to be interested in obtaining information on any and everyone," Ilias replied.

Not surprising. There was no greater power than knowledge.

"Has he tried locating the Graeae or Medusa?"

He wondered if the god might try to circumvent using the Graeae, since it seemed that the gorgon was his target.

"He has sent the maenads to investigate various channels in the market but has had no luck yet, though it seems many knew he was in possession of the sisters. The bounty's increased on Medusa's head. She's caused quite a stir among hunters. They're ravenous to find her."

It was concerning to Hades that no one in the market had yet to snitch. Usually, it didn't take much. People in the underground were there because they liked to make deals that benefited them. There were no loyalties, only a good bargain.

Which made Hades think that perhaps the Graeae had moved beyond the market.

"I did ask Euryale as you instructed. She does not know Medusa."

Strange, Hades thought. He'd expected otherwise, given that they were both gorgons. Perhaps Medusa had not always been a gorgon. Perhaps she had come under some divine curse.

"See what my brother is up to," Hades instructed.

"Which one?"

"The wet one."

Poseidon was always scheming, and he was likely working with Hera on her plan to overthrow Zeus. It would not surprise Hades if the god was trying to gather his own advantages and allies.

"Very well," Ilias said. "Are you ready for the unhappy news?"

"That wasn't unhappy enough?"

"We've detained a man," Ilias said. "We expected you would want to...interrogate him."

"And why would I want to do that, Ilias?" Hades spoke carefully, but his irritation had spiked.

"He threw a glass bottle at Persephone."

Hades waited, and when the satyr didn't continue, he demanded, "Did he hit her, Ilias?"

"No, of course not," Ilias replied. "I would have told you far sooner."

The rush of fury that had erupted inside Hades quieted, replaced mostly by horror. He wondered what had spurred the attack. Had it been Persephone's article about Apollo or her relationship with him? Perhaps both. Nevertheless, he'd see that the man paid for his actions.

"Where is he being held?"

"Your office," Ilias said.

Hades needed no more information, and he teleported to Nevernight, to his office, where he found a man bound and gagged.

He was unremarkable—a pale man with a mop of dirty brown hair and dull eyes that widened at the sight of Hades. To his credit, he did not beg, though he did begin to shake, and a wet spot soaked through his khaki trousers.

"I heard you threatened the love of my life," Hades said, shedding his jacket. He folded it and draped it over the back of the couch. Then he began to unlink his cuffs. "I'm here to discover why. Though, you should know, there is no excuse—no reason you can give that will end your suffering."

As Hades rolled up his sleeves, the man began to beg, a muffled cry that Hades could decipher as "Please."

Hades continued fixing his sleeve, and when he was finished, he removed the bind from the man's mouth.

"Please, please," he repeated in a shaky voice.

"Please what?" Hades asked.

"Don't." The word was a whisper, a plea, laced with fear.

Hades bent, eye level with the man as he spoke. "Don't worry," he said. "This is not how you die."

And as he shoved the gag back into the man's mouth, he drew on his magic, and shards of black glass shot from the floor and speared the mortal's feet, anchoring him in place. Blood pooled on the floor, and the mortal's pained screams brought about a different kind of release, a means through which Hades could channel his anger and grief.

With the torture started, he retrieved a bottle of whiskey and an empty glass and dragged a chair from the bar, positioning it before his victim. He sat opposite the man and poured himself a drink, downed it, and poured another before removing the gag from the mortal's mouth once more.

He moaned, leaning forward in his chair.

"It may do no good, but I will hear you speak," Hades said. "Tell me why you threatened my lover."

The man took a few heavy breaths. "It was stupid. I'm *sorry*."

"It *was* stupid," Hades agreed. "Unfortunate that you did not realize it sooner."

He drained his glass once more and slammed it on the edge of his chair, gripping a large sliver and jamming it into the man's thigh. He arched, but the movement only placed more strain on his impaled feet, which caused more pain.

"I am certain you are full of regret."

The man's chest heaved, and his head lolled about, an unnatural wheeze escaping his mouth.

The torture continued like that. Hades would take a drink, ask a question, and jab another sharp piece of glass into the man's body. When he ran out of larger pieces, he summoned his own.

"I don't...I don't even like Apollo," the man said in a breathy moan.

"So you are a sheep," Hades said. "A follower who thought to rise to the rank of leader with your actions."

The man groaned, though Hades did not know if he meant to agree or not.

"Let this be a lesson to think for yourself."

Hades rose and used his magic to dislodge every shard of glass in the man's body. It was a torture of its own, and as the pieces rose, they disintegrated. In the next second, he sent a surge of magic toward the man, and his wounds were healed.

"Th-thank you," he said.

"Oh, it is not for your benefit," Hades replied. "It is for mine. Perhaps I wish to begin anew."

The man began to sob. The sound grated against Hades's ears, and to stop it, he shoved the gag back into the man's mouth. Then he sat back in his chair and finished off what remained of his whiskey.

Some time had passed when Hades rose, and the movement caused the mortal to flinch, but Hades had no intention of continuing the torture. He did, however, intend to threaten his entire afterlife if he spoke one word against Persephone or himself. After he was certain the man understood, he would have Ilias take him home.

Hades fixed his sleeves, secured his cuff links, and pulled on his jacket, but as he adjusted the collar and straightened the lapels, he felt the distinct roar of Persephone's untamable power. He felt dread and tasted her distress. It was both cloying and bitter, a conflict of her magic.

He started for the doors when they burst open.

"*Persephone.*"

There was something devastating in the way she looked at him, an emotion within her eyes that communicated something unspeakable, but Hades knew this pain. His soul recognized it and called to it, familiar with the ache it would inspire within his chest.

"Hades! You have to help! *Please*—"

Her words dissolved into a choked cry, and all Hades could do was take her into his arms and hold her against him as she shook. He felt helpless, and he hated it because he only ever felt helpless with her. As quick as it had begun, she composed herself and lifted her head from his chest.

"Hades—" she started, and it was then he realized she had noticed his prisoner, though it was hard not to because he had begun to scream, albeit muffled.

"Ignore him," he said, preparing to teleport the man to a holding cell when Persephone's hand clamped down on his own.

"Is that—is that the mortal who threw the bottle at me today?"

When he didn't respond, she turned her gaze on the man. Whatever she saw was answer enough. He was prepared to hear her demand to release him, but instead, she asked, "Why are you torturing him in your office and not in Tartarus?"

The mortal must have expected more of a compassionate response, because his cries grew louder.

"Because he's not dead," Hades said. He could only take souls to Tartarus if their thread had been cut. He gave the man a withering look as he added, "Yet."

"Hades, you cannot kill him."

"I won't kill him." It wasn't his time to die, and he wasn't willing to sacrifice another soul for this man. Besides, it was far more gratifying to have him live so that he could tell the tale of his torture at the hands of the God of the Dead. "But I will make him wish he were dead."

"Hades. Let. Him. Go."

And there it was. He had expected it sooner, but perhaps he should consider it a victory that she waited this long.

"Fine," he said and sent the man to the holding rooms a level below, and blessedly, she did not demand to know where he'd gone. He led her to the couch with a hand on the small of her back, guiding her to sit on his lap. "What happened?"

She started to breathe heavier, and as he tilted her head back, her mouth quivered so badly, she couldn't speak. Hades manifested a glass of wine and held it to her lips as she drank. When she was finished, he nodded.

"Start again," Hades said. "What happened?"

"Lexa was hit by a car," she said, and it was as if her breath had been knocked from her lungs.

Her words shocked him because he had not expected them. Despite many humans believing otherwise, Hades did not have a hand in orchestrating life-threatening injuries. Those were designed by the Fates, and while all were tragic, they often served a greater purpose, if not for the victim, for those in their lives.

"She's in critical condition at Asclepius Community Hospital. She's on a ventilator. She's...*broken*."

She spoke through tears and stumbled across words laced with pain and disbelief, and while he despaired over Lexa, he hated to see Persephone suffer. Though there was a dark part of him that rose, clawing at the fringes of his mind, bringing on a familiar dread that caused him to fear the direction this conversation might go.

"She doesn't look like Lexa anymore, Hades."

She wept harder, and she covered her mouth to contain her cries.

"I'm so sorry, my darling."

They were the only words he had for her, because there was nothing he could do. Even now, he could feel along Lexa's thread, which was not cut but rather bent—she was in a state of limbo.

In other words, her soul was undecided.

Persephone twisted to face him as much as she could.

"Hades, please."

She didn't need to explain; he knew what she asked. Her eyes were desperate, and because he could not see her like that, he averted his gaze, frustration making his jaw tight.

"Persephone, I can't."

He had had this conversation so many times, with mortals he had no personal connection with and gods he held in contempt. He had never faced it with a lover. Even if Hades could save Lexa, the consequences of such actions were dire, especially when the decision to live or die rested with the soul.

She scrambled off his lap, standing a few steps away. He did not try to reach for her.

"I won't lose her."

"You haven't. Lexa still lives." She was so afraid, it was like she already considered her dead. "You must give her soul time to decide."

"Decide? What do you mean?"

He sighed, unable to contain the dread he felt at this oncoming conversation.

He answered as he pinched the bridge of his nose, an ache forming at the front of his head for the second time today. "Lexa's in limbo."

"Then you can bring her back," she reasoned.

That was not how limbo worked.

"I *can't*."

"You did it before. You said when a soul is in limbo, you can bargain with the Fates to bring it back."

"In exchange for the life of another. A soul for a soul, Persephone."

"You can't say you won't save her, Hades."

He was saying that, as hard as it was to admit. This was a situation of choice on Lexa's behalf. To interfere, to bring her back when she was not ready, or worse, did not want to come, would mean a harrowing return to the world of the living. The consequences were endless.

"I'm not saying I don't want to, Persephone. It is best that I do not interfere with this. Trust me. If you care for Lexa at all—if you care for me at all—you will drop this."

"I'm doing this *because* I care!"

"That's what all mortals think—but who are you really trying to save? Lexa or yourself?"

She wanted to escape the loss and the grief. She didn't want to think of a life without Lexa, and while he could not blame her, it was never for the living to decide, though they tried often.

"I don't need a philosophy lesson, Hades," she sneered.

"No, but apparently you need a reality check."

He rose to his feet and removed his jacket, and when his fingers moved to the buttons of his shirt, Persephone snapped.

"I'm not having sex with you right now."

He scowled, frustration making his body feel tight and warm. He shrugged off his shirt and stood bare-chested before her, dropping the glamour he used to hide the black threads marring his body. The newest was a thick band that wrapped around his arm and went across his back. It was Briareus's, and it had burned a track into his skin as he'd taken the giant's soul. They were all painful when they were made, but some hurt worse than others, and this one still throbbed.

"What are they?"

She reached to touch him, but the thought of her tracing such a dark part of his life was alarming, so he captured her hand, halting her movement. Her eyes snapped to his.

"It's the price I pay for every life I've taken by bargaining with the Fates. I carry them with me. These are their life threads, burned into my skin. Is this what you want on your conscience, Persephone?"

She wrested her hand from his hold, cradling it against her chest, though her eyes still trailed the fine lines on his skin.

"What good is being the God of the Dead if you can't do anything?" She sounded very much defeated as she looked away and took a shuddering breath. "I'm sorry. I didn't mean that."

He gave a humorless laugh. "You meant it," he said, one hand pressing against her cheek so she would look at him once more. "I know you don't want to understand why I can't help, and that's okay."

"I just…don't know what to do," she whispered.

"Lexa isn't gone, yet you mourn her. She may recover."

"Do you know that for certain? That she will recover?"

"No."

He saw no reason to lie. The truth was, even Lexa did not know yet. He wished he could offer more comfort. He knew she wanted it, but in the face of death, there were no words that would ease her pain.

Finally, she rested her head against his chest, and her body felt heavy against his, as if she were finally giving over this burden—at least for now. He took her into his arms and teleported to the Underworld, to his chamber, where he laid her to rest on his bed.

"Do not fill your thoughts with the possibilities of tomorrow," he said and kissed her forehead, letting his magic send her into a deep, unbothered sleep, hoping she would actually rest, so he could slip away to the palace of the Fates.

He appeared in a flurry of shadows and smoke that peeled away and led him to the Library of Souls where he found the Fates at work. It appeared that Clotho was spinning gold threads, and they glimmered in the air, crisscrossing the breadth of the space. While she worked, Lachesis stood at the center, holding open a large book into which the thread was burrowing, while Atropos waited with her scissors.

Just as she began to cut, Lachesis spoke, "No, no, no, you mustn't end it there!"

"You are the allotter of life. I am the manner of death," Atropos said. "I will end this life where I want!"

"You are far too humane," Lachesis said. "This man has lived an inhospitable life. He should die the same."

"Trauma is hardly pleasant."

"It is merciful. Much better to die by disease."

"Why let him die at all?" Hades asked. "Perhaps the greater torture is continuing to live an unfavorable life?"

The three snapped their heads in his direction, though with Lachesis distracted, Atropos cut the thread. As she snipped, the end turned black and curled, disappearing into the book. Lachesis slammed the book closed and launched it at her sister. The Fate caught it and tossed it back, but before it could hit, Hades wrenched it from the air, and as it landed in his palm, the three glared.

"What do you want, Rich One?" Lachesis snapped.

"Why have you—?"

"Lexa Sideris," Hades said, cutting Atropos off. "Is she the soul you chose to complete the bargain?"

The Fates had said that Briareus's life would cost him dearly. Lexa's death would have consequences that echoed far beyond Persephone's relationship with the mortal. After tonight, it was clear it would also impact Persephone's relationship with him.

"A mortal in exchange for an immortal?" asked Atropos.

"That is hardly fair, Lord of the Dead," said Clotho.

"Completely unreasonable," agreed Lachesis.

"No, dear king, the end of Briareus's life must give life to another immortal. That is the bargain we've struck."

There was a part of him that felt relief at hearing he was not responsible for Lexa's accident and subsequent limbo, but a new anxiety filled him at the prospect of an immortal life being born or taken as a result of Briareus's death, though he always knew it was a possibility.

As much as he wanted to ask them who—which immortal they had chosen—he knew the question was futile.

"Do not fret, Good Counselor," said Clotho.
"Your bargain with Briareus," said Lachesis.
"Will only ruin your life," said Atropos.

CHAPTER XV
Fight Night

Hades returned to his chamber, where Persephone slept, and climbed into bed, though he did not sleep, his mind too active from the day's events. He could not begin to understand what Persephone was going through. Even having experienced varying degrees of loss, there was no comparing grief.

Hearts did not break the same.

They did not heal the same.

They would not beat the same.

She stirred beside him, eyes peeling open with some difficulty before whispering, "Have you slept?"

"Not quite yet," he said.

She did not respond, but she seemed more awake as she stared at him.

"Will you"—she paused, hesitating—"show me the threads again?"

He did not want to, not really, but it was a part of him he had shared, and it was not so surprising that she had more questions.

He dropped his glamour, and she lifted herself onto her elbow and reached a hand out, flattening her palm against his stomach. Her touch was gentle, her hand cold, but it still managed to make him feel warm and make the threads crisscrossing his skin burn.

"Why do you hide them?" she asked, her voice remained quiet.

"Very few warrant pride," he replied.

"If you are so ashamed, why make so many bargains?"

"Because I am self-serving. There was a time when I cared nothing about the consequences of trading souls."

Persephone's hand curled on his stomach. "They cannot all be bad."

He wasn't sure if she said it because she was hopeful he might find a way to save Lexa if worse came to worse or because she wished to see the best in him in this moment.

"There are only those I regret more," he said. "And those souls belong to children."

He called up his glamour, and they spoke no more.

———

An hour later, Persephone was sound asleep once more. Hades lay awake staring at the ceiling, recalling the vision the eye had shown him. He could still remember it in vivid detail—the crowded square, the guttural sounds of sex, the acidic smell of Dionysus's magic, and the god himself seated with his lover. Perhaps the worst part was how comfortable she appeared to be as a goddess and a queen. Had the eye been trying to tell him something? Or was it merely fucking with him because it did not trust him?

He turned his head, and as he traced Persephone's features in the semidarkness, he wondered if she were better off without him.

A pulse of magic drew his attention as Hermes appeared at the end of his bed. He raised a brow.

"You could knock," he said.

"Courtesy is for mortals," said Hermes.

"And gods who want to keep their teeth."

Hermes was not amused, but their banter was overshadowed by how quickly his expression changed to something far too serious for the God of Mischief.

"You've been summoned, Hades," he said.

He did not need to ask who had summoned him. He could guess well enough.

Hera.

"Where?" he asked.

"I cannot tell you that," Hermes said. "I can only take you there."

Hades narrowed his eyes as Hermes began to draw a line in the air, summoning a portal.

"No teleportation?" he asked.

"Hera does not allow teleportation into her...*realm*... without consent, much like you," Hermes replied just as the portal he had summoned yawned open. It was big enough for Hermes to step through without hassle, but Hades would have to bend.

He sighed, a gnawing anxiety growing in his chest. He leaned over and kissed Persephone softly before rising, summoning his clothes, and stepping through the portal.

He found himself in a room—an office. He recognized where he was only because the wall of windows opposite him overlooked a familiar part of New Athens.

This was the Diadem Hotel, and it was owned by Hera. The goddess herself stood in front of a black-and-gold desk that looked more like an art piece than practical furniture. A set of gold peacock statues flanked it while a three-piece canvas hung behind it, depicting a prowling black panther with emerald eyes.

"Hades," Hera greeted with a nod. Her brown hair was pulled back into a tight bun, and she wore a white jumpsuit and tailored jacket. The goddess usually chose gold accessories, and today was no different—a large gold chain hung around her neck, paired with a stack of gold bracelets on her left wrist.

Hades always felt that the goddess's choice to wear white was symbolic. She was communicating her innocence, in contrast to her husband, who was far from chaste or loyal to her in any regard.

"Hera," Hades replied.

"I hope I was not interrupting," she said.

Hades looked around the room. No one was present aside from Hermes.

"Perhaps we should drop false pretenses, Hera," Hades said. "There is no one present to witness your false courtesy."

The goddess smiled. "Your next labor begins in an hour," she said. "Hermes, why don't you prepare our... *guest?*"

Hades's gaze cut to the god, who was far too nervous not to be guilty of *something*. Hermes bowed his head. "Of course," he said, finally meeting Hades's eyes. "This way, Hades."

Hades had never felt this kind of tension with Hermes. It was the kind that developed when someone wasn't being truthful, and it was rapidly morphing into anger. He knew the God of Mischief felt it too, because he moved stiffly before Hades as he called for the elevator in Hera's office.

Its doors were gold and opened into a needlessly extravagant lift. The floor was carpeted, thick and plush. The walls were mirrored and framed in gold. There was even a chandelier overhead; the crystals dripping from it touched Hades's head. He turned once inside, never taking his eyes from Hera as the doors closed, sealing him inside with the God of Trickery.

Now that they were alone, Hades spoke. "Care to tell me what is going on?" he asked.

"I..." Hermes said and cleared his throat. "I can't."

"Hmm...so much for being *best friends*."

Hermes's eyes and mouth opened, and Hades did not know if it was from the shock of him using those words or the thought of actually losing his friendship, but after a moment, his gaze narrowed, and his lips pressed thin. Hermes seemed more on edge, and with good reason, because in the next second, Hades had him pressed against the wall by his neck.

The god's hand clamped down on Hades's arm and he laughed nervously. "This was far less scary in my dreams."

"For what am I being made ready?" Hades asked through clenched teeth.

"Fight night," Hermes said. "You're going into the ring, Hades."

Hades released him, and the god fell to the floor. As he rose to his feet again, Hermes pressed his fingers to his neck.

"Definitely thought I'd enjoy choking far more," Hermes said. "Thanks for ruining a fantasy."

Hades ignored the god. He was not so surprised that Hera hosted such an event. It was likely she used it to choose heroes and favored mortals.

"Who am I fighting?" Hades asked.

"I don't know," Hermes replied.

Hades looked at him, and the god flinched away.

"You're being a little dramatic, don't you think?" Hades asked.

Hermes straightened and glared. "You just pinned me against a wall and not in a good way!"

Hades stared, waiting for an answer to his question.

"The competitors are different every week," Hermes said. "That's the point. The chosen—that's you, in case you didn't know—goes in blind. It's a test of your ability to improvise and adapt."

Which probably meant no magic.

They did not speak as the elevator came to a halt, and when the doors opened, it was into a busy concrete tunnel filled with a muted, blue-tinged light. Hades recognized this as one of the underground tunnels below the streets of New Athens. It seemed many used this particular one to reach Hera's fight night.

The two gods joined the fray. Many continued forward, down a set of stairs to a large open bar, backlit with blue. An oval sunken floor created stadium-style seating where people gathered.

Hermes and Hades did not descend into the throng, however. They took a right, marching down a hall that was just as crowded with people, some bent over the edge of a metal rail overlooking the bar, while others leaned against the opposite wall, preferring the peace and anonymity the darkness offered.

That was where Hades wanted to be, swallowed by shadow. Instead, he walked unglamoured among both mortals and immortals. He could feel their apprehension as much as he could see it—averted eyes and a body that bent away from his presence.

As if either would keep away death.

He could not help thinking of Persephone at this moment. The woman who pressed close to him, who sought his warmth and even his darkness. The woman who traced the threads on his skin with curiosity, not disgust. She was why he was here, he reminded himself. At the end of the day, this was about her—it was about them. It was to save a future that had barely begun and was already under threat by the Goddess of Marriage.

Hades's fists curled.

If Hera wanted a fight, he'd give her one. He'd make it unforgettable.

The hallway curved and grew wider, branching off. One part twisted on while the other was a straight, short path to a set of black doors carved with images Hades recognized—the Nemean lion, the Erymanthian boar, the Cretan bull. They were animals that had been defeated during Heracles's labors, and now they decorated the doors in Hera's underground fighting ring in gold relief.

How fitting.

Hermes pushed open the doors to reveal a surprisingly simple room. The floor was concrete, and to the left was a narrow pool. A row of lions' heads were affixed to the wall, and from their mouths poured a stream of steaming water. The wall directly in front of him was an altar dedicated to the Goddess of Women. A gold statue made in her likeness was adorned with offerings, likely prayers made by other—what had Hermes called him?—*chosen*.

Hades would not be leaving an offering.

There was nothing else to the room other than a privacy screen, and Hades turned to look at Hermes.

"Well?" he asked. "What now?"

"You must bathe," he said.

"Why?" Hades asked tightly.

"Because...the gold won't stick."

"The gold?" Hades repeated.

Hermes sighed. "Look, this isn't ideal, but have I ever led you astray?"

"Yes, Hermes, you have, in fact, led me astray. *This* is a prime example," Hades said, gesturing to the room.

"With fashion," Hermes countered.

Hades glared. He did not want to do this.

Hermes crossed the room to a stack of folded towels and threw one at him.

"Get wet, Daddy Death," Hermes said.

———

Less than fifteen minutes later, Hades stood dressed in a skirt made of leather strips that hung midthigh and nothing more. Normally he would not mind this, but it was the fact that it was for Hera's pleasure. Not to mention that Hermes had taken entirely too long dusting gold on his skin with the smallest fan brush Hades had ever seen.

"What are you doing?" Hades asked, itching to cross his arms over his chest.

"Highlighting," Hermes replied.

"Why?" Hades gritted out.

"To draw attention to your...*assets*."

Hades looked down, noting he was almost covered in the gold dust. Hermes, who was bent eye level with his abs, looked up and grinned. Whatever he saw in Hades's gaze made him hesitate.

"I think I'm done," he said, clearing his throat and straightening.

Hades glowered. "I don't see why I have to wear this."

"Clothing is optional," Hermes replied. "In fact, the preference is to fight naked."

"I meant the gold dust, Hermes."

"Oh," he said. "It's fashion."

Hades raised a brow at that comment. "I'm sure it will look marvelous with the blood of my enemies."

"Let's hope it is their blood and not yours," said Hermes, returning the jar and brush to the altar where he had retrieved them earlier.

Hades tilted his head to the side. "Are you suggesting I will lose?"

Hermes's eyes widened. "No, of course not. It's just—"

Hades crossed his arms over his chest at the god's hesitation.

"Don't do that! You're ruining my work!"

"Then don't lie to me," Hades replied.

Hermes sighed, and his whole body seemed to slump. He scrubbed his face as he spoke. "It's not that I don't think you can win," he admitted. "It's just the thought of what you might be up against."

"And what *might* I be up against?"

"Your own demons, Hades," Hermes said.

It was the first time Hades had considered what being in this ring might mean for him mentally, and it hit harder when Hermes nodded toward the wall where an array of weapons hung.

"You only get one," he said. "Choose wisely."

Hades stared at them for a long time, unable to bring himself closer. There were swords and sickles, shields and axes.

Taking a weapon in hand would only remind him of the weight of others, ones he had used in battle after battle. With that thought came others, memories tinged with sounds and smells. He let them move through his mind—screams of terror and groans of death, the smell of blood, metal, and sweat.

There was a part of him that wished Hermes had not said anything at all, had not drawn his mind to think of those times, yet he was better off preparing for it if he was to face any opponent.

With the echoes of past battles roaring through his mind, he reached and retrieved a shield from the wall. It carried a symbol of Hera, a panther, and as much as he hated to wield it, the shield itself was an invaluable weapon. It was fashioned from adamant, an unbreakable metal that could injure a god. Its edges were sharp and it was heavy, a weight that seemed to increase the longer he held it and turned it over in his hand. After a few moments, he turned and found Hermes staring, looking very much stricken.

"It's time," he said.

Hades said nothing. There was a part of him that

could not believe he was even entertaining this. He felt like a puppet Hera had dressed and attached to strings, a vessel for enjoyment rather than an age-old god.

Still, he followed, strung along by the hope that if he did as he was instructed, his future with Persephone would be secured.

Hermes led him from the room, down the rounded corridor where it branched once more, down another concrete tunnel. Ahead, he could see light, but it was unnatural, tinged with green, and as he neared it, his body grew tense, his anxiety deepening.

What would he face in this ring?

When he came to the end, where the shadow met the light, he paused. The tunnel led to an oval stadium with seats that sloped gently upward. They were full, and the crowd was already hyped—laughing and shouting, cheering and howling. Their excitement to see blood burrowed into his ears, twined into his mind. He gritted his teeth against it, hating it.

There was a second level, a fenced-in balcony where spectators stood, their fingers looped through metal wire, and while curious, they were far more subdued.

There was no announcement, no introduction as Hermes motioned for Hades to step into the ring. As he took one step, then another, the cheering that had inspired such frustration in him died—no one had expected to see the God of the Dead.

Hades's grip tightened on the shield he had chosen as a weapon as he scanned the crowd. His eyes followed a ring of fire-lit pyres before settling on Hera, whose box was built into the second floor. The goddess herself sat on an iron throne. She had changed and now wore all black, trading most of her jewelry for a single diadem of gold coins that glimmered across her forehead.

Even from here, she looked cold, carved from solid marble.

Then his eyes shifted to someone he had not expected to see.

Theseus.

Theseus, demigod, son of Poseidon, sat beside Hera. There was no mistaking his nephew's aquamarine eyes or the arrogant air with which he held himself. There was a part of him that was not so surprised to see the two together, given that Hera wished to overthrow Zeus. Hades had suspected for a long time that it was Theseus's wish—and the wish of Triad, a terrorist group that had organized against the Olympians—to end the reign of the gods.

How long, Hades wondered, had his partnership with Hera existed?

His thoughts were interrupted by a voice—Hermes's voice—as he announced Hades and his opponent.

"Welcome to fight night," he sang. "In the ring, we have a very special guest. The one and only Rich One, Receiver of Many, the Unseen One, Lord of the Underworld, God of the Dead, Hades!"

With each name, Hades's jaw grew more taut.

Hermes did not even manage to announce his opponent when a set of stone doors opposite the ring burst open as two heads emerged. They were snakelike with pointed noses and mouths. Webbed scales fanned out from the backs of their heads and down their backs. A large, clawed foot shook the ground as the creature squeezed its way out of containment, followed by another two heads.

Something sour gathered in the back of Hades's throat. He knew this creature, knew that there were three more heads attached to its body that had yet to emerge from the darkness of the arena.

It was a hydra. A seven-headed creature that was impossible to defeat. Even if he managed to decapitate one of its heads, another two would grow back in its place. Not to mention its venom, the tar-like saliva that dripped from its mouth even now, was deadly.

The creature bellowed and screamed, and as it moved into the arena, it shook its heads, slinging its deadly venom carelessly about. Horrified screams erupted as onlookers were hit with acid.

Hera and Theseus watched on, unfazed.

Hades bolted. Perhaps the only thing on his side was speed, because even hydra venom could be deadly to gods if they sustained enough injuries. Unfortunately, the hydra's heads were just as fast, and their long necks meant its bulbous body did not have to move far to reach its victims.

The ground shook as one of its heads slammed down an inch from Hades's ankles. He turned and lunged into the air, slamming his shield down on the creature's head. It remained limp, disoriented, but the other six heads hissed and attacked.

Hades rolled away and covered himself with his shield as each of the hydra's heads rammed against the metal. Soon, the shield was covered with a mix of black venom and saliva that dripped thickly off the edges and onto the ground at his feet. Hades gritted his teeth against the might of the monster. He knew that eventually he would have to move, but he needed a plan, a way to ensure the heads could not grow back. His eyes caught on one of the lit torches around the stadium.

Fire.

He could use fire.

But first, he had to get out from under this attack.

He bent his knees and hurled the shield into the air with all his might. It flipped as if it were light as a coin, distracting the hydra's heads as he bolted for the first torch, his bare feet burning as he stepped in the hydra's venom.

The monster was not deceived long, his heavy footfalls giving his retreat away, and soon the heads slithered after him. Some nipped at his feet while others went for his head. It was a constant game of jumping and dodging, and by the time he reached the edge of the stadium, his body was fatigued, the soles of his feet on fire.

Overhead, the torches burned, a beacon that signaled an escape. Hades turned, back against the wall, and as the venomous heads raced toward him, he jumped. The heads struck, one right after the other, and he used them almost like stepping stones, diving for the torch when it was within reach. But as he grabbed it, it snapped in half, burdened by his momentum, and he continued falling to the ground, the hydra's heads chasing after him, open-mouthed, a rain of venom pouring down around him, touching his body like drops of drizzle, burning his skin.

He couldn't let the hydra catch him on the ground. So he hurled the torch at one of the open mouths, and as it hit, it burst into flames.

The creature bellowed and all its heads flailed. The crowd screamed, and Hades knew that those who had remained after the hydra's first attack were probably wishing they had left.

With the hydra distracted, Hades rushed for his shield, which lay discarded across the arena. Scooping it up, he then ran for another torch. This time, he managed to top the wall, which was wide enough for him to run atop. He snapped the torch from its place and ran for the next, tossing them to the ground below.

When he came to the final one, the hydra had recovered, and as it charged for him, he waited until the last second to jump from the wall. As its heads collided with the wall, Hades bore down on one of the necks with his shield. The impact was jarring, but the shield cut into the creature's flesh enough for Hades to shove a lit torch inside. A second head was on fire, but this time as the monster reacted, it jerked, sending Hades flying across the arena.

He hit the wall, but he landed on his sore feet, legs shaking from the pain.

He watched as the hydra worked to put out the fire burning through one of its necks. A few of the heads screamed at it, but the venom only seemed to make it worse while others tried to beat at the flames with their heads. His gaze turned toward the box where Hera sat with Theseus. Neither was paying attention, each consumed in conversation with the other, and there was something about that sight that made Hades rage.

He was finished with this.

He turned toward the hydra, took up his shield, but instead of using it to defend, he used it like a disc, heaving it through the air. It tore through the hydra, and as it did, the head that had been on fire dropped into the puddle of blood and venom left behind. The entire carcass erupted in fire, filling the arena with the smell of burning flesh. The remaining heads whipped back and forth, and as each one fell to the ground, it shook, their screams growing hoarse until, eventually, all was quiet save for the sound of crackling fire.

The hydra was now a resident of the Underworld.

CHAPTER XVI
The Battle with Heracles

No one cheered, though he had not expected celebration, not to mention most of the people who had occupied the seats of the stadium had fled during the horror that was the hydra.

Indeed, the aftermath was much like the end of a battle when a strange and dreadful silence settled heavily in the air. It was the silence of death, the sound of life stolen from all living things, not just human.

And it was over.

A ringing settled deep in Hades's ears, and before it could grow worse, he offered Hera a vulgar gesture, then turned to leave the stadium.

Except that as soon as he reached the tunnel, a door slammed down, barring his exit, and a horrible screeching filled the air.

Hades whirled to find that a second gate had opened and released a herd of giant birds. There were easily twenty, all with bronze beaks and deadly metal feathers that gleamed beneath the greenish light, and while they looked like something Hephaestus had created, Hades knew better.

These were Stymphalian birds, creations of Ares, the God of War.

Their beaks, talons, and feathers were deadly weapons and had the ability to pierce armor, which made getting close enough to kill them nearly impossible.

Hades would need a bow in hopes of even wounding one, though that too would prove to be difficult given their feathers were metal.

The birds screeched and charged, a towering stampede of sharp blades heading right for him.

Fuck.

Hades took off at a run once more, though the pain made it hard for him to maintain a steady pace. He gritted his teeth through it as he heard the distinct sound of metal scraping metal, and he knew the birds were airborne. Glancing overhead, he saw that they were circling, vultures ready to pick apart their kill.

Shelter. He had to find some kind of shelter.

Frantic, he glanced around the arena, spotting his shield. He turned toward it, just as a metal feather lodged in the earth in front of him like a spear. A second followed and then a third, barring his path to the shield. He changed course, heading instead for one of the entrances used by the monsters. The threshold over the doors was minuscule, but it would provide enough cover until he decided on a plan of action.

As he veered right, so did the birds and their feather spears, each hitting so close, the air felt like a whip upon their impact. If he slowed down, he would be impaled.

Except that the birds seemed to be aware of Hades's plans, because in the next second, the small bit of relief he'd hoped to have beneath the awning of the arena was barred from him by a row of sharp metal feathers.

Hades halted in his tracks, anger boiling his blood. He turned, eyes settling on the corpse of the hydra. It was full of poisonous things, including teeth.

Once more, he changed routes while the attacks continued from above. As each feather spear hit the ground, it tore up the earth, sending rocks and dirt into the air, making his course to the hydra more difficult. There was no relief once he arrived either, as the entire creature sat in a pool of its own venomous blood, but Hades was already wounded by the venom, and if he could manage to win this final fight, he could heal himself.

Hades launched himself into the air, landing atop one of the hydra's heads. As he did, a sharp feather cut through the air, impaling the head. Several followed after that, piercing the deceased monster, making it vibrate with the impact. His anger began to build, his exhaustion a weight, and while magic was forbidden in this duel, he felt himself calling to it, gripping the teeth within the mouths of the hydra. Ripping those sharp, poisonous teeth from their gums, he catapulted them through the air and pelted the birds, filling the air with a cacophony of horrible cries followed by a metallic crash as they fell from the sky, landing haphazardly in the stadium—some in the arena, others in the stands.

In the aftermath, Hades turned, facing the box.

"Hera!" he yelled, infusing it with a hatred beyond anything he'd ever felt before. "End this madness!"

The goddess rose languidly to her feet and stepped to the very edge of her box.

"Do you not wish to wed the young Persephone?"

Hades gritted his teeth, staring at her, so consumed by his rage that he did not even notice how badly the ground beneath his feet, soaked in blood, burned. If it had been anyone else, he would have snapped, demanded that they leave her out of this, but he knew, perhaps better than anyone, that Hera would never cease her pursuit if he did not do as she asked.

She knew where her power lay, and it was in Hades's heart.

"Am I wrong?" the goddess asked.

Hades knew she sought more than an answer. She sought his vulnerability.

"No," Hades gritted out. "You are not wrong."

"And yet you cheat by using your magic," Hera said, her head tilting to the side.

Hades had no words for the goddess, only feelings, and they were building just as quickly as they had toward the Stymphalian birds. He was angry, and he was tired.

"How do you intend to atone for your error in judgment?" she asked, nonplussed.

Hades would have liked to offer her a final, vulgar gesture before returning to his realm for the night, but there was a future on the line that was not completely his own, and he was not about to let it slip through his fingers. So he answered, slow and deliberate, "However you see fit."

"I thought so," she said, smiling, and returned to her iron throne. As she sat, another door opened, revealing a large, muscled man dressed similarly to Hades. He had a head full of golden curls, and while handsome and young, there was something wrong. Hades noted how the veins in his arms and neck bulged, how the whites of his eyes were stained red, how his breathing seemed both labored and angry.

This man was stricken with madness.

Hades was familiar with this magic, a particular favorite of Hera's. She had used it throughout her existence to make men and women alike murderous, including the one before him.

Heracles, a son of Zeus.

It had been years since Hades had looked on his demigod nephew, and it was clear that whatever Hera had done left him drained of humanity.

There was no difference between him and any other monster.

Heracles left the shelter of the gate, dragging a massive club behind him.

Hades shifted out of the hydra's blood and reached for his sole weapon, the shield. Still, the warrior advanced on him. Seeming to need no time to consider his opponent, he attacked, lifting the club over his head with both hands. Hades dodged the first blow, which rocked the earth as it hit. The second whipped toward his middle, missing only by an inch as Hades jumped back. The third blow was caught by his shield, and as it hit, Hades pushed against it, sending the club flying.

With the man weaponless, Hades reared back and shoved his shield toward Heracles's neck. He'd hoped to end this fight as quickly as it had begun, but the man was fast and just as strong as Hades. He caught the adamantine shield just before it could reach him, and suddenly they were locked in a battle of push and pull until the shield itself began to bend.

With a growl, Hades shoved against Heracles and lunged to the side. The demigod stumbled forward, shield in hand, while Hades made a mad dash for the club he had flung across the stadium. A roar left Heracles, who tossed the shield. Hades ducked as it flew overhead, lodging in what remained of the concrete arena wall. Before Hades could reach the club, Heracles dove for him, locking onto his ankle with strong hands. Hades stumbled and rolled just as Heracles jerked him toward his body, rearing back to punch his face, but the god caught his fist, hands shaking as he took on the might of the man's godlike power.

Hades lifted his knee, catching the demigod in the side. It did little to deter him, however, as he continued to raise his fist. This time, Hades could not stop the blow. A burst of pain seemed to explode from behind his eyes. A second blow brought tears. A third and his nose crunched. Finally, Hades recovered and dodged the fourth attempt, managing to land a harder blow to Heracles's side, sending him to the ground and giving Hades the upper hand. With their roles reversed, it was Hades's turn to pummel Heracles.

He got in two blows to the face—one to the eye and one to the mouth that cut the skin on his knuckles to pieces—before he attempted to reach the club again. He barely rose to his feet before he was down once more, his knee hitting the arena floor with a loud quake. He twisted and kicked Heracles in the face, sending him to his back. Hades scrambled once more to reach the club.

Gripping it with his bloodied hands, he twisted just in time to be hit with the full force of Heracles's weight.

They sailed across the arena, Hades landing blow after blow on any part of Heracles's body that was exposed, until the force of their momentum broke the concrete wall and stadium like glass, stealing his breath.

The two landed in a pile of rubble. Heracles had the high ground and a host of new weapons in the form of large concrete bricks. He reached for one and brought it down on Hades. All he could do to stop the blow was cross his arms over his face. Upon impact, the concrete turned to dust.

Heracles roared and reached for another.

Hades shifted his knees up and pushed against the ground with his feet, sending Heracles toppling into the rubble beside him. He reached for the nearest rock and attacked. Landing on the demigod with the force of his body weight, Hades aimed for the eye.

The strike did not land as Heracles caught Hades's wrists, and the two struggled. Still, Hades pushed, a horrible growl escaping his mouth, and he felt almost as mad as Heracles, uncaring that he was about to murder this man. He was beyond anything humane, aside from his motivation to get back to the Underworld to find Persephone warming his bed and the hope that in the aftermath of this fight, he'd have a chance at a forever with her.

A forever Heracles stood in the way of.

Hades's arms shook, but he felt Heracles's hold slipping, and then it was done. His grip crumbled, and the rock smashed into the demigod's face. And then Hades did it again.

And again.

And again.

And again until his nephew's features were nothing but bloody pulp, and when he felt as though he had released all his aggression, he tossed the rock aside and rose to his feet, stumbling out of the mess they had made and back into the arena. Once inside, he looked up to Hera again. He could not quite place her expression, but he thought he detected a modicum of shock, though it was washed out by her overpowering anger, present in the set of her jaw.

She nodded toward Hades and said "I'll be in touch" before vanishing, taking Theseus with her.

It was only after she left that Hades let himself stumble and then fall to the ground.

Hades came to consciousness, though he had yet to open his eyes. He took a moment to assess his body, recalling how his feet and skin had burned, how his face had ached and his knees had throbbed before everything had gone dark, but there was no pain, only a deep, hollow feeling—a complete and utter numbness that accompanied the horror of what he'd done.

The hydra, the Stymphalian birds.

But the worst was Heracles.

"He should be waking up now," a voice said.

"Are you sure? He still looks green." Hades recognized Hermes's voice.

"I think that is the light," the voice replied, still warm despite Hermes's questioning.

Hades blinked open his eyes to find a young god

staring down at him. He had wide, brown eyes, a mop of brown hair, and a matching beard.

Hades knew him.

"Paean," he said.

The god offered a kind, genuine smile. "It is good to see you awake, Lord Hades."

Paean was a minor god, but his role among the Olympians was great, as he was their healer on the rare occasion a god could be wounded.

Hades rose into a sitting position, body stiff and head spinning.

Paean pushed a mug into his hands. "Drink," he said. "It is nectar."

Hades took the mug and sipped the honeyed liquid as he took in his surroundings. He was in a small room with a single cot and a lamp. Paean occupied the only chair in the room but quickly vacated it, speaking as he rose.

"You are fully healed, my lord. You may leave whenever you wish."

"Thank you, Paean," Hades said softly.

The healer offered a gentle smile and a nod before leaving the room, then Hades's eyes shifted to Hermes, who looked very pale and very awkward pressed against the wall of the small room.

"Well, I must say," Hermes said nervously, "that was the most dramatic fight night I have been to in a long while, wouldn't you agree?"

Hades just stared.

"I mean, of course you couldn't agree. You've never been," Hermes continued, wringing his hands. "Let me tell you, though. I have never seen one so…bloody. Leave it to you to set a record."

Hades did not wish to set records, and the comment only made him feel disgusted. A sickening twist tore at his stomach. He averted his eyes, ignoring Hermes's incessant talking in favor of the greater conversation at hand.

"Theseus was with Hera," Hades said, frowning as he recalled how they'd sat together in Hera's box and conversed as if they were old allies. "Did you know?"

The God of Mischief looked affronted that Hades would ask such a question. "This was the first time I saw him here."

"And how often are you here?" Hades countered.

Hermes seemed to shrink in on himself, as if realizing why Hades might not trust him in this moment when he admitted, "Every week."

"Hmm."

Hades had long suspected Theseus of plotting to overthrow the Olympians. Given the reason for his trials, he could not help wondering if perhaps Hera had formed some kind of alliance with the leader of Triad.

But why be so blatant about their partnership?

"What?" Hermes asked.

Hades looked at the god, arching a brow.

"What does 'hmm' mean? You do it all the time."

Hades blinked, and Hermes continued. "Does it mean you don't believe me? Or are you disappointed in me? Is it both?"

"It means I am thinking," Hades said, though he'd have liked to not answer at all and let the god suffer, especially after the day he'd had.

"Oh," Hermes said, and there was a beat of silence before he replied, "Well, in that case, please continue."

But Hades rose fully to his feet, downing the rest of the nectar Paean had given him. Once he was finished, he pushed the cup into Hermes's hands and said, "Perhaps you would not be so defensive if you did not feel so guilty."

To that, Hermes had nothing to say, so Hades vanished.

CHAPTER XVII
Iniquity

Hades had been summoned to Hera's fight night nearly twelve hours ago, and though he'd been healed by Paean, he felt restless and uneasy. There was a kind of horror that thrummed through his body, a darkness he had yet to channel away. It was there when he blinked, in the form of bloodied rocks and crunching bone and the phantom pain of acid burning his skin.

He returned to the Underworld, where he had expected—or rather hoped—to find Persephone. There was a part of his brain that needed to lay eyes on her after the ordeal he'd been through, not only to ease his pain but to know that she was still here, that he had fought for her and not lost her.

He was not prepared for the sinking feeling in his chest when he did not find her asleep in their bed, roaming the garden, or at Hecate's cabin.

"What has you so uneasy, my king?" Hecate asked when she found him outside her home.

"Could it have something to do with the fact that I have been *killing* all day?" he snapped.

"Murder does put one on edge," Hecate agreed airily. "Would you like some tea?"

"What I would *like* is to be free of Hera's labors," he said.

"Hera," Hecate said. "The Goddess of Women who does nothing but punish them. How did you earn her scorn?"

"I told her I would not overthrow Zeus," Hades replied.

"Yet." Hecate paused and looked at Hades, who raised a questioning brow. "What? All things must come to an end."

Hades paused for a moment, then said, "She has threatened my future with Persephone."

"No one but the Fates can truly threaten your future, Hades."

"Perhaps, but Hera can turn her scorn on Persephone," he replied. "And that would be my fault."

"Is it your fault because you love her?" Hecate asked.

"Isn't that enough?"

"Your greatest battle, Hades, will be recognizing that Persephone too has made the decision to love you. So there is no fault, only choice."

It was a pretty sentiment, but he was dealing with gods—gods like him.

"That was before she knew the consequences."

"You think so little of her love?" Hecate asked.

Hades flinched. He opened his mouth to speak but shut it once more.

"If you continue to project your doubt on her, then you do not deserve a future with her."

They were harsh words, but Hades knew they were true.

"Now, would you like some tea? It will take your mind off things."

"I think I'd rather have a clear mind, Hecate. I know what you put in *your* tea."

She arched her brow. "Does all that alcohol give you a clear mind?"

"At this point," Hades replied, "yes."

Hades returned to his office, still on edge. His short conversation with Hecate made him want to see Persephone even more, if only to confirm that she still wanted this—*them, their future*—but once more, his fears overwhelmed him.

What would it take, he wondered, to feel such assurance?

He scrubbed his face and crossed the room to pour himself a drink. It was probably best that he put off seeing Persephone until he had a shower and real sleep anyway. Besides, it was likely she was at the hospital with Lexa, and he did not wish to intrude on their time together.

Just as he set out a glass, his phone rang. Hades answered without a greeting, though Ilias did not need one to offer his update.

"Persephone's at Iniquity," he said.

Hades was overcome with a sudden coldness that settled heavily in his stomach, but the shock quickly melted into something far more fierce. Once more, his uncertainty welled.

This was part of his life he had wanted to shield her from. It was one thing for her to know and attend

Nevernight, another thing entirely for her to attend Iniquity.

"What is she doing there?"

Ilias's hesitation assured Hades that he would not like the answer.

"She was dancing," he replied. "But Kal has summoned her to his suite."

Hades teleported, appearing beside Ilias, who had yet to hang up his phone.

Despite this, he began updating Hades on the situation as they watched what was transpiring inside Kal's rented suite via a panel that acted as a one-way window into his room.

Numerous underworld criminals worked within the walls of this club under the close scrutiny of Hades's staff, and while many of them believed they were being watched via a monitor, there was an additional element to each of these spaces that ensured they never worked outside Hades's rules, including a network of secret passages that allowed observation.

Hades could not take his gaze off Persephone, who stood opposite Kal dressed in black. He hoped she at least thought of him as she had dressed, because every curve of her body was on display. The light poured over the high points of her face, creating dark hollows under her cheeks and making her look stoic and severe.

"Who brought her here?" Hades asked.

"We do not know," he replied. "But it does seem Kal did not expect her. He sent two of his employees to confirm her identity. They have been detained."

Hades glanced at Ilias. He would refrain from asking for details for now, given that he would likely wish to punish them just as severely as he intended to punish Kal.

He turned his attention back to the two.

"I want every detail of your relationship with Hades," Kal was saying. "I want to know how you met him, when he first kissed you, and all the scandalous details from the first time he fucked you."

Persephone's mouth twisted. "You're sick."

"I'm a businessman, Persephone. Sex sells. Sex with gods sells better, and you, my sweet—you're a gold mine."

Hades's fists tightened as Kal continued to speak.

"I'm not the only one who's slept with Hades," Persephone pointed out.

"But you're the first he's committed to, and that's worth more than the words of a fuck buddy," Kal replied. "He's invested in you, which means he'll do anything to protect you and the details of your private life."

While Hades had expected Kal to do something stupid after he'd rejected his offer of partnership at the Hellene Racetrack, he had not quite expected this attempt at blackmail. The mortal was daring, to be sure, though he was about to discover just how powerless he was against a god.

"But you're rich," he heard Persephone say.

"Not like him, but that's what you're going to help me with, and in exchange, you get to save your friend from certain death."

Suddenly, Hades understood what had drawn Persephone here in the first place. He'd been angry before, but now he was incensed to discover that Kal had played on such a weakness. He had dangled hope before Persephone while also breaking the rules.

It was Kal's final strike.

Hades called to his magic, and the darkness took the form of vipers, slithering from the shadows toward Kal, whose gaze was set so intently on Persephone, he did not see them until it was too late, until they had wound their way around his body like vises, rising to strike the moment he moved. He offered a small, satisfying cry, body freezing as he faced the beady eyes of Hades's serpents.

It was then Hades entered the room, choosing to manifest from the darkness behind Persephone. He noted how she straightened with his presence. There was a part of him that had not wanted to interrupt, wondering how far she would have gone to save Lexa, but he thought he knew her choice already, and he could not let her agree to Kal's bargain. He had already explained the implications of bringing a soul back from limbo without their permission, but asking a Magi to do the work of a god was even worse.

"Are you threatening me, Kal?" Hades asked.

"No…never!" Kal's voice strained as he lied.

Hades paused only an inch from Persephone, a strange electric energy buzzing between them. He took a handful of her hair as she turned her head toward him, capturing her mouth. One of her hands moved to his chest, twining into the fabric of his shirt while the other remained trapped between them. His tongue slid lightly over her lips, and as she opened for him, he brought his hand to her jaw as he deepened the kiss. He liked how she clung to him despite the odd angle, liked how she tasted, warm and wet and sweet, and he was reminded that the only thing he wished to share with the world about Persephone was that he loved her.

He pulled away, teeth grazing her bottom lip, and asked, "Are you well?"

If she said no, he would not let her stay for Kal's inevitable punishment, but she nodded, her eyes searching his own, troubled, but he did not have time to wonder about what she saw as he turned toward Kal.

"I—I was following your rules! *She* summoned *me*!"

The mortal began moving subtly—digging his toes into the floor, tightening his fingers around the arms of his chair. It was enough to put the serpents on edge, and they began to wriggle against his skin.

"*My* rules?" Hades asked, his footsteps echoing between each word. "Are you insinuating I would approve of a contract between you and my lover?"

"That would be making an exception," Kal stated, as if he were quoting a contract from memory, though his voice quivered as he did so. "There are no exceptions in Iniquity."

"Let me be clear," Hades said, his magic bursting from the tips of his fingers in the form of five pointed spikes. He captured Kal's face between them, gripping him so hard that they sliced into his skin. Blood dripped down his face in tear-like streams, which caused the snakes to slither around his body faster, frenzied with the smell of it. "Anyone who belongs to me is an exception to the rules of this club."

Then he heaved the man from the seat he had made into a throne, and he landed on the hard, marble floor with a crack. The jarring aggravated his serpents, causing them to attack, and with each bite, Kal's screams got louder and louder. Hades watched as his body convulsed on the floor, knowing that the bite of these snakes was unlike any other. It was the sting of his magic, a shock that went straight to the soul.

"You bastard," Kal wailed, rolling onto his side, shaking.

"Careful, mortal," Hades said, standing over the wounded man.

"I followed the rules," Kal moaned. "I followed *your* rules."

"I know the rules well, mortal," Hades said. The rules were that if a mortal summoned a Magi for work, the consequences belonged to the summoning mortal.

But Persephone was not a mortal.

And Hades was not willing to let her live with the consequences of Kal's horrible magic.

"You don't fuck with me or my lover, understand?"

Kal's breathing was heavy, but he managed to roll onto his stomach and lift himself onto his shaky hands and knees. When he looked up, it was Persephone who stared back.

"Help me!" he dared to demand, his cry guttural, but Persephone did not move, nor did she speak. She just watched in serene silence, and Hades kicked him to the ground.

"Do not speak to her, mortal," Hades seethed.

Kal landed with a grunt and a wail as another snake bit into the fleshy part of his arm.

Hades turned his attention to Persephone, who stared back, almost emotionless. He wished he could read her thoughts or at least read her expression, but she had watched all this with a passivity that made him think she was either in shock or somehow approving.

He hoped it was the latter.

"Shall I continue to punish him?"

She watched him a moment longer before shifting her attention to Kal. Then she approached, lowering to study his face.

"Will his face scar?" she asked.

Hades did not know why she asked, but he answered nevertheless. "It will if you wish it."

"I wish it."

Hades was only marginally surprised; the rest of him was satisfied. At least he had not scared her away with his display.

At her words, Kal whimpered.

"Shh," Persephone soothed, mocking. "It could be worse. I am tempted to send you to Tartarus."

There was a strange pride associated with those words, and Hades found them welling in his chest.

"Tomorrow, I want you to call Demetri and tell him you made a mistake. You don't want the exclusive, and you will never, ever tell me what to write again. Do we have an agreement?"

Exclusive?

Hades's brows lowered. Was there something happening beyond the blackmail Kal had tried to secure tonight?

Whatever it was, Kal agreed, nodding emphatically.

"Good," Persephone said, her voice a quiet whisper. As she rose to her feet and turned toward him, Hades knew he would do anything she asked. If she had wanted him to die here in this room, he would have made the choice.

"He can live," she said.

Generous, he thought, then he turned his attention to Kal.

"Leave," Hades commanded, sending him seven

floors below to the stage. Kal's sudden appearance would interrupt the performers, and when the crowd looked upon his scarred and bleeding face and saw the snakes that had ensnared him, they would know he had been punished by the God of the Dead.

In the quiet aftermath of Kal's torture, the two stared at each other, and a strange tension flooded the room. It felt to Hades as though Persephone were building a wall, and while he'd have preferred to tear it down, he began to build one too.

He had so many questions, among them, *What were you thinking?* But before he could demand an answer, she charged ahead.

"You ruined everything!"

"I ruined everything?" he demanded. He took a step toward her. "I saved you from making a huge mistake. What were you thinking, coming here?"

She glared up at him. "I was trying to save my friend, and Kal was offering a way to do that, *unlike you*."

"You would give up our private life—something you cherish most—in exchange for something that will only condemn your friend?"

"Condemn her? It will save her life! You bastard. You *told* me to have hope! You *said* she could survive."

He had also said that it was up to Lexa, but Persephone was conveniently leaving that fact out.

He felt like a monster, towering over her, but she rose to the occasion, fighting back just as hard.

"You don't trust me?"

"No!" she shot back. "No, I don't trust you. Not when it comes to Lexa. And what about this place, Hades? This is your club, isn't it? What the fuck?"

She had expressed her embarrassment when she'd had to find out about his charities through someone else, so it was no surprise that she was angry now.

He reached for her, his hands gripping her shoulders. There was a strangeness beneath his skin, a volatile need to touch her. It was likely fueled by how he'd spent the past several hours of his life, and he wished to channel it into something far more productive than violence.

"You were never to come here. This place isn't for you."

Hades did not expect her to wince, and he hated that he had hurt her, though he didn't understand why until she spoke.

"Leuce works here," she countered, as if they were one and the same.

"Because it's Leuce. You told me to give her job back, so I sent her here. You...you're...*different*."

"Different?" She pushed away from him. "What does that even mean?"

Hades's frustration was acute, pounding through his head. He gritted his teeth. "I thought we'd established this. You mean more to me than anyone—anything."

"What does that have to do with keeping this place from me?"

Aside from the fact that it was dangerous?

She might not like what she saw—what it made him.

"Everything here is illegal, isn't it? The Magi are here. What else?"

He stared at her, knowing that he could not escape answering but wondering if he could prolong it.

"What else, Hades?" she demanded.

"Everything you've ever feared." *Or perhaps thought to be impossible.* "Assassins, drug lords..."

He housed crime families and madams, relic dealers and thieves, arsonists and smugglers. Anyone and anything that could benefit him was within the walls of this club, but as he watched Persephone's face pale, he questioned just how much she was ready to learn.

So he trailed off, and after a brief silence, Persephone whispered, "Why?"

"I created a world where I could watch them," he said.

Watch and control.

"Watch them do what? Break the law? Hurt people?"

"Yes," he said, his frustration at a breaking point. Why did it feel so impossible to introduce her to the scope of his world? How was he supposed to illustrate lifetimes of work, built to reach both the heavens and the depths of depravity?

"Yes? That's it? That's all you have to say?"

"For now." He was at a point where he did not want to explain. If she wished to think so poorly of him, then perhaps he should let her.

"Who brought you here?" he demanded.

"A taxi."

It was not the answer he sought, and she knew it. Someone had told her about this place, fed her the information on how it worked. Hades narrowed his eyes. "You think I won't find out?"

In fact, he thought he already knew.

"I have free will. I chose to come here of my own accord."

Hades's eyes darkened, and he touched her again, drawing her closer. His body felt rigid, run through with wire. He felt too agitated, and he wasn't going to get through this if he didn't find some kind of way to release this energy. He needed to fuck, and he needed it to be unkind and ugly, and Persephone was primed to offer it.

Except that she pushed his hands away.

His gaze hardened as he stared back at her.

She could not say she did not know his intentions. His cock pressed firmly into her stomach, and despite her initial rejection, her body bowed to his desire.

"Are you telling me no?"

Truly, if she did not want him, he would release her, but she shook her head once and his resolve crumbled. He spun her around and guided her forward so her hands pressed flat against the mirrored wall, hiking up her skirt and shoving her legs apart. He brushed his palm over her round ass before giving her a light smack, which caused her to yelp. For a moment, he thought he might have hurt her, but when he met her gaze in the mirror, she offered a small nod, and he continued, bending to kiss the skin he had touched while guiding her underwear down.

Once they were off, he placed them in his pocket and turned his attention to her center. Slipping his hand between her thighs, he let his finger trail along her entrance, slick with her arousal. She groaned and arched, her stance growing wider with the hope that she would soon accommodate more of him.

And as much as he wanted to be inside her, he wanted to prolong her pleas for pleasure more.

"So fucking wet. How long have you been like this?"

"Since I got here," she offered in a whispered moan. He liked the way she pressed into the mirror, how exaggerated her back arched and elevated her ass. "I wanted you on the dance floor. I willed you to manifest from the dark, but you weren't there."

"I'm here now," he said. Rising to his feet, he kissed her shoulder and down her back before drawing his tongue over her round ass. All the while, his fingers continued their exploration, curling inside her, isolating her pleasure. Another hand worked her clit, and beneath him, she hummed and sighed and cried.

Sweat broke out across his skin, and his head felt hot. There were so many parts of her he wanted to touch and taste, and his cock grew thicker and heavier, desperate to sink into her heat, to feel her clench around him, to fill her to bursting with his come.

This was possession, and right now, he wanted to own all of her.

"Hades...please!" She gave a guttural, breathless sob, looking at him from under her arm, and he knew she was just as desperate to come. He could see it in her eyes, feel it in the heat of her skin. He withdrew, fingers sticky with her arousal, and chuckled at her cry of frustration. When she started to straighten, he held her hips in place.

"Stay," he ordered, an edge of darkness to his voice.

She offered an angry glare, and he knew she did not like the command. Still, he smiled.

"It wouldn't be punishment if I gave you what you wanted when you demand it."

Her lips slammed into a hard line. "Don't pretend you don't want me."

The sound of his zipper followed his reply. "Oh, I'm not pretending."

He guided the head of his cock to her entrance and thrust, sinking into her heat and grip. He stayed there a moment, fully sheathed, enjoying the pressure that held his cock so firmly. He could stay here forever, lost in this heady pleasure, but beneath him, Persephone writhed, her body demanding movement.

Still, he held off, brushing his hand along her back before bending close to squeeze her breasts and tease her nipples. Finally, he began to move, small thrusts, a grinding that caused them both to groan. He reached for her hair, wrapping it around his fist like a line of rope, and drew her toward him, kissing her neck and jaw. Their mouths connected, tongues twining in a desperate attempt to taste each other's souls.

Then he released her all at once, though he kept an arm wound around her middle. She watched him in the mirror as he slowed his pace despite wanting nothing more than to slam into her.

"This is for us," he said, pulling out, holding her attention like embers in the night. "You will share this with no one else."

He thrust forward, and her breath caught in her throat.

"Some things are sacred to me," he said, repeating the same teasing motion. "*This* is sacred to me. You are sacred to me. Do you understand?"

She nodded, resting her face against the wall.

"Say it! Say you understand."

"Yes! Yes, gods-dammit. I understand! Make me come, Hades!"

He pulled out of her and lifted her from her bent position. She spun to face him, eyes wild, and he kissed her, gripping her jaw, pressing her into the wall. There was something sweeter about the taste of her now, on the other side of this anger and frustration. His hands fell, smoothing down her body until he reached her thighs and hoisted her up, leveraging her so she hovered just above his cock before guiding himself back to her entrance and letting her slide down on him.

This position offered little in the way of movement, but it was the closeness they needed. Persephone's hands were tangled in his hair, as if she were ready to pull him to her once more, but Hades remained at a distance, studying her face.

"I have never loved anyone as I love you," he murmured as if he wanted no one else to hear, though he would gladly share those words with the world. "I can't put it into words—there are none that come close to expressing how I feel."

"Then don't use words," she whispered, and when their lips collided once more, Hades turned and lowered to the floor. As soon as he hit the ground, she began to rock against him, uncaring that he had slipped from inside her during their descent, though she was quick to guide him back, slamming down on him with a force that made their bodies slap together.

He watched her use him for her pleasure, fingers twining with his own as she dragged his arms up and over his head, giving him access to her breasts. He teased them with his tongue and teeth before he could no longer handle staying still.

"Fuck!"

He broke her hold and gripped her hips, fingers digging into her soft skin as he helped her move, meeting each downward slide with an upward thrust. Their breaths came hard and fast, and when she began to tighten around him, it was enough to send them both over the edge. He came hard, in a gush of heat that continued as her head fell back in listless pleasure.

She sank against him, her heart hammering, and though they were both slick with sweat, he liked the heaviness of her body against his and he wanted this forever.

"Marry me."

The words slipped out, and once they were in the ether, there was no taking them back. Not that he would want to. Marriage to Persephone had been his plan all along.

Persephone sat back, and as she did, his cock moved with her.

"What?"

It was not the emphatic answer he was looking for. He knew she had heard him, though he could not blame her for hesitating—or even saying no. They had never spoken about marriage, even if he had mentioned their fate.

"Marry me, Persephone. Be my queen. Say you'll stand by my side…forever."

He spoke and recalled Hecate's words—that no one but the Fates could unravel their future—but what if Persephone never said yes?

"Hades…I…" She hesitated. "You were just angry with me."

"And now I'm not."

"And you want to marry me?"

"Yes."

She rose to her feet on shaky legs, and when Hades tried to help, she pushed him away.

"I can't marry you, Hades," she said, her voice breaking. "I...I don't know you."

Hades's lips tightened, and his brows slammed down over his eyes. "You know me."

"No, I don't." She gestured to their surroundings. "You kept this place from me."

"Persephone, I have lived forever. There will always be things you learn about me, and you should know you won't like some of them."

"This isn't one of those things, Hades. This place is real, and it exists in the present. You hired Leuce to work here. I deserved to know, just as I deserved to know about Leuce!"

Hades tightened his jaw. She wasn't wrong, but she also did not know what she was asking for. Did she think she could handle the truth of this world?

"Why didn't you tell me?" she asked.

"Because I was afraid," he snapped, frustrated by the hurt in her voice.

"Why?"

"Obviously because of your moral compass." He rose to his feet and restored his appearance. After a few moments, he turned to face her. "I wanted time to think about how to show you my sins. To explain their roots. Instead, it seems, everyone wishes to do it for me."

Persephone frowned, but at his admission, her expression turned gentle.

"I'm sorry, Hades," she said, voice quiet.

Hades frowned. "What are you apologizing for?"

"I guess...everything," she said. "For coming here... for telling you no."

"It's okay. It's a lot to ask of you right now," he said.

"With Lexa and your work. And I have put a lot on you tonight, shown you a side of me you haven't seen before."

"You aren't...upset?"

He would not say he was upset, not with her, and while he would have liked to end this night engaged to her, it was more for his own peace of mind when dealing with Hera.

"Do I wish you'd said yes? Of course," he said, and before he could continue, she spoke.

"I'm just...not ready."

"I know," he said, pressing his lips to her forehead.

When he pulled away, she was crying.

"Tell me," he implored as he brushed her tears away.

"I ruined everything," she said, pressing her face into his chest, her arms twining around his waist.

"You ruined nothing, my darling," Hades assured. "You were honest with yourself and with me. That is all I ask."

"How could you want to marry me now? After I have told you no?"

How could he not? She had told him no, and with good reason.

"I will always want to marry you because I will always want you as my wife and queen."

It was the truth. He felt it in his soul, though he wondered if tonight had fractured her truth.

"Will you show me more of this place?" she asked, rubbing at her face to erase the tears.

"More of Iniquity?" he asked, surprised, feeling a little of the warmth drain from his face.

"Yes," she said.

"Do I have a choice?"

They had just reconciled, and he really did not feel like fighting anymore, though he had to admit, the fact that she had asked to see more and not left him in a hurry was promising.

"If I am ever to be your queen? No."

She had a point. If she eventually agreed to marry him, she was going to inherit more than a kingdom.

She would have an empire.

CHAPTER XVIII
Fucking Cake

Hades led Persephone from Kal's suite and into the private hallway where he'd watched them earlier. She noted the one-way mirror, pointing at it with her thumb.

"So you spy on all your staff?"

"Think of them as tenants," Hades said. "And yes."

He placed a hand on the small of her back and led her through a network of passages until they reached his private suite. This one overlooked the public floor of Iniquity. Persephone went to the row of windows, which flashed bright with red light and then darkness, looking below at the crowd.

"When I was down there, I felt possessed," she said.

Hades came up behind her, caging her body, and while she watched the floor, he watched her.

"You said you wanted me," he said.

"I did," she said, then turned toward him. "But it was ruined."

Hades stared down at her. "What did you see?"

She shrugged and answered, "I wanted you and I imagined you there, touching me and filling me, and then all of a sudden, it wasn't me beneath you. It was Leuce."

He frowned and brushed his fingers along her jaw. "It wasn't real. You know that?"

"It felt real in the moment," she said. "Was it magic?"

Hades glanced over her shoulder, and Persephone followed his gaze.

"It's more of a drug," he said.

It was one of Hecate's creations, and the side effects were different for everyone.

"Are you saying you drug everyone who enters this club?"

"It is part of why people come to Iniquity. Whoever gave you the password should have warned you."

At his comment, she shut down. He could see it in her eyes and the press of her lips.

"Show me more," she said, stepping to the side to escape him, or at least that was how he felt, as if she were running from him, putting more distance between them, but he said nothing, only leading her from the overlook and back into the dark passageways of Iniquity.

This time, he took her to the lower levels, and as they rode the elevator down, she stood opposite him, studying him, as if trying to figure out exactly who he was.

He didn't like it.

"Where are we going?" she asked, as if she wanted to be prepared for whatever laid beyond this elevator.

Hades stared at her for a moment. "I'm not sure what you expect to find here, but it isn't what you are thinking."

"And what am I thinking?" she challenged.

"The worst," he replied.

She did not deny it, but then she said, "Knowledge changes perception, Hades."

When the doors opened, he offered his hand, and he felt a little more relief when she accepted. As they stepped into a darkened hallway, he spoke. "This part of the club is reserved for guests who possess a token for entry," he explained. "An obol."

"I see you have repurposed the idea of paying to enter the Underworld."

He chuckled, though coming into possession of an obol was not as easy as it was in ancient times. The ones Hades issued were gold, not silver, and they were tied to the soul, which meant as soon as the possessor died, the obol disappeared. It also made forgery impossible, as each of them was unique to the grantee.

He did not give them out lightly, and because he was the only one who could grant them, he could ensure those who were given a token were honest—at least, in the ways that counted.

He continued leading Persephone down a darkened hall and into his office. It was similar to the last in how it was structured, a wall of dark windows allowing him to peer down at the activities on the floor below. Unlike the public side, there was no dancing here, no loud music. This was not a place members came to let go of their inhibitions, though now and then, someone would get too drunk and spout off, and they were promptly escorted from the building.

This was a space to set aside differences. A place to establish connections.

It was the pulse, and Hades kept his finger on it at all times.

He watched Persephone as she peered down at the bar, and he hoped it was rather underwhelming.

No blood, he wanted to say. Or whatever she'd imagined after her encounter with Kal.

Her fingers traced a line down the window.

"Can they see us?"

"No," Hades said.

In fact, from where they sat, this part of his office was mostly in shadow but would appear as a solid black wall. Despite this, none of his members were ignorant. They knew every movement they made, every word they spoke, was being recorded. It was the price they paid for their membership at Iniquity, but in exchange, they received his resources, which were invaluable and, as many were discovering, needed to survive in this part of New Greece where he too ruled.

"So you spy on them from up here?"

She looked back at him from over her shoulder, and he liked the way the light haloed her, even if her question was delivered with an element of coldness.

"You can call it spying if you like."

She turned back to the window. After a moment, he heard her intake of breath as she began to recognize faces below.

"That's Madelia Rella," she said.

"She is in debt to me."

"How?"

"I loaned her the money to start her first brothel."

It had begun that way, at least. Now she owned the whole of the pleasure district, which meant she was, essentially, a landlord, and while she owned every building in the district, it came with a great deal of responsibility. Though Madelia was more than willing to take up the gauntlet. Prior to his deal with the madam, she was already a staunch supporter of women and sex workers' rights. It was how Hades had become interested in her proposition—she wanted to own the pleasure district and reform it. Under her direction, she had promised to create safer spaces for the workers, something she had succeeded with when it came to her own brothel.

So he agreed.

"Why?"

"It was a business opportunity, and in exchange for the money, I have a stake in her company, and I can ensure the safety of her escorts."

Though he did not have to worry as much, because Madelia was a force to be reckoned with. Those who disobeyed her rules, depending on the severity, found themselves fired or dead. It was as simple as that.

"*Send me to Tartarus,*" she had told him once. "*I will gladly face eternal punishment for the lives I take. It likely means I have saved ten more.*"

Hades had smiled at that. "*If I sent you to Tartarus, Madelia, you'd likely decide that my choice of punishments was not good enough.*"

"Who else is down there?" Persephone asked.

Hades came to stand beside her and searched below, looking for people she might know, not because of their involvement in the criminal underworld but because of how they presented themselves to the public.

"That is Leonidas Nasso and Damianos Vitalis. They are billionaires and the bosses of rival crime families."

"Nasso?" Persephone asked. "You mean...the owner of the Nasso Pizzeria chain?"

"The very one," Hades confirmed. "The Vitalises are also restaurant owners, but they make their real living from fishing."

Nasso and Vitalis both specialized in gambling and loan sharking, and only a single road separated their territories within New Athens. Under the rule of Iniquity, they could continue to expand their reach with the caveats that a percentage of their income had to be funneled into charities and they could not make or deal drugs.

"If they are rivals, why are they playing cards?"

"This is neutral territory. It is illegal to cause harm to another person on this property."

Though Nasso and Vitalis had a truce since joining Iniquity, and so long as they continued to work together, they were on track to becoming the two most powerful mortal families in New Greece.

"I suppose you are the exception to that rule?"

"I am always the exception, Persephone."

"These people...they are the elite of New Athens."

She wasn't wrong. Outside this den, they were known for their wealth, and while some might suspect their involvement in crime, there was little evidence to support such a claim.

"They are the rich and the powerful, but they are rich and powerful because of me."

Each member was attached to a string, and so long as they obeyed the rules, they were given more and more slack. Fuck up and the string was cut.

Hades nodded to a few other colorful characters.

"That is Alexis Nicolo," he said, pointing to a man with a huge wave of hair. Each time he moved to sip his drink, it bounced. "He is a professional gambler."

His services were often used by Nasso and Vitalis to catch cheaters in their underground casinos.

Then he pointed to a blond. "That is Helen Hallas. She is an art forger. I use her talents to trade relics for replicas."

He saved Barak Petra for last. The balding man sat alone in the corner of the bar and looked very mundane, dressed in a blue suit.

"He doesn't look like he belongs here," Persephone commented.

"He doesn't, but that makes him better at his job."

"And what's his job?"

"He is an assassin," Hades said.

"Assassin? You mean he gets paid to kill people?"

He did not feel the need to answer that question, and Persephone made no attempt to make him.

"I don't understand. How can you be concerned with saving souls from a terrible existence in the afterlife when you offer these...criminals a place to assemble?"

"They are not all criminals. I am not under some delusion, Persephone. I know I cannot save every soul, but at least Iniquity ensures that those who operate in the underbelly of society follow a code of conduct."

If there was going to be chaos, he would see that it at least benefited society in some way, even if the path to getting there was somewhat murky.

"How is murder part of a code of conduct?"

"Murder isn't part of the code of conduct unless the code is broken."

Even then, everything depended on the severity of the rule that was broken.

Persephone met his gaze.

"We cannot all be good, but if we must be bad, it should serve a purpose."

She did not respond, and he could tell she was still processing everything she had learned tonight.

"I don't expect you to understand. There are many reasons for what I do. Iniquity is no different. I have a network of the most dangerous men and women attached to strings. I could take them all down with one pull. And they all know it, so they do what they can to please me."

"You mean everyone but Kal Stavros?"

"I told you it was just a matter of time before someone tried to blackmail you."

"You never said anything about blackmail. What does Kal have against you?"

"Nothing." And that was the truth. "He merely wishes to have control over me, as all mortals wish."

Wasn't that what all mortals wished for? Why they all bargained? In hopes that they could defy death.

Hades studied her, and while he did not expect her to accept all this so easily, there was one thing he wished to know now.

"Are you afraid of me?"

Her eyes widened.

"No," she said instantly. "But it is a lot to take in."

There was a note in her voice that worried him, though he was beginning to understand why she seemed to think she did not know him at all. He swallowed, looking down at his feet before he met her gaze once more, swearing, "I will tell you everything."

She raised a brow, as if to say *I will make sure of it*.

"I think I've heard enough tonight. I'd rather go home."

"Would you like Antoni to take you?"

He did not think she would like to return to the Underworld with him, not after everything she had learned, but she smiled and said, "You might as well take me. We are going to the same place, after all."

He drew her close, and with her body pressed against his, a wave of relief shuddered through him, and he took her home.

When they appeared, she drew away from him and disappeared into the bathroom to shower. He did not follow, choosing instead to have a drink before shedding his clothes and lying down to rest.

When Persephone returned to the room, she was dressed in a long shirt that hit midthigh. His eyes traveled up her body until he met her gaze. She had halted upon leaving the bathroom and stared at him from across the room.

"Are you well?" he asked.

She nodded slowly, and his question seemed to thaw her frozen body. She rounded the bed and climbed in on her side. They faced each other in silence, and after a moment, Hades touched her face, a light brush across her flushed cheek. She surprised him by turning her head into his palm and pressing her lips to his skin. As she did, he leaned in to kiss her, slow and soft and sweet.

When he pulled away, they shared breath as he spoke.

"Let me make love to you," he said, his voice low and warm, imbued with the gentleness he intended to show her. She nodded, and he kissed her once more. When he shifted to straddle her, he kept his weight on his hands and did not crush her, brushing his lips along her jaw, neck, and collarbone. As he explored, her breaths grew shorter and uneven, and her hands played across his skin, fingers gliding through his hair. He dipped to kiss between her breasts, plying each peaked nipple with his tongue through the fabric of her shirt.

When he came to her stomach, he sat back on his heels to lift her shirt, but Persephone took over, remaining on her back as she wiggled the fabric up and over her head. When she was still once more, he pressed his lips to her stomach, moving down her body in a slow, predatory climb.

He could smell her arousal. The air around her center was almost damp with it, and he was eager to touch his tongue to her clit, to circle her flesh until she came against his mouth. He was also eager to praise and to worship, so he sat back once more and kissed from the inside of her knee to the apex of her thigh, repeating the process down her other leg before pressing a kiss to her center. Persephone's hands clamped down on his head, and as she held him there, he offered a soft laugh, looking up at her from where he hovered.

"Do you want something, my darling?" he asked.

She stared down at him, eyes gleaming. "You said you would make love to me," she answered.

"Yes," he agreed.

"Then do it," she said. "Now."

A smile curled his lips as she spread her flesh, and he let his tongue slide along her silken skin and circle her clit. Above him, Persephone sighed, and her fingers tightened in his hair to the point that his scalp stung, but he didn't care because she had begun to press harder against his mouth, seeking depth that he could only offer with his fingers, so he curled those inside her too and moved in rhythm, her cries growing in intensity.

"Yes," she breathed. "Yes."

Her hands slipped from his hair and her body tensed.

"Do you want to come?" he asked.

She gave a guttural cry, and her answer was her release, a gush of warmth and wet that coated his fingers, and as he let them slide from inside her, he took them into his mouth to taste her.

Beneath him, she was limp, but he climbed up her body and placed his weight against hers while he kissed her, his cock cradled between her thighs. Her hand drifted down his body, and she reached between them, closing her hand around him as she jerked him up and down. He groaned into her mouth.

"Fuck. *Fuck.*"

He would have let her continue if he had not intended for this to only be about her, so he took her hand and pinned it by her head, rising to spread her legs apart with his knees. With his cock poised at her center, he slipped inside. Once more, he settled close, holding his weight on his forearms, and kissed her deeply, and while his lips were locked with hers, he began to move.

Persephone lifted her legs, wrapping them firmly around him, her heels pressing into his ass. With each thrust, they dug in harder, as if she wanted to absorb him.

He moved his arm beneath her head and looked into her eyes.

"There are few truths in this world," he said, "but the one you must always remember is that I love you."

"I love you too," she whispered and brought his mouth to hers.

His words came with a shift in the way they moved, and suddenly there was an urgency to their pace that had their bed rocking and their bodies dripping with slick sweat. Their breaths grew ragged and rough, and they prayed to each other to let the other come. When they finally did, it shattered through their bodies, rocking them deep to their cores until they were both boneless.

After, Hades rose with her and bathed before returning to bed, where he curled himself around her and fell into a deep sleep.

Later, he awoke suddenly to find he was alone. He sat up and looked around the room, but Persephone was gone. For a brief moment, he thought she had left the Underworld entirely, but he could feel her here, so he rose and went in search of her. As he stepped into the dim halls of his palace, he smelled warm cocoa and knew he would find her in the kitchen. She had a habit of baking when she was stressed, and it was only now that he realized she had not done so since she'd taught him how to make sugar cookies at her apartment.

He moved through the dining room, where he found Cerberus, Typhon, and Orthrus resting near the door to the kitchen. They looked up as he passed, and he entered, finding Persephone on the floor of the kitchen, sitting with her knees pressed to her chest, staring into the oven, its yellow light illuminating her somber face.

"Couldn't sleep?" he asked, and she turned toward

him looking very much exhausted and sad. He knew she was thinking of Lexa.

"No," she said. "I hope I didn't wake you."

"*You* didn't wake me. Your absence did," he answered truthfully.

"I'm sorry," she said, frowning.

"Don't be—especially if it means you are baking."

He sat beside her on the floor and stared into the oven window for a few seconds before looking down at her and finding her watching him.

"You know I can help you sleep," he said, voice low.

"The cake isn't finished," she whispered in reply.

He could tell she was exhausted, that she wanted to sleep.

"I would never let it burn," he promised and placed his arm around her shoulder as her head rested against his chest. It wasn't long before she was asleep, and he drew her into his arms and carried her back to bed before returning to the kitchen just in time to have an alarm go off.

The sound startled him, and he turned swiftly toward a small white timer Persephone had left on top of the oven. It was still ringing when he picked it up and tried to silence it, except that the knob came off in his hand.

"What the fuck?" he said and set it back down, covering it with a bowl to try to muffle the sound, but as soon as he did, everything went quiet. "Fucking Fates," he muttered, turning his attention to the cake and then shifting his gaze around the kitchen, realizing he had no idea where anything was stored.

If I were oven mitts, where would I be? he thought, opening cabinet doors and drawers until he found a pair...except that they did not fit his hands.

"Gods-dammit," he cursed.

Why was this so fucking difficult?

He searched the drawer for another option but did not find one. He supposed he would have to make do with what he had.

He opened the oven, and a wave of heat accosted his face, causing his eyes to sting. He reached inside in an attempt to pull the cake forward on the rack, but his knuckles hit the top, instantly burning them.

"Ouch!" He pulled back and growled.

This time, he tried shoving his hand inside the mitt, but only his thumb and forefinger fit. Still, it was better than nothing. As he reached in once more, he pinched the edge of the pan, dragging it off the rack, when it slipped. Without a second thought, he reached to catch it between his bare hands.

"Motherfucker!" he yelled, managing to toss the cake onto the oven.

He stood there for a moment while the pain throbbed in his hands before sending a shock of magic to heal his blisters.

"Fucking cake," he said, glaring at it. "You better be delicious."

CHAPTER XIX
Helios Is an Asshole

It had felt like an age since Hades had managed to handle anything related to the Graeae and Medusa, between Hera's tasks and Persephone's struggle with losing Lexa. He needed to make plans to lure Helios into helping him locate the sisters, but before he did that, he wanted a moment with Leuce.

The next day, he manifested outside the nymph's apartment door and knocked furiously until the door cracked open. He knew he had just woken her from sleep. She was bleary-eyed, and her white hair was a tangled mess.

"Good morning, Leuce," Hades said, pushing open the door.

The nymph stumbled back, tugging her robe around her.

"Ha-Hades," she said. "What can I do for you?"

"You can tell me truthfully," he said. "Did you give Persephone the password to Iniquity?"

She was silent.

"Tell me!" Hades yelled.

"What else was I supposed to do?" she demanded. "You weren't there. You didn't see her crumble!"

Hades blanched. "What are you talking about?"

Leuce huffed a sigh. "She had a panic attack while we were out because of something that happened to her friend. The one in the hospital. It *scared* her, Hades. I don't have much, but I wanted to help, so excuse me for trying!"

"You sent her to *Iniquity* for help," he said.

Despite the fact that Leuce had not been in the modern world long, she understood the purpose of Iniquity and knew it was not a place he'd want Persephone to know about. It was hard for him to believe that she thought sending her there was a sound decision, rather than believing it might create a divide. "You could have had coffee!"

"*We did*, you idiot bastard!" Leuce seethed. "How dare you think a hot drink will cure what she's going through!"

There was no curing this, he wanted to yell. Therein lay the problem—Persephone was *grieving*.

"You expect me to believe you sent Persephone to a Magi because you wanted to help?"

"What are you suggesting?"

"That you sent her into a trap!"

"Because I could never do something nice for someone, is that it?"

"How many times do I have to say, sending Persephone to a Magi was dangerous. Not to mention you *knew* I would find out. Were you hoping to create a divide between us?"

She had already tried once when she had introduced herself as his lover. Hades had suspected then that her intention was to cause trouble. Why should he believe any differently now?

"This is why our relationship never worked! You never trusted me."

"Obviously, I had good reason."

Leuce turned and reached for the nearest object—a winged statue—which she flung at Hades, who dodged it. "Get out!" she yelled as it crashed into the wall behind him.

Hades straightened slowly, glaring at Leuce.

"Fine, but mark my words, Leuce. I will find out who you are working for. In the meantime, stay away from Persephone."

Upon leaving Leuce's apartment, Hades returned to the Underworld and now stood among fifty heads of snowy-white cattle. When he had taken them from Helios, he'd only intended to choose the best among his herd, but he had run out of time, so he'd stolen them all. Later, Helios would refuse to drive his golden chariot through the sky if Hades did not return them, and Zeus thought it such a threat that he called Council over the ordeal.

In the end, Hades refused to return the cattle, and the sun still shone. Though, Hades had to admit, he did not exactly understand what it meant to suddenly own fifty new animals.

"You all stink," he said. "I will never understand why Helios likes all of you so much."

"I think they're wonderful," Hecate had said when

he brought them back. She'd been so ecstatic, she'd named each one and made garlands for their necks, though Hades could not tell them apart. Now all he really needed was to choose the best among them so he could lure Helios into helping him locate the Graeae and maybe even Medusa, though he feared bringing up the powerful gorgon. He did not trust the God of the Sun.

How did one choose a prized cow?

He turned in a circle while they grazed around him, looking for signs of superiority, but he was at a loss. They were all the same color and the same build, as if Helios had merely made clones. Perhaps this was a job for Hecate, who seemed to appreciate the finer details and differences of the animals she took responsibility for, though before he could summon her, his eyes caught on Thanatos approaching almost apprehensively.

It was strange enough that Hades stopped and stared. Thanatos's presence was always vibrant despite his black robes and his pale face and hair, and while he never looked particularly overjoyed, he did always look serene and peaceful.

Except today.

Today he looked stricken, which put Hades on edge.

"Thanatos," he said as the god drew nearer, his heart hammering hard in his chest.

"Lord Hades. I..." Thanatos paused and took a breath, then began again. "I went to see Lexa today. To...prepare for the next phase. It's...almost time."

Hades swallowed hard. He had no words, because there was nothing to say. As much as he did not want this for Persephone, it was the way of things. Lexa had made her decision, and it would be hard to grasp, given that

Persephone would never quite understand why Lexa would choose to leave her.

"While I was there, Persephone…"

Thanatos's voice trailed off, and instead of speaking, he chose to project his magic into Hades's mind. What he saw play out before him shocked him. He could see Persephone through Thanatos's eyes, demanding, "*You're working. I want to know who you're here to take.*"

"*I can't tell you that,*" Thanatos responded.

Persephone's gaze flashed, and three words slipped from her mouth like a weapon.

"*I command you.*"

"*Persephone.*" Hades could hear the desperation in Thanatos's voice. Those words had hurt the God of Death because they had communicated Persephone's mistrust of him, and despite the fact that she did not want Lexa's soul reaped, all Thanatos was trying to do was make the process comforting.

"*I won't let you take her,*" Persephone snapped.

"*If there were another way—*"

Thanatos felt desperate to communicate to Persephone, to help her understand he was not the enemy but Lexa's advocate, and her soul had called to him, had decided it was time to leave.

"*There is another way, and it involves you leaving!*"

Then she pushed him, and Hades did not know whose shock he felt more acutely—Thanatos's or his own.

"*Get out.*"

"Enough!" Hades shouted, and the images vanished from his mind.

A heavy silence followed. Hades stood still as a stone,

processing what he had just seen. His feelings raged, a storm of emotions that he couldn't quite place. In that moment, he had seen Persephone's raw fear, but he had also seen a side of her that was angry and a little manipulative.

The greater issue was that she was still trying to stop Lexa's inevitable death.

"How long does she have?" Hades asked.

"A day," Thanatos replied. "Maybe two."

Another long bout of silence.

"She's ready, Hades," Thanatos added softly, and the note in his voice was exhausted.

Hades could just imagine that was how Lexa felt. She was tired.

He could do nothing but nod.

"Reap when you are ready, Thanatos," Hades instructed. *And I will deal with Persephone*, he thought, even as he dreaded the encounter. She would not understand, though there was a part of him that did not understand either. He liked Lexa, knew that she was a good friend to Persephone. Every interaction they'd had was fun and pleasant. Despite this, the girl still wanted to leave, but Hades was not one to deny pure souls, and he would not deny this one rest, even if it hurt Persephone more than anything in the world.

Hades approached Thanatos, placing a hand on his shoulder. He had hoped it was a reassuring gesture, but the contact only made his dread deepen because he could sense the chaotic emotions in the god's energy.

"I'm sorry, Hades," Thanatos said, and it was a reminder that despite their familiarity with death, some things never got any easier.

Hades left the meadow and made his return to the

palace on foot to give himself time to process what he had seen through Thanatos's eyes. By the time he made it to the throne room, he was no closer to releasing that strange frustration, disappointment, and pain. He considered how often he had talked to Persephone about this, how he'd attempted to prepare her for the possibility of Lexa's death and still she seemed determined to prevent it, and that worried him far more than anything else, because she had already tried to bargain in exchange for Lexa's life.

Perhaps she needed to hear the consequences from the King of the Underworld, not her lover.

He sat on his throne, hands curled around the arms, closed his eyes, and searched for the familiar pull between them, the strange link he shared with no one else. He always knew when he found her because he felt instantly at peace, as if he were somehow more complete. This time, as he latched on to her magic, he pulled her to him, teleporting her to his realm.

It was, for the most part, a move designed to illustrate his power, and when she appeared in the dark-reddish light of his throne room, she looked severe, angry, and hurt. She didn't even speak to him when she arrived before she was already attempting to teleport. When her magic did not work, she snapped.

"You cannot just remove me from the Upperworld when you please!"

"You are lucky *I* removed you and not the Furies."

"Send me back, Hades!" Her voice was raw with anger. It was a tone he had never really heard from her before, but grief was strange, and it transformed emotions into monsters. For Persephone, it also made her magic riot. It boiled between them, thickening the air, and he wondered what she would do with all that energy building inside her. Would flowers bloom at her feet, or would vines burst from the floors?

"No."

He wouldn't keep her against her will, but he wasn't going to let her leave until they discussed how she had treated Thanatos. Persephone's magic seemed to have other ideas, and he felt it ripple and watched in horror as thorns erupted from Persephone's skin like blades—at her shoulder, her side, and her calves. She was immediately covered in blood, and she sank to her knees with a cry. Hades's shock brought him to his feet, and he raced down the precipice to her side.

"Stop!" she sobbed, shaking from her pain. "Don't come any closer!"

There was no fucking way he was going to leave her alone. She'd nearly exploded in a bloody heap of thorns, and he didn't think that was an exaggeration. Her magic had done this. It had gained power from her anger, and when it had nowhere to go, it just manifested like this.

He knelt beside her, unsure of what to do. She had gone so pale, and it was made worse by the light, which made her blood look black.

"Fuck, Persephone. How long has your magic been manifesting like this?"

"Don't you ever listen?" The words slipped from between her clenched teeth.

"I could ask the same of you," he said humorlessly as he lifted his hand, intent on healing her, though he hesitated a moment, waiting for her to protest. The pain must have won out because she said nothing.

He winced as he placed his hand on the first wound.

The thorn was sharp and wet from her blood, the skin around it shredded. He gritted his teeth as it healed and moved to the next one on her side, then the two that protruded from her calves. When he was finished, he sat back, hating the feel of her blood on his hands so much, they shook.

"How long have you kept this from me?" he asked, knowing it had not gotten this bad overnight.

Has she told Hecate? he wondered.

"I've been a little distracted in case you haven't noticed," she replied bitterly, her breathing still not quite right. "What do you want, Hades?"

She sounded defeated as she spoke, and the tone of her voice put Hades more on edge. He felt as though she were pulling away from him once more, but this time it was worse. It should have made him desperate, but instead, he was angry.

"Your behavior toward Thanatos was atrocious. You will apologize."

She glared. "Why should I? He was going to take Lexa! Worse, he tried to hide it from me!"

"He was doing his job, Persephone."

"Killing my friend isn't a job! It's murder!"

That word—*kill*—he hated it. It tore through him like an arrow to the heart. She acted as if he wanted this to be Lexa's fate, as if she'd forgotten who exactly he was.

"You know it isn't murder! Keeping her alive for your own benefit isn't a kindness," he hissed. It was the harshest he'd ever been with her. "She is in pain, and *you* are prolonging it."

"No, *you* are prolonging it. You could heal her, but you have chosen not to help me!"

"You want me to bargain with the Fates so that she might survive? So you can have the death of another on your conscience? Murder doesn't suit you, goddess."

Throwing the word back at her must have hit her just as hard because she tried to hit him, but he caught her hand and pulled her close. The blood that coated his palm was drying and felt sticky as he held her. Being this close added another level to his pain, as it reminded him of the night before, when they had come together so passionately.

Was this their love? These two extremes that felt so desperate all the time?

Then her hand curled into a fist, and her head fell against his chest as she began to cry.

"I don't know how to lose someone, Hades."

It was moments like this when he realized that his heart no longer belonged to him.

"I know," he said, taking her face into his hands. "But running from it won't help, Persephone. You are just delaying the inevitable."

"Hades, please," she said, desperate, and then whispered, "What if it were me?"

No.

He released her. "I refuse to entertain such a thought."

"You cannot tell me you wouldn't break every Divine law in existence for me."

Hades's power preened at the thought.

"Make no mistake, my lady, I would burn this world for you."

He had said it before, but perhaps she did not quite understand what that meant. There were no rules, Divine or otherwise, when it came to her. She was the exception. It did not matter that no one else thought so. He did, and he was the end.

"But that is a burden I am willing to carry. Can you say the same?"

She did not speak, and he was not surprised. Likely she was thinking of all those threads burned into his skin, though that was not even the worst part.

The worst part was the guilt.

"I will give you one more day to say goodbye to Lexa. That is the only compromise I can offer. You should be thankful I'm offering that."

Later that day, Hades stood unseen in a large, open meadow. On the springy, green grass, he placed one of Helios's pristine cows. By the time he had returned to the Underworld to retrieve a cow, he no longer cared about choosing the best, and the only reason he saw this plan through was because he'd like to locate the Graeae. It made him anxious that there had been no contact from their abductors, no hint of where they had been taken. He considered that perhaps Medusa had something to do with their disappearance, in which case it would have been more of a rescue. Perhaps that was why no one had come to collect the eye.

The cow mooed, drawing Hades's attention.

There was a flash of light across the way, at the very edge of the field, and Helios appeared. His purple robes fluttered around him, as if seconds behind his movement. There, he paused and scanned his surroundings, obviously suspecting a trap. Still, he vanished once more and appeared closer to the cow, again peering into the trees surrounding the meadow. The next time he appeared, it was beside the cow.

He rested his head on its back and threw his arms around its middle.

"Oh, Rosie!" He moved around to her front and lifted her long face in his hands, touching his nose to hers. "I have missed you."

Watching this exchange made Hades feel very uncomfortable.

"I'll take you far from here where you can never be taken away from me again."

He kissed the cow's nose—once, twice, and as he went in for the third, Hades appeared.

"I'm sorry. I just can't watch this."

Helios released the cow and stepped back, glaring.

"*You*," he said, gnashing his teeth. "I knew it."

"Yet you came anyway."

"Where are the rest of my cows?" he demanded.

"Waiting to be returned to you," Hades replied.

The God of the Sun narrowed his unsettling amber eyes. "You want something."

"Of course I do. I know you've been watching the trials Hera's put me through."

Helios saw everything that transpired on Earth, even the things he pretended to ignore. The entire reason Hades had abducted his cattle in the first place was because he'd refused to give the location of Sisyphus, the man who had stolen souls with a relic he had obtained from Poseidon.

The god gave a lazy smile. "I watched long enough to see your face get beat in by Heracles. That was a satisfying fight. Pity he did not win."

"Or better that I won," Hades said. "Or your cows would have become permanent residents of the Underworld."

There was a beat of silence.

"Is this your peace offering? Rosie? Or are you offering the whole lot?"

"Think of Rosie as a start," Hades said. "The more cooperative you are, the more Rosies you get back."

Helios's mouth tightened. "What do you want?"

Despite knowing that the God of the Sun was very aware of what Hades needed, he decided it was best not to quarrel with him—as much as that was possible given his mood.

"I need to know where the Graeae are located. They were taken from Dionysus's club."

Helios laughed and Hades frowned, uncertain about what exactly his response meant.

"You are so busy searching for the gray monsters, you haven't even noticed what is unfolding around you."

"And what exactly is that?"

"Unrest," he said. "And do you know what unrest breeds?"

War.

Hades did not say the word aloud because he did not wish to speak it into existence, but he knew what Helios was implying.

The god laughed again. "I predict another war soon. Olympianomachy," he said in a lofty voice, smiling. "It has a certain ring to it, doesn't it?"

"So certain we will lose?" Hades asked.

"I have no doubt."

Helios was loyal to only himself. Even his choice to

side with the Olympians rather than his fellow Titans was born out of a wish to maintain his well-being rather than loyalty to Zeus.

"You forget that you are all seeing, Helios," said Hades. "Not all knowing."

"I've always chosen the winning side," said Helios. "That has never been by chance."

"Treason is a poor look, Helios."

"I have taken no action," said the god. "And I am helping you. That is far from treasonous."

He was helping, albeit resentfully.

"What does all this have to do with the location of the Graeae?"

Hades could speculate all day long, but he asked because he wanted a direct answer.

"Everything," said Helios. "I am doing you a great service in telling you that the Graeae were intended to be a weapon. Their gift was supposed to be the foundation on which a war was built against the Olympians."

Hades was not surprised.

"Intended?"

"We both know you are in possession of the eye, and without it, the sisters are blind...*useless*."

Hades gritted his teeth. They were not useless, even without the eye. In fact, Hades felt like the greatest power they possessed was the secrets they kept.

"You said they were intended to be the foundation on which a war was built. What do you mean?"

He did not want to mention Medusa, even if Helios was aware of the gorgon. He'd rather the god bring her up on his own.

"Hades, don't play dumb. Their eye gives access to

the future. It is a valuable tool for anyone in battle. In the…wrong…hands, it is an avenue to lay the foundation for victory."

It was a thought that had crossed Hades's mind before.

"Who took the Graeae, Helios?"

"Is that what you wish to know? Who took them, or where they are? You only get one question, one answer. I have already given you a mine of gold."

"Are you not interested in obtaining the rest of your cattle?"

"Rosie here will do," Helios said, patting her back. "With her, I can breed a new herd."

Hades curled his lip in disgust.

"Choose wisely, Hades," said Helios.

He did not need to think long. The most immediate need was obtaining the Graeae. Hades would find out who abducted them later. In fact, he thought he could already guess who was responsible. There was only one organization bold enough to think they could go against the gods—Triad.

Though that thought was paired with the image of Hera and Theseus sitting side by side during his second trial. Had Hera found an avenue through which she intended to overthrow Zeus?

"Where are the Graeae?" Hades asked at last.

Helios offered a wicked smile.

"Lake Tritonis," he said. "You'll find them held in the caves."

The God of the Sun pulled Rosie close, his great strength allowing him to carry the animal under his arm.

"You are about to find out, Hades, that you're on the wrong side."

Hades narrowed his eyes at the message but said nothing. Not that Helios would have listened, because in the next second, he was gone. Hades could safely say that while he'd suspected an inevitable uprising against the Olympians, he had always thought that relics would be the avenue through which an opposition would attempt to gain power over them—not via literal divine monsters. Worse yet, divine monsters could be created, and if Triad was responsible for this, if they had managed to gain the support of a handful of Olympians, then they were far more of an adversary than Hades had thought.

At least now he had a path forward, and it began at Tritonis.

He called up his magic to teleport when Hera appeared in the clearing.

"Fucking Fates," he said, the words coming out slowly as a hiss.

"Hades," she said, a wicked smile on her face. "I've been looking for you."

CHAPTER XX
The Amazons

Now is not the time, he wanted to say, but he knew what she would threaten.

His future with Persephone, though he had done enough to damage that himself during their last encounter. His chest ached at the thought of how he'd left her—with no comforting words, only a countdown to say goodbye to her friend—and even though he had fucked up, he did not need Hera making it worse. It was that thought that made him relent, despite the pressing matter of locating the Graeae.

He would just have to send Ilias to Lake Tritonis. For a brief moment, he'd considered including Dionysus in the retrieval, but he did not know the god's loyalties, and with a potential revolt on the horizon, he did not want to take any chances.

"What is it?" he snapped. He saw no reason to hide his resentment of the goddess. Especially after what she had put him through during the last two labors, though that only made his stomach churn. What did she have planned for him next? Was it to be something far worse?

"I'd like you to retrieve Hippolyta's belt," she said, almost casually.

Hades's brows lowered. That was a relatively tame ask given what she had saddled him with before.

"Hippolyta's belt," Hades said. "Why?"

"Do not question my wants, Lord Hades. It is none of your business."

Hades narrowed his eyes. "Does Ares know of your wants?"

"The belt was his gift to Hippolyta. I see no reason to ask him."

Hades glared. There was nothing particularly stunning about the belt. It was leather, and Hippolyta wore it to symbolize her status as Queen of the Amazons. Its only power was that it gave its wearer superhuman strength, a useless power for both Hippolyta and Hera, who already possessed such a skill.

Unless, of course, it was an attempt to gain another weapon in her fight against Zeus. The belt could give an Impious mortal the power to face a god.

Hades's mood darkened, and suddenly he wondered just how much his labors had intertwined with her ultimate goal of overthrowing Zeus.

He did not let himself think on that long, though. He filed the information away for later. Perhaps he was onto something—something that would allow him to end Hera's labors and prevent her retaliation against Persephone.

"Do whatever you must to trade," she said. "You have until sunset."

Hades gave a frustrated growl as she left. He took out his phone and called Ilias.

"Yeah?" the satyr answered, out of breath.

Hades arched a brow. "Are you in the middle of something?"

"Running a marathon," Ilias replied, a sarcastic edge to his voice.

Hades did not question it. "When you are finished," he said, "I need you to travel to Lake Tritonis and secure the Graeae. Tell no one. I will be back as soon as possible."

"Got it," Ilias replied, and when Hades hung up, he vanished.

The Amazons lived in Terme, which was north of New Greece, and while part of the mainland, it existed on no mortal map. A smaller island extended off the coast, which they called Themyscira and used as a training ground. The landscape of Terme was lush and green, the terrain made of cresting hills and deep divots where white water flowed over great rocks. Their city was encased in a tall and expansive wall of stone and graying brick. Its towers and gates were heavily guarded as there was always a brave mortal or two trying to scale the walls, and depending on their intentions, they were either released or held in prison under Queen Hippolyta's discretion.

It was at one of those gates that Hades appeared. While it was likely he could have appeared at Hippolyta's sanctuary, doing so would have been considered in poor taste, and since he was going to ask a favor of the Amazon queen, he decided against it.

The two women at the gate were tall and stood at

attention, dressed in bronze hoplite armor, including a helmet, breastplate, and greaves. They carried bronze shields that reached from their chins to their knees and spears in their right hands. They were stoic and strong.

While they stood still before the wooden gate, he could tell by how they stiffened that they did not expect to see him.

"Lord Hades," the one on the left said. "To what do we owe the pleasure?"

"You don't have to lie," he said. "I need to speak with Hippolyta."

The Amazon on the right used her spear to knock on the gate thrice, and the doors opened to reveal the interior of the Amazons' oasis, which was just as lush, packed with evergreen oaks, cypress, and flowering myrtle and oleander. Dirt paths wound through identical homes that were composed of sun-dried mud bricks and covered in a flowering vine that smelled strongly of honey.

On the other side of the gate, another Amazon waited. She was dressed the same as the two guards and said nothing to him, only turned and led him down the winding road. Hades followed between the tightly built homes. The floral smell was stronger here, and Hades noticed plump bumblebees moving from flower to flower, zipping between him and the Amazon he followed.

The path led to a round courtyard that was several feet below ground level and accessible by a set of stairs that extended around the entire perimeter. Despite the center being covered in sun-dried brick, the Amazons had managed to make the space look just as lively as the surrounding landscape, filling great stone pots with flowers and greens. Opposite this gathering place were more of the same homes, and from over the tops of their roofs, the mountainous terrain of the rest of Terme was visible, where clouds hung low to meet their peaks.

Despite the fact that the Amazons had a queen, there were no palaces here, and Hippolyta did not even sit on a throne. She was queen because of her knowledge and expertise in battle.

Nothing else mattered.

The Amazons not on guard wore white peploses and cloaks. Some wore gold or leather belts while others chose ribbons, and their hair was braided into intricate styles that kept it off their necks and out of their faces—a completely practical choice, both due to the heat and because of its interference in battle.

Hades followed the guard down the steps into the lower courtyard. There was a large fountain in one corner where the women could draw drinking water and a firepit where they cooked community food, but the thing that caught Hades's attention was a metal pole protruding from the ground and the woman tied to it.

Hades nodded toward her.

"What did she do?"

The Amazon did not look in her direction but answered, "Slept with a man outside the mating ritual."

Hades said nothing. The Amazons procreated once a year with a tribe called the Gargareans, keeping only the female children born from the couplings—males were returned. It wasn't that the Amazons hated men; they found them unnecessary for anything outside of sustaining their society, so to seek one out beyond necessity was considered shameful.

And dishonor among the Amazons was a death sentence.

Hades could not help looking at the woman who was staring down at her feet, and while she appeared stoic and unbothered by her punishment, he could see her pain in the details of her body—the way her toes curled into her sandaled feet, the tremor that shook her legs, the hard fists she made behind her back, the set of her mouth that seemed to make her jaw far more prominent. The metal at her back had to be scorching, and if he had to guess, her skin was covered in blisters.

They continued across the courtyard, though as Hades looked ahead once more, he found Hippolyta approaching. There was something enchanting about her face. Perhaps it had something to do with her eyes, which were pastel green and heavy-lidded. She looked perpetually bored but stern. Her blond hair was braided away from her face and she wore white. Cinched around her waist was her leather girdle. It was a plain piece of ornamentation that laced closed at the front, though as far as relics went, it was probably best it was so unremarkable. No one expected mediocrity from the gods. They'd assume it had no power save its utility.

"Lord Hades," she said. "You are here to see me?"

"I am," he said. "I've come to ask for your belt."

He saw no need to be anything other than direct. He did not have time, and neither did Hippolyta.

There was a pause. "I appreciate that you do not dally, though your request seems out of character."

"It is."

He said nothing more, not wishing to offer an explanation, and Hippolyta did not ask for one, likely because she did not care. The Amazon queen studied him for a moment, then said, "I am not opposed, though it would need to be a fair exchange."

"I have a trade in mind," he said. "Though it is not conventional."

He was not certain Hera would like it, though she had not said *when* he had to obtain Hippolyta's belt, and her final message had given him more room for interpretation than she had probably intended—*do what you must to trade.*

"Go on," she said.

"I am in need of an aegis," he said, indicating behind him with a nod. "And one of your own is in need of honor."

"Zofie is young," Hippolyta said and, like the other Amazon, did not spare her a glance. "She has a wandering eye that causes her to lose sight of what is truly important."

She was speaking of discipline.

"Perhaps a charge will give her focus," Hades said. "If she brings honor, then I will return her to you in exchange for the belt. If she does not—"

"You will kill her," Hippolyta said.

Hades was not surprised by the queen's quick command. It was likely their plan for her to begin with, so he nodded.

Not one to delay, Hippolyta nodded.

"We have an agreement, Lord Hades," she said and glanced at the Amazon who stood a few paces behind Hades. "Bring her."

The guard left to retrieve Zofie, and with her departure, Hippolyta turned her attention to Hades.

"There is unrest out there," she said. "I feel it in my blood."

That premonition was something she had inherited from Ares. It was a type of magic that stirred their lust for battle, and it only confirmed what Helios had said about war.

"You are not wrong," Hades replied, grimacing.

Hippolyta inclined her head. "You do not like war despite its benefit to your kingdom."

"There is no benefit for traumatized souls," Hades said, and as much as the Underworld could offer healing in peace, receiving souls who had died in battle was not an easy thing to witness.

The queen said nothing, and the guard returned with Zofie. Hades turned to observe the woman. He had been right about the blisters. Her skin was bubbled, not only from where the metal pole had touched her but from where the sun had beat down on her shoulders and arms. It was likely her scalp looked the same, though it was hard to tell given her dark hair, which was long and braided. Her hands were still bound, but she no longer looked down. She met his gaze with piercing green eyes.

"Lord Hades has offered you a chance at honor," said Hippolyta, and when the Amazon heard her speak, her eyes lowered to the ground once more. "If you are found to be inadequate at any point, he has been ordered to kill you."

There was a moment of silence.

"Look upon me once more, Amazon," said Hippolyta,

and Zofie obeyed. The address communicated the hope Hippolyta had that she would succeed.

"Thank you, my queen," Zofie said.

Zofie said nothing more, and Hades could not tell what she thought. There were some who might see being in his care as a worse sentence than dying by exposure.

"Goodbye, Hades. Perhaps I will see you again," Hippolyta said, though there was an element of dread that came with her words, given that she had spoken of war.

He nodded, and the armored Amazon returned them to the gate in silence.

Once outside it, he faced Zofie and tapped her shoulders, healing the blisters while releasing her from her bonds. Her eyes widened as her arms fell to her sides, and as she lifted them to rub each wrist, she whispered, "Thank you."

"It is not for me to judge what has been viewed as an indiscretion by your people," Hades said. "All I care about is that you protect my future queen. Do you understand?"

Her expression shifted from surprise and gratitude to one of serious acceptance. She nodded. "Of course, my lord."

He had to admit, he felt a little less fretful, knowing that Persephone would be actively protected, but his peace was soon disrupted by a call, which he took outside the gates of Terme.

"Yes?"

"They're dead," Ilias said, and Hades felt his stomach clench. "All three. Recent too."

Hades found Ilias in a cave off the side of a rocky cliff that faced Lake Tritonis. The satyr stood over three dead bodies. Each appeared to have attempted to crawl away from their attacker, with a hand outstretched and a foot curled into the dirt. It had been a long time since he had seen the three sisters, but even in death, they looked no different. Aged faces, hooked noses, and deep frowns. Their bodies were cloaked in black, their snow-white hair peeking from beneath a hood.

"They were stabbed," said Ilias.

Hades could not see the blood for the black cloaks, but he could tell that the cloth had been sliced everywhere. The attack had been brutal and cruel. Still, the fact that the three sisters lay dead at his feet was shocking, considering they were deities in their own right and their powers included the ability to heal wounds, though these were numerous.

The wind outside howled and whistled, a harrowing wail that seemed to mourn the deaths of the witches. Hades made a circle around them, pausing to kneel near one—Deino, he believed. He reached out and touched one of the wounds. His fingers came away stained with red and black—blood and poison that burned.

"Hera," Hades said quietly.

"What?"

Hades rose to his feet and smeared the mixture of blood and poison on the wall.

"They were stabbed with hydra blood–tipped blades," Hades said. "I fought and killed the hydra days ago. I was on my way here when Hera ordered a new labor, which is why I sent you instead."

It had been a distraction, and it had given Hera the

time she needed to order the deaths of the Graeae. The question was why?

After a moment of silence, Hades nodded to Zofie, whom he had brought along, seeing no point in wasting time depositing her elsewhere.

"This is Zofie. She is Persephone's new aegis. She needs armor and weapons. Get her settled. After that, I need you to look into Hera's dealings with Theseus."

He was beginning to see an end to her labors and any hold she had over his marriage to Persephone.

CHAPTER XXI
Divine Retribution

Night had come, and Hades was in search of Dionysus. He'd first gone to Bakkheia, only to be stopped at the doors and informed that the God of the Vine was not there. When Hades had asked where the god might be, he received no answer.

There were few places he might be, or at least to Hades's knowledge, but one of them included the Theater of Dionysus, which had been erected to honor and worship him. It was there Hades ventured, to the horseshoe-shaped theater that was located downtown near the Acropolis where Persephone worked.

On this night, a comedy called *Lysistrata* was being performed. The play's title character decides to end the Peloponnesian War by encouraging her fellow Athenian women to abstain from sex with their husbands, a tactic that eventually succeeds. Onstage, the actors and chorus wore grotesque masks with an array of expressions, and despite some that were to appear serene and content, they were all somehow horrifying with wide, gaping mouths and hollow eyes. Some wore wreaths on their heads wrapped with ivy and berries. Peals of laughter broke out during song and dance and spoken word, though Hades did not hear the performance, his gaze focused on the crowd.

He found Dionysus sitting at the very front of the orchestra. The seats to his left and right were empty, likely a request he'd made so that he could sit alone.

Hades approached and took a seat beside him. Dionysus kept his gaze on the performance as he spoke. "Have you come to tell me the Graeae are dead?"

"I assumed you would know by now," Hades said. "Seems I was right."

Dionysus did not offer any information on how he had found out, but Hades guessed that one of his maenads had spied Ilias handling the situation and communicated their discoveries.

There was silence between them, though all around, the performance continued and the crowd reacted, laughing and cheering.

"I don't understand," Dionysus said at last.

"Don't you?" Hades countered.

It was the first time the God of the Vine looked at him. "What is that supposed to mean?"

"The Graeae were just as much a weapon as the secrets they kept," Hades said. "It's clear whoever killed them preferred to sacrifice their use rather than allow the power to fall into our hands."

"You keep saying 'our,'" Dionysus pointed out. "We are not on the same side."

"Then what side are you on?"

Hades never thought he'd feel any kind of way about Dionysus's allies until now, and he had to admit, he hoped that he'd align with him.

Though, he did not know what it meant to take sides yet. All he knew was that someone—potentially Hera and Theseus—was learning to kill the divine. The divide was complicated. Aligning against them seemed to mean siding with Zeus, which was not something Hades particularly wanted.

"I am on my own side," Dionysus said.

As much as Hades respected that, this was not a situation where being neutral would work.

"You realize the death of the Graeae means more than the loss of Medusa," Hades said. "It means that someone has found a way to kill us."

"Then it sounds like I need to be on their side," Dionysus said.

Hades's lips flattened. "Is that your plan?" he asked, then tilted his head. "I wouldn't have thought you'd be the first to kneel."

Dionysus's jaw tightened. "This isn't about submission, Hades. It's about lying low until the opportune moment."

"And what moment is that, Dionysus? When everyone stronger than you is dead?"

"You're not very strong if you're dead."

They were quiet for a few moments before Hades said, "I've never really liked you."

"Nor I you."

"But I respected you because I thought you were a protector." Hades thought about all the women he'd pulled out of harmful situations, how he had trained them to protect themselves. He had helped them take back their power, yet here he would let the Graeae's deaths go unavenged. He would hide. He was a coward. "Turns out, you are...but only of your own interests."

He noted how Dionysus swallowed at his comment, and Hades rose to his feet.

"I am not saying choose a side," Hades said at last. "I'm telling you to choose allies. This is not a war that will see any of us unpunished."

With that, he left the theater.

It was late when he returned to the Underworld and found his bed empty.

He had not expected to find Persephone there, but it reminded him of how they parted and made his chest feel like an open chasm. Despite this, he tried to sleep, but all he saw when he closed his eyes was her on the floor before him, sobbing and bleeding.

I don't know how to lose someone, Hades, she'd said, and as much as he knew what that was like, he realized he didn't know how to lose her, but that was exactly what was happening. The ironic part was that all he'd been doing this whole time was fighting to keep her—or at least the possibility of their future together.

He must have fallen asleep eventually, because he woke later with a pounding headache. His mouth felt dry and his tongue swollen. He stumbled out of bed and poured himself a drink, but before he could take a sip, a strange feeling straightened his spine, and an unnerving silence blanketed the room. He set his glass down with a click and headed for the balcony, summoning his clothes as he did.

In the distance, beyond the mountainous peaks of Tartarus, the gray sky had begun to whirl and rumble.

The Fates were angry.

What the fuck had happened?

He started to teleport as dread gathered heavily in his stomach, but a hand on his shoulder stopped him. He turned to find a pale-faced Thanatos.

No. It can't be.

He knew what the God of Death was going to say. He could already feel the betrayal in his bones, grinding away.

"She did it," Thanatos said. "Persephone did it. She made a deal with Apollo to heal Lexa."

There was something about this that dissolved his previous feeling of regret and turned it to rage. His body shook with it. How could she have been so reckless, and to involve *Apollo*? After he had been so clear about his hatred for the God of Music? After he had bargained to get her out of owing him anything? Had his sacrifice meant nothing to her?

Hades curled his fingers into fists and met Thanatos's haunted eyes.

"Release the Furies," he commanded.

Hades did not often like to call on the Furies. They were not discreet creatures, and their presence in the Underworld—as well as on Olympus—was always known.

He did not even flinch when their horrific cries breached the air, pricking his skin as he turned to see three winged creatures explode from the depths of Tartarus to retrieve Persephone and Apollo.

Hades felt like he was being torn to pieces from the inside out, his anger was so acute.

Was there no end to this turmoil?

He had killed friends and monsters, bargained and sacrificed. He had made deals to protect and promise a future that he was beginning to think only he wanted.

Hades teleported to Nevernight, where he waited for the Furies to bring his captives. He'd have done this in the Underworld, but he did not want to offer Apollo another invitation into his realm. It was not long before he sensed their approach, an energy so volatile, it made the hair on the back of his neck stand on end.

He watched as Persephone and Apollo landed at his feet. Persephone was deposited gracefully, landing in the position she had fallen when the Furies had captured and paralyzed her with their venomous snakes, while Apollo was dropped right on his face. Hades appreciated the satisfying crack that followed his landing and probably would have grinned had he not been so fucking angry… devastated…betrayed.

His eyes shifted to Persephone, who rose to her feet on shaking legs.

The first thing he noticed about her was how tired she looked. She was pale, her eyes were red, and the shadows beneath them looked deep and dark. She likely had not slept last night if she'd been with Apollo, but it still worried him, more so when she met his gaze. Her eyes had no luster, and he could feel her apprehension and fear. It built between them, as sharp and tangled as thorned vines.

"Fucking Furies," Apollo groaned.

Hades's attention shifted to the god as he got to his feet. The Furies must have pulled him from sleep, because he wore a floral robe and his usually pristine hair was a mess.

Hades would have liked to pummel him into the ground until he reached the depths of Tartarus but refrained from making a single move. Once he began, he wouldn't stop. This kind of rage had no rationale. It coiled through him, tightening every part of his body until he wanted to burst.

"You know you could upgrade to something a little more modern to enforce natural order, Hades," Apollo said, oblivious to Hades's fury. "I'd rather be carried off by a well-muscled man than a trio of albino goddesses and a serpent."

"I *thought* we had a deal, Apollo." Hades spoke slowly, his face growing hot from his anger. He had not invited Apollo into his realm to bargain for *this* to happen.

"You mean the deal where I stay away from your goddess in exchange for a favor?" Apollo's voice dripped with sarcasm.

Hades waited, actively suppressing the overwhelming urge to punch the god's teeth down his throat.

"I'd have been more than obliging, except your little lover showed up at Erotas demanding my help. *While* I was in the middle of a bath, I should add."

"No, you shouldn't," Persephone said, the words slipping from between clenched teeth.

Hades's jaw flexed. Erotas was a brothel in the pleasure district where clients bid on men and women they wanted to fuck. Apollo was a regular visitor, bidder, and, he imagined, fucker, and the thought of Persephone walking those streets and entering that house made Hades feel sick.

"She can be very persuasive when she's angry. The magic helped. You never said she was a goddess. No wonder you snatched her up quickly."

Hades's mood darkened further at that comment, and he glanced at Persephone. This was the last thing she should want for herself. Apollo had gained more than just a bargain with his lover. She had given him power over her in the form of a secret. He imagined she knew by now that the God of Music wouldn't let that go to waste.

"I could hardly deny her request when she had razor-sharp thorns pointed at my nether regions."

Hades's mood lightened at that comment, and he almost smiled at the image of Apollo being castrated by Persephone's magic. Then he remembered that he had probably been naked during this entire encounter and frowned.

"So we struck a deal. A *bargain*, as you like to call it. She asked me to heal her little friend, and in exchange, she provides me with...companionship."

"Don't make it sound gross, Apollo," Persephone hissed, glaring at the god, and while Hades watched her, she did not look at him.

"Gross?"

"Everything that comes out of your mouth sounds like a sexual innuendo."

"Does not!"

"Does too."

"Enough!" Hades snarled.

Persephone startled, her eyes finally meeting his, and

once more, he saw her fear. There was a part of him that wanted her to be afraid, because he wanted her to understand the severity of what she had done. This had consequences beyond anything he could control.

He held her gaze as he continued to address Apollo. "If you are no longer in need of my goddess, I would like a word with her. Alone."

Apollo did not hesitate. As arrogant and irritating as he was, he knew when to push buttons.

"She's all yours," he replied and vanished without another word.

Silence stretched as Hades stood opposite Persephone, trying to understand what she had done, why she had done it.

I don't know how to lose someone, Hades, she'd said. So had she just decided not to learn at all?

"What have you done?"

Persephone's eyes flashed. Normally, he would have fed her defiance because he loved her passion, but this—this was misguided.

"I *saved* Lexa."

"Is that what you think?"

He took a step toward her, and his magic snaked around him. He couldn't tell if it was trying to protect him or Persephone because he was losing his temper, and by the time he stood inches from her, he no longer bore his mortal glamour.

"She was going to die—"

"She was *choosing* to die!" Hades shouted. She stared back, her eyes glistening. "And instead of honoring her wish, you intervened. All because you are afraid of *pain*."

"I am afraid of pain," she yelled back, her voice

imbued with a hatred he had never heard before. "Will you mock me for that as you mock all mortals?"

"There is no comparison," he spat. "At least mortals are brave enough to face it."

Her whole body seemed to flinch in that moment, igniting her magic and pushing thorns from her skin. Hades watched once more in horror as her body became covered in bleeding spikes. They ran down her arms, over her back and stomach, and down her legs. If she did not learn control, she would tear herself to pieces. He reached for her because he didn't know what else to do, and despite everything, he could not stand watching this. He wanted to heal her—not just these physical wounds but the ones on her heart and soul.

"Persephone—"

But she took a step back, shutting down his advances. She inhaled sharply as she made a miserable attempt to cover the thorns by crossing her arms over her chest.

"If you cared, you would have been there."

"I *was* there!" He had been there every time she had come to him, and each time, she had begged him to save Lexa's life.

"You never once came with me to the hospital when I had to watch my best friend lie unresponsive. You never once stood by me while I held her hand. You could have told me when Thanatos would start showing up. You could have let me know she was...choosing to die. But you didn't. You hid all that, like it was some fucking secret. *You weren't there.*"

His eyes widened, and the heaviness in his chest expanded into his stomach. It was true he had not considered many of those things, but that was because he had never given courtesies in death. He'd also been pulled away nearly every other day by something. If it wasn't the Graeae, it had been Hera's trials.

"I didn't know you wanted me there," he said, his voice quiet. He had thought the time she spent with Lexa at the hospital was time she wanted to herself.

"Why wouldn't I?" she asked, brows lowering.

"I'm not the most welcomed sight at a hospital, Persephone."

"That's your excuse?"

The edge to her voice made him feel defensive. "And what's yours?" he asked, voice raising once more, despite how badly he wanted to remain calm. "You never told me—"

"I shouldn't *have* to tell you to be there for me when my friend is dying. Instead, you act like it's as…normal as breathing."

"Because death has forever been my existence!"

"That's your problem!" she said, letting her hands fall to her sides, flinching as she did. Her arms ran red with blood and it dripped to the floor. Hades's stomach twisted and his throat felt tight. He wanted to fix this. "You've been the God of the Underworld so long, you've forgotten what it is really like to be on the brink of losing someone. Instead, you spend all your time judging mortals for their fear of your realm, for their fear of death, for their fear of losing who they love!"

"So you were angry with me," he said, and the more he continued, the more incensed he felt. "And once again, instead of coming to me, you decided to punish me by seeking *Apollo's* help."

Why was it always Apollo?

"I wasn't trying to punish you. When I decided to go to Apollo, I no longer felt like you were an option."

There was a pain to those words that lanced through his chest. Did she know how badly that hurt him?

"After everything I did to protect you from him—"

"I didn't ask that of you," she snapped.

"No, I suppose you didn't," he replied bitterly. "You have never welcomed my aid, especially when it wasn't what you wanted to hear."

"That's not fair." Her voice shook.

"Isn't it? I have offered an aegis, and you insisted you do not need a guard, yet you are regularly accosted on your way to work. You barely accept rides from Antoni, and you only do now because you don't want to hurt his feelings. Then, when I offer comfort, when I try to understand your hurt over Lexa's pain, it isn't enough."

"Your comfort?" she shouted. "What comfort? When I came to you, begging you to save Lexa, you offered to let me grieve. What was I supposed to do? Stand back and watch her die when I knew I could prevent it?"

"Yes!" he shouted, throwing up his hands. "That's exactly what you were supposed to do. You are not above the law of my realm, Persephone!" Not even he was above the law of the dead, and he wore that reminder on his skin. "I don't see why her death matters. You come to the Underworld every day. You would have seen Lexa again!"

"Because it's not the same!"

"What is that supposed to mean?" he demanded.

She crossed her arms over her chest once more. Each time, she flinched, and he thought that maybe her anger made her momentarily forget her pain. But as she stood there facing him, she seemed to fold in on herself, as if she were afraid to say whatever she was truly thinking.

"What happens if you and I...if the Fates decide to unravel our future? I don't want to be so lost in you, so anchored in the Underworld, that I don't know how to exist after."

A thickness gathered in his throat. Losing Lexa to the Underworld was too great of a risk in the event that they did not make it, and the worst part was that everything he had been doing up to this point—the absurd labors, seeking out the Graeae, the truce with Dionysus—was for her. To ensure they had a future.

Was she so uncertain?

"I'm beginning to think that maybe you don't want to be in this relationship," Hades said.

"That's not what I'm saying."

"Then what are you saying?"

She looked confused and afraid as she answered. "I don't know. Just that...right when I was really starting to figure out who I was, you came along and fucked it all up. I don't know who I'm supposed to be. I don't know—"

"What you want," he finished.

"That's not true. I want you. I love—"

"Don't say you love me," he said, looking away. "I can't...hear that right now."

The words would hurt. They did hurt. If she loved him, why was she planning for a future without him?

After a stretch of silence, Persephone spoke in a sad whisper. "I thought you loved me."

"I do," he said, frowning, and he considered that

perhaps he put too much faith in the threads that wove them together. "But I think I may have misunderstood."

"Misunderstood what?"

"The Fates," he answered, eyes lifting to hers. How was it possible that she looked more stricken now than before? "I have waited for you for so long, I ignored the fact that they rarely weave happy endings."

"You cannot mean that," she said, her voice breaking.

"I mean it," he said, and his tone was just as sad. "You'll find out why soon enough."

Because it was likely she would blame him for anything that happened to Lexa moving forward. He called up his glamour and straightened the sleeves and lapels of his jacket.

He looked at her one last time. She was a haunting image. Pale and sad and bleeding, and he knew he would regret leaving her like this, but he would regret it more if he stayed.

"You should know that your actions have condemned Lexa to a fate worse than death," he said, then left Persephone behind in Nevernight.

CHAPTER XXII
A Desperate Plea

Hades tried to channel his aggression into a productive torture session, and while that usually helped lighten his dark mood, this time, it only succeeded in making him feel far more chaotic. He could not unsee Persephone's pain, could not unhear her words.

You weren't there.

The accusation tore through him as he considered what he would do differently, but did any of that matter now that they were here? On the other side of her decision to go to Apollo for help? She had explicitly broken the rules of his realm.

He wondered if she had been proud of herself when she'd discovered an alternative to healing Lexa in the God of Music. Had Apollo explained that his bow and arrow only healed bodily wounds? Had he been clear that it could not heal a broken soul? Had he been so mesmerized by Persephone's offer of companionship that he'd failed to consider the consequences of his own actions?

Likely he had not cared at all.

And that was another thing—*the companionship.*

Hades gritted his teeth. Now he had to watch Persephone frolic about New Athens with the same god who had fucked his former lover, and while he felt that Persephone resented Apollo too much to fall victim to his wiles, he worried that the god would force her into situations that would harm her.

He'd have to think of a great enough threat to keep the god in line. Otherwise, he'd never feel comfortable with that arrangement.

When Hades finally left Tartarus, he went in search of the Graeae, finding them nestled in a rocky, cave-like area at the edge of Asphodel that mimicked their home in the Upperworld. While he did not approach, he watched them from afar, sitting on a set of large rocks while a fire danced before them. They talked and cackled and passed a bowl from which each of them drank, and the only solace Hades took from their deaths was that at least here, they seemed at peace.

Eventually, Hades returned to the palace, though he felt a great sense of foreboding knowing Persephone would not be there. It was made worse when he found his way barred by Cerberus, Typhon, and Orthrus. They stood on all fours, lips curled back, showing their teeth as they growled.

"So you are betraying me too?"

"No one has betrayed you," Hecate said, approaching. It was as if the goddess had formed from the darkness behind her.

Hades flattened his lips and glared. "I recognize Persephone is far better than me, but you cannot ignore her blatant disregard for the rules of my realm."

"You sound like a child," Hecate chided.

"Hecate, I am in no mood—"

"Likely not. You are rarely in a mood for anything other than sex, which, from what I have seen, will not happen anytime soon."

Hades curled his fingers into fists and turned on his heels, but Hecate had teleported and blocked his way once more.

"As much as Persephone must deal with the consequences of her actions, so must you, and one of those is hearing what I have to say to you."

"And what can you have to say to me that I don't already know?" Hades snarled. "That I fucked up? That I should have been more present?"

"Maybe you should have been more present, but you weren't, so what are you going to do now?"

Hades stared and Hecate repeated herself.

"What are you going to do now, Hades?"

"I...don't know," he admitted. He hadn't thought beyond what had happened today, hadn't even processed it completely, though he had taken a few key things from their interaction, and one of those was that Persephone wasn't even certain about the future of their relationship.

"I heard that," Hecate snapped, and Hades's eyes flashed.

Hades grit his teeth. "We had an agreement, Hecate, that you would not read my mind."

"And I respect it when you aren't being a complete

and utter idiot," she replied. "You are just as uncertain about your future as Persephone."

"I have every reason to be," he countered. Had he not just spent the past few weeks entangled in a battle with Hera to ensure that the goddess sided with him when it was time to ask Zeus for permission to marry Persephone?

"You are so centered on securing her hand in marriage, you aren't even focused on laying the foundation for it. Just because the Fates have entangled your future doesn't mean you have no work to do."

Hades stood in a tense, angry silence. In part, he was not ready to hear any of this, but he also knew that Hecate was right.

"You have bent to Hera's will out of fear, yet I ask you, does her blessing mean more than the love you have for Persephone?"

"Of course not," Hades snapped. She was simplifying Hera's intentions. It wasn't just about approval of their future but assurance that she would not harm or curse Persephone as a means to get back at him.

"Perhaps the worst part of all this is that she doesn't even know what you've been fighting for. You haven't told her. You've told her nothing. You did not even tell her the consequences of bringing Lexa back."

"She should trust me."

"Fuck you, Hades."

He stared, a little shocked by her vitriol.

"You want her to be your queen, to stand beside you in judgment of souls, yet you could not even tell her that broken souls never come back right. You could have *shown* her the consequences. She is not some mortal who came to beg at your feet for a bargain."

A thickness gathered within Hades's chest. It was almost suffocating and nearly impossible to swallow it down.

"People like Persephone, who have been told half-truths and lies their whole life, need more than words, Hades, and you—you have to realize this isn't even about love or trust anymore. It's about you. Your fears. Your insecurities. You cannot continue to live a life and not show her the world you have created, no matter how awful or hard or scary. She deserves to know what it means to love you fully. Do you not wish for that?"

"I wish for it," he admitted. "But I do not believe she will love all parts of me."

"That is unfair to her," Hecate said. "You think her darkness cannot love yours? She was made for you."

Hades lowered his eyes and felt the weight of his defeat.

"Now what are you going to do about this?"

"I…don't know yet."

"You do not have to know today," she said. "But you will have to decide, because Persephone is about to learn what it means to bring Lexa back, and she will need you, more than anything."

Hades frowned. He suspected that whatever lay before her with Lexa would be far worse than what was behind them now.

"Come, boys," Hecate said. "We have work to do."

Hecate left the hallway, and each of his Dobermans glared at him before turning one by one to follow the goddess.

Hera did not come to collect Hippolyta's belt, which further confirmed Hades's suspicion that she had not truly cared about the labor so much as she wished to use it to distract him. He was certain now that he understood the goddess's motives, though he had yet to confirm her alliance with Theseus.

When he'd refused to participate in her revolt, Hera had sentenced him to labors that would benefit her. The death of Briareus was revenge but also ensured that Zeus would not be able to call on a great ally who had defeated her in the past. Fight night had likely been a test to evaluate the use of the hydra, the Stymphalian birds, and Heracles as weapons against the gods. Obviously, they'd found a use for the hydra's venom, and while Hades did think that Hera could have used Hippolyta's belt, he knew now that it was a decoy.

She'd unwittingly managed to manipulate Hades into benefiting her cause, and he resented it—but he would find a way to get back at the goddess. She would regret her entanglement in his life.

In the meantime, Ilias had prepared Zofie for her assignment. They'd agreed that she would keep her distance by using a particular power Hades had been surprised to learn she possessed—the power of shape-shifting. The power itself was not unusual; he'd just not expected the Amazon to morph into an average white cat. Still, it meant Zofie could keep a close and discreet eye on Persephone, which gave Hades peace of mind considering they were currently not speaking. As much as he wanted to, he did not know how to move forward yet. Apologies seemed too trivial here, but perhaps that was the only way to begin again.

"Are you even listening?" There was an edge to the voice that brought Hades out of his thoughts, and he met a pair of brown eyes. They were set in the face of a mortal man with dark, curly hair and thick glasses. He was Hades's first bargain of the night, and potentially his last.

He could not focus on this right now.

"No," Hades admitted, and as hard as it was, he offered an apology. "I'm...sorry. Please continue."

The young man's lips were pressed thin, a reflection of his anger, but he sighed and continued. Before Hades had zoned out, the man had explained that his grandmother had been his guardian since the age of five and she was now dying.

"The doctor has given her two months to live," he said. "Please...she's all I have."

Hades frowned at the young man. "I will not bargain for the life of a soul," he said, and though they were the words he always used to deny a request like this, they were harder and more painful to say this time.

His rejection just seemed to spur the mortal on.

"Then I need to bargain for something else," the man said, searching for ideas. "The money to get her the care and medicine she needs. Maybe there's a chance—"

"Have you asked your grandmother what she wants?" Hades interrupted him.

He blinked. "What do you mean?"

"Have you asked your grandmother if she is at peace with dying?"

"She doesn't want to leave me," he said defensively.

"I did not ask you if she wanted to leave you," Hades said. "I asked if she is at peace with dying."

The mortal did not respond.

Hades rose to his feet. "Ask her. Respect her answer."

It was what he wished he had told Persephone.

He left the suite and headed into the lounge, where mortals were gathered beneath low light playing poker, blackjack, and roulette among other games.

"Will you take another contract?" Ilias asked, coming to stand beside him.

"No, no more tonight," Hades replied.

Ilias nodded. "Then I'd like you to meet me at the Grove in an hour."

Hades raised a questioning brow.

"This is something you have to see," the satyr promised.

Hades did not question him beyond that and left the lounge. As he passed Euryale, the gorgon inhaled, her head rising, casting light over her scarred and blindfolded eyes.

"Troubled, Lord Hades?" she asked.

"More than you can imagine, Euryale," he said, continuing to the balcony that overlooked the floor of Nevernight.

As he looked down at the floor, he recalled the first time he had seen Persephone. If she had existed during the Trojan War, it would have been her beauty that had launched a thousand ships.

She'd sat with Lexa, Sybil, and Adonis. He remembered worrying over whether she liked Adonis and if she'd leave with him, though he had known then he wouldn't let her leave because the urge to claim her, to mark her, almost sent him to her side then. He had been both bewildered and disturbed by his fierce need for her and had returned to the Underworld only to find that her thread was woven with his—that she was his fate, and even now, in the face of all this pain and anguish, he did not want it any other way.

He sighed, rubbing a spot just over his heart that felt tense and knotted, when his phone rang. When he saw the caller was Antoni, he answered with dread in his stomach, because this likely had something to do with Persephone.

"Yes?"

"Ha-Hades?" Antoni asked.

"Who else, Antoni?" he asked, frustrated already.

The cyclops laughed nervously. "Of course, my lord. I am sorry, my lord. It's just…uh…I was on my way to pick up Persephone, you see? At the Pearl where she insisted on going after work, and…uh…she's gone."

"*Gone?*" Hades repeated.

"She just…vanished. Zofie said she was there one moment and gone the next."

"Fuck," Hades said under his breath. He hadn't considered that Zofie likely could not follow when Apollo chose to call on his bargain with Persephone.

"Where is Zofie?"

"She's…with me."

Hades was quiet for a long moment as he attempted to locate Persephone through her magic, but the connection was dead, which only added to his irritation.

"Wh-what would you like us to do?" Antoni asked.

"It's likely you can do nothing," Hades said, though he would try to send Ilias's team to search for her. There were a number of clubs Apollo was known to frequent.

"We're sorry, my lord," Antoni said.

He sighed, frustrated, and then managed, "How is Zofie?"

"Ah, well, she's...I think she expects to be... *murdered*."

"Tell her it isn't time yet," Hades replied and hung up.

He seethed for a moment, his frustration renewed, though he was less angry at Persephone than he was at the situation she'd put herself in. She was at the mercy of another god, and as much as he hated that, he knew she hated it more.

Hades did ask Ilias to send a few of his men out to search the various clubs for Apollo while he did his best to stay occupied as he waited for Persephone's magic to flare to life once more, and when it did, he teleported, appearing in her room. He heard voices coming from the living room—Sybil, Zofie, and Antoni.

"What did Apollo make you do?" he heard Sybil ask, and he held his breath as she answered.

"He wanted me to judge a karaoke contest," Persephone replied. "And he threw a fit when I did not choose him as the winner."

Hades felt a sense of pride that she had refused to name Apollo as the winner, though anxiety quickly followed at the thought of what he'd do in retaliation.

"Tell me you didn't, Persephone," Sybil said, sounding shocked. "Apollo does not lose."

"Well, he did tonight," she replied smugly. "He could not hold a candle to Marsyas. I doubt he will be eager to have me judge him again. He ended the night with a kick to the balls."

A smile curled Hades's lips.

She was definitely the opposite of Leuce.

There was a beat of silence.

"Any updates on Lexa?" Persephone asked. It was a

question delivered with care and a little trepidation as if she feared the answer, though she knew it would not be death.

"She was still asleep when I visited," Sybil answered.

Another bout of silence followed, and there was an energy running through him that made him impatient to see her. He had no idea what kind of struggle she had faced when Apollo had snatched her to do his bidding, had no idea what sort of stress and anxiety she was feeling in the aftermath of Lexa's...*healing*...but it did not sound good or pleasant.

"I'm going to bed," Persephone said after a while. "See you guys tomorrow."

She noticed him immediately upon entering her room and closed the door. She did not pause in surprise or hesitate to be alone with him.

"How long have you been here?" she asked.

"Not long," he said.

There was a pause as she threw her purse on the bed. "You know what happened?"

"I overheard, yes."

She swallowed and asked in a quiet voice, "Are you angry?"

"Yes, but not with you."

He took two steps forward, which brought him close enough to touch her. He placed his hands on her arms, swept them up to her shoulders, and then touched her face. Her skin was warm, and she smelled like vanilla and lavender—pleasant and sweet.

He wanted to pull her close and bury his face in her hair. He wanted to kiss her and make love to her. He wanted to promise her things that were beyond this world.

"I couldn't sense you," he said, staring hard at her. He wanted to know how she did it, how she cut him off from her magic. "I couldn't find you."

"I'm here, Hades. I'm fine." Her tone was hushed, and she stared up at him, placing her hands on his forearms.

Fine.

She was fine.

That word rattled through his head wrong, and he released her, reaching to turn on the light. When he looked back at her, she was squinting.

"You will never know how difficult this is for me," he said. He wasn't even sure what he was talking about—if it was Lexa or Apollo or just the distance he felt between them, a dark chasm that lay at their feet, though Persephone obviously thought she knew, because she had a reply.

"I imagine as difficult as it's been for me to deal with Minthe and Leuce, except that Apollo has never been my lover."

Hades glared. He did not like Apollo's name and the word *lover* spoken so close together, and if he could, he would take them from her mouth and spit them on the ground.

"You have not been to the Underworld." He tried not to make it sound like an accusation, but he could not help it. When she was angry, she seemed to avoid it altogether. She crossed her arms, as if she wanted to deflect his words.

"I've been busy."

"The souls miss you, Persephone." *I miss you.* "Do not punish them because you are angry with me."

She glared at him. "Don't lecture me, Hades. You have no idea what I've been dealing with."

"Of course not," he said, surly. "That would mean you'd have to talk to me."

"You mean like you talk to me?" she countered. "I'm not the only one with communication problems, Hades."

He pressed his lips together and took a step away from her.

"I didn't come here to argue with you or lecture you. I came to see if you were okay."

"Why come at all? Antoni would have told you."

She'd have probably preferred that. He looked away from her, scowling. "I had to," he said and took a breath. "I had to see you myself."

She stepped toward him. "Hades, I—"

"I should go," he said. "I'm late for a meeting."

And while it was true, he knew he was really running from her.

Hades teleported to the Grove, which, while he owned it, was operated by Ilias. He preferred anonymity and applied the same practice to his other restaurants scattered about—a couple of pubs and cafés, even a few street carts. If there was one thing Hades had learned in the time he had been alive, it was that people tended to talk more when drink and food were close at hand. It was a great way to gather intel on the various happenings across New Greece.

He manifested beside Ilias, who stood in the shadows on the rooftop restaurant, observing operations. Staff buzzed about carrying trays of drinks and food, and there was a low murmur that ebbed and flowed as people conversed and ate and moved dishes about. It was the only indication of how busy it truly was, since parties were hidden in pockets of lush flora.

"Right on time," Ilias commented, glancing at Hades once and then nodding as a host led two familiar individuals to a table out of sight.

One was Theseus.

The other was Ariadne.

"Shocking," Hades said, though his voice was monotone, and he was not so much surprised as he was disappointed. Now he wondered what the detective's objective had been when she had begged for his help.

"They dated very briefly," the satyr explained. "But it seems Theseus was more interested in Ariadne's sister, Phaedra."

This was the first time Hades had heard that Ariadne had a sister, and if that were the case, why were they at the Grove?

"Thank you, Ilias," Hades said before he called up his glamour to move unseen between gardens, lush alcoves, and canopied groves. He found the pair at a round table nestled in a recess of vines.

"I am in need of a favor," Theseus was saying.

"I'm sure we can come to some kind of agreement."

He seemed to ignore her comment and continued. "I need you to help remove any suspicion your fellow detectives may have that I am involved with the Impious."

"Why?" Ariadne asked, her voice on edge.

"Rumor has it they are about to become more... vocal."

She did not ask what that meant, but Hades thought he had an idea, and he didn't like it. The Impious were mortals who did not worship the gods. It was more of a belief system than it was an institution, though some chose to organize under the banner of Triad. It was an organization that used to terrorize the public to prove that the gods were passive, but with Theseus at the helm, they pretended to put aside their aggressive tactics in favor of appearing peaceful, though if Hades had to guess by Theseus's ask, he'd found a new avenue to execute his violence, and he didn't want the connection known.

"How can I possibly be responsible for what people think, Theseus?"

"You can. I do it all the time."

"Just like you've done with my sister?"

The demigod did not flinch at her retort, though Hades was certain she meant it as an insult.

"Since you brought her up, I'll remind you what's at stake."

"You already owe me one visit with her, Theseus," she said, leaning across the table as she spoke through her teeth. "I helped you find the Graeae."

"And they were useless," he said.

"Like you?" she countered with her usual venom.

Theseus glared. "I am not the one who consistently fails to deliver."

"I deliver. You just don't like the results."

"And you must not like seeing your sister."

She sneered at him, but Hades noticed how Theseus stared at her, eyes set intently on her mouth. It was a predatory gaze, and after everything he had said to her tonight, it made Hades want to pluck his eyes from his head and shove them down his throat.

"Put that mouth of yours to good use and do as I say," said Theseus.

A tense, hateful silence followed, then Ariadne spoke. "If I do as you say, when can I see my sister?"

"That depends entirely on you," he replied.

Hades did not like whatever hold Theseus had over Ariadne's sister—or Ariadne, for that matter. It was as if Theseus was holding her prisoner and only granting access to Phaedra when Ariadne performed like he wanted. Knowing the detective like he did, it was unlikely she'd see her sister again. Ariadne wasn't someone to be controlled.

Now he wondered why she'd come to him about the missing women in New Greece. Had she thought her sister was among Dionysus's maenads before she'd discovered otherwise?

Hades frowned and returned to Ilias, who he found directing staff in the kitchen. He tried to ignore how the clamor of dishes and chatter ceased at his presence.

"Theseus has Ariadne's sister," said Hades. "Find out why and who she is."

Ilias nodded, though he did not take his eyes off his task, which was rolling silverware into black napkins.

"And keep an eye on them, especially Ariadne," Hades said, biting the inside of his lip as he thought about the detective. He worried for her and feared the longer Theseus strung her along, the less he would need her. Knowing the demigod, he was already planning how to dispose of her. She knew too much and wasn't someone he could charm, which meant he couldn't keep her around long term.

"Of course," said Ilias.

"Hey! You can't go back there!" someone shouted, disrupting his debrief with the satyr. For a moment, he thought that perhaps Ariadne had somehow spotted him, but when he turned, he found Leuce bursting through the kitchen doors.

"Hades!" She said his name, but he couldn't tell if she was surprised or relieved at his presence. His lips flattened as he watched the pale nymph approach, wide eyed and out of breath.

"What do you want, Leuce?" He was still angry with her about Iniquity, not to mention he still believed she was working against him and Persephone.

"I just..." she began, then hesitated. "Will you take me home?"

Hades and Ilias exchanged a look before the god asked, "Why?"

"I...I just feel *afraid*."

"You feel afraid?" he repeated. Leuce was a lot of things, but never afraid.

"When I was walking home from Iniquity, I got the sense someone was following me," she said, and Hades frowned. Likely, she wasn't wrong. Now and then, a few unsavory characters would linger outside Iniquity and attempt to track various attendees to darkened allies. Usually, they were interested in obtaining an obol to get into the club. "I stopped here because I thought Ilias might be able to help." Her eyes shifted to the satyr.

"I can take her home, Hades. It's nothing."

"No," he said. He'd rather have the satyr here watching Theseus and Ariadne. It was far easier for him to take Leuce. Though he did not relish time spent with her, he would hate to discover that something had happened to her.

"Keep watch," Hades reminded Ilias before ushering Leuce out of the kitchen and into a waiting elevator. They did not speak as they took it to the first floor of the parking garage and exited onto the street. Hades looked about as he set off east down the road, and though he saw no one moving in the shadows, he did not trust that whoever had been following her had not walked on to head her off while she was in the restaurant.

"Hades, wait!" Leuce called, and in the next moment, he felt her hand reach for his. Her touch slithered through him, and he jerked his hand away.

"Don't touch me," he said.

"Sorry. I was just trying to keep up."

Hades said nothing but slowed his pace, which allowed her to walk beside him, the steady tap of her heels grinding on his nerves.

"I hope you have forgiven Persephone for attending Iniquity."

"There was nothing to forgive," he replied.

"Then have you forgiven me?"

Hades did not respond, because the answer was no.

Leuce scoffed. "Where is this understanding for me? Where was it when we were together?"

Hades cringed. "I have no interest in reflecting on my past with you, Leuce."

"You've changed for her."

"You only think that because you were gone so long," Hades replied. "You know nothing about me. Not anymore."

"I...I'm not saying that because I am angry," she said.

"I'm saying that because I like Persephone. Despite what you think, I do not wish her harm."

"Perhaps if you'd admit that Demeter gave you life, I'd be more willing to believe that."

"If you want answers, you'd have to do more to protect me, Hades," she replied.

Those words gave him pause, and he wondered what she meant—or rather, what she feared. They said nothing else until they had made it to Leuce's apartment. She unlocked the door and stepped inside.

"If protecting Persephone meant protecting you, I'd do whatever it took," Hades said.

"You can start by giving me a new job," she said and then offered a small, sad smile. "I've already said too much."

Then the nymph slammed her door in his face.

Before Hades returned to the Underworld, he stopped by Persephone's room, where he intended to tell her about his night—namely that he had seen Leuce home. However, when he manifested, he found her asleep, and given that she had been so tired earlier, he did not wish to wake her, so he smoothed his hand through her hair, inhaling her sweet scent before pressing a kiss to her forehead.

"I love you," he whispered and vanished.

CHAPTER XXIII
A Game of Pride

"You are really going to hate this," Ilias said and dropped a copy of the *Delphi Divine* in front of him as he sat at the Nevernight bar the next morning.

Before the words were out of his mouth, Hades already felt a heaviness in his throat and stomach. Somehow, he knew what was coming.

The headline read:

**HADES STEPS OUT WITH
MYSTERIOUS WOMAN**

Below that was a picture, snapped at the precise moment Leuce had reached for his hand. It was as if someone had been waiting to take it, and in that frozen second, it appeared that he had been holding her hand, dragging her hurriedly down the shadowed street. There was a lot someone could infer from it, but all he cared about was that Persephone knew the truth.

As he stared at the photo, he studied Leuce's face, who had schooled her features into a placid mask, the opposite of how she had looked when they had faced each other.

I'll help you when you admit that Demeter gave you life.

Well, if this wasn't fucking proof.

She had set him up.

A sharp, black spire shot from the tip of his finger, and he used it to shred Leuce's face before rising to his feet.

"I'll be back," he told Ilias before vanishing.

He manifested on the sixtieth floor of the Acropolis, at the entrance of *New Athens News*. There was a young blond at the front desk who gasped and stood. As he walked past her, she started to speak. "Can I...?"

"No," Hades growled, having already found the object of his visit—Persephone, who rose to standing, dressed in black. She was beautiful and striking, and her anger and pain hit him with a force that nearly stole his breath.

He swallowed down the dread crawling up his throat and continued toward her.

"You need to leave," she whispered furiously, though it was so quiet on the floor that her words carried.

"We need to talk."

She leaned forward just an inch, eyes alight, determined in her refusal to hear his explanation. Clearly, she'd already decided what to believe, and there was a sharp pain in his chest that made his heartbeat feel slow and sluggish.

"*No.*" The word was harsh and definite.

His features hardened. "So you believe it then? The article?"

"I thought you had a meeting," she threw back at him, and it was the first time he heard the hurt leak into her voice.

"I did." It was frustrating that she didn't believe anything he had said.

"And you conveniently left out the fact that it was with Leuce?"

"It wasn't with Leuce, Persephone."

She looked away, clenching her jaw. "I don't want to hear this right now. You need to leave."

She came around her desk and walked past him toward the elevator. He turned to follow.

"When are we going to talk about this?" he asked.

"What is there to talk about?" she asked, jamming the button for the elevator. "I have asked you to be honest with me about when you are with Leuce. You weren't."

"I came to you immediately after I saw Leuce home, but I didn't feel good about waking you. When I saw you yesterday, you looked exhausted."

She whirled to face him. "I *am* exhausted, Hades. I'm tired of you and sick of your excuses."

That was a lie. Well, part of it was, anyway. She wasn't tired of him.

"Leave!" She pointed to the open doors of the elevator, but if she thought he would go without discussing this, she was wrong.

He drew his arm around her waist and hauled her into the elevator with him, choosing a floor at random just so the doors would close. Once they were alone, he sealed the lift with magic. It wouldn't move and it wouldn't open for anyone.

Hades placed Persephone on her feet, his hands on

her waist, and he leaned into her, bracing one hand on the wall.

"Let me go, Hades! You're embarrassing me," she said. Hades felt a twinge in his chest at the sound of her tired and defeated voice. Her hands were on his chest as if she wanted to push him away, but she didn't. "Why did you have to do this *now*?"

"Because I knew you'd jump to conclusions. I'm not fucking Leuce."

She paled at his words and shoved against him. "There are other ways to cheat, Hades!"

"I'm not doing any of them!"

And a horrible sickness twisted through him, knowing that she thought he had. Though it seemed after hearing those words, she'd lost her energy to fight. She stood between him and the wall, her arms at her sides, staring at his chest.

"Persephone." He closed his eyes against her name. "Persephone, please."

"Let me go, Hades," she said quietly.

He wanted to touch her, to lift her face so he could look into her eyes. So he could beg her not to think what she was thinking, but he realized she was not ready to hear anything right now, and while he hadn't wanted to give her time to think, to agonize, to wonder what had really happened, this wasn't how he'd wanted to have this conversation—not through force.

"If you won't listen now, will you let me explain later?"

"I don't know," she whispered.

"Please, Persephone. Give me the chance to explain."

"I'll let you know," she said, her voice thick with tears.

"Persephone."

He moved to brush her cheek, but she turned away. There was a strangeness to this pain between them, and it went deeper than Leuce. His heart felt very broken, a shattered thing that moved about in his chest, puncturing whatever it came into contact with. After a moment, he stepped back, giving her space. She wouldn't look at him, keeping her burning, glistening gaze on the elevator wall. Still, he studied her profile—the turn of her nose and the pout of her mouth and the way her hair curled around her ears and neck, like tendrils of his shadowy magic cupping her face.

He memorized her as if this were the last time he'd see her, and without another word, he left.

Hades found himself on the island of Lemnos, knocking on Aphrodite's front door.

He hated what he was about to do, but Hecate had asked him over and over what he was going to do, and while Aphrodite never seemed to be able to handle her relationship with Hephaestus, she was still the Goddess of Love, and it was likely she could offer some insight.

Or at least tell him what to avoid.

He peered through the glass door of her home, looking for any sign of Aphrodite or Lucy, the animatronic maid Hephaestus had made who was far more lifelike than necessary in his opinion, but the hallway was empty.

He knocked again and sighed.

"I know you're here," he growled.

A loud yawn broke from behind him, and he turned

to find Aphrodite stretching. She was dressed in peach, and her golden hair fell in waves down her back.

"What is it, Hades?" she asked. "I am tired."

Now that he faced her, he suddenly felt very stupid and wanted to leave.

"This was a mistake," he said. "I... Sorry."

He started to leave when Aphrodite's presence flashed as she teleported closer to prevent him from going.

"Did you just apologize, Hades?" she asked. He did not speak, and a smile curved her lips. "Something must be wrong," she said. "Come."

She led him down a walkway that ran parallel to her home and opened to a patio that overlooked the ocean. He had seen the water in all forms throughout his visits to this island—deep blue and green, golden and orange—but today it churned beneath the bright sun, making it gleam like millions of diamonds. It almost hurt to look at it.

Aphrodite made her way to a lounge where it was clear she had been resting before Hades interrupted her. A book lay facedown on a table beside a large hat and some kind of pink drink.

"I would tell you to sit," she said, "but I doubt you would be comfortable enough."

She was right. Instead, he remained on his feet, hands in his pockets, standing on the line where the shadow met the light, and stared off at the horizon, squinting against the bright day.

"I know you have not come all the way to Lemnos for the view," Aphrodite said. "Tell me why you are here so that we might both get back to our day."

While her words were dismissive, Hades knew she was far too intrigued by his visit to be too impatient.

"As if your schedule was packed," Hades countered.

"If you are going to beg for my help, you could at least respect my time."

"I have not come to beg."

"Perhaps not," she said. "But if you keep delaying, you will be on your knees before you leave my sight."

Hades ground his teeth and finally relented. "I fucked up," he said, and he held his breath as he added, "I need advice."

Aphrodite's eyes gleamed, amused, but as he began to tell her what had transpired between him and Persephone—the goddess's desperate wish to save her best friend, the bargain with Apollo, the aftermath of their anger and pain—that warm glow in her eyes dimmed.

Aphrodite knew the pain of loss, and she understood it from the perspective of love—all love, not just romantic—because love did not end when life did. It carried on in the absence of it.

"I cannot even begin to decide how to make amends. She was right. I could have supported her more, prepared her for Lexa's decision and Thanatos's eventual reaping, but I didn't. I treated her situation like every other mortal, thinking it was no different, but it was different because it was Persephone."

He dragged his fingers through his hair, frustrated, and it fell from its tie around his face.

"Have you told her that you are sorry?"

He met her gaze. "I *tried*. She didn't want to hear from me." He paused. "I want to *do* something."

"Sometimes grand gestures are not as important as words, Hades," Aphrodite replied.

Hades frowned. He couldn't deny that he was disappointed in her response. "Odd that you would give such advice when you cannot even bring yourself to talk to Hephaestus."

Aphrodite's mouth hardened, then her eyes flashed. It was the only warning he had before a hard hit sent him to his knees. He looked up to find that the Goddess of Love stood inches from him holding a gold rod that was taller than she was. It was the weapon she'd used to knock him off his feet, and now she pointed the sharpened end at his face.

"You don't have to like what I say," Aphrodite said, "but you must respect me."

Hades nodded once. "Fair. I'm sorry."

It was the second time he had apologized to her today—he was definitely not in his right mind.

She stared at him, as if assessing whether he meant what he said, and after a moment, she nodded, righting her spear.

Slowly, Hades got to his feet. After a moment, he spoke, still uncertain that words were enough to convince Persephone that he was sorry.

"I just…cannot imagine that she wants to hear from me."

He had no reason to believe otherwise, given their earlier encounter and how it had backfired.

"Perhaps she just needs time," Aphrodite said. "I will not pretend to know her mind or answer for her. Plan something grand and beautiful, but remember that the only way forward is to ask her what she wants."

Hades nodded, and after a moment, he met her gaze. "Any chance I can convince you to never bring this up again?"

"Never," she replied with a wicked smile.

―――――

Throughout the day, Hades returned to his conversation with Persephone and Aphrodite's words. The two were in such conflict, he did not know what to do, but he hoped that at some point, Persephone would let him explain what had happened with Leuce.

Hades was still deciding what to do about the troublesome nymph. He couldn't exactly get rid of her. He knew, despite Persephone's hurt over the article in the *Delphi Divine*, that she would not approve of him sending Leuce away, and as much as he believed she was working with Demeter, it likely meant that she felt she had no choice in the matter, even with Hades's offer of protection.

Essentially, Leuce was caught between two gods who could do very brutal things if she disobeyed, and while he considered confronting Demeter about the situation, he knew he'd only make things worse. Not to mention he had other, more pressing matters to attend to, among them ensuring that their plans did not actually succeed in tearing him and Persephone apart.

He'd begun to map out an idea for how he might proceed when Hermes appeared in his office dressed in all white. His shirt was halfway unbuttoned, and he looked very flushed.

Hades raised a brow at the god and was about to comment on his attire when he spoke instead.

"We need you," he said.

Hades's brows slammed down over his eyes, and Hermes's next two words had him out of his seat.

"It's Persephone."

He did not need to say anything more, and they were teleporting, appearing before a curtained lounge with white couches. The air was thick with a suffocating white smoke that flashed bright with colors as music roared around them. Hades knew this club. It was the Seven Muses, and it was owned by Apollo, who sat on one of the couches, looking bored while Persephone lay on the one opposite at an odd angle, as if she'd collapsed there. Her eyes were closed and she wore nothing but mesh and gold leaves. While he liked the dress, he would have preferred being the sole person to have seen her in it. She needed a gods-damned blanket, but the best he could do now was call up his glamour to conceal the booth.

Hades ground his teeth. This had to be part of her fucking bargain with Apollo.

"What happened?" he demanded.

"What does it look like?" Apollo asked. "She drank too much."

Hades glared at the god, who was perfectly sober. Persephone had not had years to build up a tolerance to alcohol like the rest of them. She could still get drunk, though unlike mortals, her body could recover far faster.

"I tried to get her to leave after she threw up the first time," said Zofie. "But she refused."

As he stared down at Persephone, she opened her eyes. She did not seem to realize where she was and her brows furrowed.

"There you are, Sephy," Hermes said, sitting near her head. "You had us worried."

She kept staring at him, and Hades wasn't sure she heard the god at all. Finally, she glanced up at him and asked, "Why did you call him? He hates me."

Hates me? Hades's whole body recoiled at those words. When had he given the impression that he hated her? He'd gone to her work hours ago to beg her to hear him out about the Leuce situation. He took a breath, reminding himself that she was, in fact, incapacitated at the moment. Though the words still ate at him.

Instead of denying her statement, Hermes said, "Blame Zofie."

Hades gazed at the god questioningly, but if he had to guess, since Zofie was the aegis, she'd insisted that Hermes get help. He felt a bit of relief that the Amazon had accompanied them. Likely Persephone would have continued to lie here under the scrutiny of the club otherwise.

He lowered to his knee beside her. "Can you stand? I'd rather not carry you out of this place."

Once more, she frowned. A touch of hurt bled into her eyes before anger pushed her into a seated position. He tried to hand her a glass of water Zofie had pushed into his hands, but she refused it, mouth tight.

"If you don't want to be seen with me, why don't you teleport?"

Obviously, she had forgotten how jarring teleportation could be. "If I teleport, you might throw up. I've been told you've already done that once tonight."

Hades got to his feet as she rose and swayed. He caught her around the waist. For a moment, she sunk into him, and he welcomed the way she let her head rest on his chest, but when his arm tightened around her, she pushed against him.

A wave of frustration made Hades feel heated. He wasn't doing a very good job of schooling his features either. He felt the coldness of his gaze in his core.

"Let's go," she said and turned from him, holding her head high as she made a path out of the club.

Hades cast a spiteful glance at Apollo, Hermes, and Zofie before following her.

Antoni waited, opening the door as soon as he saw them emerge from the club, and despite their obvious dark moods, he smiled.

"My lady."

"Antoni," she said with a crisp nod, which was far from her usually warm reception of anyone who wasn't Hades at this point. He watched as she bent and crawled into the back of the Lexus on her hands and knees. Thank fuck he had continued to cloak them in glamour so that the world hadn't seen her ass.

Once the door was closed, they were locked inside with their anger, a tension that built and made him feel electric. Usually, he'd work through this physically, but there was a long list of reasons he couldn't do that this time, among them that Persephone was not sober. It didn't stop him from fantasizing, though, which was both satisfying and torturous.

He considered what he would do first, which likely would be pressing his mouth to hers and drawing her thighs apart. He would slide his fingers along her core, then sink into her silken heat. They would both moan because of how long it had been since they had become lost in each other. And after she was spent by his hand, he would draw her into his lap, take out his cock, and help her ride him until he came inside her so hard, she could taste it in the back of her throat, and even in that aftermath, he would lay her down and put his mouth on her clit and revel in how she tasted like him.

He shifted in his seat, his cock hard with these thoughts. There was a certain relief that came when they arrived at Nevernight, knowing he would soon be out of this suffocating cabin where their emotions were too high and too heavy. Persephone must have thought the same thing, because she was out the door before Antoni could open it. Hades followed as quickly as he could, but not before she fell on the hard cement sidewalk.

"My lady!"

"I'm fine," she said as the cyclops offered a hand to help her to her feet, though as she shifted to sit, they both saw what a mess her knee was. It was more than a scratch; the skin was broken and blood welled in large bubbles, sliding down her leg.

She stared at it and frowned, then looked up at them. "It's okay. I don't even feel it."

She tried to stand twice, during which Antoni moved behind her just in case she started to fall. When it was clear she wasn't going to get up on her own, she took a breath.

"You know, I think I'll just sit here for a little while."

This was getting ridiculous. Hades realized she didn't really want his touch, but he wasn't going to wait outside while she sobered up, especially while she was bleeding, so he gathered her into his arms and carried her into Nevernight, nodding to Mekonnen, who had come outside to hold the door open for them.

He took her downstairs into the empty club, having closed nearly three hours ago. Persephone had definitely been out later than usual. He headed behind the bar and sat her down before lifting her onto the counter. Then he reached for a glass and filled it with water.

"What are you doing?"

He pushed the glass into her hands. "Drink."

To his relief, she obeyed, which left him to focus on cleaning her knee. He felt far less frantic about this wound—it was nothing like witnessing her body perforated by thorns. Still, that thought did not help him here, because it reminded him of how much danger she was in even from herself.

He removed his jacket and filled another glass with water to use on her injury. He would have used his magic to heal her, but it had to be clean first, so he set to work, folding a cloth to go under her leg before cleaning away the grime. Once he was finished and the area was dry, he healed it. There was a strange relief that came with seeing her whole.

"Thank you," she whispered.

He had not heard those words in a long time. He took a step back until he could lean against the opposite counter, drawing his arms over his chest. He stared at her in her leaves and her lace. She was beyond stunning, and as much as he liked the outfit, there was a part of him that wanted to rage that so many had witnessed her in it before him.

"Are you punishing me?"

She frowned. "What?"

"This," he said. "The clothes, Apollo, the drinking?"

She looked down at the dress and back up at him. "You don't like my clothes?"

That is not what I said, he thought as he stared at her. Then he noted the defiant set to her mouth as she pushed off the counter and reached for the hem of her dress.

Hades stiffened...everywhere. "What are you doing?"

"Taking off the dress," she said.

"I can see that," he said, eyes narrowing, though he tried not to smile. "Why?"

"Because you don't like it."

"I didn't say I didn't like it." His voice lowered.

But he wasn't going to stop her, and once she stood naked in front of him, his eyes made the climb from the apex of her thighs where curls darkened her center, up her stomach to her breasts, which hung heavy and round. His mouth watered and he swallowed hard.

"Why weren't you wearing anything under that dress?" he asked, because as fucking hot as he found it, he couldn't help remembering where she'd been before she was here.

"I couldn't... Didn't you see it?"

Oh, he'd seen it.

"I'm going to murder Apollo," he muttered.

She looked confused. "Why?"

"For *fun*."

She laughed, her eyes glittering. "You're jealous."

"*Don't* push me, Persephone."

He really would murder Apollo, and he hadn't wanted to because his existence was far more cruel than a life in the Underworld. He turned and plucked a bottle of whiskey from the bar, pulled off the cap, and took a long drink.

"It wasn't like Apollo knew," she said. "Hermes was the one who suggested it."

Hades's fingers curled around the bottle so tight, it shattered and suddenly the floor was covered in glass and whiskey.

"*Motherfucker.*"

Hades was well aware of Hermes's sexual preferences, which while not limited, likely did not include Persephone. Still, he did not like the liberties the god took.

Best friend, my ass.

"Are you okay?" Persephone asked.

His gaze shifted to hers as he answered. "Forgive me if I am a little on edge. I have been forced into celibacy."

She rolled her eyes, and he ground his teeth. "No one ever said you couldn't fuck me."

"Careful, goddess. You don't know what you're asking."

"I think I know what I'm asking for, Hades. It's not like we've never had sex."

He could fuck her. He would too. Hard. Fast. Unapologetic. He'd turn her to face the counter and enter her from behind so he could control her. He'd shove his fingers into her hair and use it to move her body. He'd bend her to his will until he came.

It would not be about her. It would be about him and his aggression, and that was not what he wanted, as much as he did want her.

"Are you wet for me?" he asked. His voice was low, and despite the shiver that visibly shook her body, she tilted her head in challenge.

"Why don't you come find out?"

He took deep breaths until even those were only filled with the scent of her magic and arousal. He moved to holding his breath and clutching the counter behind him. This night was a fucking challenge. Why did she have to be aroused now? *Why didn't she reject him now?*

"Why didn't you let Apollo see Hyacinth after his death?"

Fucking Fates.

"You really know how to kill a boner, darling, I'll give you that."

He chose a second bottle from the display behind him, and by the time he turned around, she had put on his jacket. As much as he liked seeing her completely naked—and in heels—there was something about also seeing her draped in his clothing, too big for her small frame. It almost possessed her, much like he wished to do now.

"He said he blamed you for his death."

Even gods misplaced their anger over deaths. He couldn't count the number of times one of the Olympians had blamed him for the death of a hero, a lover, an enemy they had not finished torturing.

"He did. Much like you blamed me for Lexa's accident."

Saying that probably made him an asshole, but it was the truth, and she knew it, despite what she said next.

"I never said I blamed you."

"You blamed me because I couldn't help. Apollo did the same."

He expected her to argue, but instead, she took a breath. "I'm not...trying to fight with you. I just want to know your side."

He took a drink from the bottle before explaining

the truth behind his feud with Apollo. It went far beyond Leuce, who, in the end, was really just a victim. She'd been caught in the middle of a Divine feud, much as she was now. Hades grimaced at how life never really changed.

"Apollo didn't ask to see his lover," he said, realizing in this moment how hard it was to actually speak these words, to dig them up from a past that had been buried so deep, one that he'd wanted to forget but had been forced to face. "He asked to die."

Hades remembered the day well. Apollo had stood at the Lerna Lake entrance to the Underworld screaming his name, and when Hades obliged to meet him, he'd demanded that Hades take his life.

"Of course it was a request I could not—*would not*—grant."

At the time, Hades had believed that Apollo wasn't fit to make any decisions, that he would regret the sacrifice he'd made to die, but now he wasn't so sure.

"I don't understand. Apollo knows he cannot die. He is immortal. Even if you were to wound him…"

"He wished to be thrown into Tartarus. To be torn to pieces by the Titans. It is the only way to kill a god." Or, at least, it should be, his thoughts turning to the Graeae. Someone had managed to kill them without the might of gods. A strange feeling twisted in his gut, and he pushed that aside, focusing on Persephone. "He was outraged, of course, and took his revenge in the only way he knows how—he slept with Leuce."

Persephone's eyes widened and her mouth fell open in shock. "Why didn't you tell me?"

"I tend to want to forget that part of my life, Persephone."

Though it seemed to not want to forget him.

"But I—I wouldn't have—"

"You already broke a promise you made. I doubt my story of betrayal would have prevented you from seeking Apollo's help."

His words hurt her. He could tell by how she seemed to fold in on herself, and a surge of guilt made his entire body feel weak. Perhaps his honesty would have influenced her behavior differently, but he had not even given her the chance.

He set the bottle aside and pushed away from the bar.

"You are probably tired. I can take you to the Underworld, or Antoni will see you home."

He gave her two options, not knowing where she'd like to go, but instead, she asked him, "What do you want?"

You, of course, he thought, yet found himself putting the choice to her. "It is not my decision to make."

When she averted her eyes, he knew he'd made a mistake.

"But since you asked," he added, and she looked at him. "I always want you with me. Even when I'm angry."

There was a little less sadness to her expression.

"Then I'll come with you."

He approached, crunching the broken glass beneath his feet as he drew her body against his. Despite their proximity, there was still so much distance between them. He would take this for now, though, her closeness and her presence in his bed.

At least for this night, she would be home.

CHAPTER XXIV
Answers

Hades should have guessed he would not sleep, though he did rest, which was easy given that for the first night in what felt like forever, Persephone lay beside him. Eventually, he rose, though reluctant, and left their room. In the halls, he passed staff carrying bundles of flowers and leafy garlands, and the smell of savory foods permeated the air. He followed the activity, finding Hecate in the ballroom giving instruction on the placement of banquet tables and flowers.

"What's going on?" he asked.

"Tonight is the solstice celebration," she said.

Right. He had forgotten. Usually these festivities were relegated to the Asphodel Valley, but Persephone had insisted on moving more of them to the palace, and it had begun with the Ascension Ball.

"Will you join us?" Hecate inquired.

"I'll try," he said.

"Persephone will want you here."

Hades was not so certain, but he would actually make an effort.

He left Hecate to her work and wandered to the stables, where he released Orphnaeus, Aethon, Nycteus, and Alastor from their pens. He followed them out into the field and, at the last minute, mounted Alastor, riding fast across the Underworld. He had no particular destination in mind, but it had been a long time since he had just existed somewhere without expectation, and that was what he wanted to do right now.

Alastor galloped hard and fast until he came to the edge of the Underworld, where a steep cliff met the gray Aleyonia Ocean. Hades considered jumping into its cold depths, if only to feel cleansed of the chaos that had riddled his body over the past few weeks. As enticing as the thought was, he remained seated and, soon after, turned Alastor away. It was on their way back toward the palace that he dismounted, allowing the horse to run free across his realm, though he was not alone long before Hermes appeared.

Hades did not speak, finding that he was still irritated about last night. In particular, he was not happy that the God of Mischief had chosen Persephone's dress.

"I came to say I am sorry," Hermes said.

Still Hades did not speak, nor did he stop, continuing toward the palace.

"Don't do this, Hades." Hermes followed on his heels. "The dress was for your benefit, and you know it."

He hated that the god knew what he was so angry about.

"My benefit?" Hades countered. "How so, when I was the last person to see her in it?"

"Well, that's the purpose, isn't it?"

"Do you really think I don't want to fuck Persephone?" he spat, whirling to face him. It wasn't even the dress that made him so angry; it was the reason behind it. It was meant to make him jealous. It was meant to make him yearn. "There's more between us than sex, and if you must know, everything outside that is the problem at this moment."

Hermes dropped his gaze. "Look, Hades. I didn't mean to make things worse. At the end of the day, I just wanted to help...and yeah, the dress was meant to send a message, but I thought it might help you see what's most important."

"And what is that?"

"The woman in the dress, you idiot."

"I *know* that, you fucking imbecile. You didn't have to put her in fucking *mesh* for me to get the message."

"And what if that's what she wanted?" Hermes asked.

Hades just stared.

"Stop being toxic about the things that don't matter. You'll miss out on what's really important, which is that she loves you." Hermes shook his head and continued. "A lot of us love you, and you don't make it easy, especially when you're like this."

"Like what?"

"*This*," he said, gesturing toward him. "Broody."

"I am not broody," Hades replied, crossing his arms over his chest.

"You are, and sometimes it's hot, but right now, it's just pathetic."

"Take that back!"

"I'll take it back," Hermes said. "But only when you accept that you deserve more than loneliness."

Hades was still frustrated by Hermes's words hours later when he was summoned to Nevernight by Ilias, who informed him that a detective had arrived to speak with him. At first he had assumed it was Ariadne, but he soon discovered that was not the case when he found a man in his office.

He was short, stout, and balding, and he stood with his hands resting on a thick belt that holstered his gun, extra rounds, a Taser, and handcuffs and still managed to hold a folder clasped between his fingers.

"Lord Hades," he said. "Thank you for meeting with me."

"What can I do for you?" Hades asked, glancing at Ilias, who lingered near the doors.

"I am Captain Baros. I believe one of my detectives has been to visit you recently."

"Enlighten me," Hades said, not wanting to out Ariadne, as he had suspected she'd come to him without this man's knowledge. "I see a lot of people."

The detective frowned, then reached into the folder, pulling out an official portrait of Ariadne in her uniform.

"Detective Ariadne Alexiou. She's gone missing."

Once more, Hades glanced at Ilias, whose expression had become tense. They were both thinking the same thing. Had Theseus decided to dispose of the detective already?

"That is very unfortunate," Hades said, not wishing to admit that he knew the woman at all. There was something about this that did not sit right with him, and it had nothing to do with the fact that Ariadne was gone. "Why come to me?"

"It's just a hunch I have," said the captain. "See, she's been investigating these disappearances across New Athens, and shortly before she went missing, she asked if she could go to the gods for help. Specifically, she wanted your help."

The last sentence was delivered like an accusation. Hades did not like it.

"I am very aware of the Hellenic Police Department's disdain for the gods," Hades said. "So it seems unlikely you would approve such an endeavor."

"I didn't," the captain replied mildly.

"Then what would lead you to believe your detective came to me?"

"Ariadne is...difficult."

"Difficult or determined?"

"Ignoring orders doesn't make anyone look good, Lord Hades."

"It certainly doesn't make you look good," Hades said. "It makes you look like you don't have control of your people. Is that why you are really here, Captain?"

The man glared. "I'm here because I'd like to locate my detective and happen to know that she did, in fact, come to you against my orders. What do you have to say to that?"

"Are you accusing me lying, Captain?" Hades asked, and before the officer could respond, he continued. "Be very careful with how you respond, as I happen to know some truths about you, and I have no fear in disclosing them."

The detective continued glaring and, after a moment, picked up the photo of Ariadne. "I'll leave my card."

"Don't bother," Hades said. "I know where to find you."

The captain said nothing but left stiffly, as if he could feel Hades's gaze on his back as he went. Once they were alone, Hades looked to Ilias.

"I thought I said to watch her," Hades said.

"We have," the satyr replied, defensive. "This wasn't Theseus."

If not Theseus, then who? There was only one other person interested enough in the detective to be responsible for her disappearance.

"Dionysus."

———

Hades had a theory that Dionysus had discovered Ariadne's association with Theseus, likely because he'd had his maenads stalking her since her unwanted visit to Bakkheia. He decided not to waste time arriving the mortal way and chose to teleport instead, appearing in Dionysus's darkened office at his club.

"How discourteous," the god said when Hades appeared.

"Do you have Ariadne?" Hades asked.

"As if anyone could control that wicked, mouthy—"

"I did not ask for a list of traits you admire about her," Hades cut him off. "*Do you have her?*"

Dionysus glared. "She's mine to punish, not yours."

"She doesn't deserve your punishment," Hades said.

"She betrayed me," he said.

"You cannot blame her for the deaths of the Graeae. I doubt it was her who held the knife, but she can tell us who did."

"I am not a child, Hades," Dionysus said through clenched teeth. "I know her value."

"That, coming from someone who won't choose a side."

The God of the Vine glared. "I'm letting you in, aren't I?" he countered. "Is that choosing a side?"

Hades lifted his head. "It's a start."

Dionysus pushed past Hades. "Come."

They left the office for the elevator on the way to the basement.

"No dungeon?" Hades inquired, glancing at the god, who seemed more on edge.

"No," he said with none of his usual sarcasm.

Hades raised a brow but said nothing.

Once in the basement, Hades was surprised to find Ariadne in the common area among the maenads, though she kept her distance, sitting in a large chair farthest from everyone in the room, reading. He'd expected her to be locked up in one of the dorms, though he recognized that was probably not wise, considering the Graeae had easily been taken from there. At least if she were in a crowd, there would be witnesses to a potential abduction.

Ariadne looked up as they approached and stiffened.

"What do you want?" she snapped.

Hades rolled his eyes. "I see you haven't lost any of that venom."

She offered a malicious smile. "It doesn't seem to deter you."

"Not when you happen to have answers to my questions," said Hades.

"I'm not sure what you think I can give you," she said.

"Don't you? The Graeae?"

There was a long pause as Ariadne stared at the two gods. Her eyes began to water.

"I hate you," she said between her teeth. "You think he won't know that you've taken me? You think he won't guess what you want?"

"I told you I would protect you," Dionysus clipped.

"And what about my sister?" she yelled, her voice raw and pained.

Hades watched Dionysus look away, jaw clenched. Clearly there had already been some discussion around what kind of information she was willing to offer.

"Where is your sister?" Hades asked. He realized he still did not know why Theseus seemed to have her.

"Her sister is married to Theseus," said Dionysus, speaking for her. "And he uses her to manipulate Ariadne."

That explained why she seemed to have to earn the right to see her.

"What she doesn't seem to realize is that there's nothing we can do for her," Dionysus said.

"You can't," Ariadne said. "But I can and the only way to ensure that is to not tell you a fucking thing."

"Do you really think Theseus will grant you access to his wife?"

"Don't call her that," she said between her teeth.

"Tell me," said Dionysus. "How long has it been since you've seen her?"

When Ariadne did not respond, he asked again, and this time, she screamed. "Three years! Three. Years. You. Bastard," she seethed. "And now, because of you, I will never see her again!"

There was silence in the aftermath of Ariadne's

outburst, though Hades did not blame her. He could feel the love she had for her sister. It shook her body and broke her voice, and he wanted to do everything in his power to ensure she saw her again.

"Perhaps you should have thought about that before you came here with the intention of locating the Graeae," Dionysus said, because he did not know when to shut up.

"I didn't!" she seethed. "I came here hoping you might help me rescue my sister, but when I discovered how *difficult* you were, I decided it was easier to just go along with Theseus's instruction."

Hades looked between the two, and after a moment, he knelt. "Look, Ariadne. We can get your sister back… but I have to ask, does she want to be saved?"

"She doesn't know what she wants anymore," she replied, and she took a shuddering breath.

"That's not what I asked," Hades said.

"He abuses her," she countered.

"Ariadne," Hades said, his voice quiet, and truly, his heart broke for her. "You know you cannot rescue people who do not want to be saved."

She buried her face in her hands as a few deep sobs racked her body. After a moment, she looked up and took a breath.

"You will help me get her back no matter what she wants," said Ariadne. "And I'll give you the information you need."

Hades looked up at Dionysus, who stood aside, mouth set hard. He did not wait for the god to agree before he said, "Deal."

It still took Ariadne a few minutes to begin, but when she did, everything fell into place.

"Theseus already knew where you were keeping the Graeae. It was just a matter of distracting you long enough so Hera could retrieve the sisters."

Dionysus's mood darkened at the mention of Hera, and Hades knew why. The Goddess of Women had been the bane of his existence in antiquity. She'd struck him with madness, made him travel the world endlessly and listlessly. She was also responsible for killing his mother, Semele.

"So the woman in the bathroom?" Dionysus asked. "Was she a setup?"

"No! I would have never..." She paused and huffed. "I know what you must think of me, but Theseus does not control every part of my life. I came here with my own motivations."

"Because you thought I was trafficking women," Dionysus replied sourly.

"I came because I thought you might be able to help me," she snapped, her words silencing Dionysus who stood, stunned. Then she added in a quiet voice, "He doesn't know about Medusa, and I did not tell him. I couldn't bear the thought of putting another woman in danger."

Hades had to admit, that piece of information was a relief and likely an advantage they had over the demigod.

"When they came without the eye, he was angry, but he kept them alive for a time, and he only decided to kill them when he thought that you might be able to rescue them," she said, looking at Hades. "Hera gave him access to hydra venom, and he thought killing the Graeae was a way to test how much he needed to murder the Divine. Of course, Theseus didn't actually make the kill. He sent his soldiers to do it."

"Who are his soldiers?"

"Other demigods, mostly," she replied. "There are mortals too, but he only finds them useful when he wants the public to think the Impious are acting alone."

Other demigods, Hades thought. There were a number scattered about New Greece, and he had no doubt that most carried a lot of resentment toward their Divine parents.

"He wants to overthrow the Olympians," she said. "Even the ones who side with him now."

"Do you know his next move?" Dionysus asked. "If he intended the Graeae to be a weapon and they turned into his victims, what's next? He needs more weapons and new targets."

Ariadne shook her head, and Hades frowned deeply. While he was not surprised by what she had shared, it brought on an immense amount of dread.

Perhaps the worst part was that he would have to tell Zeus, though the only good that might come out of that was leverage against Hera, who still thought she held power over Hades with her labors.

She was about to discover quite the opposite.

Dionysus looked toward Hades. "I'll send maenads to scout. Maybe they can discover his next move." He looked at Ariadne. "And start planning an escape for Phaedra."

"I thought you didn't take sides," Hades replied.

"Yeah, well, fuck anyone who sides with Hera," Dionysus said.

CHAPTER XXV
The Forest of Despair

It was late when Hades returned to the Underworld to find Persephone waiting up for him. She turned to face him as he entered their room, dressed in a full-length gown. It was black and gold and the sleeves were long but split, so she looked as if she wore a cloak that touched the ground. On her head was a crown with jagged edges. It was black in color and encrusted with diamonds and pearls. It complimented his own, and he knew that it had been done purposefully, likely by Hecate.

She took his breath away, though she gazed at him unhappily, looking like a queen—*his queen.*

"I did not think you would be awake," he said.

He had expected her to be asleep, exhausted after celebrating with the souls. Instead, she looked bright-eyed, almost lustful, and there was an excitement that curled in the bottom of his stomach.

"Where were you?" she asked.

"I had a few things to take care of," he said. Explaining

what had happened with Dionysus and Ariadne needed too much context. It also opened up a whole new part of his world that, while he'd eventually be glad to share, was too uncertain.

Luckily, she did not seem interested in pursuing his whereabouts.

"Were these *things* more important than your realm?"

"You are angry that I was not at your party."

He frowned, in part because she knew why he did not often attend celebrations. He made people uncomfortable, as much as she believed otherwise.

"Yes, I am angry," she said. "You should have been there."

"The dead celebrate everything, Persephone. I won't miss the next one."

"If that is your view, I'd rather you not come at all," she snapped.

His brows lowered. Obviously, she was searching for an answer he could not give. "Then what do you want from me?"

"I don't fucking care how much they celebrate. What's important to them should be important to you. What's important to me should be important to *you*."

"Persephone..."

"Don't," she snapped, and he pressed his lips together, repressing the surge of frustration that erupted at her command. "I understand you don't know what I don't tell you, but I expect you to be aware of what I am planning and show interest—not only for me but for your people. You never once asked about the solstice celebration, not even after I asked you for permission to host it in the courtyard."

He stared at her in silence for a long moment. It

was true he hadn't taken it seriously. Even after Hecate's reminder, he had dismissed the importance of attending, and for that, he felt ashamed.

"I'm sorry," he said at last.

"You aren't. You are only saying that to appease me, and I *hate* it. Is this why you want a queen? So you don't have to attend these events?"

"No, I wanted you, and because of that, I wished to make you my queen. There are no ulterior motives."

Did he respect her more because she loved his realm and his people? Yes, but those characteristics came from her compassion and her kindness, and that was why he loved her.

After a moment, she took a breath and closed her eyes. "Look, Hades. If you don't...want this anymore, I need to know."

He stared at her, confused, and waited for her to look at him again. "What?"

"If you don't want me, if you don't think you can forgive me, I don't think we should be in a relationship, the Fates be damned."

The words were out, and they lingered in the air between them. Hades spent a few moments processing them before making his way toward her.

"I never said I didn't want you," he said. "I thought I made that clear yesterday."

"So you want to fuck me? That doesn't mean you want an actual relationship. It doesn't mean you will trust me again."

He paused before her, towering over her small frame, and despite the difference in their statures, she held her own, glaring furiously back at him.

"Let me be perfectly clear," he said, leaning close as he spoke. "I do want to fuck you. More importantly, I love you—deeply, endlessly. If you walked away from me today, I would love you still. I will love you forever. That's what Fate is, Persephone. Fuck threads and colors...and fuck your uncertainty."

"I'm not uncertain," she said between her teeth, her eyes searching his. "I'm afraid, you idiot!"

"Of what?" he demanded. "What have I done?"

"This isn't about you! Gods, Hades." She turned her head. "I'd think you of all people would understand."

He studied her profile for a moment—her angry, glistening eyes and the hard set of her mouth.

"Tell me," he begged.

It took her a few tries, a few deep swallows before she managed, "I've longed for love all my life. Longed for acceptance because my mother dangled it in front of me like something I had to earn. If I adhered to her expectations, she would grant it; if I didn't, she'd take it away. You want a queen, a goddess, a lover. I can't be what you want. I can't...*adhere* to these...expectations you have of me!"

He had to admit that he was stunned. He had never imagined that calling her his queen would come with so much weight.

He turned her head toward his, and she met his gaze, eyes red and watery. "Persephone, what do you think of when you think of a queen?"

"I don't know," she said. "I know what I would like to see in a queen."

"Then what would you like to see in a queen?"

"Someone who is kind...compassionate...*present*."

The last word was meant for him.

"And you do not think you are all those things?" he asked. He let his thumb brush over her lips. He wanted to kiss her because he hadn't in a very long time. He wanted to bring her comfort and to assure her that there was no title she needed to live up to because she was already enough. "I'm not asking you to be a queen. I'm asking you to be yourself. I'm asking you to marry me. The title comes with our marriage. It changes nothing."

"Are you asking me to marry you again?" she asked, her words quiet and slow.

"Will you?"

She stared, and he already knew the answer, even as the tears slid down her face, and he had never felt so conflicted—so desperate to hear her say yes but so content with her no. She'd shown him tonight how willing she was to defend his people, how she had adopted them as her people, and he knew that meant she loved him.

"My darling," he whispered. "You do not have to answer now. We have time—an eternity."

Finally, he kissed her, and the release was instant but quickly overpowered by an all-consuming need to be inside her. Then she touched him, sliding her hands down his stomach and over his cock before unbuttoning his trousers, fingers curling around his bare flesh. He groaned, loving the feel of her on him, and he wanted more.

He let his tongue and teeth play across her lips, over her jaw and down her neck, and the harder she breathed and moaned, the more he teased and sucked her skin, which was why he was surprised when she pushed him away. She took a moment to stare at him with hungry eyes, then placed her hand on the center of his chest, pushing him back until he felt the edge of the bed behind him.

"Sit," she ordered, and as he obeyed, she removed the crown from her head and set it on the nearby table. She placed her hands on his knees, holding his gaze as she lowered to the floor.

"You look like a fucking queen."

She always did.

She smiled as she answered, "I am your queen."

Then she touched him, her hand working up and down his cock. He took a breath, the heat of her touch going straight to his head.

"Persephone." Her name felt rough on his tongue, and while her hands felt good, her mouth felt better, closing around his crown, tongue trailing around his head before she brought him fully into her mouth.

He drew her hair into his hand and held it away from her face so he could watch her take him deep. She was warm and wet, and the pressure her mouth offered was far different from being inside her. There was something all-consuming about this, and he had an acute awareness that she was somehow in every part of his body, though she touched just one. After he came, he brought her to her feet with him and devoured her mouth while his fingers worked to unlace her dress. Once she was naked beneath his hands, he lowered her to the bed until she was on her back, rising once more to shed his own clothing.

She watched him from where she lay, and his eyes never left her body, so exposed in the firelight of his room, cradled in the darkness of their sheets. As good as her mouth had been on his body, he couldn't wait to be inside her.

He climbed on top of her and rested his body against hers. There was nothing like the feel of her against him, nothing that felt more like home. She placed a hand on his face, then twined strands of his hair around her fingers.

"Why do you wish to be married?" she asked.

He wasn't exactly sure how to take her question, though they had never discussed each of their perceptions of marriage, and perhaps that was part of the problem. He had asked her twice without knowing how she felt. He was definitely an idiot.

"Haven't you always dreamed of marriage?" he asked, curious, though he imagined she hadn't thought it was ever going to be a possibility, considering her mother had probably never encouraged her to think beyond four glass walls.

"No," she answered. "You didn't answer my question. Why is marriage important to *you*?"

"I don't know," he admitted. "It became important to me when I met you."

They stared at each other for a few moments, then their bodies shifted so that their hips met, and Hades reached to guide himself into her heat. He entered her hard, but once he was fully sheathed, he paused, bending to press kisses to her forehead. There he stayed as his hips began to move, taking her in slow, deliberate strokes, but the harder she held on to him, the harder he moved.

"So fucking sweet," he said as his mouth pressed against her skin, tasting and sucking and nipping. "Take me deeper, darling."

He shifted, snaking his arm under her leg, which

lifted and parted her flesh even more. She gasped, her head digging into the bed. The deep fissures her fingers had made into his skin turned into scratches down his back.

"Harder!" she cried in a breathless plea, and he obeyed, completely disarmed as he watched her pleasure. He held on to that, unrelenting until she clenched around him.

"Come, darling."

Feeling her come was the end of him too. He felt his whole body quake as he released into her, pulse after heated pulse.

Breathless, he bent to kiss her, then settled his weight on her before shifting so he could lie on his back with her draped across his body.

"Gods, I missed you," she said and pressed a kiss to his chest.

He laughed and looked down at her as she stared up at him. He could tell she had something to say and understood why she was hesitating when the words came out of her mouth.

"You were going to tell me about Leuce."

"Hmm. Yes," he said, and he tugged on her until she shifted on top of him, resting with her arms crossed on his chest. "I had a meeting with Ilias at my restaurant. I didn't know Leuce was there. She hurried after me as I was leaving and grabbed my hand. Old habit."

He wasn't sure why he added the last part, because he did not so much believe it had been a habit now. Persephone must not have liked it either, because she gave him a dull look, and he pressed his fingers to her lips, smiling wryly.

"I jerked away and kept walking. She was asking for a new job."

It was a half-truth, but he did not wish to go into the details of Leuce's own lie or deception. That would come later when he could prove it.

"That's it?"

"Afraid so."

She dropped her head, and he drew his arms around her.

"I feel like an idiot," she said.

"We all get jealous. I like when you're jealous... except when I think you might actually leave me."

She sat up fully, her hands pressed flat against his chest, gliding to his stomach. Her eyes glittered in the dim light and her skin was flushed. He liked the look of her, liked being beneath her.

"I was angry, yes, but...leaving you never occurred to me."

He studied her a moment, then rose into the same position, keeping his hands on the bed for stability while her arms wound around his neck.

"I love you. Even if the Fates unraveled our destiny, I would find a way back to you."

"Do you think they can hear you?" she asked in a whisper.

He gave her a smile. "If so, they should take that as a threat."

She laughed, and their mouths collided. Hades dropped back to the bed while Persephone sought his erect cock, positioning him once more near her entrance before bearing down on him. He inhaled as he watched her move, setting her hands against him so that her breasts pillowed and rose together. He held them as she rose up and slammed down, and when she was too tired to move, she went to her side, and Hades entered her from there and brought them both to release.

Hades woke hungry, which wasn't usual. If he ever felt that gnawing rumble, he usually quenched it with a drink, but tonight, he found himself slipping from bed while Persephone slept and wandering the halls of his palace to the kitchen, where he discovered tons of leftover food from the solstice celebration, both sweet and savory smells competing for dominance. At first he thought he'd prefer something salty, but as he searched what remained in the array of dishes, he found something he did not expect.

Cake.

He remembered his previous battle with Persephone's molten monstrosity. He'd never gotten to taste it, and while this was not her creation, it was still chocolate and it was cake. He shifted to look around the kitchen, which, while he technically owned it, was not really his. It was Milan's, and the result was that he did not know where the fuck anything was. He started to look for a plate or some kind of bowl to put the cake on, but when he found a fork first, he decided he would eat straight from the container.

As he cut into the springy and fluffy cake, his stomach growled even louder, but then a horrible feeling trickled down his spine and he froze. It was like his body was being attacked by some invisible force. Chills raced down his arms, and there was a weight in his chest that kept his lungs from expanding. He could not take in breath, could not swallow, could not move.

Persephone.

He dropped the cake, fled the kitchen, and raced back to their bedchamber, where he found their room empty. Then he noticed the balcony doors open, and from there, he felt Persephone's magic detonate. It was the only way to describe it. It dropped like a bomb, and the shock waves echoed throughout his realm. He had never felt anything like it, and his magic was not prepared to handle the sudden spike.

His world began to wilt. Even the garden below him wept, trees bowing, limbs curling, flowers disintegrating beneath the weight of Persephone's magic. Within a matter of minutes, the Underworld was a desert of coarse black sand that stretched for miles and miles, only interrupted by desolate rivers and the ominous mountains of Tartarus.

What is happening? Hades thought.

She had bared the true nature of his realm, and throughout it all, a wail carried across a violent wind. It was anguished, much like his world.

His heart raced. Her power made him breathless.

Persephone.

He teleported from the balcony to find her in Tartarus—in the Forest of Despair. He felt acid burning the back of his throat at the thought of what horror she had discovered here. It was a place within the boundaries of Tartarus that fed off fears. Whatever she'd seen here was real to her. It had her shaking with a violent energy he could feel rumbling the earth at his feet.

If he didn't stop her, she would destroy his realm.

"Persephone!" he called, desperate.

"*Don't* say my name!"

He blanched at the sound of her voice, a horrible grating echo that carried across the space between them.

"Persephone, listen to me!"

He took a step toward her.

"*Don't!*"

Her voice boomed, and the ground ruptured and yawned as a deep ravine fractured far and wide between them.

"Persephone, please!" If she didn't stop on her own, he would have to use his power against her, and that was the last thing he wanted.

But the more he said her name and the more he begged, the more agonized and angry she became. She screamed, and he did not know if it was from her rage or the power of her magic, which usually felt so pleasant against his own, but tonight felt more like war—a goddess prepared to deliver death, heedless of prayer.

He watched in horror as she brought her hands together, and the power she had drained from life in the Underworld—his magic—gathered between her palms, then she turned them outward, and all that power hit him. He was thrown back by the force of it, and as he landed, he dropped his glamour.

This was a nightmare.

His chest and heart ached—both from the impact of her blow and for what he was about to do. He gathered his magic, and it tore from him. As it charged for her, she threw up her hands and screamed, anguished and enraged, and his shadows froze as they hurled toward her, long black spears just suspended in the air, vibrating as they were caught between the push and pull of both of their powers.

There was a moment of stark silence. It pressed against Hades's ears until they popped, and suddenly his magic was racing back toward him. He managed to recover enough to gain control of them and turn them into ash, the remains of which were carried away with Persephone's raging wind.

"Stop!" Hades said. "Persephone, this is madness."

And it was madness—everything about it. Just weeks ago, Persephone had been unable to control her own magic. It had burst from her in the form of thorns, leaving her torn and bloody, and suddenly, fueled by whatever horror the Forest of Despair had offered, she was turning Hades's magic on him? It was unheard of.

It was dangerous.

Then she spoke, and despite the roar of her magic, her voice carried like a spell.

"You would burn the world for me?" she said, and there was an energy gathering around her that was both feral and volatile. "I will destroy it for you."

The sky opened, and roots that looked more like giant trees breeched the vast expanse, slamming into the earth below. The ground shook and debris rained down on the entire Underworld.

Fuck. Fuck. Fuck.

He only seemed to be making it worse. She was heedless of anyone beyond her pain, but whatever that was, it would not compare to what she would feel when this was all over.

"Hecate!"

The Goddess of Magic appeared beside Hades, her

robes whipping in the wind, and she brought her hand up to shield her eyes against the debris.

"What happened?" she asked.

"I don't know. I felt her anguish and came as soon as possible."

Persephone seemed to grow stronger. The roots that she had summoned from the sky grew larger and tunneled into the ground, curling around trees and mountains, squeezing until they were rubble. Hades attempted to counter that, his magic spiraling like matching vines to tangle with Persephone's, while Hecate's power joined the miasma. Only she did not attack Persephone. She kept her spells defensive, casting a shield over them in an attempt to contain the damage Persephone was doing to the Underworld. At the same time, though, Hecate's magic had a weight. Even Hades could feel it bearing down on him. It made his shoulders shake and his concentration wane. He ground his teeth against the intrusion and knew that Persephone did too. There was an interruption in the power of her magic—a give, a break—and he watched as tears began to track down her face, her eyes locked with Hecate's.

"What are you doing?" he demanded.

But Hecate did not respond, focused on Persephone. Then, all of a sudden, her magic was gone and a horrible silence followed, as if she really had sucked the life out of everything within his world.

Persephone swayed, and Hecate teleported to catch her just as she vomited at her feet.

"It wasn't real," Hecate whispered, brushing Persephone's hair from her face. "It wasn't real, my dear, my love, my sweet."

Hades watched as Persephone buried her face in Hecate's chest.

"I cannot unsee it. I cannot live with it."

"Shh," Hecate soothed, and as she did, she looked at him, and for the first time since this had all begun, he could see what had sent Persephone into her rage.

Him.

Hades wanted to vomit.

Even now, his stomach twisted into hard knots, and his throat felt tight as the vision Persephone had seen played through Hades's mind—Leuce locked in his embrace, pressed against a tree, their mouths colliding in a passionate kiss.

He knew how the forest worked because he had created it as a weapon for torture. The souls who were sentenced there constantly lived a reality of their greatest fears. They felt and looked real because, in a way, they were.

When she had stumbled on them, she would have had no reason to believe what she was seeing wasn't real. It would not have occurred to her, such was the way of the forest.

He watched Hecate rise with Persephone in her arms.

"I will take her to the palace," she said, "while you restore order."

He did not argue. He would have preferred to be the one to take Persephone, but he also knew that she would not want him right now, so he let Hecate leave and focused on restoring order to his realm.

While it was something he could do within seconds, he took his time, turning the roots Persephone had brought into the Underworld to ash, leveling the ground she had disturbed, before calling up his magic to create lush, rolling hills, thick forests, and extensive gardens full of blooming flowers.

When he was finished, he returned to the palace and found Hecate in his bedroom. She sat beside the bed while Persephone slept.

"How is she?" he asked.

"Exhausted," she replied. "She just stopped shaking."

Hades's frown deepened.

"I don't understand how she managed to wander into the forest."

"Enchantment," Hecate said.

"Enchantment," Hades repeated.

"I have been thinking, the fear is all wrong too."

Hades's brows knit together. "What do you mean?"

Hecate kept her gaze on Persephone as she spoke.

"Persephone has no fear of you cheating with Leuce. She trusts you. Her greatest fear is losing Lexa. Which leads me to believe this was meant to tear you apart."

Hades considered her words and, after a moment, asked, "Was Leuce at last night's celebration?"

"I believe so," Hecate said. "Which is why the fear seems off. Even after that picture surfaced in the *Delphi Divine*, she was unbothered enough to bring Leuce to celebrate."

"You said it was an enchantment?" Hades asked.

The goddess nodded.

"A potion, if I had to guess," Hecate said. "Likely from a Magi."

Hades had no doubt that Leuce was involved somehow. Her deception was about to end. He left the bedroom and headed outside, where his realm had been restored to order, and called for Hermes, who appeared almost immediately, as if he had been waiting for Hades's summons.

"You called, Daddy Death?" Hermes arrived grinning, but that smile quickly died. "You look awful."

Hades *felt* awful.

"Find Leuce," he said.

"Oh no," Hermes said. "What did she do this time?"

"Nothing different from before," Hades replied. "She just fucked with the wrong god."

"I'll locate her."

"Don't just locate her," Hades said. "Bring her to me."

Hermes nodded and vanished.

When he was once again alone, Hades took a deep breath and wandered away from the front of the palace, around its many gardens. He was anxious to have Persephone awake, to talk to her about what she had seen and beg for her forgiveness. Despite the fact that he had done nothing wrong, he had created the monster that had affected her so cruelly, and for that, he felt guilt.

He rounded the garden wall that separated the garden outside his bedroom from the Asphodel Fields and came face-to-face with Persephone.

She was pale and dressed in white. Without energy to keep up her glamour, her Divine form was on full display, and beneath the muted Underworld sky, she looked both beautiful and haunted.

For a moment, all he could do was stare. There had been so many times in the past when he had feared that she would disappear right before his eyes, that every moment they'd had was some kind of torturous game the Fates had woven into his life only to unravel, and he'd never felt that more than in this moment.

He swallowed hard and asked, "Are you well?"

She stared back, the gold of her hair glinting as a light wind teased the strands, and in that moment, her cheeks flushed a light pink.

"I will be," she said softly.

The silence that followed was not so heavy, and Hades hoped that healing from this would be easier somehow.

"May I join you on your walk?" he asked.

"This is your realm."

He frowned at her response, which was less enthusiastic than he'd hoped, though he supposed he could not blame her for putting distance between them after what she had seen. She moved ahead, walking in the direction he'd come from, and he fell into step beside her. He wanted to touch her, at least hold her hand, but he recognized that he was seeking comfort, seeking confirmation that they were okay, and he could not expect her to be ready for that.

He curled his fingers into fists as they continued on in silence, coming to the end of the garden, facing the Asphodel Fields, and the tension between them was so great, Hades could no longer handle it.

He turned to her, and while her body was angled away, she stared up at him.

"Persephone," he murmured, wishing so much that he could reach for her. "I...I don't know what you saw, but you must know—*you must know*—it wasn't real."

Which was mostly true. Hecate had pulled memories from Persephone's mind, and those had been filtered through her pain and her anguish and her trauma. He would never truly know what she'd seen, only how it had affected her, and that somehow made this all worse.

"Shall I tell you what I saw?" she asked, a raw note to her voice that made it rasp. "I saw you and Leuce together. You held her, moved inside her like you starved for her."

She squeezed her eyes shut and trembled.

"You took pleasure from her. Knowing she was your lover was one thing. Seeing it was...devastating, and I wanted to destroy everything you loved," she said, her voice cracking as tears spilled down her face. "I wanted you to watch me dismantle your world. I wanted to dismantle *you*."

Her words were like claws digging deep into his chest, and despite his previous reservations about touching her, he reached for her now, wishing to meet her gaze.

"Persephone," he said and she opened her eyes, brimming with tears. "You must know that wasn't real."

"It felt real."

That was the horror of it—the torture of it.

"I would take this from you if I could," he said, and he meant it. He would take it from her so she would not feel the pain of a betrayal he did not commit, so she would not look at him like she did now—with the shadow of suspicion in her eyes.

And yet even with the doubt swimming in her expression, she drew nearer.

"You can take this," she said, then whispered, "Kiss me."

He was doubtful at first but eager all the same, and he touched his lips to hers. His intention was to be gentle, but Persephone left no room for soft caresses. Her hand snaked behind his neck, and her mouth pressed hard against his, so he let his tongue taste hers. Hades drew her closer, his fingers digging into the fabric of her dress while her hands cascaded down his body to his cock, which had grown long and thick as their kiss had continued, and he drew away with a guttural inhale.

Still, Persephone held him, and despite the layer of fabric between them, he felt hot in her hands.

"Help me forget what I saw in the forest," she begged. "Kiss me. Love me. Ruin me."

She never had to ask, though he cherished the invitation. They shed their clothes as they kissed, and Hades reached between Persephone's legs, cupping and teasing her heat before drawing one of her legs to hook around his hip and sliding two fingers inside her. She offered a breathless moan, arms twining around his neck as she sought a way to steady herself, but Hades kept a firm hand wrapped around her waist and moved slowly. Their faces were inches apart, and he watched her as her expressions morphed from a focused intensity to something far less controlled—as if she could no longer control how her body reacted to him. Her head fell back, her mouth fell open, her eyes rolled, and when she became weightless in his arms, he knelt to the ground with her.

He stared at her openly as she reclined on his robes amid the tall blades of grass that rustled around them. Naked, hair gleaming, bathed in his light, she was ethereal.

"Beautiful," he murmured. "If I could, I would keep us here in this moment forever, with you spread out before me."

She tilted her head down, and though her eyes were

eerie and bright, there was a darkness to them that made the pit of his stomach ignite with fire.

"Why not fast forward," she asked, "to when you are inside me?"

He offered a lopsided grin. When he had said this moment, he meant all of it.

"Eager, darling?"

"Always."

He crawled forward on his hands and knees until he was between her thighs, where he kissed her skin until he found her center. She was soft against his tongue, and he lapped at her arousal, pushing her legs farther apart while Persephone hooked her arms beneath her knees. She was a vision, glorious and glowing, and she writhed beneath him as he pushed her toward release with both his mouth and his hand.

When she could no longer control her body or the sounds that came from her mouth, he knew he had her and he pushed forward until she came.

"Hades," she spoke his name, her legs limp around him, her fingers threading through his hair, then tugging on the strands to bring him up her body to her mouth. He kissed her for a long time, the heat between them unbearable even as he paused exploring to stare into her eyes.

"There was no greater torture than feeling your anguish." There was a part of him that hated bringing this up, especially after all his effort to make her forget what she saw, though she knew just as well as he that there was no forgetting the Forest of Despair. "I knew I was somehow responsible, and I could do nothing about it."

Persephone was less inclined to speak on what

happened, because she touched his lips while dragging her tongue over her own and said, "You can do something about it."

She arched beneath him, then her hand found his cock, which she tugged generously, sending a wave of pleasure to his head, and he understood. As much as they had to talk eventually, this was what they needed, what they did.

So he settled between her hips and entered her. The first few strokes were slow and deep, and his reward was watching Persephone, breathless, beneath him, but he found it hard to maintain this pace when what he really wanted to do was fuck, and if they were trying to make this far more memorable than their exchange in Tartarus, then it had to be different.

So things shifted between them, and Hades kissed her harder and moved harder, and Persephone's fingers dug into his skin. Neither one held on to their cries of passion, pleasure—and pain.

This was it, the vessel through which they released and processed their emotions, and it was raw and wild and desperate.

Persephone came first, her entire body clenching around him, even her nails, which pierced his skin.

"Fuck!"

He drew in breath between clenched teeth, but not from the ache of breaking skin. It was more from the pleasure of it and a fierce need to come inside her, to claim this moment, and he took her hands and guided them over her head, holding her in place as he slammed into her. Moving inside her was its own euphoria, and the pressure built in his cock and the back of his throat until he came so hard he collapsed atop her.

They were still for a long moment, just breathing. Persephone's hands came around him, fingers trailing down his back. He got the sense she was looking for injuries, but they had already healed. When he had collected himself, he rose onto his elbows and stared down at Persephone.

"Are you well?" he asked, drawing pieces of her hair from her face.

"Yes," she whispered.

"Did I... Did I hurt you?"

It occurred to him that he hadn't been completely grounded or aware at some point during their coupling, but then she smiled and touched his face, her finger dancing lightly over his features.

"No," she said. "I love you."

Those words flooded him with a sense of relief. He had said before that words held no meaning, but that was before Persephone had uttered those three.

"I wasn't sure I would hear those words again," he admitted, unprepared for the shock those words would have on Persephone, who immediately began to cry.

"I never stopped," she whispered.

"Shh, my darling," Hades comforted. "I never lost faith."

But his words did nothing to quell her tears. Her body shook with them. Maybe she needed this—another form of release. He lifted her into his arms and carried her inside, where he laid her on their soft bed and kissed her until she was calm.

"I love you," he said, because he had yet to say it back, and then, "I am sorry."

She shook her head. "Things have been hard."

It was true for both of them in very different ways.

He bent to press his lips to her forehead and settled between her thighs. Despite the fact that they had just come together outside, he wanted to make love to her, and he wanted it to be both delicate and desperate. At the end of it, he didn't want to know where he ended and she began.

She widened her legs as he guided himself to her entrance but froze as a knock sounded at the door. He met Persephone's gaze, then grinned.

"Enter," he said, and Persephone's eyes widened.

"Hades!"

He chuckled as he rolled off her into a sitting position, and she rose too, pulling the blankets to her chest right as Hermes entered.

The god gave a lopsided smirk.

"Hey, Sephy," he said, a note of warmth in his voice.

"Hermes," Hades said, and his gaze shifted to him.

"Oh yeah." For a moment, Hermes's smile widened, then he took on a more serious expression. "I found the nymph, Leuce."

"Bring her," Hades ordered, and the nymph appeared before their bed, looking stricken and pale.

"Please—" she began, already sobbing.

"Silence!" Hades's voice was like a lashing, and Leuce immediately quieted, tears tracking down her face. "You will tell Persephone the truth. Did you send her to the Forest of Despair?"

At his question, more tears spilled down her cheeks and she nodded. There was a very small part of him that felt remorse for Leuce—not for what she had done to Persephone but for how sorry she truly seemed.

"Why?" Persephone asked. The betrayal in her voice

made him feel terrible for bringing this to her, but she needed to know.

"To tear you both apart," Leuce answered in a whisper, her eyes on the floor.

Hades could not tell what Persephone was thinking, but he thought she might be in shock, because all she could ask was "Why?"

Leuce pressed her lips tight and shook her head, body shaking with renewed sobs.

"You will answer," Hades commanded.

She collapsed in a heap on the floor. "She will kill me."

"Who?" Persephone asked, looking from Leuce to Hades.

"Your mother," Hades said. "She's talking about your mother."

Persephone's eyes widened and she looked at Leuce. "Is this true?"

Hades didn't like the shock in her voice. This was a woman who had taken Leuce in. Not only had she invited her into her home, but she had offered to mentor her. Even if Leuce hadn't wanted to, she still deceived Persephone.

"I lied when I said I didn't remember who gave me life," Leuce said. "But I was afraid. Demeter reminded me over and over that she would take it all away if I didn't obey. I'm so sorry, Persephone. You were so kind to me, and I betrayed you."

There was a moment when no one spoke—not even Hermes, who still stood by, watching this interrogation take place. But then Persephone shifted, wrapping the sheets around her as she left the bed, exposing his nakedness, though he did not care as he watched her approach Leuce and kneel before her.

He wanted to protest. The only person he would ever kneel to was her, but Persephone was not like him, nor did she need to be.

"I don't blame you for fearing my mother. I feared her for a long time too. I won't let her hurt you, Leuce."

Persephone spoke with a note of understanding in her voice that Hades did not share, but her kindness comforted Leuce, and the nymph fell into her, sobbing. Hades watched the strange display, his feelings mixed. On the one hand, it was what he had expected of Persephone, but he was angry with Leuce and frustrated that she had received such an easy pardon, though he supposed she had been punished enough by him.

"Hermes," Persephone said once Leuce had collected herself. "Will you take Leuce to my suite? I think she deserves some rest."

He smirked, bowing as he accepted her instruction.

"Yes, my lady."

Persephone rose with Leuce, and they shared an embrace before Hermes led her from their room. Once they were gone, Persephone's gaze returned to Hades, her eyes dipping to his exposed flesh, as if she'd just realized he'd been sitting there naked.

Then her eyes darted to his face.

"What?" she asked, likely because he was staring and smiling at her.

"I am just admiring you."

She raised a brow, her eyes momentarily darkening, but then she sighed. "I suppose we should summon my mother to the Underworld."

"Shall we call on her now?" Then he suggested,

"Perhaps we should make love so that she has no reason to suspect her plan worked."

"Hades!" she scolded playfully as he reached for her, pulling her between his thighs. She dropped the sheets and pressed against him skin to skin, and they fell back onto the bed, descending into their madness once more.

PART III

"What we were once and we are today,
we shall not be tomorrow."
—OVID, *METAMORPHOSES*

CHAPTER XXVI
Survival of the Fittest

Later, they dressed, and Hades sent Hermes to summon Demeter.

"I think you just want her to disfigure my face," Hermes said. "She will bite my head off when I tell her you've commanded her appearance in the Underworld."

"Then don't tell her Hades sent for her," Persephone replied. "Tell her I command it."

Hermes smiled at that. "Will do, Sephy," he said and left the Underworld.

"Are you nervous?" Hades asked as they walked, hands linked, to the throne room, where they would receive her mother. Hades thought it was the second-best option, the first being their bedchamber, though Persephone had shot that idea down. And to be honest, he looked forward to witnessing this—Persephone looking radiant in her Divine form, wrapped in a white peplos, being who she was meant to be, a goddess and queen.

"No," she said and looked at him, and as their eyes met, a warm smile spread across her face. It felt like a long time since she had looked at him that way, and it made his throat feel tight. "Not with you by my side."

His lips curled, and he squeezed her hand. It was all he could manage for the moment. Anything else and he would pull her to him, kiss her, and he wouldn't stop.

"Remember what I taught you in the meadow," he said.

"With your hands or your mouth?" she countered, breathless.

"Both," he said. "If it helps you with your magic. Plus, I will take great pleasure in knowing you are thinking of my mouth while you put your mother in her place."

They entered the throne room, which while dark was not cast in the red light that had made Persephone's wounds look so much worse. Instead, his halls were brightened by the glow of Hecate's lampades.

Leuce already waited at the base of the steps to the dais where Hades once sat alone, where two thrones now stood—his a jagged obsidian and Persephone's a smooth ivory embellished with gold and florals. When Persephone saw it, she looked at him.

"You missed an opportunity, Lord Hades."

He quirked a brow in question.

"I could have sat on your lap."

He grinned as he helped her up the steps, and as Persephone turned, he asked, "Is that a suggestion or a request, my queen?"

"Something to consider," she replied. "For next time, perhaps. I fear we may have pushed my mother too far with our request."

"She has little power here, my darling." Hades guided her to sit and did the same.

"Stand beside me, Leuce," said Persephone, and as she did, the nymph shook.

Persephone frowned. His goddess had far more sympathy for Leuce than he did, though he was not surprised. It was in her nature, but Persephone also knew what it was to live beneath the constant and critical eye of Demeter.

"She will lash out," Leuce said, her voice trembling. "I am sure of it."

"Oh, I expect it," Persephone replied with no hint of dread in her voice. "She is my mother."

There was a strange anticipation to this, one that wasn't unpleasant but almost freeing. Hades wanted this, he realized: to present to Persephone's mother united, to show her they were stronger than her ploys and games.

"Hermes has returned," Hades informed them when he felt the god's magic erupt. It was like sweet citrus and fresh linen, clean and crisp, and it mingled with Demeter, who should smell like a rotting corpse flower but instead smelled like fragrant wildflowers.

The doors at the end of the room yawned open, and Demeter strolled in ahead of Hermes with a confidence that faltered. The air grew heavy and charged with her anger. It had been a while since Hades had looked upon the goddess, though he noted nothing about her had changed, except that perhaps she appeared far more resentful than before.

Hades wondered if she'd thought she had been summoned to retrieve her daughter, only to find her sitting at his side, a queen to his king. Her stony gaze slid from him to Persephone, bitter with contempt.

"What is this about?" she demanded, and there was a sharpness to her voice that Hades imagined Demeter had often used with Persephone, but if it had frightened her before, it did not now.

"My friend tells me you have threatened her," Persephone said, and Leuce shook beneath the attention.

"You would believe your lover's whore over me?"

"That is unkind," Persephone said with an edge to her voice. "Apologize."

"I will do no such—"

"I said '*apologize.*'" Persephone's voice echoed throughout the chamber, and Demeter hit the ground with a loud crack.

Hades knew Demeter had felt Persephone's magic rise but had not considered it a threat, which was evident in her stunned expression as she knelt on the floor before them.

Her shock quickly melted into fury, however, and when she spoke, the air vibrated with her animosity.

"So this is how it will be?"

"You could end your humiliation," Persephone said. "Just...apologize."

It was difficult for Hades to remain stoic when he had never watched anything more entertaining in his entire life than this—Demeter on her knees in his realm, seething.

At Persephone's suggestion, Demeter's lips had gone pale and pinched.

"Never."

Demeter attempted to rise and sent her power

barreling outward, a tremor that was likely an attempt to both break Persephone's hold and call forth some kind of destructive magic. Whatever it was never manifested. Persephone managed to hold Demeter in place on the broken ground, and Hades's magic lay in wait, ready to defend if hers failed.

Against Demeter's suffocating wave of magic, Persephone rose and advanced on her mother, who had not relented in her efforts to break Persephone's hold. As she drew nearer, her magic grew stronger and heavier, and it sank Demeter farther into the ground as if it were soft earth and not stone.

"I see you have learned a little control, Daughter," Demeter said, allowing her magic to dissipate. Hades noted that it left her body shaking, and he wondered if the goddess was frightened.

He was.

Not of Persephone, but for her.

He thought of the power she had displayed in Tartarus. Her anguish had fueled that magic. It had overpowered *him*. Now she had managed to overpower Demeter.

It was an ominous prospect, a dreadful one, given that if she was a threat to them, she was a threat to anyone—to Zeus—and his brother liked to dispose of threats.

"All you've ever had to do was say you were sorry," Persephone said quietly, but there was a power to her voice that commanded attention. "We could have had each other."

"Not when you're with him."

Demeter spoke with venom. He had always known

the Goddess of Harvest would not approve of a union between him and Persephone, but she took it a step further by refusing to have a relationship with her, all because of her choice.

"I feel sorry for you," Persephone said at last. "You would rather be alone than accept something you fear."

"You're giving up *everything* for him."

"No, Mother, Hades is just one of many things I gained when I left your prison."

As those words left her mouth, she took a step back, and the hold she had over Demeter broke. The release was sudden, and it was clear Demeter had not been prepared, because she nearly hit the ground when it no longer held her up.

Hades watched the goddess stare up at her daughter with no hint of affection in her face, and his heart twisted painfully. He knew he would never fully understand what it meant to live beneath the reign of such a mother—one who could turn her love on and off at will—but he imagined it had left Persephone feeling very unworthy, and it was likely why she had so much doubt when it came to their relationship.

Sometimes he forgot the baggage she carried, forgot that her need for reassurance did not necessarily mean she had doubts, only that she needed comfort, and this was why.

It made him resent Demeter even more.

"Look upon me once more, Mother, because you will never see me again."

Demeter's expression changed, and a faint smile curled her lips. Hades did not like it, and he did not like what she said next.

"My flower. You are more like me than you realize."

Hades watched Persephone closely, and at her mother's words, he noted how her back stiffened and her fingers curled. As much as he hated those words, he knew that she feared their truth.

You are not like her. You never will be, he thought.

Demeter vanished, but the silence felt heavy with her presence. It was Leuce who broke it, taking a few cautious steps before she hurried to Persephone, throwing her arms around her.

"Thank you, Persephone."

The goddess hugged her back, and despite the smile on her face, Hades knew she was changed by this.

Hades's gaze slid to Hermes, who still lingered in the room. When their eyes met, he knew they had both reached an understanding about what had occurred here.

Demeter was no longer Persephone's family. They were, and they would do anything to protect her, to give her what she never had—even in the face of war.

While Persephone seemed more confident in the days following her encounter with her mother, she was also more anxious. Hades knew that was mostly due to Lexa, who remained in the hospital for another two weeks. Despite Persephone's happiness upon her release, he worried she expected things to go back to *normal*. He was not certain she understood that she lived in a new world, one where Lexa would never be as she once was. "Do you think Lexa will be able to attend the gala?" Persephone had asked one evening while they sat in the library.

The upcoming gala was hosted by the Cypress Foundation and would illustrate the impact of its charity work. Before Lexa's accident, she had a role in planning the event, and while Hades would like Lexa to be present, he didn't know if she was prepared for such an intense evening, and he said as much to Persephone.

She was quiet for a long moment, and when she spoke, her voice was thick with emotion. "How long do you think? Until she's..."

Her voice trailed off, but he knew what she wanted to ask. *How long until she's normal again?*

He rose and came to kneel before her, their eyes level.

"Darling," he said quietly.

"I know," she said, tears already streaming down her face. "You don't have to say it."

So he didn't.

While he'd have liked to have his attention solely on Persephone, he couldn't. Since the death of the Graeae, Hades had Ilias attempting to track Theseus's contacts in the black market. His goal was to discover what relics the demigod had managed to obtain or might be seeking. Hades also had to deal with Hera, but first, he needed to make Zeus aware of what had happened to the Graeae. He wasn't yet prepared to tell Zeus of Hera's alliance with Theseus...unless she refused his ultimatum.

Hades found Zeus at his estate in Olympia, which was a modern version of Olympus. The gods had homes in both locations, even Hades, though he was loath to use them. The God of the Sky was in his backyard, a golf club clasped between his enormous hands as he attempted to hit a small white ball by twisting his entire body around. The first few swings sent grass and dirt flying across the lawn. When he finally hit the ball, it sounded like thunder as it tore through the air, zooming far past the flagged target in the distance. It likely landed in the ocean and belonged to Poseidon.

Zeus growled in frustration, an indication that the club in his hands was likely to follow wherever the ball landed.

"Starting a new hobby?" Hades asked, making himself known.

Zeus whirled, the scowl darkening his bearded face turning to one of jovial surprise, though Hades knew it was likely not because his brother was glad to see him. There was an art to Zeus's demeanor, and he crafted it carefully so that no one knew his true thoughts or feelings.

"Brother," Zeus boomed. "To what do I owe this great honor?"

"I have brought you something," Hades said, though as he reached into his pocket to retrieve the box that held the eye of the Graeae, his stomach knotted. There was a part of him that wanted to hold on to the eye, but a greater part of him needed this leverage for his future with Persephone.

While Hades was still not certain how the eye worked—or even if the vision it had shown him was true—giving Zeus anything with relative power made him anxious. Not to mention the eye was sentient. Would it resent him for this exchange? Would it retaliate by showing Zeus something that would destroy his whole world?

As Hades handed Zeus the box, he said, "I fear I have bad news to accompany it. I found the Graeae dead. They were killed by a hydra blood–tipped blade. I fear it may be the first of many attempts on the lives of the Divine."

Zeus stared down at the open, black box before snapping it shut and resting his hands atop the club.

"Who was responsible?"

"I suspect this is the work of Triad."

Zeus did not speak, but Hades knew how he felt about the organization of Impious. As much as he hated them, he did not see them as a true threat.

"We should call Council," Hades suggested.

"No," Zeus said suddenly.

Hades glared. "No? You've called Council for less." Including Helios's cows.

"For what purpose would I call Council?"

"To warn other gods," Hades said, angry.

"The Graeae were blind," Zeus said. "They were at a disadvantage. You do not honestly think another god could fall prey to this parlor trick?"

"Parlor trick? The Graeae are dead, Zeus."

Hades did not know how often he would need to say this before Zeus understood. The Graeae—Divine beings—had been murdered.

"You cannot honestly think Triad will stop with these three deaths? They will try again, and they will seek more ways to replicate what they've done."

"And who will they target next? Hephaestus, perhaps? Aphrodite will likely thank them."

Hades ground his teeth until his jaw popped. "So this is your response? To the death of deities?"

Hades usually operated without expectation of his brother, but he had failed to do so here. He had thought the King of the Gods, the one responsible for the well-being of everyone and everything on Earth, would be appalled by the death of the Graeae. Instead, he seemed to think Triad had somehow granted a kindness to the three sisters.

Zeus looked at Hades and placed a hand on his shoulder. "Do not worry, Brother. If it were you, I'd call Council in an instant."

Hades imagined that was meant to be some kind of compliment and shoved his brother's hand away.

"Action doesn't matter once you're dead, Zeus."

"If deities are dying, then perhaps they have no business being Divine," Zeus replied, once more returning to his practice—widening his feet, gripping his club, and manifesting a white ball. He swung and hit the ball with a crack that echoed through the air, shielding his eyes to see how far it flew, but it was already out of sight. Hades wanted to tell him he was supposed to aim for the red flag in the distance, but he had a feeling his brother had decided to play differently—especially when he could not play right.

"It's survival of the fittest, Hades," Zeus said at last. "Always has been, always will be."

CHAPTER XXVII
A Proposal

Hades left Olympia for Nevernight. The only thing that quelled his frustration toward his brother was thinking about what he had planned for Persephone this evening. He'd decided to show her a little more of the Underworld and, in the process, himself. He hoped it would be healing and perhaps lay a foundation so that he could share more things—harder things—but those thoughts were put on hold as he appeared on the floor of Nevernight and knew he was not alone.

Hera.

He turned to face the goddess.

"Hades," she purred.

"No," Hades said.

He was done with her and her labors. The goddess looked stunned for a second before her cheeks grew flushed with anger.

"You forget you are under my control," she said. "I decide your future with your beloved Persephone."

"I would think carefully on how you decide my fate, Hera," Hades said. "Because I decide yours."

She blanched. "What do you mean?"

"I was not eager to get involved when you decided you wanted to overthrow Zeus again, but since then, I have learned of your alliance with Theseus, and now I have no other choice but to choose a side."

Her eyes darkened. "Are you saying you are with Zeus?"

"No," he replied. "I am on no one's side but my own."

"Why am I not surprised?" she said through her teeth. "Your only loyalty is to yourself."

"Wrong," Hades said. "I am extremely loyal to those I care about, though you are not one of them. Perhaps you could say the same if you truly cared for anyone."

She lifted her head. "So what are you going to do now? Tell Zeus? Have him hang me from the sky?"

"No," he said. "But I want your favor in exchange for the secret, and I'd like to cash it in now."

"Let me guess. You want my blessing for your marriage?"

"I don't just want your blessing," Hades said. "I want you to defend it."

The goddess swallowed hard, and Hades knew she was weighing her options. She had been punished by Zeus before for her insolence, but this was different and she knew it. She'd helped Theseus kill three deities, and it was likely when Zeus found out about her involvement with Theseus, he'd call forth the Furies to enact Divine retribution. The only reason Hades had not done so was because only Zeus could punish his queen.

"Fine," Hera said at last. "You have my blessing."

Hades did not thank her. Instead, he started toward the stairs but paused to look upon her once more before offering a final warning.

"This is not a war you survive, Hera."

It would be up to her to believe him or not.

Hades returned to the Underworld and changed into the clothes Hermes had left for him. He had almost dreaded asking for help, knowing the god would react with an overwhelming amount of enthusiasm—and Hades had not been wrong—though Hermes had made him work for it.

"You need my help?" he'd asked.

"Yes, Hermes," Hades had said, frustrated. "I need your help."

"With fashion."

Hades did not consider this fashion. He was asking to be dressed down, and those were clothes he did not own. Still, he knew Hermes would not appreciate that.

"Yes," he hissed, trying to remain calm.

"Hmm. I may be able to pencil you in...though, I am *always* willing to do favors for my best friends."

Hades glared, and Hermes raised his brows.

"Persephone is your best friend. This is for her."

"But Persephone *admits* she's my best friend," Hermes said.

"Does it mean as much when I say it?"

"It's like saying I love you," Hermes explained. "I might know it, but it's good to hear."

There was a long pause, then Hades mumbled, "You're my best friend."

"What was that?" Hermes asked. "I couldn't hear you."

"You're my best friend," Hades repeated quickly.

"Ah, once more, with *feeling*."

Hades glared and said deliberately, "You're my best friend."

Hermes preened. "I'll have something for you by the evening."

And he had held to his word, leaving a black shirt, pants, and a pair of riding boots for the evening. Once he was changed, Hades went to the library, where he waited for Persephone to return to the Underworld.

Luckily, he did not have to wait long, though when she spotted him, she halted, as if surprised.

"What are you wearing?" she asked at seeing his outfit, a smile curving her pretty lips.

"I have a surprise for you."

"Those pants are definitely a surprise."

The corner of Hades's mouth lifted, despite not knowing how to take her reaction. Did she like these clothes? Perhaps he should have just worn his suit, though riding horseback would have been decidedly uncomfortable. He decided not to ask and instead reached for her hand.

"Come."

He led her outside, where Alastor and Aethon waited for them. Of his four sable-black horses, these two could not be more opposite. Aethon was impatient and dreaded being locked in the stables at night. Alastor was far more calm, and he preferred being alone. Despite this, Hades knew he was the best horse for Persephone due to his loyal and gentle nature.

"Oh, they're beautiful," Persephone said, and the horses liked her praise, snorting and bobbing their heads. Hades didn't blame them—he felt the same beneath her approval.

"They say thank you," he said with a laugh. "Would you like to ride?"

"Yes!" she said with more enthusiasm than he expected, but it made him happy. Then she hesitated. "But...I've never..."

"I'll teach you," he said quickly and once again took her hands, guiding her forward.

"This is Alastor."

"Alastor," she said and stroked his nose. Alastor lowered even more, urging her to scratch his head. Persephone giggled and obeyed. "You are magnificent."

Aethon gave an envious bray.

"Careful," Hades warned. "Aethon will be jealous."

Persephone smirked and reached to pet Aethon too. "Oh, you are both magnificent."

"Careful, I might get jealous," Hades said, then took up Alastor's reins. "Put your foot in the stirrup," he instructed Persephone. "Lift yourself up and swing your leg over, then sit down gently."

She followed as he advised, and once she was seated, he continued.

"If you become afraid, sink your weight, lean back, and firm up your legs, but my steeds will listen if you speak. Tell them to stop, they will stop. Tell them to slow down, they will slow down."

"You taught them?" she asked, holding the reins in one hand while petting Alastor's mane.

He mounted Aethon and answered "Yes," though it

was not difficult. The four steeds were Divine, and they had been together for a long time. They knew Hades's moods just as well as he knew theirs. He did not even need to speak. "Don't worry. Alastor knows what he carries. He will take care of you."

They started slow, wandering into the fields and gardens beyond the palace. Alastor and Aethon ambled side by side. Hades could not help watching Persephone as she rode, her hands wrapped gracefully around the reins, her hair catching beneath the light of his realm. She was beautiful and happy and *beaming*. It made his heart beat almost erratically.

"This is a wonderful surprise," she said.

An excitement shivered through him as he answered, "This isn't the end."

They wandered through Hecate's green meadow, where Alastor and Aethon only briefly became distracted by the goddess's wild mushrooms before they were redirected, heading around the ominous mountains of Tartarus.

"How was your day?" It wasn't a question Hades asked often, mostly because he didn't want the same asked of him. He never had a good answer anyway, but it always presented more ways for him to omit the truth, and that only made him feel more guilty for the things he felt he had to hide—the truth of him and his life. Asking now was progress—a way to start anew and be more transparent.

"Good," Persephone said and paused before adding, "Lexa's been making coffee in the mornings. It isn't how she used to do it, but I think it's a sign she's going to be okay."

Hades said nothing, knowing there was still so much uncertainty around Lexa's livelihood. Just getting her out of the hospital had been a feat. Now that she was home, she'd have to face the reality of routine, and sometimes that was harder than the confinement of a hospital.

Persephone did not ask him about his day, and he wondered if she saw the point, if she assumed he would not be honest.

They continued along, winding through landscapes that changed from mountainous to forested to fields of purple and pink flowers. Against the backdrop of the darkened mountains, which mostly housed prisoners of Tartarus, they looked aflame.

"How often do you…change the Underworld?" she asked.

"I wondered when you'd ask me that question."

She raised a brow. "Well?"

"Whenever I feel like it," he answered. Sometimes he changed it when a deity left just in case they thought they could find their way back. Mostly, though, he expanded his realm. He created new spaces within Asphodel for the souls, because as the world changed above, so did their needs below. Elysium was another challenge and often evolved because each soul was there to heal. Outside of that, his world changed as he wished—and it would soon change as Persephone wished.

"Perhaps when my magic isn't so terrifying, I will try."

"Darling, there is nothing I'd like more."

The field they had crossed narrowed to a path that cut between more forested mountains. They were just on the other side of Tartarus, close to Elysium. The same solitude that blanketed the air there also reached here, and Hades could feel it settle on his heart, a pleasing calm that he had not felt in a long while. They were near their destination, and when he heard the waterfall, Hades stopped to dismount, then came to Persephone's side. As she threw her leg over, Hades gripped her waist and helped her slide off the horse. He kept his hands on her even after her feet were on the ground.

"You look beautiful today," he said, staring down at her. "Have I told you?"

"Not yet," she said, smiling and rocking onto the tips of her toes. "Tell me again."

He answered by kissing her, hands tangling into her hair. During their ride, his body had grown warm, and now he was boiling, but as eager as he was to channel this heat, to release it into her, he pulled away and nuzzled her nose, whispering once more, "You're beautiful, my darling."

He led her through the tree line to a spot in the mountains where water ran off the rocks into a shallow and shimmering lake, and though the muted light of Hades's sky cut through parts of the canopy above, they were mostly in shadow.

Beside him, Persephone's breath caught in her throat, and she spoke, awed. "Hades...how gorgeous."

But he had never stopped staring at her, and when she finally looked at him, they came together once more, their mouths colliding. Hades's hands slid around her body, holding her hips in place as he rolled into her, his length trapped between them, hard and throbbing.

"Hades," she whispered as his mouth left hers long enough to remove their clothes. He lowered them both to the ground, where he worshipped her body with his mouth. He loved every part of her—her heavy breasts, her stomach, and the space between her thighs—and when they were both wound tight, he settled his arousal against her and rocked his hips forward.

Sliding into her was an out-of-body experience, and she was there, swelling and gripping, and he froze, his forearms braced on either side of her face. For a moment, she was still, her head back, chin tilted up, but then she seemed to relax, release her breath, and open her eyes.

Their eyes met, and all Hades could see when he looked at her was his queen.

"Marry me," he whispered as her finger traced his face, and though he had asked her twice before, this time felt different. It felt *right*, and he guessed it was for her too, because she answered with a quiet "Yes."

They smiled at each other, and he kissed her before he moved, thrusting deep, and she arched beneath him. There was a part of him that felt almost powerful as she writhed—powerful but humbled, because she let him in. She let him drive her toward release, and after he came, he noticed that tears welled in her eyes.

He bent to kiss them, whispering as he did. "My darling, why are you crying?"

"I don't know," she said and reached to wipe her eyes, laughing once more.

Hades thought he understood a little of what she was feeling—a happiness that went beyond anything he had ever known. As much as he felt being here was a victory, he also felt like he had more to lose.

"I love you," he said and carried her into the water, where they bathed.

After, they dressed and headed for the palace.

Unlike their ride to the waterfall, their return was quiet. For the first time in a long while, Hades felt unburdened. In this place and time, nothing existed beyond this moment—not the labors Hera had put him through or the death of the Graeae. He did not think of Theseus or even of Zeus. Those were not things he was fighting for—they were things he fought against.

He fought for Persephone, for this love that she inspired in his heart—for these feelings he never expected to feel, much less so deep. He knew things were changing. He could feel it in the threads that moved beneath his glamour, but he hoped that whatever the Fates wove, it included a future for him and Persephone.

Even if that future meant turmoil.

When the palace came into view, Hades noticed Thanatos waiting, and his mood instantly darkened. The high he'd felt from the start of their evening crashed so hard he felt shaky. When he'd thought of turmoil, he hadn't expected it to come so soon, but he knew what this meant.

He knew.

And already his heart was breaking for Persephone.

A few more paces and they were within range of Thanatos, who looked stricken. He was always pale, but there was a yellow sheen to his skin that made him look sickly, and even the hollows of his cheeks seemed deeper, his eyes more hooded. Hades dismounted, and as he helped Persephone off Alastor, he noted that she couldn't take her eyes off the God of Death either. Her dread was just as heavy.

As they approached, Hades kept his hand on the small of Persephone's back, a precaution in case she crumpled.

"Thanatos," Hades greeted.

"My lord, my lady," he said and swallowed, trying twice to speak, but whatever words he had thought he would start with fell dead on his tongue. Instead, he admitted, "I don't know how to tell you this."

It was not often Thanatos was at a loss for words, not often when he could not provide comfort in difficult situations, and the fact that he could not now showed how much he truly cared for Persephone and her friend.

It was a few more moments before he managed to speak, and by then, Persephone was quivering.

Finally, he managed, "It's Lexa."

The first sob tore from her mouth in a rush of emotion, and Hades drew her to him, holding her tighter as Thanatos continued.

"She's gone."

CHAPTER XXVIII
On the Way to Elysium

Hades had watched a lot of people die, and he had watched a lot of people lose.

Nothing prepared him for watching someone he loved losing someone they loved.

It was a feeling he couldn't quite explain. It was as though someone gripped his heart, as if they were squeezing it within their palm, and there was no release, no way to shake the hold. It was ever-present and constant, and it was hopeless.

"Persephone," Hades said, but her eyes were unfocused. She had stopped crying soon after the first wail had burst from her lips, and now she was quiet and distant. As much as he wanted to give her time to process this, he needed her attention for a few moments longer.

"*Persephone*," he said, touching her face, and when her eyes met his, she burst into tears once more.

"My darling," he said gently, brushing away her

tears, but she just cried harder. "We don't have much time."

He gathered her into his arms, teleporting to the pier at the Styx where Charon would be arriving soon.

When she heard the rush of the river, she pulled away, looking off toward the horizon.

"Hades, what are we——?"

Her words faltered when she saw Charon's boat cutting across the black waves, his robes a bright beacon against their darkness. There was a single figure beside him, a woman who looked far younger in the Underworld landscape than she did in the world above.

"*Lexa*," he heard Persephone whisper, and when Charon docked with the soul, Persephone stood so close, Lexa barely had space to climb out of the boat, but she seemed just as eager to see Persephone. They held each other and cried. All the while, Hades stood aside and let them, because beyond this time together, nothing would ever be the same.

Not for Lexa and not for Persephone.

Hades tried not to listen to their conversation, but it was hard given that he stood only a few feet away. There were apologies and expressions of pain, and the dread came when Persephone turned to him and asked, "Where is she going?"

She was going to Elysium to heal because she had taken her own life, and to do that, she would have to drink from the Lethe, which meant she would have no memories from her time above—not of anything, not even Persephone.

He knew Persephone had asked because she hoped he would say otherwise, but when he did not speak, he knew she understood. He waited for her anger, but Lexa was quick to speak, drawing her attention.

"Seph," she said, squeezing her hands. "It's going to be okay."

Persephone's mouth trembled. "Why?"

Lexa opened her mouth to speak but shook her head. It was likely she didn't even understand the decision she'd made. It was just that her soul had wanted so badly to remain in the Underworld the first time, it couldn't handle returning to a world it did not want—no matter how much she loved Persephone.

"I did this," Persephone said, her voice trembling, and Lexa brought her hands to her chest.

"Persephone, this was my choice. I am sorry it had to be this way, but my time in the Upperworld was over. I accomplished what I needed to."

"What was that?" Persephone asked, miserable.

Lexa smiled. "To empower you."

Persephone shook her head and fell into Lexa's arms. It wasn't something she was ready to hear yet, but there would come a time when she would recognize the impact of this loss. She would see how strong she truly was.

They remained together until Thanatos arrived to escort Lexa to the Lethe. This time, he was far more prepared to offer the benefits of his magic, and a sense of calm overcame everyone gathered, even as Lexa hesitated.

"Wh-where am I going?" she asked.

"You will drink from the Lethe," Hades explained. "And then Thanatos will take you to Elysium to heal."

Even as Hades spoke the word—*heal*—he noted the glow in Lexa's eyes. She was ready.

"I will visit you every day, until we are best friends again."

Persephone's promise made Hades's heart hurt, but he had no doubt she would hold to it—no matter how hard it would be.

"I know," Lexa whispered, and for the first time since she arrived, there were tears in her eyes, but Thanatos took Lexa's hand, and she seemed comforted by his presence. She let him lead her away, and when Hades and Persephone could no longer see them, they returned to the palace.

Once in their bedchamber, Hades encouraged Persephone to rest, and after she had fallen asleep, he found himself in Hecate's meadow, where the goddess invited him for tea. Inside her small cottage, he felt like a giant, barely able to sit at her table, though he managed as she made a blend—one in particular she said would calm nerves.

"I hear our dear Persephone has had quite a harrowing evening," she said.

Hades nodded, reflecting on the day. They had gone from one extreme to another—an intense high to a devastating low. He wavered between each of those memories—Persephone's genuine happiness to her shocking pain. There was a part of him that hated himself for this, that blamed himself for Lexa's ultimate end. If he had been more forthright about his world, maybe none of this would have happened.

Hecate slammed a hand against the table, snapping Hades out of his thoughts.

He met her gaze, mildly annoyed.

"Stop that," she said, setting a steaming cup of tea beside his arm. It smelled like chamomile, lavender, and mint.

He raised a brow at the goddess. "I thought we——"

"I don't need to read minds to know when you are brooding because you scowl," she said. "What's done is done. There are no decisions that can take us back in time, only ones that move us forward. Right now, Persephone needs an attentive...*boyfriend*."

Hecate seemed to shudder at that word, and despite everything, he smirked. "Fiancé," he said.

Hecate blinked. "Excuse me?"

"Fiancé," he said once more and added, "Persephone agreed to marry me."

A slow smile broke out across Hecate's face.

"Are you saying," she said carefully, "that I get to plan a wedding?"

"I think you'll have to talk to Persephone, but I doubt she would tell you no."

"Engaged," she said, as if she did not believe it, and sank into her chair across from him.

"Yes," Hades said, amused by her response.

"*Married*," she said.

"Eventually," Hades said, though he hoped sooner rather than later.

Then she shook her head. "I never thought this day would come."

"Oh, ye of little faith," Hades said, though he had not been so certain either.

"You're not exactly charming or good at communication," Hecate said. "And you're an alcoholic."

"Is there anything I am good at, Hecate?" Hades asked, and the goddess smiled.

"Learning."

Hades spent another hour at Hecate's cottage before returning to the palace, where he met Thanatos in his office. The God of Death offered an update on Lexa's trip to Elysium, which had been, gratefully, uneventful. There were times when souls who drank from the Lethe became hostile and lashed out at the god, but Lexa had been pleasant, quiet, almost shy.

"I fear it will be some time before Persephone can visit with Lexa," Thanatos said.

"I will tell her," Hades said and added, "Thank you, Thanatos, for taking care of her."

Hades noticed a faint blush color the god's cheeks, and he opened his mouth to respond but settled on a simple nod before leaving.

It was then, while alone, that the day crashed down on him, and he was filled with a restless energy he couldn't shake. His thoughts stormed through his mind, as relentless as the flames in the fireplace he stood before.

This time, rather than dwelling on how he might have prevented Lexa's end, he felt fear—fear that Persephone would blame him, that once she had time to think about how this had unfolded, she would see that he had failed her.

The guilt made his eyes sting, and when the door opened, he stiffened. There was a part of him that was preparing for her rage and a part of him that feared seeing the weight of her sadness, feared that when he looked upon her, he would break too.

He felt her draw near, though hesitant, and he was surprised when she asked, "Are you well?"

He swallowed hard around the thickness in his throat. He should be asking her. "Yes, and you?"

"Yes... Hades," she said, and he knew she was waiting for him to look at her. He took a few deep breaths, until the wetness behind his eyes did not feel so threatening. When he met her gaze, he did not see what he expected—no resentment or anger or hatred. He just saw...her, beautiful and raw and open.

"Thank you for today," she whispered.

Her gratitude made him uncomfortable. He had only tried to make up for what he had done so wrong before.

"It was nothing," he said and turned back to the fire, but Persephone reached for him. He held her gaze, and as much as he wanted to give her distance in this moment, he realized she was asking for the opposite.

"It was everything," she said, her eyes heated, her lips parted.

He angled toward her and took her mouth against his, and they knelt before the fireplace. The heat from the flames made their skin hot and slick. Hades took his time with her once more, much as he had done in the mountains, and when he found himself sliding into her, she spoke.

"You were right," she said, her body shifting beneath his, legs widening, back arching.

"I did not want to be right," he said as he began to move.

"I should have listened."

"Shh," he soothed, bending to kiss her mouth. "No

more talk of what you should have done. What is, is. There is nothing else to be done but move forward."

He recognized he needed to take Hecate's advice just as much as she did, but the words worked to calm her, and soon they were moving together, hard and fast and measured, and when Persephone started to moan his name, his lust for her knew no bounds. He gripped her hips and slammed into her, liking the bite of her nails as they scored his skin, and he came so hard inside her, he collapsed when he was done.

They rested like that for a long while, shifting only to be closer to the fire, as they'd moved a considerable distance during sex.

"I'm going to quit *New Athens News*," Persephone said.

"Oh?"

It was the first time he had heard of this plan, but he could not say he disapproved. He hated Kal Stavros, and while he did not think the mortal would bother her anymore, he'd rather she not work for him.

"I want to start an online community and blog. I'm going to call it *The Advocate*—it will be a place for the voiceless."

He smiled a little, knowing that this was what she was passionate about—offering a space for those who felt like they were not heard, much as she had felt throughout her life.

"It sounds like you have thought about this a lot," Hades said.

"I have."

He placed a hand beneath her chin and drew her gaze to his. "What do you need from me?"

"Your support."

He nodded, brushing his thumb across her cheek. "You have it."

"And I'd like to hire Leuce as an assistant."

He raised his brows, though he wasn't surprised. "I'm sure she'd be pleased."

"And...I need your permission."

He almost laughed at her list of requests, but he was intrigued, unable to imagine what she might ask his permission for, though he would grant anything if she asked.

"Oh?"

"I want the first story to be our story. I want to tell the world how I fell in love with you. I want to be the first to announce our engagement."

His chest felt tight at her words, and while he'd never consider offering their life to anyone willingly, he would do it for Persephone.

"Hmm," he said, pretending to consider her demand. "I will agree under one condition."

"And that is?"

"I too wish to tell the world how I fell in love with you."

She smiled and offered a breathy laugh as he took her mouth against his, and when she shifted to straddle his body, he gladly let her take him.

———

Hades had attended few mortal funerals, and when he did, it was often when he was cloaked in glamour, but this one—Lexa's—was different. He attended with Persephone because she asked, and even if she hadn't, he would have been there for her. It was a morose affair, with many dressed in black.

"She would have hated this," Persephone said. "She would have wanted a celebration."

Hades smoothed her hair and pressed a kiss to her temple. "Funerals are for the living."

It wasn't long after that her anxiety began to rise. Hades did not need to look to know what had upset her—mortals. Those in attendance knew who he was, knew who she was, and did not understand why he had allowed Lexa to die. He could feel their gazes, angry and discontent, though all he cared about was how Persephone felt.

"You could never make them understand," he said in an attempt to quell her nerves.

She stared back at him, not only sad for Lexa but for him. "I do not want them to think poorly of you."

"I hate that it bothers you. Does it help if I tell you the only opinion I value is yours?"

"No," she said, but despite her pain, she managed a smile.

CHAPTER XXIX
Pirithous

**MY JOURNEY TOWARD LOVING
THE GOD OF THE DEAD**

***It was the first article on Persephone's new website,** The Advocate,* and while Hades had been prepared for it, she hadn't let him read it until it was live.

"You'll have to wait like everyone else!" she had said.

When he'd asked why, she'd blushed.

"Because I don't want to be here when you do."

Now that he had read her words, he understood. She had wanted him to read it alone so he could feel the full weight of her confession—and did he ever.

He'd read it over and over again.

Fuck. He loved her, and it took everything in his power to remain focused on his work when all he wanted to do was go to her, but today was a big day for her. She had launched her website, this…*love letter to him*…and she was quitting her job at *New Athens News*. She was taking back her power, and he was *proud*.

In the meantime, he had an errand to run—one that felt even more right on the heels of this article—and he was eager to see it complete, which was how he found himself returning to the island of Lemnos, but this time to visit Hephaestus. He wandered through the god's lab, a cluttered and cavernous workshop built into a volcanic mountain, filled with his inventions. The God of Fire had created weapons, armor, and even human life for the Olympians and their heroes. His skills, while invaluable, were often overlooked by the other gods, who were content to forget he existed until they needed something, though Hades did not think Hephaestus minded, as it allowed him to pursue his own interests.

As he wandered through the empty lab, he heard a loud clanking coming from below. Hades followed the sound into the darkened corridors of Hephaestus's lab, down a set of stone steps, to a forge that was bright with fire. Hephaestus stood before it, sweat dripping down his bare chest, his muscles bulging from the work he had already put into shaping the metal he had pressed against his anvil.

A few more hard strikes and Hephaestus dropped his hammer, turning his attention to Hades. Perspiration and black coal stained his face, making his gray eyes somehow look brighter. He wiped a hand across his brow, then used a cloth sticking out of his leather apron to clean his hands.

"Lord Hades," he greeted. "Come to retrieve your ring?"

Not long ago, Hades had commissioned Hephaestus

to craft a ring for Persephone, but shortly before he had gone to retrieve it, Persephone had discovered his bargain with Aphrodite, which had caused her to question everything—even his love for her. He knew how it had looked then, knew how it looked even now, but that had not made letting her go any easier, and it had made seeing the ring he had designed for her even worse.

Hades had expected to never see the ring again, but Hephaestus had known better and promised to hold on to it until he needed it again.

"I didn't know you were psychic," Hades said.

"It is not so easy to fall out of love," Hephaestus said, and there was an uneasy silence that followed those words. Likely Hephaestus feared he had invited Hades to comment on his relationship with Aphrodite, but Hades said nothing, though he knew Hephaestus spoke from experience.

The God of Fire crossed to a workbench and plucked a black box from one of his crowded shelves and handed it to Hades. He was overcome with a comforting energy as the soft velvet touched his palm, and when he opened the lid to gaze upon the ring—a ring of flowers and gems that gleamed in the firelight—he felt nervous.

"Thank you," he said quietly, closing the box.

Hephaestus nodded.

"What are you working on?" Hades asked. He was always curious about the god's projects.

"Nothing of worth," the god replied, but Hades caught sight of it—the metal he was shaping—and he had questions.

"Is that...*adamant*?" Hades looked longer. "Is that a *trident*?"

Then his gaze leveled with Hephaestus's.

"Are you trying to re-create Poseidon's trident?"

The God of Fire was frozen in place, but not out of fear. This was different. He was stiff all over, his muscles rippling, as if he were about to have to defend himself.

"It's not what you think," he said, his tone darkening.

"I hope it's exactly what I think," Hades replied. "Hephaestus, tell me you've chosen a side."

Hades returned to Nevernight with the ring safe in his pocket. He kept his hand around the small box, comforted by the weight of it, though that comfort was disrupted by a feeling that something was wrong. There was a discontent that tangled his veins, and it was like the world was too quiet and too still.

Persephone.

Antoni and Zofie burst through the doors of Nevernight. Behind them, a girl followed, the blond from Persephone's work—Helen—who sat at the front desk. Hades could feel their hysteria, knew they were about to deliver fatal news.

"She's gone!" Zofie exclaimed. "Persephone! She's missing!"

Black spots clouded his vision and he growled. "Where was she last?"

"We were about to leave the Acropolis when she went downstairs," Helen explained, her breathing uneven. "She said she had to say goodbye to someone. When she didn't come back, I went to look and found...well...*this.*"

She handed a notebook to Hades, and he snatched it from her hands.

"What is it?" he demanded.

"It's not good," Antoni said. "Someone was stalking her."

Hades opened the book and read one of the entries—they were all dated and handwritten.

Date: 6/27

Persephone had lunch with me today. She told me that her god was angry with her. If she were with me, I'd never be angry with her. I'd make her feel real good.

Date: 7/1

Today Persephone wore pink. Her dress was so tight, I could see each time her nipples hardened. She had to be thinking of me.

Hades felt bile rise in the back of his throat as he read entry after entry. They were all like this: short, dated paragraphs that detailed what Persephone was wearing, conversations the man had had with her, and gifts he'd left her. Whoever this was had planned this abduction. He'd wanted to hurt her, torture her, rape her.

Hades's body shook with a fury he could not contain as his glamour melted away.

What if he was too late?

"Who is this man?" he demanded through his teeth.

"They call him Pirithous," said Helen.

Pirithous.

"He was a janitor," she added. "No one ever took notice of him…except…Persephone."

And it was likely her kindness he had abused.

Hades's magic welled, and in the next second, a

familiar screech broke the air as the Furies—Alecto, Megaera, and Tisiphone—erupted from the floor around him. They hovered in a circle, their pale bodies adorned with black snakes that hissed as they slithered around their arms and their stomachs and their legs.

"Lord Hades," they said, their voices a horrible, strange echo.

"Find Persephone," he said. "Do what you must to keep her safe."

The Furies screamed as they accepted their orders, and their black wings beat, whipping the air as they rocketed toward the ceiling, breeching the pinnacle of Nevernight, sending chunks of obsidian flying across New Athens.

"What can we do?" Helen asked.

"There is nothing you can do," he snarled, and she stumbled back at his rage. He did not care that he had startled her, because he had silenced her, and that was what he needed right now—the quiet, so he could follow the Furies' magic. While he held on to them, a finger twined around thread, his mind felt like a battlefield, erupting with nothing but thoughts of the consequences of finding her too late, and that only fueled his agony.

He knew when the Furies had located her because the tension between his magic and theirs lessened, and while he felt the smallest sense of relief, he would not be okay until he laid eyes on her, until he was certain she was unharmed.

He teleported, manifesting in the shadows of his own magic to find Persephone bound to a wooden chair. Her face was stained with tears—eyes red, lashes wet—and all around the room was what looked like wood debris. Then his eyes fell to the man who had abducted her.

Pirithous.

He was unassuming—thin and willowy with dark hair and high cheekbones. There was something to his features that made Hades think he had Divine blood. He was crumpled against the wall, a massive stake protruding from his chest.

He was dead, but not for long.

Hades called on his magic, and Pirithous gasped, then moaned, the pain of his wound shuddering through him. When he saw Hades, he began to whimper.

"I brought you back to life so I can tell you that I will enjoy torturing you for the rest of your eternal life. In fact, I think I will keep you alive so you can ruminate in your pain."

Hades snapped his fingers, and a chasm opened beneath Pirithous's body. As the Earth fell away, he took pleasure in the sound of the man's screams echoing as he fell to Tartarus.

"Alecto, Megaera, Tisiphone, see to Pirithous," Hades ordered. The three would guard him until he could take over. They bowed and vanished, and Hades was left to care for Persephone.

He released her from the coarse bindings Pirithous had used to restrain her, noting the redness on her wrists. As he knelt before her, she fell into his arms, and he gathered her to him, teleporting to the Underworld. Once in their bedroom, she burst into tears, and he felt helpless to do anything but sit with her and hold her and let her expend every ounce of her fear.

"I'm so sorry," Hades said as he rocked her. "I did not know. I'm so sorry."

While he held her, he felt like breaking too. He could not control the beat of his own heart, could not stop his stomach from twisting or the nausea from climbing up this throat. He was angry for so many reasons, but at the end of the day, he was devastated that she had not been safe, that there was a possibility she would never feel safe again.

He did not know how long Persephone cried, but there came a time when she quieted, and when she pulled away, she took his heart with her.

"I need to scrub him from my skin."

Hades said nothing because he feared what he would say and instead took her to the baths. Once there, he sat apart from her while she undressed and entered the hot pool. He watched as she washed every part of her skin until she was red from head to toe, and all he could think was that he had touched her there—everywhere. By the time she finished, his hands were fisted so tightly, his nails had cut into his palms.

He only healed them when she crawled into his lap and wrapped her arms around his neck. He was grateful for her closeness and held her tight.

"How did you know I was missing?" she asked.

"Your coworker, Helen, got worried when you didn't come back from the basement. She went to search for you and found the journals."

When he thought of them, he wanted to kill Pirithous a thousand times over—and he would. He had no tolerance for abusers of women and children, and the fact that Persephone was involved made it even worse.

"She didn't know who to tell. For better or worse, she told a security guard. Zofie had been patrolling outside when she was notified, and she realized she'd watched Pirithous leave with you—in a tilt truck. When she told me, I sent the Furies. You had already been gone so long...I wasn't sure what I would find."

"He was a demigod," she said, her voice quiet. "He had power."

Hades's earlier observation had been right, then. He grimaced.

"Demigods are dangerous, mostly because we do not know what power they will inherit from their Divine parent." Not to mention many demigods did not know their parentage, and it was not always apparent even after their powers developed. Hades could not help thinking about Ariadne's comment, that Theseus had gathered an army of demigods—soldiers, she had called them.

Pirithous was just one example of how little they actually knew about demigods—including their numbers, their powers, their capabilities.

"What was Pirithous able to use against you?"

"He put me to sleep, and when I woke, I couldn't use my magic. I couldn't focus. My head...my mind was in turmoil."

Hades's brows lowered. "Compulsion. It can have that affect."

It took a lot of training to keep from being compelled too. Persephone would have had no chance to fight it.

After a moment, he asked in a quiet, rough voice, "Tell me what happened?"

She studied him for a moment, looking very

troubled. Perhaps she worried over what he would do once he knew the full truth, and she had every reason to, because he was not stable at the moment.

"I will tell you if you will promise me one thing."

Hades studied her face, waiting.

"When you torture him, I get to join you."

He hugged her tight as he swore, "That is a promise I can keep."

It might have been a promise Hades kept eventually, but it was not one he would keep tonight. Once Persephone was sleep, he teleported to Tartarus. Pirithous had been taken to his office and tied to the same chair he'd used to restrain Persephone. The stake that had left him lifeless on the floor in the Upperworld was still embedded in his chest, and with each breath the demigod took, he whined.

When Hades finally came face-to-face with him, he lashed out, kicking the stake farther into the man's chest. Pirithous gave a pathetic cry and began to wheeze as blood spattered across the floor and dripped from his mouth.

"You touched my lover, my fiancée, my future," Hades bellowed. "An unforgivable crime."

"It's not my fault!" Pirithous gave a gargled howl.

"Not your fault?" Hades repeated, the fury burning his blood. "Go ahead and tell me how it wasn't your fault. You stalked her. You wrote horrible things about her. You abducted her. *You. Touched. Her.*"

He was raging, and once more, he kicked the man in the chest. This time, Persephone's stake went right through him and fell to the floor, though Hades managed to hold on to the man's life thread. He would not die yet. He would face immeasurable pain, and despite the pleasure Hades would take from inflicting it, he knew it would not atone for what this man had done to Persephone.

"No," Pirithous moaned, his words barely intelligible. "Th-Theseus said...we... Theseus said..."

"Theseus?" Hades repeated, his body stiffening at the sound of the demigod's name. "Did you say Theseus?"

Pirithous nodded.

"*He...was...friend.*"

Hades took a moment to collect himself, then used his magic to heal the demigod. It would be hard for him to explain himself with a mouth and throat full of blood.

"What about Theseus?" he demanded.

"We made a bet," Pirithous explained, his voice high-pitched and keening. "To carry off goddesses. He said... he said we couldn't get in trouble because of Hera."

"You made a bet to carry off goddesses, and you chose *my* goddess?" Hades asked.

"It was Theseus who suggested it," said Pirithous. It was as if he thought he shouldn't be punished because it was not his idea, though Hades wondered why Theseus had put Pirithous up to this. Had he merely wished to see what happened when someone fucked with him? Or had he done this as a type of revenge?

Either way, Pirithous would not be the one to suffer for what happened tonight, though he would be the first.

Hades used his magic to summon Persephone's stake from the ground, and as he hovered over the demigod, Pirithous began to wail.

"She was not yours to take," Hades said, and he jammed the stake into the man's neck. As he jerked it free, he seethed. "She was not yours to touch! She was not yours! She was not yours!"

As he raged, he shoved Persephone's stake into the demigod's body, bathing in his blood, and he only stopped when he had lost his voice.

CHAPTER XXX
The Start of War

Hades's stomach knotted with anticipation. Tonight, his nonprofit, the Cypress Foundation, was hosting a gala to illustrate the impact of his charity work. Among them was the Halcyon Project, which held a special place in both his and Persephone's hearts. Without her, it would not exist. Everything he poured into it was inspired by her. It was also a project Lexa had worked on before her death, and he had something planned to honor her legacy.

It was just one reason he was unusually excited about tonight's event. The second had to do with the black box in his pocket. As he stood outside his bedroom door, he took it from the inside of his jacket and looked at the ring. Nestled in black velvet, it gleamed, and by the end of the night, it would glitter on Persephone's finger, a symbol of their commitment to each other.

Once more, his chest felt tight with nervous energy. He took a breath. He could do this—she had already said yes.

He closed the box and returned it to his pocket before entering their bedchamber, where he found Persephone already dressed for the evening in a red off-the-shoulder gown. While the top was lace, her skirt was made of layers of tulle, and he could not help thinking that Hecate had chosen it specifically to make things difficult for him.

"You look lovely," he said.

"Thank you," she said, a flush creeping over her cheeks. "So do you. I mean...you look handsome."

He chuckled at her nervousness, though he couldn't deny he felt the same, and it gave him some comfort that even after everything they had been through, they could still feel this sort of flustered excitement.

"Shall we?" He offered his hand and she accepted, allowing him to pull her close and teleport to the surface, where Antoni waited for them outside Nevernight.

The cyclops smiled when he saw them and opened the door to the limo.

"My lord, my lady," he said. "Looking divine this evening."

"Thank you, Antoni," Persephone said and laughed as she climbed into the back seat.

Hades followed close, inhaling her sweet scent. "And what is so amusing?"

"You know we could just teleport to the Olympian."

"I thought you wanted to live a *mortal existence* when in the Upperworld," Hades said, though to be fair, it had been a while since she'd said anything like that, which made him think she had grown more and more content with the balance of her life.

"Perhaps I am only eager to begin our night

together," she said, and there was a sensual edge to her voice that sent Hades's blood rushing to his head—both of them.

He raised a brow. "Why wait?"

She shifted, bunching her ridiculous skirt into her hands so she could straddle him, but even as she sank against him, he could barely feel her for all the layers.

"Who chose this dress?" Hades growled as his hands sought her skin.

"You don't like it?"

Like wasn't the word he would use.

"I'd really rather have access to your body," he answered as his palms finally skimmed her bare thighs.

"Are you asking me to dress for sex?"

He smiled and leaned close as he whispered, "It will be our secret."

He kissed her, and his hands shifted upward toward the apex of her thighs, while hers skimmed down his chest to the button of his trousers.

"Persephone," he breathed as she freed his sex and took him into her hand. Her palm was warm, and she kept her thumb at his crown, rubbing circles over the come that beaded there.

"I need you," he growled. "Now."

He thought she might resist, drag this out until he was feverish and desperate, but she seemed to feel the same because she mounted him, sliding on with a groan that rocked each of their bodies.

"You have ruined me," Hades said, holding on to her hips, fingers digging into her skin and the gods-damned fabric of her billowing dress. "This is all I ever think about."

"Sex?" she asked, breathless. She alternated between sliding up and down his shaft and grinding against him. It made his head spin, and he wanted to fuck her harder.

"You," he said between his teeth. "Being inside you, the feel of you gripping my cock, the way you tighten around me just before you come."

"You just described sex, Hades."

He laughed, though he panted too. "I described sex with you. There is a difference."

They lost themselves at some point, and they came together viciously, kissing and thrusting, and there was nothing to hold on to but each other.

"Fuck, fuck, fuck," Hades said, and he sought her clit, touching her there until she came apart, and though she had come, she still moved for him, whispering erotic things until his release exploded inside her. In the aftermath, Persephone collapsed against him, and his body sagged with exhaustion and pleasure.

He tangled his hand into her hair and kissed her face, groaning. "Fuck me. I'm like a fucking teenager."

"Do you even know what it's like to be a teenager?"

"No," he said truthfully. He had been swallowed as a baby and born an adult. "But I imagine they are always horny and never quite sated."

He could take her again if she'd let him.

"Perhaps I can help." She shimmied off his lap to the floor and wrapped her hand around his cock before he stopped her, hands on her face.

"No, darling."

"But—" she protested.

"Trust that there is nothing I would love more than

for you to go down on me, but for now, we must attend this gods-forsaken dinner."

"Must we?" she asked, a pretty pout to her mouth that made him want this even more, but they were nearing the hotel where the gala would take place, and this event…it was important.

"Yes. Trust me, you will not want to miss it."

She held his gaze for a moment, and her hand slipped up and down his cock in defiance, though eventually she rose to sit beside him, and they restored their appearances, which was easier said than done, especially because Persephone kept her eyes on his cock.

"*Goddess*," he warned.

She offered a sheepish smile before her attention turned to the window, and he noted how she stiffened at the sight of the crowd that had gathered outside. Though they were still a few miles from the hotel, the sidewalks were packed with people hoping to catch a glimpse of divinity. He reached for her hand, offering a reassuring squeeze. He did not blame her for being nervous at the sight of so many people—so many strangers—and when the limo stopped and the door opened to a blinding wall of flashing lights, he felt her anxiety spike even more.

He exited the car and turned to her, reaching for her hand. He would not let her go through this alone.

"Darling?"

She latched onto his fingers and allowed him to help her from the car, and together they walked down a red carpet that led to the front of the Olympian Grand Hotel. As they walked, people shouted their names and demanded pictures, even reached across the barriers erected on either side of the walkway in hopes that they might brush their skin.

Hades kept Persephone close, and when the carpet widened and gave them more distance from the crowd, they both felt at ease.

"Zofie!" Persephone cried, and Hades turned his attention to the Amazon who approached, looking very uncomfortable in her blue gown and with the hug Persephone pulled her in to. Hades had requested Zofie join them tonight, both as Persephone's aegis and her friend.

"Persephone, are you well?" she asked, frowning a little, perhaps confused by Persephone's excitement. The Amazon was not used to being valued beyond her skills as a warrior, so it was likely she did not understand what friendship really meant.

Though Hades knew Persephone would teach her.

"Yes," Persephone answered. "Just happy to see you."

The Amazon smiled.

They continued on, and Hades kept a firm hand on Persephone at all times, though the goddess was handling every request with grace. They stopped for a million photos, and by the time they came to the end of the media circuit and were led into a large reception hall, all Hades could see was flashing lights. The hall was less crowded, but there was a roar to the room that was somehow worse inside. Perhaps that was because the noise was contained. Still, people gathered into small groups to chat, while servers darted around carrying trays of drinks.

Hades noted that Persephone kept her gaze on the ceiling, which was, essentially, an art piece—a field of glass-blown flowers in an array of striking, bright colors. She did not get to enjoy the view long because they were approached by people who wished to make Persephone's acquaintance. Luckily, they were people Hades liked, mostly donors, some who ran within the circles of Iniquity and some not.

"Sybil!" he heard Persephone shout, and she left his side to embrace the oracle.

Hades hung back, watching her as she spoke animatedly with the mortal. He braced himself for Hermes's arrival, which, true to his nature, was dramatic. He appeared behind her and gathered her into a tight hug, swinging her around, coming to a stop before Apollo.

Hades looked away when he noticed the God of Music, gritting his teeth. He had yet to forgive the god for the bargain he'd struck with Persephone.

As much as Hades hated that he could not prevent what had happened to Lexa, Apollo had a role in the game too.

When dinner arrived, the nervousness Hades had felt before they left the Underworld returned, simmering in the bottom of his stomach as he tried to focus on eating. The only thing that kept him grounded was Persephone, who sat beside him, laughing and talking to everyone near. She was charming and beautiful, but the longer dinner went on, the quieter she became, and he got the sense she was thinking about Lexa.

He placed a hand on her thigh and felt an immense amount of relief as Katerina took the stage to begin the event's program. She welcomed everyone and offered an overview of the Halcyon Project, touching on how it had begun and its purpose. Then it was Sybil's turn, and as she took the stage, Hades moved his hand from Persephone's leg, lacing his fingers through hers.

"I am new to the Cypress Foundation, but I fill a very special position. One that was once occupied by my friend, Lexa Sideris. Lexa was a beautiful person, a bright spirit, a light to all. She lived the values of the Halcyon Project, which is why we at the Cypress Foundation have decided to immortalize her. Introducing...the Lexa Sideris Memorial Garden."

Behind Sybil, a screen showed pictures of Lexa and illustrated images of the garden. Persephone's fingers squeezed his as Sybil continued.

"The Lexa Sideris Memorial Garden will be a therapy garden for residents of Halcyon and will include a magnificent glass-like sculpture at the garden's center, representing Lexa's soul—a bright and burning torch that kept everyone going."

He leaned toward her and whispered against her ear, "Are you well?"

"Yes," she said, looking over her shoulder at him with tears in her eyes. "Perfect."

He kissed her, and when they finished dinner, they left the dining hall to dance. Hades was not ready to release Persephone just yet and drew her onto the floor, his hands pressing into her body as he held her close.

"When did you plan the garden?" she asked.

"The night Lexa died," he admitted. He'd thought of it the moment there was a possibility she might not make it, as morbid as it seemed, but he had always liked the idea of offering people peaceful spaces to mourn and remember.

Persephone was silent.

"What are you thinking?" Hades asked, suddenly anxious that he had somehow made her sad.

But then her eyes met his and she answered, "I am thinking about how much I love you."

Hades smiled, drew her close, and whispered in her ear, "I love you too."

When the music shifted to something more electronic, Hades took his leave so she could spend time with her friends. He snatched a glass of whiskey from a tray as he retreated to the shadows, keeping her within sight, mistrusting of anyone but those closest to them.

He was not there long when he saw Ilias enter the ballroom, and he stiffened. The satyr was supposed to be at Nevernight, and for him to have come all this way—and in person—something had to be dreadfully wrong.

"Hades," he said.

"Ilias," he replied with a nod. "What is it?"

"Normally I wouldn't give much weight to rumors, but this one you need to hear. The market's saying the ophiotaurus has been...resurrected."

Hades's first reaction was shock. A sudden heaviness descended on his whole body. The ophiotaurus was a monster, part bull, part serpent. It was said that whoever slew the creature and burned its entrails would obtain the power to defeat the gods. During the Titanomachy, the creature was killed by the Titans, but before they could burn its entrails, they were captured by one of Zeus's eagles, thwarting their plan.

If it was alive once more, it would likely be a target for Triad—for Theseus—and it was the perfect weapon to use to overthrow the gods.

And Hades knew exactly how it had come to be.

"*Fucking Fates.*"

He'd expected the murder of Briareus to haunt him, but not like this. He remembered their words to him.

"*Do not fret, Good Counselor.*"

"*Your bargain with Briareus...*"

"*Will only ruin your life.*"

Just when everything was within his grasp, he thought, the Fates did this. He wondered at their decision to resurrect the ophiotaurus. Did they want the Olympian reign to end? Had they woven a future where the demigods ruled a new era? Or were they merely entertaining themselves? He would not be surprised if it were the latter, though their fun would end in bloodshed. Everyone would look for the ophiotaurus because everyone wanted the chance to kill divinity, even gods themselves.

"Sorry to ruin your evening," Ilias said.

Hades focused on the satyr once more. "No, thank you, Ilias. We'll begin searching tonight."

The satyr nodded, and as he departed, Hades slipped his hand into his pocket, clutching Persephone's ring as he searched for her on the floor, noting that she was gone, and he went in search of her. In the face of Ilias's news, she was even more important. He had not fought so hard to have her, to love her, only to have her taken away.

He found her on the balcony overlooking New Athens.

"There you are," he said and drew his arms around her, sealing her back to his chest. Her warmth was a comfort to his chaotic mind, and he took a deep breath, inhaling her scent once more. "What are you doing out here?"

"Breathing," she said with a laugh, though he could

feel how hot her skin was and knew she needed a break from the crowd.

He chuckled and they fell silent, content for the moment to stand in each other's energy.

"I have something for you," he said, kissing her hair.

Persephone turned in his arms, her hands pressing firmly to his chest. "What is it?"

He studied her for a moment, like he did when he wanted to memorize her face. This time, he wanted to memorize this moment before everything changed. Then he shifted, reaching into his pocket for the box.

He knelt before her.

"Hades—"

"Just...let me do this. Please."

She closed her mouth and smiled. Then he opened the box, revealing the ring he had Hephaestus forge so long ago. She brought her hands up to cover her mouth as her breath caught in her throat.

"Persephone," he said. "I would have chosen you a thousand times over, the Fates be damned. Please... become my wife, rule beside me, let me love you forever."

Her eyes glistened and she swallowed as she whispered her answer.

"Of course. *Forever.*"

Hades grinned, and for a moment, he forgot to put the ring on her finger. He fumbled as his large fingers clasped the small piece of metal. Once it was in place, he rose to his feet and took her into his arms, kissing her until she was breathless.

"You wouldn't have happened to overhear Hermes demand a rock, would you?" she asked once they parted.

"He might have been talking loud enough for me

to hear," he said, amused. "But if you must know, I have had that ring for a while."

"How long?"

"Embarrassingly long," he admitted. "Since the night of the Olympian Gala."

But he had known then that she was his forever. Fuck, he had known before that, from the moment he had laid eyes on her on the floor of Nevernight.

"I love you," he said, pressing his forehead to hers.

"I love you too," she said, and this time, her lips pressed to his.

He drew her close, wishing to become completely lost in this moment, to forget what lay on the horizon, but there was a sudden chill on the wind that made his blood run cold. When he pulled away, he saw snow.

Snow in the middle of summer.

There was only one god who might be responsible, one god who used weather to torture the world into submission—and that was Demeter.

"Hades," Persephone whispered, drawing closer to him. "Why is it snowing?"

He did not look at her as he spoke, staring angrily at the flurries whirling over New Athens.

"It's the start of a war," he said.

And you—you're at the center of it.

BONUS CONTENT

Read ahead for a sneak peek into *A TOUCH OF CHAOS*, coming from Bloom Books, September 2023.

The burn in his wrists woke him.

The headache splitting his skull made opening his eyes nearly impossible, but he tried, groaning, his thoughts scattering like glass. He had no ability to pick at the pieces, to recall how he had gotten here, so he focused instead on the pain in his body—the metal digging into the raw skin on his wrists, the way his nails pierced his palm, the way his fingers throbbed from being curled into themselves when they should be coiled around Persephone's ring.

The ring. It was gone.

Hysteria built inside him, a fissure that had him straining against his manacles, and he finally tore open his eyes to find that he was restrained in a small, dark cell. As he dangled from the ceiling, body draped in the same heavy net that had sent him to the ground in the Minotaur's prison, his gaze locked with familiar aqua eyes. He was not alone.

"Theseus," Hades growled, though even to him, his voice sounded weak. He was so tired and so full of pain, he could not vocalize the way he wished; otherwise, he would rage.

The demigod was not looking at him, but at a small object clutched between his thumb and forefinger. He looked so at ease—and why not? He had the advantage.

"This is a beautiful ring," he said and paused, twisting it so that even beneath the dim light, the gems glittered. Hades watched it, his stomach knotting with each movement. "Who would have guessed it would be your downfall?"

"Persephone will come," he said, certain.

Theseus laughed. "You think your bride can go up against me? When I have managed to ensnare you?"

Hades took a breath, as deep as he could manage, though the weight of the net pushed against his sternum—it pushed against his whole body, made him feel like he was crumbling. Then he spoke, a quiet promise that shook his bones.

"She will be your ruin."

Author's Note

If you've followed me for any length of time, you know I began the Hades Saga because of my readers, though I always felt that Hades was up to something in the time he wasn't with Persephone in the main series. I especially knew this to be true during the events of *A Touch of Ruin*, but I'm not sure even I expected what would unfold in *Retribution*.

This book was a bitch to say the least, and I fought hard against writing it. I think there was an element of dread because I was returning to a book that dealt heavily with grief and I am only a year into my own journey with grief.

I dreaded facing the feelings, drudging them up. I dreaded the feedback, too. I was afraid people would compare Hades and Persephone and once again elevate his character above hers, and we all know how much I identify with my girl.

I have a soapbox I like to stand on when people

compare the two—and I'm going to use it now because this is important to me, and because it's important to me, I know it will be important to my readers—to *you*.

There is no comparison between Hades and Persephone. There is no elevating one above the other. The foundation I am laying is one of equal partnership, and these books are meant to illustrate their progress toward that. Hades lives in a very big world. He is an immortal god who has existed for thousands of lifetimes. The challenges he faces day-to-day look very different from Persephone, whose world is much smaller. I am so dismayed when I see people—women, especially—bash Persephone while they glorify Hades. He has just as many issues to work through, no matter how much he professes his love for Persephone.

So I just ask you to instead consider their backgrounds and celebrate their differences. I ask you to remember how hard it is to face loss and to grieve—and if you cannot remember, then imagine. If you do not wish to imagine, then do not judge, because until you've gone through it, there is nothing to say.

With those words, I'm going to dive into some of the myths I wove into this story.

Let's start with the greatest theme in this book:

The Labors

First, I knew I would not be rehashing all twelve labors because that would have been awful (mostly for me). I also knew some of what Hera was working on outside of the obvious labors (the Graeae, Dionysus, Ariadne, even Persephone) would all be some type of labor.

Of the labors I used these:
- The hydra (which you see in *Malice*)
- The Stymphalian birds
- The Girdle of Hippolyta
  - I have a longer note on the Girdle of Hippolyta. I don't like either of the original two myths about Heracles and Hippolyta. The first is that she was so enchanted by Heracles that she gave him her belt without argument and the second ends in her death after the Amazon's attack Heracles and his crew, thinking they are abducting his queen. Still, I felt she would respect a god who would honor her by an equal exchange rather than simply taking. I feel this is truer to character for Hippolyta, who, I believe, knows how to pick her battles.

Of the labors, I made a nod to these via symbolism:
- The Nemean lion
- The Erymanthian boar
- Cretan bull

You will note that one of the "labors" is Hades fighting Heracles—while not a nod to the labors themselves (there is one where Heracles retrieves Cerberus from the Underworld), it is a reference to an account by Pausanias, who details a story of Hades being shot with an arrow by Heracles in Pylos. He was later healed by the god Paean, who we also see in the book. I wanted to reference this because I felt it was an opportunity to also reference Hera's angry pursuit of Heracles. Because he was a son of Zeus, she struck him with madness, and he later killed his entire family. In the aftermath, the labors were born.

Last, we'll talk about the first labor, and perhaps the hardest—the death of Briareus. This reference, as I have explained in the book, was a nod to Hera's previous attempt to overthrow Zeus. I felt that she would begin her next attempt with the execution of those who had thwarted her in the past. It made for a devastating scene and still makes me sad.

The Graeae & Medusa

I must admit, I did not expect the Graeae—or, the Grey Sisters—to appear in this book, but as I began writing the opening scene, I realized Hades was attending the races for a reason and the more I wrote, the more I realized the Graeae were involved. Now, you may recognize the Graeae from an iconic Disney movie, *Hercules*, which has a ton of issues, among them, that they lead everyone to believe the Graeae are actually the Fates.

It was the Graeae who shared an eye and tooth between them, and they really only did one thing in mythology, and that was tell Perseus the location of the Medusa (only after he threatened to throw their eye in the sea).

Dionysus & Ariadne

Oh, Dionysus and Ariadne. I've known these two would make an appearance in this series eventually and did they ever. I love them so much.

Let me begin by explaining Ariadne.

What a boss babe—even in mythology. She is literally responsible for Theseus's success. Without her, he would have never made it out of the labyrinth once he killed the Minotaur. Do you know how he repays her? He leaves her on an island while she sleeps. Somehow, on that island, she meets Dionysus and they wed.

I have always seen Ariadne as a detective. I worried it was a little cheesy, but I just felt like she had such a dedication to justice. I like to imagine that she was tired of her father sacrificing seven men and women to the Minotaur every year (rather than the original myth which says Ari fell in love with Theseus. Gross.) and that is what motivated her to help Theseus. Later, she flees with him to avoid facing punishment.

Theseus does later marry Ariadne's sister, Phaedra, and what unfolds during their marriage is such a clusterfuck. I'll let you do your own research. In the end, I feel like Theseus is a user in mythology, so that's exactly what I make him in my retellings.

Dionysus, God of the Vine, is the son of Zeus. He actually has a very robust set of myths, unlike some gods, and his cult is probably one of the most interesting in myth. Like Heracles, he was also relentlessly pursued by Hera and struck with madness that led to him wandering the ends of the earth. Dionysus also has the ability to strike people with madness and he does so often—not only his followers who are called Maenads, but also anyone who spurns him.

An example was with King Pentheus, who refused to accepted Dionysus as a god and prevented the women of his kingdom from participating in worship. Dionysus was so angry, he struck Pentheus's daughters with madness (essentially, they became Maenads) and they tore their father to pieces…literally. It was because of this myth that I decided modern Maenads should be assassins. I liked the idea that they were women who were fleeing abusive situations and could find comfort with other women who had gone through the same thing while learning to protect themselves.

In modern times, Dionysus is known as a bit of a party god, and while I felt he had some of those traits, I also felt that he had likely become more disciplined over the many millennia he had been alive. To me, he is a god of sin, and I can't wait to see how this comes out in his own book.

I do reference a few other stories in regard to Dionysus—the death of his mother, Semele; the Theater of Dionysus (which is real); and, of course, Bakkheia, which is a festival that celebrated Dionysus.

Theseus and Pirithous

The final scene where Pirithous says that it was Theseus's idea to abduct goddesses was pulled from the myth of Theseus and Pirithous who were literal bros. They decided to steal daughters of Zeus. Theseus took Helen and Pirithous was the idiot who thought he could steal Persephone from Hades.

Spoiler alert: It doesn't end well.

I am sure I did not include every nod to mythology in this author's note, but I always hope these additions give you an idea of how critically I think about these retellings.

Thank you so much for giving me the chance to share my stories with you. Thank you for helping me live my dream. I am forever grateful.

All my love,
Scarlett

About the Author

Scarlett St. Clair is a *USA Today* bestselling author, a citizen of the Muscogee Nation, and the author of the Hades X Persephone series, the Hades Saga, the Adrian X Isolde series, *Mountains Made of Glass*, and *When Stars Come Out*.

She has a master's degree in library science and information studies and a bachelor's in English writing. She is obsessed with Greek mythology, murder mysteries, and the afterlife. For information on books, tour dates, and content, please visit scarlettstclair.com.

Find her on social media:
Facebook: AuthorScarlettStClair
Instagram: @authorscarlettstclair
TikTok: @authorscarlettstclair